Connect the Scotts

EVAN MUNDAY

Published by ECW Press
665 Gerrard Street East, Toronto, Ontario M4M 1Y2
416-694-3348 / info@ecwpress.com

LIBRARY AND ARCHIVES CANADA CATALOGUING IN PUBLICATION

Munday, Evan, author
Connect the Scotts / Evan Munday.

(The Dead Kid Detective Agency ; 4)
Issued in print and electronic formats.
ISBN 978-1-77041-333-7 (softcover); ISBN 978-1-77305-220-5 (ePub); ISBN 978-1-77305-221-2 (PDF)

I. Title. II. Series: Munday, Evan. Dead Kid Detective Agency ; bk. 4.

PS8626.U54C66 2018   jC813'.6   C2018-902513-1
                    C2018-902514-X

Editor: Crissy Calhoun
Cover and interior illustrations: Evan Munday
Cover and text design: David Gee
Author photo: Rodrigo Daguerre

Printed and bound in Canada by Friesens
5   4   3   2   1

The publication of Connect the Scotts has been generously supported by the Canada Council for the Arts which last year invested $153 million to bring the arts to Canadians throughout the country, and by the Government of Canada. Nous remercions le Conseil des arts du Canada de son soutien. L'an dernier, le Conseil a investi 153 millions de dollars pour mettre de l'art dans la vie des Canadiennes et des Canadiens de tout le pays. Ce livre est financé en partie par le gouvernement du Canada. We also acknowledge the Ontario Arts Council (OAC), an agency of the Government of Ontario, and the contribution of the Government of Ontario through the Ontario Book Publishing Tax Credit and the Ontario Media Development Corporation.

Connect the dots. La la la la.
Connect the dots. La la la la.

— Pee-wee Herman

Black Sunday

The moon was high in the clear April sky. It was a Sunday night like any other Sunday night in Sticksville, a small town in Southern Ontario, which is to say that a thirteen-year-old girl and her five dead friends were in the midst of breaking and entering (or committing a "905") at the historic Sticksville Museum. And that aforementioned thirteen-year-old was one October Schwartz, the protagonist of this series of books (but you probably already knew that).

This was not the first time October and the dead kids had broken into the Sticksville Museum in the pursuit of a mystery. And this time, there was no need to use one of the dead kids' heads to break open a window, nor were there any troublesome ghost pirates (or substitute teachers *posing* as ghost pirates) to worry about. (If you haven't read the three books that precede this one, you really should. *Ghost pirates!*) October's dead friends, as ghosts themselves, had no effect on the motion sensors (or whatever burglar alarms use — this is a book about child ghosts, not an Alarmforce training manual). They were also fully aware of where the burglar alarm was located and how to deactivate it. After allowing their living friend to enter, they all crept quietly down the narrow hallway that led from the kitchen and up the uneven steps to the museum's private administration area, where materials, documents, and artifacts not currently on display were stored. October and the dead kids marvelled at the rows and rows of metal shelving overstuffed with bankers boxes.

"What exactly are we looking for?" Derek, a Mohawk boy who died only a few decades ago, asked.

"I'll know it when I see it," October answered, scanning the boxes' labels for guidance as if one might read, *Clues You Desperately Require (1 of 2)*.

"Super," Kirby sighed, adjusting the belt of his khaki shorts under his gut. "Improvised detective work is my favourite."

Though it was the dead French-Canadian quintuplet Kirby LaFlamme's tendency to provide unconstructive criticism, his snark was justified. The kids had been raised from the dead by October a week ago during the full moon and — as per the seemingly lunar rules of child resurrection — they had only a few more weeks until they'd have to return to the cold ground.

So what, exactly, was October hoping to find hidden in the labyrinthine storage system of Sticksville's only public museum? As long-time readers of the escapades of the Dead Kid Detective Agency well know, ever since the black-clad dark makeup enthusiast October Schwartz accidentally raised from the dead the five kids with whom she was currently committing a felony, she has been bound to the corpsified tweens — first through their aid in solving the mysterious death of her kindly French teacher, Mr. O'Shea, and then through her offer to help each of the kids discover how and why they died in the historical eras in which they first took dirt naps. As it happens, the dead kids were rather good at detective work (read, "*illegal* building entry"), being able to walk through walls and get around largely undetected. But they required the shrewd mind (and warm body) that only — let's presume — October Schwartz could provide to actually solve the riddles of their own demises. In the past six months, October and her ghost friends had solved the mysteries behind the untimely deaths of United Empire Loyalist Cyril Cooper (in 1783) and Scottish immigrant Morna MacIsaac (in 1914), and in both cases something way more sinister than a case of tuberculosis was to blame.

Of the two dead kids' deaths that October and the team had already solved, 100% of them could be tied back to a seemingly ancient secret society in Sticksville named Asphodel Meadows — a society that may also have ties to long-dead Sticksville resident

Fairfax Crisparkle, who may or may not have been a witch. (Reports varied.) Murderer number one was an impostor of a *Titanic* survivor, Dr. Alfred Pain (who was *really* Udo Schlangegriff), while murderer number two was the alleged Crisparkly witch himself. More recently, young October discovered that the very same Asphodel Meadows may also have had something to do with the disappearance of her own mother, who departed without much explanation when October was three, leaving her and her father (Mr. Schwartz to you) on their own.

The excursion to the Sticksville Museum — a must-see in any historical murder investigation — was part of October's search into the cause of death of a third deceased friend of hers, Tabetha Scott, a girl who was born enslaved in 1800s Virginia, escaped to Sticksville via the Underground Railroad (a bit more on that later, just you wait), but died in the relatively placid (and, then, slavery-free) settlement of Sticksville, Ontario. Though even money had it that the dastardly Asphodel Meadows was somehow to blame for Tabetha's death, October wouldn't be much of a detective if she just attributed the mystery to Asphodel Meadows without asking the whys and wherefores, right? That impulse to be a competent detective was what led her and the dead kids to the Sticksville Museum, searching for some material on Tabetha and her family or, at least, Sticksville's role in the Underground Railroad.

However, as it was April and not February — that very short window also known as Black History Month — all the information about the town's Black history was no longer on display and had been filed for later use (next February). This included, tragically, any information regarding Sticksville's role as a point in the Underground Railroad — that causeway to freedom for so many oppressed and imprisoned by slavery in the United States. That a soul-crushingly boring and predominantly white town like Sticksville could have ever been a beacon of hope to people escaping slavery was mind-boggling to October (and your humble narrator). October spotted a bankers box with *Black History Stuff* scrawled on the label in Sharpie, and Derek clambered up the metal shelving to retrieve it. The dead kids opened the box and spread the documents, prints, and objects across the office floor.

"So you're telling me there's a Black History Month every February?" Tabetha asked, turning a replica of Eli Whitney's cotton gin invention over in her hands. Being, for all intents and purposes, a part of Black history herself, she was unaware of the annual observation.

"Yeah," October said, riffling through papers. "And maybe it's wrong for me to assume so, but I figured if there was anything about your death in this museum, that's where we'd find it."

"Nice how they decided Black History Month should be the shortest, coldest month of the year," Tabetha grumbled.

"I don't understand," Cyril confessed, though one could assume this of him in most situations. "Don't we all have the *same* history?"

"Really, white boy?" Derek said, displaying for his Loyalist friend an example of manacles used on a slave ship.

October sighed. "Cyril, you may not realize this because when you were alive, it was assumed by white people that they were, like, God's chosen ones and destined to be lords of all domains or whatever, but most of history is written from the perspective of certain groups of people who've spent, like, a lot of the past ruling over, controlling, and even owning other people. And Black History Month is just one way of trying to counteract that."

Cyril, thoroughly chastened for his archaic (though, sadly, still quite popular) ideas, returned to searching. But as he was unable to read, he honestly was not much help.

"Given this town was supposed to be an endpoint of the Underground Railroad," Kirby started, "you'd think they'd have a display up year-round. That would be a pretty big deal."

"Right?" Tabetha said. For once, she and her constant nemesis agreed. "Thank you."

"I'll have to talk to Ms. Fenstermacher about that," October said. October's high school history teacher (who took the place of her former murderous one) worked part-time at the Sticksville Museum.

"Wait," Morna said. "Sticksville had a subway? I don't remember tha'."

As Morna had died in 1914, she had heard of electric underground railways (or subways) in London, New York, Paris — even her home country's own Glasgow — but nothing in Canada. (Toronto didn't open its subway system until 1954.)

"No, not a subway, Morna," October explained. "The Underground Railroad wasn't an actual transit system. It didn't have tracks or tickets. The Underground Railroad was a nickname for a secret group of people and travel routes to help people like Tabetha, born into slavery, escape the American South and get to freedom in Canada."

October was paraphrasing for the sake of brevity, but she was mostly correct. As October Schwartz and most human beings around the world (let's hope) are well aware, the cruel and barbaric practice of slavery had been practised by Europeans throughout the Americas and Caribbean since the first English colony in Jamestown, Virginia. This system, whereby Africans were kidnapped from their homes in West-Central Africa, Sierra Leone, and elsewhere and sold by slave traders to farmers and landowners as enforced labour ironically was thriving when the American Declaration of Independence, asserting that "all men are created equal," was signed. (As with most laws written by white men in America, exceptions applied when it came to men and women of colour.) Shortly after the end of the Revolutionary War, right about the time that Cyril Cooper died in Sticksville, most northern states

5

passed laws to abolish slavery, though the practice grew and calci-fied in the Southern states, where one in four families owned other people. Black men, women, and children were sold on auction blocks like cattle, whipped and beaten in a cruel effort to impose obedience, and even hanged.

In the early 1800s, the Underground Railroad emerged, though it didn't *emerge* so much, since secrecy was the key to its success. As October explained to Morna MacIsaac, perhaps more patiently than I might have, the Underground Railroad was not an actual rail system, but more a covert movement against unethical laws and institutions. It's been said the resistance used the lingo of railways, with safe houses being "stops" and "stations" and organizers being "conductors" who would guide small groups of freedom seekers from one station to the next. To maintain secrecy, con-ductors — made up of free Black Americans, Native Americans, Quakers, and white abolitionists — often knew their section of the "track," but not full routes. Railroad "passengers" would, by way of foot, wagon, or boat, move from barn to cave to church basement on indirect routes from the Deep South to the northern states or Canada. (Canada was preferable, as bounty hunters and federal marshals would pursue and apprehend escaped slaves only as far north as upstate New York.)

Over the Underground Railroad's history, over 30,000 enslaved people escaped to Canada, with most of the Black families arriving through the station of Fort Malden in Amherstburg, Ontario. Many settled in Southern Ontario in the Lake Ontario and Michigan Peninsula, though many returned to the United States during or following its Civil War (after which, slavery was — in theory — abolished).

But before any Canadian readers feel too smug about Canada's role as "Promised Land" and end destination of many Underground Railroad routes, please keep in mind that slavery was only abolished in this country in 1833. Though the slave trade in Canada was never the massive institution it was in the United States, there were thou-sands of Africans enslaved during Canada's early history, including those brought by Loyalists fleeing the newly independent U.S.A. (much like Cyril's family). And even after slavery was abolished, discrimination against Black people in Canada was rampant. (In Saint John, New Brunswick, the town legally banned Black residents from practising a trade or selling goods until 1870!)

Apparently, another Underground Railroad terminus — not as celebrated and heralded as Amherstburg, 'natch — was Sticksville, Ontario, the home of our own intrepid heroes. Not that you'd know it from looking around the Sticksville Museum. (October *was* going to have to speak to Ms. Fenstermacher. Kirby was correct: it was a really big deal.)

"Over here," Kirby called. "I found something that may be of interest."

Kirby, not typically one for understatement had, well, understated. Resting on the mottled carpet was a placard clearly used in the Black History display, with information about the town's role in the Underground Railroad. More importantly, the placard was accompanied by a map showing what was believed to be the terminus of the Underground Railroad in 1860 Sticksville.

"October, d'you know where that is?" Tabetha asked, pointing at the storehouse marked on the map.

"Sort of," she answered. "Don't you? I mean, this map is more from your time than mine. And you were actually there at one point."

"That's Acheron Creek," Derek asserted, pushing his finger through the blue gulf on the map.

"So, this is fairly far north in town," October said.

"We lived near the creek," Tabetha said. "Me n' my dad. He built a house not far from where we arrived, near a storehouse by the mill. White folks didn't like people who came up on the Railroad to move too far from where they came from."

"If it's north by the creek, this has to be where the fairgrounds are now," October decided. "There won't be anyone up at the fairgrounds these days — not until June, at least."

"Maybe we can snoop around and see if we find any clues," Derek said.

Tabetha, encouraged by the first real break in her mystery since ever, was overwhelmed with enthusiasm: "We could go tonight!"

"It doesn't look like we'll find anything more about Tabetha or the Underground Railroad here," Kirby said, riffling through the remaining contents of the *Black History Stuff* box. All that remained were posters about Elijah McCoy and Portia White: important Black Canadians, yes, but ones who never lived in Sticksville nor had any connection to the Scott family.

October glanced at the office wall clock, to discover it was past 1 a.m. "I don't know . . . the fairgrounds are pretty far . . ." Though far more nocturnal than most thirteen-year-olds (and possums), she was acutely aware that tomorrow was a school day and her father was liable to check on her empty bedroom at any given hour, given how many times she'd snuck out in the past several months. "Maybe we could leave this until tomorrow?"

"Why wait?" Morna asked. "I've been dead so long, I don't even remember what it's like to sleep anymore!"

Morna: helpful as always.

Having placed the maps and historical objects and bric-a-brac back into their proper boxes, the group descended the stairs from the office area into the museum proper. October was not relishing the several additional hours during which she would now have to be awake, nor was she entirely sure how she and the dead kids would get to the fairgrounds, the pathetic Sticksville bus service having ended around ten. But, like a proper detective, she asked Tabetha to recount what she remembered of her life over 150 years ago in Sticksville, so as to give her some rough guide to what she should be looking for at the Sticksville Fairgrounds.

"Tabetha, when did you arrive in Sticksville, at the warehouse by Acheron Creek? How did you and your father get here?"

"I dunno," she said. "I was pretty young. I think about seven?"

Tabetha Scott's childhood recollections were cut short by the sound of a low hum, like a far-off riding lawnmower, emanating from the darkened part of the stairs. Cautiously, the six continued downward until a bright white shape took form in the darkness, revealing itself to be a snarling, agitated Dalmatian — an unorthodox choice for a guard dog, but a choice, nonetheless.

"That's new!" Kirby said.

☠   ☠   ☠

2

Birds of a Father

Though I'm not going to be mistaken for Simone Biles or even Melissa McCarthy any time soon, the sight of an unhappy dog about to attack pushed me to dig deep and find my inner acrobat. The dead kids were ghosts and didn't have to worry about the pain (and resulting infection, probably) of dog bites. But I did, so I took a running leap over the Dalmatian and landed in a roll, managing to tumble right into the base of a display case of 19th-century personal grooming items, which sent glass, ivory combs, and straight razors skittering across the stone floor.

Cyril hoisted me up from the crumpled heap I was in and helped me run to the lobby doors, which I shoved open and sprinted through. (The dead kids, being above such mortal things as French doors, simply raced through the walls.) The guard Dalmatian was also, apparently, not into doors. He crashed through the lobby entrance in a geyser of broken glass like a spotted battering ram. We had to keep running if we were to avoid this canine crusader. We sped through the front doors, exiting the museum entirely, with Derek wisely picking up a tall candlestick on his way out.

"Wait up, you traitors," shouted Kirby, who — improbably — was even more out of breath than I was.

"No can do," I panted. "This dog isn't chasing *you*. I've got my own living flesh to worry about."

As soon as we'd all cleared the front doors, Morna and I slammed them shut and Derek slid the candlestick through the door handles, trapping the fire dog inside.

"That reminded me a lot a' whatcha were just askin' about," Tabetha said, slapping Derek on the shoulder. "One a' the few things I remember is my dad n' me running off the plantation."

The Dalmatian, though it continued to snarl and push at the front doors, seemed securely imprisoned, so I managed to pay attention to Tabetha's entire story of escaping from the plantation where she worked as forced labour — the Scott Plantation — and hopped upon (figuratively, of course) the Underground Railroad. Perhaps because I knew it would be important, or perhaps because the heightened adrenalin or endorphins or whatever rushing to my brain made the story that much more vivid, when Tabetha told me her harrowing story, it was almost as if I were there, like I'd entered a particularly good VR simulation of one of the worst times in history.

☠   ☠   ☠

Tabetha began to describe her father and her midnight run from the plantation. Her father, Lunsford, strode ahead, his large frame casting even wider shadows in the moonlight. He led Tabetha — only seven at the time — west from the slave quarters of the Scott land, and, before long, they had entered an area that was mostly bog, with tree roots criss-crossing the muddy ground. Tabetha remembered having to hop and skip more than run to avoid tripping and falling on her face. Tabetha's mother did not accompany the two of them on their secret mission, having died years earlier from overwork.

Tabetha brought her boot down into some sucking mud, and the resulting splash caused her father to turn and raise his index finger to his lips. Realizing the terrain was probably too rough for a seven-year-old to navigate, he lifted Tabetha from the ground and cradled her in his arms, then continued westward, before turning north at a wooden cross planted in front of a willow tree. They had been fleeing for about a half-hour with no sign or sound of pursuit, thankfully.

There were no fences nor walls that imprisoned the Scotts' slaves. There was no reason for there to be. Lunsford and Tabetha, as every other person born enslaved or sold into the Scotts' fold, were well aware of the fate of slaves who had attempted escape: seasonal whippings and brandings had built invisible fences much stronger than wood or wire. Yet even with the constant threat of thrashings and even death, Lunsford took his daughter Tabetha and decided to make a break for it. And why?

Part of the reason for this daredevilry came into Lunsford and Tabetha's field of vision. Sitting atop a coach drawn by two horses blacker than the night sky was a heavyset white man, with a top hat and greying brown beard that ended just below his collar, and a Black driver, with a closely cropped beard and streak of black in his snow-white hair. The coach was parked outside a no-longer-used stone mill beside a muddy creek bed that had once featured a moving waterway. In the carriage were dozens of dome shapes draped with rough burlap canvas. The white man was Alexander Milton Ross, and this wasn't the first time Tabetha had seen him. The coach driver was introduced as William Lambert, from the Detroit area. Ross leapt from the coach seat — far more spry than she expected a man his size would be — and greeted the father and daughter using both of his hands to shake theirs and stage-whispering, "I'm so glad you made it."

☠ ☠ ☠

Early that morning — the work day of the enslaved started about 5:30 a.m. on the Scott Plantation — Tabetha had seen Alexander Milton Ross for the very first time. Accompanied by an overseer astride a horse, he meandered through the cotton fields, lifting a pair of binoculars to his eyes every now and then and scanning the trees that served as the cotton fields' outer perimeter. As the two wandered closer to Tabetha and her father, busy pulling cotton bolls from the plant branches and — at times — instructing his daughter (who would soon need to harvest cotton in the very same fashion) on the tricks and finer points, Tabetha couldn't help but stare at the large man. He certainly wasn't dressed as a Southerner, clothed in a heavy blue-grey tweed suit that looked like it must have been extremely warm. The shine of his forehead and cheeks seemed to confirm that hypothesis.

"Boy," the overseer barked at Lunsford, though Tabetha's father was in his mid-thirties. "Watch your little runt. Make sure she keeps her eyes on your work an' offa the guests."

Tabetha's father, having long ago learned it was best not to respond to an overseer, no matter what your response, nodded.

The overseer thwacked Lunsford's back with the butt end of a bullwhip. "You hear me, boy? Keep her wandering eyes facing forward, or I'll take you out to the whippin' post."

Tabetha saw the bearded northerner's mouth turn to a grim horizontal line just before her dad rotated her by the shoulders to face the wall of cotton plants. The two white men continued on through the cotton fields.

Lunsford began to sing a song: "My Lord, He calls me . . . He calls me by the thunder . . ."

Georgina, head down a few rows over, joined him in song. Tabetha recognized the spiritual as "Steal Away," and almost immediately her heart vaulted into her throat. Her dad had spoken about the Underground Railroad for months, providing Tabetha with snatches of hope — first thing in the morning, or in the evenings when the overseers were away. In earnestness, she sometimes thought it wasn't a real thing — more a fairy tale he told her to raise her spirits. But she recognized her father singing "Steal Away" for what it was: secret code alerting her and the other enslaved of the Scott Plantation to their imminent escape.

Tabetha's father, however, showed no tell-tale signs of elation or anxiety. He continued his work on the cotton plants until she stopped him by tapping his shoulder.

"Does this mean —?" she began.

Her dad, peering at her beneath a sweat-beaded brow, shot her a glare that ended her question mid-sentence. This was not a conversation for daytime, when overseers and other white folks were thicker in the cotton fields than locusts. Tabetha just smiled and made a little locking motion with her hand in front of her lips. Though she had no idea how or exactly when their

escape would take place, she realized this would be — should fate be on their side — her last morning on the Scott Plantation. Her insides roiled with an unsettling compound of excitement and terror. Though Tabetha relished a life outside of slavery, she knew escape was anything but easy.

Both buoyed and troubled by her father's secret planning, Tabetha was fully preoccupied in her own thoughts when she saw the bearded man again. The white man made lazy circles around the area where her father and a team of about a dozen field slaves pulled cotton. They were right in the middle of a second rendition of "Steal Away," so Tabetha and Lunsford almost didn't hear when the visiting stranger said, just a few levels above a whisper, as if he were calmly waking up a friend from slumber, "You, with the little one."

Add to this that the white man was not facing them or standing in any manner which could be said to address Lunsford and Tabetha. In fact, he stood about three paces away, his back to them, scanning the trees with his small binoculars and holding a notebook in his free hand. Tabetha heard but wasn't sure her father did — also, she was very confused who he was speaking to. The birds?

"Excuse me," he repeated. "You, with the girl."

Tabetha tugged at her father's sleeve, rolled up to the elbows in his labour. "Dad, I think he's talkin' to you."

"Tabby, I told you —" Lunsford began, raising his voice to his only child.

"Your overseer, Malcolm, is nowhere to be seen," the bearded man said, still gazing up at the trees. "I assure you."

Now, Tabetha told me — while we casually walked across the museum parking lot — that her and her dad's previous experiences with white people had given them reason to put about as much stock in their assurances as in those of a venomous snake. But still, because this was the 1850s, and he was being addressed by a white man, Lunsford was obliged to turn toward the solo birdwatcher.

"No, keep working!" the man said, trying to maintain his poise and calm, though it was clear a little panic had gripped his voice box like an overeager toddler meeting her first kitten. "Don't look at me. We don't want to arouse any suspicion."

"Uh-huh," Lunsford said, who returned to cotton picking, though he moved from a cappella vocals to whistling.

"My name is Alexander Milton Ross," the man said, his back still to Tabetha and her father. "I'm an ornithologist. That's someone who studies birds. And I'm here to look at Cuban Emeralds. They're extremely rare in this part of Virginia. That's why I'm allowed to roam freely among the cotton fields."

"You're a friend a' the Scotts," Lunsford said. "Seems you can do whatever you want."

"Fair point," the bearded man said. This was like an alien world. Tabetha noted that had her father said that to any other white person, despite how tame a barb it had been, he'd have been at the receiving end of a serious beating. Or, at the very least, a backhanded slap. "Nevertheless, I'm not here to see birds. I'm here to help you escape."

"Escape?" Tabetha said, her large eyes lighting up like the incandescent light bulbs that had yet to be invented. Was this white bird-lover what all the singing was about? For some reason, Tabetha expected . . . someone else. As did her father.

"Escape?" her father echoed, though his eyes were far more cynical. He kept his voice to a whisper. "You?"

"Shhh," Ross said.

Lunsford nodded and returned to work.

"I'm a conductor of the Underground Railroad," the ornithologist continued. "A friend named William suggested I pay you a visit at this plantation. He said another man he helped escape, Garrett, provided him with your names."

Lunsford's hands froze at the mention of Garrett. "So you're gonna help me n' my daughter escape, huh?"

Like most slaves who had lived past thirty, Lunsford had learned to be mistrustful of most men — white men, in particular.

"That's correct," he coughed. "Ideally, tonight."

"Y'know, when I talked with Garrett about the Underground Railroad," Tabetha's father said, "I was expectin' someone Black."

"I assure you, there are many Black conductors in our organization. Should things . . . progress, you will even meet a number of them. But you will agree it's difficult for those conductors to connect with 'passengers' working under such conditions," the man said. Suddenly, his eyes widened.

Tabetha's father continued singing and his daughter, catching on quickly, joined him. The white man who may or may not have been aiding them in escape had already moved ten paces from them and was adjusting his binoculars. The overseer, perched atop a slowly cantering horse, passed by and spat tobacco in their general direction. About two full verses later, their new white friend spoke up.

"I believe it's safe to speak again," he said. "Are you able to steal away tonight?"

"Hold up. Why exactly should we trust you?" asked Tabetha's father.

"The only things I am passionate about are avians and abolition, mister . . ."

"Lunsford," he answered. "Just Lunsford."

"Oh, yes," the birdman said quietly. "Well, we'll have to get you a proper last name once you arrive in Canada. But we have a long journey ahead — you and your daughter more so than me."

"We are not planning on going anywhere," Tabetha's dad decided. "I planned things with Garrett, n' — t'be honest — I expected to be hearing from Garrett himself. Not you." He then returned to full-volume singing.

"Mr. Lunsford," Ross said, making the same mistake again in his exasperation. "Garrett, obviously, could not just saunter back onto a plantation — even if it's not the one from which he escaped. You realize what danger that would put him in. So I am to be the first of your many guides on your voyage to freedom. I'm afraid you must take a chance on me. This may be your only chance at escape."

"Or," Lunsford whispered dramatically through his crooked teeth, "it's my chance t'get me n' my daughter killed for runnin' around like fools with some fat birdman."

A long pause followed that exchange — as heated as an exchange could get with two men not facing one another and neither willing to rouse the suspicion of any cotton pickers or overseers who might be within snooping distance of their argument. The matter seemed over, and it appeared that Alexander Milton Ross would walk on to stalk more feathered friends or find some other mush head working outside to lead into his nefarious trap. Tabetha, however, was crestfallen. If her father had planned escape for tonight, why wouldn't it be this birdman? But before the birdman continued on his way through the cotton fields, he left them with one more sentence: "Garrett — he goes by Garett *Freeman* now — says you owe him a ham from that game of Old Maid you played back on Dunn Plantation."

Finally, unable to help himself, Lunsford turned to face the ornithologist, though the white man kept up the charade and refused to move from (what one would assume to be) his bird-viewing vantage spot. Tabetha's father must have calculated there was a chance Ross was some sort of sadistic slave-catcher who could have earlier plied the same trick on his friend Garrett, then made him confess to Lunsford's growing Old Maid debt under torture or duress, but — for the moment — he was willing to take the chance that was not the scenario. After all, Lunsford *had* made arrangements to escape via the Railroad, and was expecting to connect with a conductor at some point this day. That the birdman Ross knew so much about Garrett seemed to suggest he was his unlikely contact.

Lunsford began to quietly whistle again. "You tell us where we need to be and when."

Though she tried to suppress it, so as not to alarm the overseers, Tabetha's face split into a wide smile.

☠   ☠   ☠

Tabetha then described how, when she and her father made their late-night rendezvous with the proverbial Birdman and his partner in the forest, the Birdman immediately showed

them how they'd be travelling northward to the Underground Railroad's next station — and it was certainly not in style.

With Alexander Milton Ross being a self-professed bird enthusiast, perhaps Tabetha and her father should have expected something like what was under the burlap tarps. But, in all fairness, the birdcages were very unexpected.

"You want us to hide in those?!"

Lunsford was incredulous, but the ornithologist did, indeed, want him and his daughter to travel in oversized bird-cages. Ross and his fellow conductor William Lambert nodded apologetically. The carriage of Ross's coach was filled with cages of nearly every size, some of them containing birds native to this part of Virginia, others vacant. Lunsford and Tabetha were to occupy the two largest ones, which could have fit very healthy vultures or certain falcons.

"I realize it will likely prove extremely uncomfortable and more than a little humiliating, but there truly is no other way," Ross quietly pleaded. "You can't travel in this part of the country with two Black passengers up front with the driver. And even if I put you in the back, but *not* in the birdcage, we could be spotted by authorities or bounty hunters once word gets out that the two of you escaped — if it hasn't already."

"Why don't I pretend t'be your driver," Lunsford politely asked, gesturing toward William, "n' *he* can sit in the birdcage?"

William Lambert shook his head. "We been workin' together for years now. We both like to sit up front."

Tabetha didn't care much about travelling in a birdcage. In all honesty, she'd been transported in far more shameful ways in her young life. "C'mon, Dad. It'll be fine. Let's just go."

But Tabetha's father remained unconvinced.

"The journey won't be far," Ross said. "But it will be far, far more treacherous for all of us unless you sit in those birdcages and I cover those birdcages with that canvas."

"Do we have to make bird noises too?" Tabetha asked.

Ross sighed. "I assure you, if you get in, I'll have you to your destination within a day without incident. The other cages are there as a camouflage — some of them have actual birds inside. Even the nastiest slave-catchers don't particularly like putting their fingers anywhere near caged birds."

Lunsford grumbled, "I'll have t'bring this up with Garrett if I ever see him again."

As Tabetha Scott told it, the Birdman was mostly accurate — she and her father hid inside the birdcages, pretzeled up into their tiniest selves, with only the opaque burlap blanket as scenery. The plaintive warbling of birds, the rhythmic crunch of the coach wheels rolling on gravel, and the intermittent singing of their driver comprised the only soundtrack for about four hours. But sometime after that, the sound of other horse hooves interrupted. Then they heard shouts and the wheels slowed to a halt. It being the middle of the night, Tabetha couldn't even see shadows beyond the canvas, but she could hear other voices accompanying that of Alexander Milton Ross.

"Hold on, friend. Where might you two be headed?" asked a voice thick with Southern drawl.

In reply, Ross gave his traditional introduction, which he had treated Tabetha and her dad to just that morning — about him being an ornithologist and all that jazz. Of course, this not being Ross's first rodeo — if a death-defying mission on the Underground Railroad can ever be called a "rodeo" — Ross left out the part about he and Lambert actually being conductors for the Underground Railroad. Tabetha had no idea whether the other voices belonged to slave catchers, bounty hunters, or someone from the Scott Plantation, but if *any* white folks were alerted to the presence of two escaped slaves in Ross's cartage, it could spell utter disaster for everyone involved.

"An' who might this fella be?" the Southern voice asked. "Ain't I seen you workin' the cotton this mornin'?"

Laughs all around.

"That's my driver, William."

"So what's under all the lumpy canvas in the back of your cart then, mister bird man?" a second Southern voice asked.

"Well . . . birds," Ross answered. "I'm taking a number back with me to my aviary up north."

"I don't suppose you'd mind if we took a closer look then," the first voice chimed in.

"Of course not," Ross said. Tabetha had never heard such a cool customer in her life. Two Southern gentlemen just said they'd be looking through the goods he was transporting — in which, of course, he'd secreted two recently liberated individuals — and he was all like, "NBD." Naturally, he was in less danger than Tabetha and her father, who were as good as hanged if found. But there's no way Ross knew he wouldn't be hanged, as well. The punishment for aiding slaves to escape, particularly across state lines, could be death no matter *how* white you were. And they wouldn't care that William Lambert was a free Black man.

Under Tabetha's bottom, the coach shifted as two men hauled themselves up into the back. Though Tabetha couldn't see a thing, she could hear their heavy footfalls and the sound of fabric lifting as they, presumably, took a look inside the birdcages at the far end of the coach bed. The swish-swish of the cage reveals, often followed by the interjection of birdsong, slowly grew louder, nearer.

"Please replace the canvas coverings," Ross asked. "The birds get so agitated if I travel with the cages uncovered."

"Sure, sure," one Southern man's voice muttered.

"I can barely see a thing," the other said. "Bring that lantern closer."

Ross, somehow, didn't begin to shriek in horror. Tabetha could hardly believe it. Her heart was rattling in her chest like the chain in a roller coaster (not that those existed yet) and she feared her heightened breath might alert the search party to her location.

Another rough swish. The call of a common nighthawk followed.

Even louder, a swish sounded and was answered by an oystercatcher.

The men were so close to where Tabetha sat she could hear their breathing and see the silhouettes thrown from the light of their lantern. Surely, they could hear her heart as it just about detonated. Another canvas was removed, but this time the call came from a man — one of the search party shrieked out in pain.

"Ah, you found the laughing gull," Ross said. "I'm sorry. This one does like to bite."

"You okay, Clem?" a voice asked.

The laughing gull made its cackling sound.

"Ugly thing nearly took my finger off!" Clem shouted.

"Mister, you best control your birds!"

"Control?!" Clem shouted. "Imma kill that bird — laughing at me!"

"Gentlemen," Ross said. Tabetha could hear he'd turned around in the driver's seat as he attempted to calm the bungling catchers and minimize the loss of bird life. "I assure you, the gull is not laughing *at* you."

The laughing gull continued to chuckle.

"It ain't laughin' *with* me."

"That is merely the sound of its birdsong," he continued. "Must I remind you that we are dealing with *wild* animals here? Ones that will bite and lash out if feeling threatened?"

"My fingers," the one called Clem continued to moan.

"I situated the more . . . rambunctious specimens closer to the driver's seat, I'm afraid. If someone would care to hold the horses, I'd be happy to show you the remaining birds myself — so you don't risk your fingers."

"No, sir, that's fine," someone who was not Clem answered. "I think we seen enough. Let's get outta here, Clem."

The coach rocked as the men hopped out of the carriage and continued on their way. After a few moments, Lambert prodded the horses, and the travel continued. However, the coach must have driven twenty minutes before the Birdman felt comfortable enough to whisper, "Now *that* was a close one."

Close for who? Tabetha thought, though she didn't dare speak. William Lambert began to sing once again, and Tabetha's heart rate finally slowed to something resembling normal. Never, for the rest of her days, could she handle the fact she owed her life to a laughing gull.

☠   ☠   ☠

When Alexander Ross pulled the canvas from the birdcages, he woke Tabetha from a deep slumber. She was completely disoriented, as the sky was dark, though a full day must have passed since she last saw Ross's face. He opened the massive birdcage, and Tabetha stood up and began to stretch her sore limbs. William Lambert uncovered her father's cage.

"How long have we been travellin'," was the first thing he asked. "Feels like days. And I never thought freedom would involve so much time in a cage."

Ross made a face that was part smile, part grimace. "My apologies. The only safe time to reveal the hiding place of a couple fugitive slaves this side of the Mason-Dixon line is under the cover of night. The time is nearly dawn, but a full day has passed since we left."

Tabetha's father grunted in reply as he extracted himself from the birdcage and extended his legs.

"Where are we?" Tabetha asked.

"Your next station on the Underground Railroad. From here, another conductor will take you farther along your path," William said. Tabetha had never heard a Black man with a

Northern accent before. Then, less cryptically, he added, "But more accurately, you're still in Virginia."

Ross led them to a barn and opened the front door.

"You'll spend the day resting here at the station," Ross said. "The barn is safe — we've used it dozens of times before. Word has been sent to the next conductor, who is planning to arrive just after dark tonight. Until then, William and I will stand watch. I can bring you some supper later in the afternoon."

Tabetha didn't remember much beyond that, as she had nestled into a fresh pile of hay and begun to doze off.

☠ ☠ ☠

From the abandoned barn, they were taken by a second conductor, Solomon Drury. Drury wore a bowler hat, and his triangular face was framed by large mutton chop sideburns. He had an even less comfortable spot for Tabetha and her father to hide: the two of them were forced to wedge themselves into a large steamer trunk in Drury's carriage, where they lay folded like misshapen origami and tensed up with every single deviation from the soothing calm of the carriage's rolling wheels.

After the fitful and uncomfortable ride through the night, the carriage stopped, and Tabetha and Lunsford were greeted by the smiling face of Solomon Drury as he unlocked the steamer trunk. Beyond his face stood yet another barn. This one differed from the previous one in that it was mostly painted a sky blue. (But, like, barns were everywhere back then. They were like Starbucks.)

"We're here!" he announced cheerily, though quietly.

The sun was just beginning to slide over the horizon, and though Tabetha was resentful at having to spend hours in a cramped spot beside her dad, she was relieved the night's journey hadn't resulted in any further close calls or visits from search parties. Drury tied the horses to a post outside the blue barn. He led Lunsford and Tabetha through the barn doors and announced it was the next station.

"We're nearly in Maryland now," he said, with a fair amount of glee.

"And will you be conductor for our next leg of the journey?" Lunsford asked. "Or will another conductor be taking over?"

"You know, you ask a lotta questions fer a slave," Solomon Drury noted, closing the barn door behind the three of them.

"We're not slaves anymore," Tabetha insisted.

"Is that so?" Drury said.

From the dark corners of the barn's interior, two men emerged with pistols drawn.

☠   ☠   ☠

"Wait, what do you mean?" I asked.

"It was an ambush, October!" Tabetha shouted. "That man wasn't part of the Underground Railroad; his name wasn't even Solomon Drury. He was a slave catcher. He must have discovered one of the stations!"

"And the Birdman?" I gasped.

"Nah, he got tricked too, as we later found out," Tabetha said, adding some further intrigue. "Conductors often didn't know much about other conductors."

"You escaped from the Scott Plantation," Derek asked, confused. "But your last name is Scott too?"

"How d'ya think I got that name?" Tabetha said, more disappointed than angry. "We were given them by the Plantation owners. My dad didn't name me; some white slave owner did."

"That's the saddest thing ever," Morna said, seemingly unsure if she should pat her dead friend on the shoulder or if that would make things worse.

"Some Black folks gave themselves new last names when they finally got free," Tabetha said. "Dad kept the Scott name. Said it reminded him of what we fled n' how hard we struggled."

"Tabetha, I'm so sorry," I added.

That's when the front doors of the museum blew open and the formerly wedged candlestick fell clattering to the ground. The Dalmatian barked loudly to announce his independence and sprinted into the parking lot. It wasn't enough that they had exited the museum, the fire dog was still on the hunt. Kirby sighed as they broke into a run again.

The dogged Dalmatian barked, spittle flying in several directions. Kirby took a while to pick up speed and, despite being dead, still seemed to garner a lot of the guard dog's interest. And Kirby's eyes showed that he knew it too.

"So," Morna puffed. "Obviously this fake Drury guy was the one who killed ya, right?"

"I was seven!" Tabetha shouted. "Do I look seven now?! *Obviously* I survived that."

"Shut up, you two!" Derek shouted. "Look!"

Somehow, the dead kids and I had managed to run all the way back to the Sticksville Cemetery, and the Dalmatian still hadn't relented. I'd never run so far in my life. If you chased me with an angry dog, I could probably finish a marathon.

"We're at the cemetery," Cyril announced.

"So? Dogs can enter cemeteries," I said. Duh. "There's no animal force field. Keep running!"

"But who is that?" Derek asked.

A lone automobile was parked in the Sticksville Cemetery lot, which was a very unusual occurrence for a Sunday at one o'clock. But I figured this was a mystery that could wait until way later. Cyril, the doofus, unfortunately didn't feel the same way and had stopped dead in his tracks to ponder the car. Which meant that I ran headlong into his United Empire Loyalist back and toppled backward with the impact. That's when the Dalmatian pounced on my prone body and chomped down on my left ankle.

☠   ☠   ☠

Pet (in the) Cemetery

As if October Schwartz were made entirely of soup bones — and I'm not confirming she's not — the guard Dalmatian tucked into her ankle, which was protected only by the thin canvas of her Chuck Taylors and black woollen socks. The barrier proved to be insufficient protection, and October howled like she was murdering a Cranberries song at karaoke.

"Get him off me!" October pleaded, trying to pry the fire dog's mouth open with her hands, which only put her biteable fingers in even *more* danger. Things were rapidly devolving from bad to worse, like a season of *Grey's Anatomy*. Were it not for the quick-though-predictable thinking of Tabetha Scott, October might well have changed her name to Purina. (Or, if we're being fancy, Science Diet.)

Tabetha turned to stop Kirby, still mid-run. In truth, he was relieved October was the one being eaten by a dog, given he was the slowest runner among them. But his relief was short-lived.

"What?" he asked.

Tabetha rolled up her sleeves and gave Kirby the "gimme" fingers. "Show me yer arm."

Kirby quickly realized what was being asked of him.

"No," he said, shaking his head with such insistence, his short blond hair ruffled back and forth. "Why me? It's *your* idea!"

"We're solvin' *my* mystery, Kirby," Tabetha reasoned. "I'm probably gonna need both my arms ta solve it."

"Take Derek's . . . or Morna's," he pouted.

"Nah. You've got more meat. We need to keep that mutt occupied."

Kirby refused to submit his arm to Tabetha while October continued to struggle on the ground with the dog like they were two ill-prepared MMA fighters.

"I know you guys aren't allowed to hurt living *people* . . ." she shouted, "but can you hurt *animals*? Because, even though I love dogs, that would be really handy right now . . ."

Tabetha gestured to the girl and dog locked in mortal combat outside the cemetery gates. "Yer livin' friend's life hangs in the balance."

"We're not that close."

October cried out in pain as the Dalmatian bit down deeper.

"Okay, okay," Kirby relented.

Tabetha used both hands to clutch Kirby's wrist, then hoisted her leg and pushed her boot into her dead frenemy's gut.

"Sure you're strong enough?" he taunted.

Tabetha heaved, and Kirby's arm popped out at the shoulder with an unsettling wet sucking sound. She then began to spin like an Olympic discus thrower and finally released the pale arm high into the air.

The spotted dog looked up from its meal and saw the body-free

arm of Kirby LaFlamme flapping in the night air. The Dalmatian paused to follow the arm with his eyes, gazing intently as the appendage sailed across the road, landing with a damp thud on the other side of a lawn sign that advertised masonry. The furry fiend, seeing a potential meal that had already been broken into more manageable pieces, released October's still-attached leg and scurried away to find Kirby's (possibly) delicious arm.

Morna and Derek rushed to October's side to help her off the ground. Kirby would likely have assisted, too, but so many mechanical actions had just become far more difficult.

"Are you okay?" Derek asked, lifting October up with his shoulder. "Can you walk?"

"Yes," she said, wincing as she hobbled along. "It just hurts."

"I don't think it broke skin," Cyril said, eyeballing October's ankle.

"Well, I'm glad *one* of us isn't harmed," Kirby said.

"Quit whinin'," Tabetha said, the Darth Vader to Kirby's Skywalker.

"Thanks for donating your arm to the cause of my continued existence," October said. "I'm sure it will be awkward for a while, but at least I don't have to explain to my dad how my leg got amputated."

"Shh," Derek said. "Let's get further into the cemetery. Maybe we can lose that dog."

"Okay," said October. "But why are we being quiet? Everybody out here is dead."

"Not so," said Cyril. "Observe this suspect automobile."

Cyril gestured as the Dead Kid Detective Agency made their way across the cemetery parking lot, where a somewhat dusty Toyota Yaris was the only car in sight.

"Weird," October remarked, having now been convinced to lower her voice. "That's Alyosha Diamandas's car."

Obsessive readers may remember that the Sticksville real estate agent who has more than one time antagonized the dead kids, and made October's life generally more aggravating, drives a fun yet sensible Yaris.

"What is he doing in the cemetery?" Kirby asked as they left

the parking lot and progressed up a hill on which a small mausoleum sat. He had not yet adjusted to the loss of his arm and
was listing heavily to one side. The Mystery of the Dusty Yaris
— easily the simplest mystery yet featured in these books — was
quickly solved once the Dead Kid Detective Agency surmounted
the hill. In the middle distance, not far from the wooded area with
the large tree where October would often raise (and meet) the
dead kids, they saw a theatrically dressed man speaking to Alyosha
Diamandas. They stood in the middle of a circle of white sand or
powder.

"Theatrically dressed" can mean so many things, but in this
case, it meant the stranger was dressed as if he were leaving for an
evening at the theatre, provided the theatre was located in 1880.
Not only was his attire formal, it included white evening gloves
and an honest-to-goodness cape. (All he lacked was a top hat.)
Dramatically large round glasses were perched on his nose and,
though he had no moustache, a jet-black goatee that matched his
hair projected a couple inches from his chin. Whatever this man
and Alyosha Diamandas were plotting in the Sticksville Cemetery,
they made no attempts to be subtle about it.

"There's Alyosha," Derek said.

"Who's tha' man wi' him?" Morna asked.

"And why are they in a ring?" October added.

Kirby shared an unlikely theory: "Maybe they're starting a circus?"

Nearly as soon as October and the dead kids had time to take in the spectacle before them, Alyosha and his friend left their circle and began walking toward the hill.

"They're coming this way," October said, panicking a tad. "Let's hide."

"Hide?" Tabetha whispered. "Where? All the tree cover is over there!"

Alyosha and his companion continued their casual conversation as they climbed the hill. From their super-chill pace, it was clear they hadn't seen October or any of her ghost friends yet.

"We're going to have to hide in here," Kirby said, pointing at the tomb with his remaining arm.

"Ewww, really?" October slid her tongue between her teeth. She was fine with palling around with a bunch of corpses, but October Schwartz still found something unpleasantly wrong about breaking into the departed's final resting places — particularly when they were strangers. But desperate times — or near-Alyosha encounters (same thing, really) — called for the dismissal of such objections.

"Okay, fine," she relented. "Open the door for me, please."

The five dead kids slid through the locked wooden door to the mausoleum and opened it from the inside. Before either Alyosha or the man unfortunate or deranged enough to be his friend looked up from their in-depth conversation, October hopped inside and locked the door behind her. Inside, she found a stone coffin set in the centre of a narrow stone room. Unlike other family mausoleums — the apartment complexes of the graveyard — this tomb was the dead's equivalent of a bachelor pad: just one coffin. October stood there, noting how strange it looked on its own, when she heard the door handle begin to clatter. Panic mode: achieved.

"Why are they trying to get in here?" she hissed in the general direction of the dead kids, though she was not really expecting them to have the answer. "Whose tomb is this?"

However, there were considerably more pressing questions that October had not posed — such as, where was she to hide, given she was faced with three stone walls and a door through which a real estate agent and his opera-going friend would soon be entering, and she was yet unable to walk through walls like the dead kids. Derek, however, often a step ahead of most, was already developing a solution. He planted his feet and began to shove the stone cover of the coffin aside. The other dead children, grasping his idea, joined him. With a gradual scrape they hoped the men outside wouldn't notice, the kids pushed the stone tablet lying across the coffin loose.

"Think they have keys to this tomb?" October asked.

"I think we should assume Alyosha Diamandas has a key to every room in this town," said Derek.

"You had better get in," Cyril suggested.

The padlock outside rattled again.

"We all had," October said as she stumbled in. "Remember that Alyosha can see all of you."

"We'll just go through the back wall instead," Kirby said. "No fuss, no muss."

"What's muss?" Cyril asked.

Before anyone could answer, they became aware that Kirby was stuck halfway through the mausoleum wall.

"Havin' a problem there, Kirby?" Tabetha asked.

"I don't think I can get through the wall," he cried.

"Did you hear something?" the voice of Alyosha said from beyond the locked door.

"I can't get out," Kirby said.

"They're coming!" Morna whispered as loudly as she could.

"Hurry!" October exhaled like a pressure cooker releasing its steam valve. "Everybody, get in the coffin."

October held her breath and tried to ignore her concerns about hiding on top of a dead body. (She had to prepare for what-ever shape the body was in — skeleton, if she was lucky). She clambered into the stone coffin and crouched into a ball. Luckily it was dark (what with it being a tomb and the middle of the night), but unfortunately that darkness only heightened her sense of touch, and she could feel the cold skull of the coffin's occupant pressed against her own cheek. She felt tingles running up and

down her legs, but couldn't be certain if that was fear or if the coffin was full of spiders. October attempted to angle her body in a way that didn't put her in direct face-to-face contact with a dead person's skull, but her foot slipped, and she fell further into the skeleton's arms. Rotting teeth banged into her face. No matter how harrowing October envisioned her first kiss, she couldn't have imagined it coming from a corpse.

In moments, however, the unwanted embrace of an old skeleton was no longer top of mind, as the dead kids shut the coffin's lid and ghosted through the sides to squish themselves beside her. The six of them (plus the original dead guy) were wedged like sardines in a stone can, with about as much free oxygen as a week-old balloon. To be quite honest, if Kirby still had two arms, they might not have even fit. October groaned as she felt someone's knee press into her back — probably Kirby's — and had just started to complain when they heard footsteps. Alyosha and his pal had entered the tomb.

October and the dead kids maintained (aptly, I'd say) utter silence, hoping (a) they'd overhear the two men discuss the reasons they were in the cemetery and making circles out of oatmeal or whatever they were up to, and (b) the two men had a shred more decency than the six of them did and wouldn't be disturbing the coffin in which they hid. Hopes were partially answered, as they often are. The two graveyard-dwelling gents left without disturbing the coffin, and not before having a conversation that October managed to catch at least a portion of:

"And you believe this will work?" the unmistakable voice of Alyosha Diamandas came, complete with its strange rhythm.

"One does not enter this business if one doubts his abilities," said the other man.

The man's voice, like everything else about him, was theatrical. October wondered what line of business, save grave robbing, brought two adult men to a cemetery this late at night.

"Yes, of course . . ." Alyosha answered. "In that way, your work and mine — real estate — are very much the same."

The following eerie silence suggested Alyosha's friend doubted their jobs' similarity.

"What kind of salt is that?" Alyosha asked, finally breaking the silence. "Just, like, Morton table salt? Pink Himalayan?"

"I'm afraid that's a trade secret, Mr. Diamandas," the other man said.

"As long as it works, Nicodemus."

Somehow, Alyosha had found a friend with a name just as unusual (in the cloistered town of Sticksville, at least) as his own. The odds on such a feat were staggering.

"It *shall* work," Nicodemus assured. "Though I'd feel much more comfortable about it if you knew who these children were."

The coffin being blacker than a puddle of tar, the dead kids couldn't see October's wide-eyed "check-it-out" face that trailed the last comment of Nicodemus. Obviously, these two were after the dead kids, though what they were planning to do with them, she had no idea.

The men's voices faded and the door clicked shut. October counted ten full Mississippis in her head before she said a word.

"I think we can get out of this coffin now."

The ghost knee retracted from her spine and the blood began to flow through her extremities once again. The dead kids slowly exited the coffin, then pulled open the lid for October. She got to her knees, careful not to lean too heavily on the skeleton underneath her, and clambered out, joining the other dead kids in the crypt. The room looked entirely unchanged, save for a white circle that went around the tomb's perimeter. A salt circle, given the men's conversation.

"What d'ye think they were doing in here?" Morna asked, as she'd clearly not been paying as much attention to the conversation as October had.

"Do you think they're Asphodel Meadows? It sounds like they're both part of some secret society," Cyril noted.

The question was a fair one: Asphodel Meadows was the name of a mysterious group that had bedevilled October and the dead kids' investigations for months now, and all they knew about them was they were a secret society of some sort that had something to do with a long-dead witch. Why couldn't two middle-aged men chilling out in a cemetery overnight comprise the entirety of the nefarious Asphodel Meadows?

"Quiet, Cyril," October said. "One of you who can read, please tell me whose tomb this is and how long they lived."

Derek Running Water went to open the door to read its

inscription but stopped as he approached the border of the salt circle.

"Um . . . I'm having a bit of a problem."

"What's the problem?" Tabetha said.

"I don't think I can move," Derek answered. However, he stepped backward — clearly, he could move in *some* directions — then tried to push forward again, but stalled at the salt on the stone floor. "I can't go any further."

"See, the same thing happened to me when I tried to leave through the back wall," Kirby insisted.

"This is ridiculous," huffed Tabetha. She pulled Derek back by his black T-shirt and marched forward, running smack-dab into the same invisible wall that stymied Derek.

"Come on!" she shouted.

October, just as confused as any of the dead kids, thought to try for herself. She walked to the salt circle's edge, bracing herself for impact with the force field that was apparently there, but the impact never came. She was able to take a sprightly step over the salt and open the door, revealing the name of the occupant: *Isaac Fitzgibbon, 1822–1832*.

"Ten years old," October whispered to herself.

"Where are ya goin'?" Tabetha shouted.

"Yeah, don't leave us here in this tomb," Kirby added.

An epiphany that most likely had already occurred to you smarter readers finally occurred to October: "This is a tomb for a kid," she said. "Those two guys — Alyosha and Nicodemus — they're looking for children's graves. They're looking for you dead kids."

"For what purpose?" Cyril asked.

"To trap you, obviously," October said, gesturing broadly to how none of them could exit the salt circle. Duh, everyone. "There's another circle around the outside of the mausoleum. That explains why you couldn't ghost your way out, Kirby."

"Why would they want to do that?" Kirby said.

"Maybe because we ruin Mr. Diamandas's life?" Morna suggested.

"Don't call him 'mister,'" Kirby insisted.

While the dead kids bickered over how well or how poorly they had treated Sticksville's most prominent realtor over the past few months, October was having a much more uncomfortable realization. Alyosha Diamandas wanted to prevent the dead kids from ever leaving the cemetery.

"Here," October said, kicking a big gap into the line of the salt with her shoe. She took a step outside and did the same with the second ring. "I don't know why a circle of salt should prevent you guys from leaving, but this should help."

The dead kids, now free to roam wherever they so pleased, left Isaac Fitzgibbon's final resting place and walked out into the wider cemetery. Nicodemus, Alyosha, and his Yaris were nowhere to be seen.

October felt a strong need to develop a plan to counter this new and pressing threat from Alyosha and his new, seemingly more-magical-than-David-Blaine friend, though she wasn't sure how they'd manage that.

"We need to keep Alyosha from guessing which graves are yours," October reasoned.

"Unless they just make one of them salt circles around the entire cemetery," Derek said.

"That'd be a *lot* of salt," Kirby said.

"Can you take me to each of your graves?" October asked. "Maybe we can do something to disguise them."

"I don't think that matters," Derek said. "Now that we've been raised from the dead, the grave is just where our dead bodies are — the salt wouldn't trap us."

The group strolled past Derek's own grave and saw it, too, had been encircled with salt. Alyosha and Nicodemus had been busy this evening. October kicked the salt circle to dust, just in case.

"Should we check all our graves, just t'be safe?" Morna asked.

Before October could decide, she was sideswiped (sucker-punched) by a revelation from Tabetha.

"That's gonna be hard. I'm not even buried here," Tabetha said.

"What do you mean, *you're not buried here?*" October asked. Though she didn't plan to make a habit of exhuming her friends, a body had come in handy when investigating Cyril's mystery. Not having Tabetha's grave close by could be a serious wrinkle. "Where are you buried?"

"I'm not," she said. "Not anywhere I know. When I'm raised from the dead, I show up in the cemetery, but just in the middle of some trees rather than near any grave. We've all looked fer our own tombstones. I'm not here."

One would hope, dear readers, that October is that brand of peculiar person who says she loves a challenge.

☠ ☠ ☠

School of Rock (and Other Popular Music Genres)

"And who can tell me what specific latent heat is?" my dad asked the science class as he faced his chalkboard. Somehow Sticksville still managed to have chalkboards, and somehow my dad still managed to get the chalk from those boards all over his white work shirts, day-in, day-out.

"Anyone? We went over this just last week," he said, apparently hurt none of us were that chuffed about latent heat. And then, as if I weren't his only child and were instead some random student who didn't speak up in class: "October Schwartz?"

This had been happening a lot — a ton! — since the semesters switched over and I now, horrifyingly, had to take science class with my own dad. He was definitely calling on me way more than anyone else and being extra-hard on me whenever I got something wrong. I had to make sure I didn't mess this up.

"Specific latent heat is the amount of energy needed to change one kilogram of a substance from a solid state to its liquid state at the same temperature," I said, giving the textbook short form.

"Okay, good," Dad said, facing the class and folding his chalk-stained forearms across his chest. After that, he gave me — I think — a barely perceptible wink and my stomach dropped. (Here's hoping I was the only person to perceive it.) Dad turned back to the board and continued his lecture. I was thankful he'd singled me out on what was a relatively simple question, as I had been preoccupied all day with the Underground Railroad.

The remainder of last night had been spent clearing the salt from as many graves as we could find — not just the dead kids', but any kids'. (We didn't want to give Alyosha any clues as to who the dead kids *really* were.) Tabetha's story about the Birdman and her adventurous escape got me thinking: if Sticksville had once been a final "stop" on the Underground Railroad, then couldn't I reasonably expect some sort of historic site or museum or — at the very least — a very informative plaque where that stop was? But prior to meeting the ghost of Tabetha Scott, I had no idea Sticksville and the Underground Railroad were in any way connected. (I guess it made some sense, given how close the town was to the American border.) Plus, Tabetha said they built their house close to the stop, up near Acheron Creek. If her body wasn't in the cemetery, maybe it was buried up there. Or maybe there was something left of her old house.

I'd have to wait until class was over before taking a bus to the fairgrounds to find out for myself just how much there was to learn about Tabetha and her dad at the old Underground Railroad site. You'd think I could just skip school for detective work — after all, it's not like what I was planning to do wasn't informative. It was basically a history field trip, even though my history classes with Ms. Fenstermacher — and Mr. Page before that — ended last semester.

In the midst of all these thoughts on Sticksville's history, my history class, and special treatment for detectives, I hadn't realized that my father, the science teacher, had called on me again. Were there no other students in this class with the ability to speak?

"Could you repeat the question?" I asked, blinking dramatically.

"For you," my dad said, smarm spreading across his face, "anything. I was asking what the formula was for the specific latent heat of a substance, since you so accurately defined it earlier."

Again, it was only pure luck — unless there was some sort

of guardian angel watching out for kid detectives — St. Hardy or something like that — that Dad asked me about something I knew like the back of my hand. Better, even — I doubt I could draw the back of my hand from memory. I gave the obvious answer — $L = Q/m$, for you science buffs — and the speaker tone that indicated the switch between periods sounded. Between semesters, they'd updated the school P.A., so instead of it sounding like a fire alarm whenever we had to switch classes, it now sounded like a sad robot moaning.

As I pushed out from my desk, Dad frowned and shook his head, clearly disappointed by my divided attention. Maybe if he'd known my attention had been diverted by thoughts of historical significance — the Underground Railroad, for Pete's sake! — his disappointment would have lessened. But maybe not. He was very Neil deGrasse Tyson: nothing was more important than science. I weaved through the corridor, gliding around the skaters and band geeks on my way to the cafeteria. On the surface of almost every wall in the school, the same poster had been tacked up.

BANDWARZ
Sticksville Battle of the Bands
WEDNESDAY NIGHT

Grand Prize:
bragging rights & a $500 gift card
to Rhythm Impossible

That vital information was paired with a photo of an intense looking teen rock trio — some stock photo site's concept of a high school band, I guess. I must have passed twenty posters just like it on my way to meet Yumi and Stacey.

Another thing (or person, more accurately) I passed was Ms. Fenstermacher, who waved so emphatically I was kind of forced to stop and talk to her.

"Ms. Fenstermacher," I said. "How are you? How was your weekend?"

"Not great," she huffed, pushing her thick glasses up the bridge of her nose with an index finger. "We had a break-in at the Sticksville Museum. The guard dog even got loose — one of the interns spent most of this morning chasing it down."

"You have a guard dog?" I made the best surprised face I could. There was no way I could let on I knew a single thing about it. "That's terrible . . . not the guard dog. The break-in. Did they take anything?"

"The director of the museum says a few displays were overturned, but she doesn't think anything was stolen," she said, relieved. "And you think you live in a quiet town . . ."

I had to escape the conversation before I said anything incriminating. "I have to get to class, Ms. Fenstermacher." She didn't need to know my next class was, technically, lunch. "Sorry to hear about the museum."

My best friends in the whole world were — as per usual — draped across the cafeteria table in the far corner like they were the entrails of a vulture about to be inspected by a sloppy augurer. Stacey MacIsaac was double-fisting tuna sandwiches while Yumi Takeshi poked at some leftover stir fry in a cloudy Tupperware container. She was apparently a lot happier to see me than she was the day's designated lunch.

"October Schwartz, as I live and breathe." Yumi dramatically sighed and shifted over to make room.

"If you call this living," Stacey joked. At least, I thought he was joking.

"How were your weekends? You do anything fun?" I was all

of thirteen and had already transitioned to a full-blown mom in my conversations.

"Well, Stacey hooked up his old family VCR, and we were supposed to spend Saturday night playing Catan and watching *Decline of Western Civilization 1* and *2*," Yumi began.

"But at some point, my dad recorded over the tape with my aunt's Hawaiian wedding," Stacey finished.

"So we watched Stacey's weird aunt get married while we played Catan. You do anything more interesting?"

Uncovering maps of historical significance and witnessing skullduggery — possibly *major* skullduggery — go down in a cemetery is, by mere definition, "interesting," but it's not like I could tell Yumi and Stacey that. They didn't know about the dead kids at all, even though Yumi thought she'd seen them once, and Stacey was distantly related to Morna.

"No. I had to help my dad do a bunch of housecleaning," I said, which both of them would know was a lie if they saw the current state of our house.

"It must be weird having class with him," Yumi said. Though it had been a few weeks, she still couldn't get over the reality that the school was forcing me to take science with my own father. The entire situation seemed wrong to her, like a surgeon doing a kidney transplant for her own child. "I'd rather jump into boiling oil than be taught any class by my father."

"How is being taught by your dad?" Stacey asked.

"Okay, I guess," I said. "Though I feel like he's extra-hard on me . . . and last week he called me *pumpkin*."

"I'm so sorry, Schwartz," Yumi said. "You going to Bandwarz?"

I wasn't the only one the posters were influencing.

I finished my bit of turkey sandwich. "I don't know. Should I? Are there bands at this school I'd want to see?"

I'm not sure why I acted like a grizzled indie-rock veteran. I'd literally been to one concert in my entire life: the Plotzdam Conference show at the Y that Yumi and Stacey had taken me to at the start of the school year.

"My cousin says that Phantom Moustache almost always wins, mainly because most of the other bands are either terrible bunches of dudes imitating Nickelback or sad girls with weak voices who sing songs about their parents' divorces," Yumi explained. "But we still might go. As you might have *surmised* from our riveting Saturday night, our social calendars aren't exactly jam-packed."

"Idle hands are the devil's playthings," Stacey added.

As if on cue, a searing electronic whale sound split the cafeteria air, making everyone's heads perk up like a mild electric shock had been run through every cafeteria bench. (Maybe this was an innovation the school was saving for next semester.) Eyes swivelled to the stage at the front of the cafeteria, where our student council president stood behind a microphone, his black baseball cap (invariably advertising some sort of youth camp) defiantly turned backward. Refusing to apologize for his obvious audio blunder, he made his announcement:

"Hello, this is Zogon, your student council president." He paused for applause that failed to arrive. "Okay, so as most of you know, this Wednesday night is Bandwarz, Sticksville's only youth Battle of the Bands competition. This is the school's fourth year doing Bandwarz. You may remember last year's winner, Phantom Moustache . . ."

At the mention of the band, the applause Zogon so dearly coveted arrived.

"Well, they'll be back to defend their title. And we want to make sure Bandwarz has a big crowd this year, so each lunch, your student council — or me, ha — will introduce to you one of the bands competing at this year's Bandwarz."

It was then that I became aware of three kids standing beside the stage, lingering around like the dust cloud on Pig-Pen from the *Peanuts* comics. Henry Khan, who had been electronically matched with me by an ill-advised computer romance service that was part of a near-criminal student council Valentine's Day campaign, shuffled his feet in his understated preppy clothes. Another boy in a black metal T-shirt and Doc Martens, and a girl who looked like a JCPenney summer model except for hair that resembled a goth cheerleader pom, stood beside him. Zogon from the student council introduced the three as Crenshaw House.

"This is Levi, Henry, and Matilda. Guys, what kind of music do you play?" Zogon asked, treating the weird announcement like he was Ryan Seacrest at an Oscar red carpet. He probably had no greater wish in life than to be Ryan Seacrest. Zogon first put the microphone in front of Matilda, who shrugged with such exaggeration, it really required no amplification.

Levi, clearly the band's frontman, was not nearly so uncertain. He took the microphone from high school Seacrest's hand. "Thank you. We are really excited to play for all of you tomorrow night and it's really an honour, but Crenshaw House

is not a band," Levi clarified, then began to shout. "We are a musical revolution — and we're going to blow down the walls of this suburban prison of a school like the walls of Jericho."

The sleepy-town student body of Sticksville Central were audibly unsettled by the at-first polite, then suddenly aggressive frontman of Crenshaw House. He knew how to get people's attention, for sure. Levi shoved the microphone into Henry's face, who quietly added, "Mostly we play pop punk, though."

Watch out, walls of Jericho! As the crowd in the cafeteria grumbled and made hyperbolic confused faces to one another, Zogon ushered the members of Crenshaw House off the stage (to no applause). He then outlined all the vital details of this week's Bandwarz. Well, they didn't leave the stage to *literally* no applause. Yumi and Stacey were applauding quite loudly, though it seemed they were the only ones.

"Who are those kids?" I asked Yumi. Yumi knew who everyone was. She was like a high school Wikipedia.

"Matilda Coffin's in grade ten, and she has the school's best name and best hair. Levi Marylebone is grade eleven, I think, and is one of the school's, like, eight Black kids," she said.

After Yumi pointed that out, I realized how strange it was that Sticksville had a relatively small Black population. Wasn't it, at one point, the end of the Underground Railroad? Then again, according to Tabetha, it sounded like there once was a larger population of Black residents, mostly living by Acheron Creek. But perhaps the unsolved death of a twelve-year-old Black girl made most of them decide to relocate to friendlier towns.

"And isn't that other guy your boyfriend?" Stacey asked.

"Yeah," Yumi finished. "And Henry Khan is your one true love."

I could feel blood rushing through my usually very pale cheeks. "He's not my boyfriend. I barely know the guy. It was just a stupid computer algorithm."

"Do you know how good computer algorithms are nowadays?" Yumi said.

My face was rapidly turning hotter than the cellophane cover on a microwaved TV dinner; I had to change the subject.

"How is —"

"What in the name of Marilyn Manson?" came the irritating voice of my arch-nemesis (I thought it was fair to call her that now), Ashlie Salmons. "Who were those kids?"

Ashlie Salmons had been tormenting me in levels from mild to dangerously spicy ever since I started at Sticksville Central High School, and, despite some almost tender moments between us, showed no real signs of stopping. Coincidentally, the detective in me couldn't help noting that she'd dated a member of Phantom Moustache, Devin McGriff, whose older brother Skyler turned out to be a homicidal member of Asphodel Meadows. And word in the schoolyard was that she'd recently started macking on another Phantom Moustache member, Boston Davis, their objectively adorable (if unpleasant) lead singer. So, no matter how good Crenshaw House and any other band was — literally, if OneRepublic did a surprise show at Sticksville Central's Bandwarz — Ashlie would still be in the pocket of Phantom Moustache. Before anyone could answer Ashlie — not that she was seeking an answer — she responded to her non-question with a quick karate chop of her elegant hand through her auburn hair.

"It doesn't matter *who* they are, anyway. Phantom Moustache is going to win Bandwarz."

"Nobody cares," moaned Yumi.

"People care about Phantom Moustache," Ashlie insisted. "They're this school's favourite band."

"That's like being a favourite terminal illness," Yumi said, rolling her eyes. "Besides, everybody is talking about how Crenshaw House is a way better band than your boyfriend's little group. I hear they've had interest from record labels."

As far as I knew, Yumi was entirely fabricating this information to infuriate Ashlie. I don't think "record label" is even a thing that exists.

"You know, they kind of look like you losers," Ashlie added, pointing to the members of Crenshaw House, who were still loitering around the cafeteria stage.

This observation was a bit too much for my dear friend Yumi Takeshi.

"Clearly, *they* are punk, and *we* are goth, Ashlie," she shouted, slapping her palms onto the cafeteria table and sending everyone's milk cartons quivering. "Open your eyes!"

Ashlie stared in disbelief at Yumi. The whole situation was becoming about two hundred percent too tense for me.

"I'm not goth," Stacey added, eyes flitting back and forth between Yumi and Ashlie. "Am I?"

Ashlie pivoted her gaze from Yumi to me, under the mistaken belief that I was somehow the ringleader of our trio, and issued a warning: "You three have become entirely *too* comfortable around here recently, and I think that's bad for everybody," she said, then picked up my half-full milk carton and overturned it in Yumi's Tupperware of stir fry. "I'd hate to see you get too complacent."

I watched in horror as Yumi's left hand rose as if in slow motion — about to connect with Ashlie's perfect, stupid face — only to pause mid-air when my other school arch-nemesis — the pastel-suited, handlebar-moustachioed, probably wig-wearing

Mr. Santuzzi, who was, thankfully, no longer my mathematics teacher — arrived.

"Mr. Santuzzi!" Ashlie greeted the burly vest enthusiast, gleefully unaware of the smack Yumi had nearly delivered her. "Will you be going to Bandwarz this Wednesday evening?"

Santuzzi, obviously unsettled by the close proximity of Ashlie Salmons and me during lunch hour, hesitated before answering.

"Yes. I'll be one of the teacher chaperones that evening," he said. "What is happening here?" he asked, twirling his massive finger at our cafeteria table as if an escaped raccoon had died upon it.

Yumi, Stacey, and I maintained dead silence as Ashlie, staring at me with murder in her eyes, explained, "I was just asking October and her friends the very same question. My boyfriend is in Phantom Moustache, you know, so I want to make sure there's a good audience."

Ashlie then smiled with a ferocity that made even Mr. Santuzzi wince. Knowing we couldn't be trusted together, he broke up the conversation. "Okay," he said, "I'm sure you can leave that job to the student council. Back to your friends now . . ."

Ashlie scurried back to the girl in the novelty T-shirt and the little girl with the big laugh (the usual suspects), but Mr. Santuzzi continued to hover by our table, like he were a cloud of Stacey's overpowering boy deodorant.

"How about you, Ms. Schwartz?" Mr. Santuzzi asked, possibly the broadest question ever conceived. "Staying out of trouble?"

"You know me." I shrugged.

"Yes," he said, his face turning suddenly grave. "I certainly do."

Santuzzi then slowly marched out of the busy cafeteria, arms folded behind his back. He side-stepped a toppled cafeteria tray full of pierogies on his exit and made no attempt whatsoever to pick it up or alert anyone to its presence.

"Yikes, what a jerk," Yumi said as soon as he was

(presumably) out of earshot. "I don't know how you survived his math class, Schwartz. He seems to have taken an interest in you. Stacey and I have class with him and he's always upset at us for talking in the back corner."

"Sounds like Santuzzi," I said. "He used any military terms on you yet?"

"The other day I think he referred to someone as a 'tail-end Charlie' — what does that even *mean*? It's going to be impossible getting through that class without talking at *all*," Yumi concluded.

"Won't be easy," the mostly-silent Stacey argued.

Yumi rose from the bench and emptied the milk-drenched rice from her container into the garbage can in the centre aisle. "What are you up to this afternoon? Want to join Stacey and me? We're going to the bookstore to buy the newest *Fangoria*."

"Hundred best zombies in movie history," Stacey said, which I deduced was the theme or focus of the issue.

"Can't. I have to work on a school assignment," I lied. The trouble with the second semester was that I no longer had history class to use as an excuse when I wanted to check out the Sticksville Museum or some old historical site. My English and social studies assignments from Mr. Copeland and Mrs. Theriault were going to have to get a *lot* more elaborate.

"Okay, just let us know if you want to borrow the issue later," Yumi said.

We exited the cafeteria together. The fact was, I could see five kid zombies whenever I wanted, and as talented as the special effects wizards featured in *Fangoria* might be, they could never match the real deal. I made my way to Mr. Copeland's class already anticipating the hardships and dangers of trying to find the site of Sticksville's Underground Railroad or Tabetha's former house this afternoon — and most of them just involved the process of using Sticksville's public bus.

☠   ☠   ☠

I've Been Workin' on (Findin') the Railroad

October Schwartz was right to be apprehensive regarding her journey via Sticksville's public transit — for it was not a bus for the faint-of-heart, nor the short-on-time. The long and winding route to the fairground took a full hour by wheezing city bus. October boarded at a stop near her school, and the driver made so many right turns, October could only assume the bus was spiralling outward in larger and wider concentric circles. Additionally, the bus itself was populated by no children her own age, but rather a motley assemblage of the elderly and beyond all hope. After the eighteenth right turn, a generously bearded man in a military-style beret stood up from his seat and moved into the one beside October and began to regale her with his most beloved prog metal bands and songs. This conversation culminated in him taking his Discman (clearly first purchased twenty years prior) in his fingerless-glove-clad hands and placing the headphones over the unwitting October's ears, subjecting her to a song by someone or something called Hawkwind. Just as October's discomfort had reached the point where she considered smashing the window and diving into oncoming traffic, the Sticksville Fairgrounds slid into view.

October slowly removed the large noise-cancelling headphones with a manufactured smile and reached for the yellow cord above her head. Her new bearded friend looked disappointed as the bell chimed and the driver eased the bus over to the curb.

Finally free from public transit, October Schwartz stretched her arms and legs but already dreaded her journey home. Given the duration of her bus ride there, she knew she only had a couple hours to find the Underground Railroad site and do some investigating before the sun fell. She assessed her surroundings: a line of lonely bungalows stood on one side of the street, faced by a wide-open field across the road. The open field was the outer boundary of the Sticksville Fairgrounds, which were unused at this time of year. The fair opened in mid-June to correspond with the town's confusingly titled Spring Fling. In the distance, October could see some tents and fencing, as well as a couple of the permanent structures, like the bandshell and a few of the rides and attractions. The rest of the fair consisted of temporary structures that would be built or re-installed in the coming weeks. October decided to begin with the fairground perimeter, then make her way inward. Maybe she'd find some sign of the Underground Railroad or — better — the old home of Tabetha Scott.

Sometimes in the world of detective work, an investigator will spend an inordinate amount of time pursuing leads that produce no evidence whatsoever. This truth of the profession seemed important to keep in mind as October spent the next couple hours searching through the mouldy canvases of semi-permanent tents, hopping around abandoned carnival rides like the Gravitron and the Scrambler. What exactly October was looking for, she wasn't quite sure. In her head, she'd pictured perhaps a plaque and informational display tucked somewhere out of the way. Or an ancient shack, set far back in the field. Or even a heritage building — "Ancestral Home of the Sticksville Scotts" — preserved much as it had looked in the 1860s, but that seemed too much to ask. Instead, all she found were dormant rides frozen mid-spin, like dioramas of taxidermied Ice Age mammals one might find at a museum. The fairground held nothing of historical significance, unless you feel carnival rides that had not undergone safety inspection since the mid-1980s fit that criteria. The only thing out of the ordinary was a plot of land where a new ride was being constructed. The sign had already been erected, though the furrows and fibreglass tubes were still being put together. The name of this ride was "The Sharktacular Plunge," which October surmised was probably some kind of log flume or other water ride, which may or may not feature live sharks — nature's serial killers. (Probably not.) If October was unable to find the site of the Underground Railroad terminus or Tabetha's old house today, as was quickly becoming apparent, perhaps she could return when the construction crew of the Sharktacular Plunge were at work and ask if they had any idea where such things might be.

One possibility that had not yet occurred to our young detective is that perhaps no efforts at historical preservation had been made. For all she knew, the shed or warehouse that once served as an endpoint for the Underground Railroad could have been demolished, wiped off the face of the earth decades ago, and no one ever thought to mark it. After all, it's not like the terminus, whatever it was, would have been known to most people when it was in use. Who knows when that map in the Sticksville Museum was drafted; it could have been decades later. And it would be odd for the city to preserve the house where two historically insignificant (relatively speaking) people lived after escaping slavery. The only historic homes October knew of in Sticksville belonged to wealthy white families with long town legacies, like Cyril's family. She thought there was a LaFlamme household also designated as a heritage site in town. Any information about historic homes owned by Black residents seemed to be stuffed in a box in the town museum.

Perhaps, October mused, this was a question best asked of someone with an intimate knowledge of Sticksville's historical preservation efforts — someone like her former history teacher, Ms. Fenstermacher. After all, her friends Yumi and Stacey now had class with her, so it was easy enough to linger around their classroom and ask her a few questions. It's not like she hadn't done it a conspicuous number of times already!

Concluding she had spent an afternoon in investigative failure and on pointless bus trips, October crossed the wide field of crispy grass not yet recovered from the winter and made her way back to the bus stop. As she reached the road again, she spotted something she hadn't seen when she first exited the bus. On a weathered telephone pole planted along the curb — across from the

lonely-looking houses — somebody had affixed a bouquet of flowers with packing tape. She inspected further and — though she was no botanist, like Dr. Ellie Sattler in the blockbuster film *Jurassic Park* — she could identify the flowers as yellow roses. Who was leaving yellow roses at the edge of this empty field? And why were they doing so? The flowers looked relatively new — they hadn't wilted like Walmart lettuce yet — and traditionally this kind of thing was done when someone was killed in a car accident. But Sticksville had avoided any vehicular tragedies for the past few months, at least. This was not the first time she had wished she had ready access to a fingerprinting kit, but good luck finding that in Sticksville. And even if she ordered one on Amazon, where would she get an archive of criminal fingerprints?

October Schwartz was in the midst of racking her brains, as futile as that may have been, for the significance of yellow roses, when the racking process was cut short by the bassist of Crenshaw House, October's ideal computer match: Henry Khan. He asked her what most people would ask a thirteen-year-old rooting around an empty field and closely studying a telephone pole: "What are you doing here?"

October suddenly felt embarrassed about her detective work in a way she never had before, and it was unclear why that was. She had spoken to Henry before, and there was nothing particularly menacing about the boy, dressed as he was in chocolate brown slacks and a V-neck sweater over a collared shirt, looking for all the world like Archie Andrews cosplay. He was about as intimidating as a croissant. And she had lied to classmates and adults and various legal authorities more than enough times for it to be nearly routine. Perhaps it was the location — looking at mystery flowers at the edge of a remote, empty field. Or perhaps, dear readers, Ms. Schwartz was allowing the results of that computer match game to get to her and her feelings for young Henry Khan were making her insides all gross and mushy. Only time will tell. At some point, October realized she had been asked a question and hadn't answered for seconds — minutes, even. Henry Khan repeated the question.

"I said, what are you doing here, October?"

"What are *you* doing here?" October spat back. Classic deflection.

"This is my street. You?"

"This might be difficult to believe," October said, preparing to lie, "but I'm working on a history project?"

Ending her explanation with a question mark didn't exactly fill Henry Khan with confidence.

"History project?" he asked, glancing around at his surroundings. "On what? The fairgrounds?"

"Sort of," October said. "Apparently somewhere around here was one of the endpoints of the Underground Railroad."

Henry's eyes widened. "Really?"

October nodded solemnly. She figured it best to leave out that the house of her ghost friend was also supposed to be in the general vicinity.

"I should tell Levi," Henry said, almost to himself. "He loves that stuff. He named the band Crenshaw House after the Underground Railroad. But why is there an endpoint here? Once people got to the border, weren't they free?"

Henry brought up an interesting question.

"I mean, it would look kind of suspicious for the final stop to be literally just north of the American border. Maybe there were people to help provide them with jobs or homes are something?" October suggested. The reasoning was sound as any. Most of the former slaves were arriving in Canada with nothing aside from the ragged clothes on their backs, facing a country full of discrimination nearly as bad as what they'd faced in the States. A sort of friendly welcoming committee probably would have been greatly beneficial. And Tabetha's suggestion that a lot of Underground Railroad passengers built homes near the endpoint hinted that maybe people would find some empathetic souls nearby.

"So, where is it?" Henry asked the million-dollar question.

October shoved her hands into her pockets. "I was hoping you might know?"

Henry shook his head in disagreement. This was not encouraging. "Why were you studying those flowers?"

Another good question from Grand Inquisitor Henry Khan, whom October resented more the longer she spent in conversation with him.

"When I couldn't find the Underground Railroad terminus, I just started looking closely at everything unusual. Did somebody die in a car crash here or something?"

"Nah," Henry answered. "Someone died here, but it was like a billion years ago."

One can assume he didn't mean the terrible thunder-lizards of our Paleolithic past.

"What?" October said, sensing a story that may or may not be a clue and/or *clues*.

"Yeah, old Beryl leaves flowers here regularly," he (sort of) explained. "She says a little girl was murdered here in the early years of the town's founding."

Now it seems fairly rude to me to call anyone "old" Beryl, especially given there were probably no "new" or "young" Beryls in town, but that's beside the point. October requested further information about this old Beryl and her seemingly robust flower budget.

"Explain," October said.

"Explain what?" Henry asked. "There's an old lady named Beryl that lives here, and she leaves flowers in that spot every once in a while. She's Levi's great-something-or-other."

"She leaves flowers for a girl that died here?" October asked. "When did she die?"

"I don't know," Henry threw up his hands in defence. "*I* didn't kill her. It was like a hundred years ago."

"Do you think it had anything to do with the Underground Railroad?"

"How should I know?" Henry pleaded. "Though I think the number one goal of the Underground Railroad was to *not*, like, kill the passengers, right?"

October just looked inquisitively at Henry Khan.

"Beryl lives in the yellow house over there," he said. "You should ask her all about it. She'd probably love the company. I don't think she gets all that many visitors. Levi rarely comes to this part of town."

October's gaze moved from the increasingly deer-like Henry Khan to the modest yellow bungalow with a grey roof down the road, then focused (obviously) on the three-storey birdhouse planted in the front lawn. Someone liked birds.

"Thanks," October said absently as she marched over to Beryl's house. She climbed the front steps and peered in the narrow vertical windows sandwiching the front door. Not a single light source could be seen inside. October left the porch and circled around the side of the house, looking in what appeared to be the house's kitchen window. It, too, was dark, and October could spy a jet-black cat snoozing on the kitchen table.

"What are you doing?" Henry Khan called out. "Ever heard of knocking?"

October, however, unlike "normies," didn't need to knock. She could tell just by the dimmed lights, the unconscious cat, the ease with which she cased the joint, that Beryl's house was currently unoccupied. She returned to the front porch and opened the mailbox, made of black metal (not the musical genre popularized by Ghost and the like), and flipped through Beryl's mail to determine her full name. October retrieved the *Two Knives, One Thousand Demons* composition book, which had long ago become a detective's casebook, and wrote down *Beryl Gibson* on a blank page. She almost never wrote about Olivia de Kellerman these days. Kind of a shame.

"That's illegal," shouted Henry, who still hadn't moved from his spot in the middle of the road.

"I'm not *opening* the mail; just looking at it."

On a second blank page in the composition book, October printed a message for Beryl Gibson:

MY NAME IS OCTOBER SCHWARTZ. I AM A STUDENT AT STICKSVILLE CENTRAL HIGH SCHOOL AND I'M WORKING ON AN ENGLISH NONFICTION PROJECT ABOUT STICKSVILLE HISTORY. MY FRIEND HENRY KHAN SAID YOU HAD A SAD BUT INTERESTING STORY ABOUT A MURDER IN TOWN, AND I WAS HOPING I COULD INTERVIEW YOU ABOUT IT AT YOUR EARLIEST CONVENIENCE.

Then October left her home phone number, still being only in possession of a land line (see Book 2, *Dial "M" for Morna*), and thanked Beryl Gibson for her time and consideration. Note that nowhere in the missive did she callously refer to her as "old Beryl."

October tore the page from her notebook, folded it precisely into four and slid it under Beryl Gibson's front door.

"What are you doing now?" Henry asked as October returned to his general vicinity.

"Waiting for the bus," she said, stopping right beside the bus stop sign. "I have to get home."

October did *not*, shockingly, look forward to the individuals she'd meet during her long bus ride home. But if this murdered girl that Beryl Gibson regularly mourned was Tabetha Scott, then the harrowing bus rides may well have been worth it.

☠   ☠   ☠

6

Guess Who's Coming to Sticksville?

Tuesday night, the dead kids and I were scouring the town library's microfiche for further clues to Tabetha's murder, but with the newly added information that it might have happened not far from her house. Since the investigation into Cyril Cooper's death, we had basically become experts in breaking into the public library unnoticed. The six of us sat around a microfiche box (or whatever they're called), which was providing the only light in the otherwise dark library. I had informed Tabetha about the flowers near the fairground and asked if that rang any mind-bells.

"I dunno," she said, watching Kirby cycle through the pages of microfiche reel. "I mean, I'm a girl who died a long time ago in town, but there musta been others. Even Morna would qualify."

Unfortunately, she had a point. Until I talked to Beryl Gibson, I had no idea if the flowers had anything to do with Tabetha.

"But Morna didn't die anywhere near the fairgrounds — and the fairgrounds are right where the Underground Railroad supposedly ended and where Tabetha and her dad lived," Derek said.

Kirby sighed heavily. "Is our plan to just read through every single issue of this stupid newspaper? Because I don't feel like that's a stellar plan."

"When did you die, Tabetha?" Derek asked from behind Kirby's shoulder. "We should just focus on that year."

Tabetha shrugged. "Maybe . . . five years after settling in Sticksville?"

"Okay, you were seven when you escaped," I reasoned. "And that was when? 1857? And you died when you were twelve? So you must have died in 1862 or 3 or something?"

"I have some unfortunate news for both of you," Kirby said, leaning back in his seat and folding his arms. Or trying to. He still only had the one arm. "These microfiche films only go back to 1901. I don't think there was a newspaper before then — or if there was, it hasn't been preserved in this library."

Tabetha looked to the ceiling and began to gulp deep breaths like a fish that had swan-dived from its glass bowl onto the shag carpet below.

"No, it's okay," I said, hoping to prevent Tabetha from losing hope. "I have an idea . . . are there reels from 1912? Let's start there. That would be fifty years later."

"So?" Derek asked.

"Well, it's possible, given how unusual and tragic it is for a twelve-year-old to die, maybe the anniversary was mentioned in the *Sticksville Loon*. Like they do with Princess Diana."

Kirby made a face that demonstrated his lack of faith in the plan, but at least Tabetha ended her weird, heartbreaking gulps.

"It's worth a shot," Morna said.

"You're not the person who has to read all these papers," Kirby said, reminding Morna — as if she needed reminding — of her illiteracy.

"October is our leader," Cyril reasoned. "I say we follow her — we managed to uncover the root cause of two of our deaths so far. Why should we doubt her?"

While the other dead kids were variously questioning or validating my research abilities, Derek Running Water had already retrieved the small paper boxes of microfiche tapes from 1912 and 1913. He hauled the first to Kirby to spool onto the machine. They began the slow process of skimming the ancient pages of the *Sticksville Loon* as I prodded Tabetha to tell me more about her journey to Sticksville.

"So what happened after you were ambushed in the barn?" I asked.

"What barn?"

"Last time we talked about this — when we were running from the dog — you said one of the stops of the Underground Railroad was a trap. That there were bounty hunters posing as conductors in the blue barn . . ."

"Yeah, but that happened before we even got to Sticksville," Tabetha said.

"Still," I said. "We don't know what information is important and what isn't. The more I know, the better."

Derek and Kirby, supported by the non-reading Cyril and Morna, continued to scroll through the pages of the 1912 *Sticksville Loon* while Tabetha told me more of her journey out of the South.

☠   ☠   ☠

What Tabetha and her father, Lunsford, had fallen into was a snare called the Reverse Underground Railroad. The system tricked escapees into thinking they were still on their way to freedom when, in fact, they were now in the clutches of villains who intended to bring them back to their owners for monetary rewards. The enslaved people themselves would face untold punishments and possibly even death. This Solomon Drury, if that *was* his real name, was one such slave catcher, and two of his goons had emerged from the darkened corners of the barn to apprehend Tabetha and her dad. Drury himself had gone outside to guard the barn doors. Both of the white men had drawn pistols and one held two pairs of shackles in his free hand. He tossed them to Lunsford, who caught them with natural ease.

"Put 'em on, slave," the man said.

But Tabetha's father had not risked his life and spent a day in a man-sized birdcage just to be apprehended by some Southern toughs halfway to freedom. Before the men knew what was happening, Lunsford had flung the manacles back into the one's face, smashing his nose. He then leapt behind the other assailant and managed to pull his arms behind him. Tabetha started to scream as the other man (with the now-busted nose) began to shoot, hitting the other man in the chest and her dad in his hand. She was frozen in place and watched in horror as the man with the gun again pulled the trigger.

Then nothing happened.

The man attempted to shoot again and again, but his revolver just clicked.

"Abernathy, you cheap louse!" he shouted. "You only gave me two bullets!"

That was the only invitation Lunsford needed. He dropped "Abernathy," shot and handcuffed, to the straw floor below, and moved toward his partner.

"Stay away!" the man warned.

But Tabetha's dad did not listen to him. Given the white man had an empty gun and Lunsford was about twice his size, there would appear to be no good reason *to* listen to him.

The tense scene was halted by the barn door swinging open wide. Tabetha and her dad, assuming that their captor, Solomon Drury, had heard the gunshots and come running, hit the deck. Imagine their surprise when they saw he was in no position to threaten them. Drury was bound by jute rope and dragged into the barn by the dynamic duo of William Lambert and Alexander Ross. Though he seemed to be sputtering and spitting like a cat that missed its dinner, Drury's mouth was gagged. The three of them were followed into the dark barn by a fourth person — a balding Black man with a goatee.

"If you two don't mind," Ross said to Lambert and the fourth man, nodding toward the remaining slave catcher. The two quickly grabbed the disoriented and fearful goon, hogtying him with more jute and stuffing a gag into his mouth.

"Stay away!" Lunsford warned the men. "I'm not goin' back t' that plantation!"

"And we have no desire to take you there," Ross insisted. "I swear."

"Then who's that?" Tabetha asked, pointing to the bald man with the beard.

"That, my child, is the *real* Solomon Drury," he explained. "William and I ran into him on our journey north. Having never met him in person, I didn't realize how different he looked from that man claiming to be him."

Obviously, Ross was referring to their now-captured captor.

"Horrified that we'd been hoodwinked by an impostor, the three of us raced back to the barn as soon as we could and followed their trail," William Lambert added. "You two okay?"

Tabetha's father wasn't sure what to think. Recent events made it rather difficult for him to trust his seeming rescuers. He clutched his damaged hand and winced in pain. "So, what do we do with them?"

They exited the barn, leaving the dead man and the other bound ones inside. The apparently real Solomon Drury shut the doors and barricaded the handles using a pitchfork. Obviously, Tabetha doubted the makeshift pitchfork lock would hold the faux Drury and his henchman for long. Her father was of the same mind and expressed those concerns to the Underground Railroad conductors.

"You need to give me a horse so my daughter and I can get outta here," he said.

"We don't know the way, Dad," Tabetha said.

Drury interjected. "I can take you as far as a stop in Massachusetts, if that'll help. Ross and Lambert, you should stay here at the barn."

Drury hoisted Tabetha on top of an auburn stallion and directed Lunsford to mount it. He himself hopped atop his black steed.

"Certainly," Alexander Ross said. "We'll stay here for the day before moving on. Better if I'm here, should we encounter any trouble from the law."

Lunsford's busted hand bled freely all over their horse's flank.

"Lunsford," Ross said. "I can't apologize enough to you and your daughter. First chance you get to safely do so, please have that hand examined by a doctor."

Then it was three of them. Two Black men and one child, riding by themselves in the middle of dangerous territory. Though Lunsford and Tabetha weren't exactly devastated to leave the Birdman behind, given how sideways things had gone, not having a white man of status among their number came with its own problems. Mainly, they couldn't risk being spotted by any white people in their ride through the woods.

"So what did you do?" I asked, still shocked by the terrible story. "How did you make it here, to Sticksville?"

"The real Drury and we rode by night, all the way to Massachusetts," she said. "There, he connected us with a nice Quaker family who helped get us the rest a' the way t' Sticksville."

"And your dad's hand?"

"Mr. Drury was able to clean it up some, but he wasn't a doctor. He was a carpenter," Tabetha said. "By the time we got to Massachusetts and the Quakers, his hand had to be amputated."

"That's awful," I gasped.

"Cool — did he get a hook?" Derek asked, overhearing our conversation.

"Nah, just a stump."

Eventually, Tabetha and her now-one-handed father arrived in the small Ontario town of Sticksville. And while there hadn't been institutional slavery in Canada for decades, the townspeople didn't exactly welcome them with open arms.

"We couldn't get land — we didn't have any money — and

no one would give my dad a job at first because he was Black," Tabetha explained. "We actually lived in the safe house at the end of the Railroad for a couple months until he could find work, and a charity provided food and clothing for the first little while. We were exiles as far as the town of Sticksville was concerned. No one wanted us around."

Though freedom in Canada was no doubt preferred than enforced lifelong servitude — what wasn't? — life for the newly freed didn't seem anything like a picnic. Tabetha's dad eventually found menial work as a barback in one of the taverns through one of the town's "vigilance committees," volunteers who would provide things like food and shelter for the formerly enslaved in the short term. Before too long, he was able to build them a very modest house near the Underground Railroad terminus, where the few other Black families in Sticksville had settled. According to Tabetha, her dad didn't want to live closer to the town centre — he didn't want to put himself and his daughter in the middle of where no one wanted them. So they lived in relative isolation like that for years. Of course, until Tabetha's untimely death, which she remembered very little about.

"Didn't you have any friends there? Were there other kids who lived nearby?" I asked.

"Not really," Tabetha said. "Most of the other people who'd come via the Underground Railroad were older. Sometimes the Sticksville vigilance committee would visit us to make sure we were doing all right. And sometimes they brought their kids with 'em, but, for all the nice things the vigilance committee tried to do, my dad still didn't want to associate with the town. He said a lot of people didn't want us Black folks livin' there, because we might draw attention t' the Railroad. Make trouble from the States or bring more Black people to town, which none a' the white folks were too keen on. Because a' that, some of the Black families moved to Owen Sound."

"Did it draw attention?" I asked. "The Black families living there?"

"Like I said, it wasn't that many families. Most left fer other parts a' Canada," Tabetha explained. "And barely no white folks 'cept the vigilance committee ever came near the Creek. Back then, it was used as the dumping ground."

"Eww." Morna pinched her nose and scrunched her forehead as if we had suddenly been transported to a dump from 1860 (which I suspected would smell worse than dumps of today).

Tabetha continued: "When I was a bit older, I started workin' as a servant in one of the houses downtown. I worked fer the mayor. He was an unpleasant person, n' paid as if spendin' money was like pullin' his own teeth. My dad didn't like me workin' there, but we needed money. He said it was like we'd escaped slavery, only fer the two of us to end up doin' what other people told us to. N' I think he still had trouble trusting white people."

"Makes sense," I said.

"I still don't trust 'em," Derek said, at which Cyril looked somewhat hurt.

"There was one other white person who was nice to us in Sticksville," Tabetha said, "but that just ended up even more trouble in the long run."

"What do you mean?" I asked.

Tabetha spun a hardcover book around in her hands. "There was this musician, Ms. Yvonne. She was always going on hikes past our house in the morning — had a lotta stuff t' dump, I guess. Eventually, she and my dad would start talking. After a couple months, she brought pies."

"That doesn't sound so bad," Cyril said, elbowing Kirby in his belly.

"Yeah, what's wrong with pies?" I asked. Never did I think I'd see the day where pies required defending.

"It wasn't the pies, it was the friendship," Tabetha said, exasperated, as if we were all missing something important. "A Black man like my dad couldn't just chat with a white woman like Ms. Yvonne."

"Ohh . . ." we all said in unison.

"Then that incident at the Stubborn Goat Tavern, that really messed things up . . ." Tabetha said, trailing off.

Before I could find out what she was talking about and how it involved stubborn goats, Derek interrupted: "Wait, check it out!"

I followed his finger to the dimly illuminated microfiche screen and read what had him so excited.

"This is about Morna," I said, disappointed.

"Oh, yeah," he said. "Sorry."

"Tabetha," I continued, momentarily distracted. "What did you say that bounty hunter's name was? The one who nearly caught you? What was his real name?"

"Abernathy," Tabetha answered, nearly vomiting the foul name.

"Do you ever think he followed you to Sticksville? Maybe he's the one who killed you. Sounds like it would have been easy enough to find you, with you working for the mayor and your dad working in a pretty public spot."

"Maybe he," Cyril added, "is part of Asphodel Meadows."

Though Cyril Cooper's ideas were not always the greatest — and it was hardly his fault, given he was from the 1700s — this was not a bad one. Whatever the secret society Asphodel Meadows stood for or were up to, they certainly seemed to have one creepy hand in all the dead kids' untimely deaths. Why not Tabetha's?

"He's not," Morna said, which was an unexpectedly confident assertion from my dead Scottish friend.

"What makes you say that, Morna?" I asked.

"Because Derek and I have been putting together everything we know about Asphodel Meadows," she said. "Abernathy isn't one of the family names."

(Minor) bomb dropped.

Derek and Morna had been busy compiling all the facts and figures and anecdotes we knew about Asphodel Meadows so far — it was a project so clever, I really wish I, Sticksville's greatest detective (I assume), had thought of it first. But instead, I said, "What do you mean?"

Derek pulled out a 4" x 6" notepad from his back pocket and handed it to me. In his black handwritten letters — looking almost like they belonged in a comic book's word balloons — were all sorts of things we knew — or *thought* we knew — about Asphodel Meadows, including some things I had forgotten about. Where we'd seen "Asphodel Meadows" graffiti, people who had claimed to be working for or with them, and — most relevant to now — the list of surnames we'd recently found in the personal effects of Mrs. Crookshanks — the ghost pirate herself.

"See?" Derek said, displaying the list again:

Crookshanks (ghost pirate lady)
Schlangegriff (Morna's killer)
O'Dare
Burton
Fairweather (October's mom?)
LaFlamme (Kirby's family)

As far as we knew, membership was limited. Crookshanks had listed six family names under Asphodel Meadows, and everyone we'd encountered had been part of that list — even Skyler McGriff, who'd tormented Yumi, was originally a Schlangegriff. Derek and Morna had even added helpful notes to each name to provide context to relevant clues or past encounters we'd had with the families.

I suddenly felt my face flood with shame. Maybe Derek and Morna should be running this unofficial detective agency.

Morna, sensing my embarrassment, ran up to me and placed her tangible ghost hand on my shoulder. "Sorry, we thought it would be helpful!"

"It is," I said. "I just can't believe I hadn't thought of it before. A compilation of all the Asphodel Meadows information in one place will be so important. How did you even find that notepad?"

"We broke into the groundskeeper's office," Derek explained. "He didn't have anything better. I guess you don't really need a notebook to maintain funeral plots."

"We need to get you something bigger . . ."

"Derek does all the writing," Morna explained, "but I sometimes remember things and come up with ideas."

"It's great," I admitted.

"But there's nothing about someone named Abernathy in there? What about Scott?" Cyril rhetorically asked, pointing at the small notepad.

Morna shook her head.

"Do we know that there aren't other members? Or that these are even members?" Kirby said. "We don't know what that list *is*."

"Just because your name is on there," Derek said, "doesn't mean it isn't what we *think* it is."

"N' we don't know that Abernathy was that creep's real name," Tabetha added.

"What about the mayor?" Cyril suggested. He'd already assumed the mayor was more than ready and willing to kill a servant. "What was his name, Tabetha?"

"Mr. Sinclair."

"No dice. What about a Ms. Yvonne, or Beryl Gibson?" I asked.

"Who's Beryl Gibson?" Tabetha asked.

"She's the woman who apparently knows about that long-ago death at the fairground," I explained. "The one who was placing the memorial flowers I told you about."

"We haven't seen either of those names before," Derek said.

I glanced over at the wall clock and its alarming face. The clock displayed nearly 2 a.m., which looked like a smug grin on the wall. The microfiche search was proving fruitless, and I feared progress on Tabetha's case, despite how much she'd remembered, would be sparse to nonexistent until I could meet with Beryl Gibson.

"We should wrap things up," I said. "It's getting late."

"What about the microfiche?" Kirby asked.

"Pack it up. We can try again on Thursday night. Maybe I'll have talked to Beryl Gibson by then."

I flipped the power switch on the microfiche machine.

"Thursday night?" Tabetha said, making no attempts to hide her disappointment. "What's wrong with tomorrow?"

"Tomorrow," I said, pausing more dramatically than I'd planned, "is Bandwarz."

☠　☠　☠

Band War and
Band Peace

Wednesday after school, October's father offered October and her friends Stacey and Yumi rides to Bandwarz that evening. As long-time readers of this book series know, Leonard Schwartz suffers from clinical depression — an ailment that sometimes prevented him from participating in school activities like Bandwarz. In truth, Mr. Schwartz sometimes struggled just to arrive at school to practise his chosen profession. But he informed October he would be attending the night's concert, and not as a "fun night out." An insistent memo had been sent to the teaching staff about attending school cultural events. October Schwartz politely declined her dad's offer, mumbling something about commitment to the "walking lifestyle," whatever that may be. (There are probably wristbands.)

October met up with her two companions on her return to school after departing it only a few hours prior. Though each of the three affected an air of nonchalance about Bandwarz, treating it as just another thing to do, in truth they were curious about this music promised by Crenshaw House. At the very least, their outfits suggested it could be music they all might like.

After a few moderately heated (lukewarm) discussions about which bands featured in *The Decline of Western Civilization, Part I* were *actually* good, October, Stacey, and Yumi arrived at the parking lot to their high school. It had been denim jacket weather for weeks, so they were a bit alarmed to find Mr. Santuzzi serving as sentry to the parking lot, directing proud (and tragically embarrassed) parents of Bandwarz participants to the appropriate parking spots, wearing what can most accurately be described as the cloak a French police officer might have worn in the late 1800s.

"Evening, Ms. Schwartz, Mr. MacIsaac, Ms. Takeshi." He greeted them with a casual salute.

"You have parking lot duty, I guess?" October asked, not really prepared or willing to have a conversation with her (second) nemesis.

"It's an important task," he said.

"As a former soldier, does the name 'Bandwarz' bother you?" Yumi added.

Mr. Santuzzi's thoughts turned to the serious. "These young men and women, with their loud music and noodle arms, couldn't handle basic training, much less a war."

Having received a response to a question that couldn't really be topped, the three ventured on to the school.

"Good luck, Mr. Santuzzi!" Yumi called behind her.

"Sorry you have to miss all the music," October added.

"I prefer the drone of car motors," their teacher said.

Inside the front double-doors of Sticksville Central, the usually sputtering fluorescent lights had been dimmed or turned off completely. Balloons hung everywhere and, located at one end of the atrium, were a couple cafeteria tables manned (or personned) by none other than Ashlie Salmons and a couple older girls that October didn't recognize. Naturally, Bandwarz wasn't free; it was a fundraiser for the school's end-of-year summer formal — a party that October and her friends would not be welcomed to, unless her classmates had some sort of *Carrie*-esque pig's blood scheme in the works. As such, October felt a bit reluctant forking over ten dollars to Ashlie Salmons, but she reasoned that at least a portion of those funds was intended for the band members.

"Are you sure ten dollars is enough?" Ashlie asked, snapping the purple plastic bill between her manicured fingernails, themselves a different shade of eggplant. October quickly glanced at her own ragged, bitten fingernails. Hand modelling was definitely out of the question for her.

"The sign says admission is ten dollars, Ashlie," Yumi growled.

"But I think there might be an added fee for degenerate losers," she said.

Yumi tossed two crumpled-up tens at Ashlie — well, as crumpled-up as plastic Canadian money gets — and dragged October and Stacey with her toward the auditorium.

As if the fates were somehow scheming to prevent them from ever seeing crummy high school bands — would that they were so lucky — October's father, who had arrived earlier (because car), became the next person to waylay them on their way to Bandwarz. A veil of dread enveloped October as she visualized the potential embarrassment that a night spent in the company of both her dad *and* her friends held. Luckily (for her), Mr. Schwartz had no intention of sitting anywhere close to his daughter during the Bandwarz festivities.

"Pumpkin," he said, already mortifying October with his opening word, "I wonder if you'd mind if I sat with Crown Attorney Salmons during the recital."

Her embarrassment over his use of "recital" aside, October was relieved her dad didn't want to, like, hang out during the concert. Of course, this also meant that things hadn't fizzled between her father and Ashlie Salmons's mom — the woman who had brought the demon-spawn into existence — which was its own set of problems.

"No, that's okay, Dad," she said.

Yumi gave her the widest-eyed stare she could manage.

"Great," he said with renewed enthusiasm. "We can meet up later and compare and contrast our favourite bands of the evening."

"Sounds good."

Against all odds, Yumi's eyes just got wider.

"Oh," Mr. Schwartz added, just as he was departing for his seat. "I nearly forgot . . ."

He patted his pants and pulled out a folded scrap of paper from his back pocket and quickly scanned it for confirmation, as if he were about to announce the Academy Award winner for Best Original Screenplay. "You got a phone call from a Beryl Gordon, who said to visit her tomorrow at five."

"Oh, good," October said.

Mr. Schwartz took his daughter two strides to their left and leaned in to whisper. "October, have you started seeing a therapist outside of the school one? Because I think that's not a bad idea —"

"No," October said, taking the paper from him, though she didn't really need the information. "It's a school project thing, an . . . an English project."

(English was quickly becoming October's course of choice for all the fake assignments that could explain away things like meeting with octogenarians on a weeknight.)

"Of course," he said, literally jogging away from the three teens after patting both of lanky Stacey's shoulders. "Have fun, you guys."

"Is Mrs. Salmons going to be your new mom?" Yumi asked, looking like she'd swallowed a spoonful of dry oatmeal.

"Don't make me think about it," October insisted.

"Why did your dad pat my shoulders?" Stacey asked.

October shrugged. "Guy stuff?"

"Let's find seats," Yumi demanded. "I want to see the crushing disappointment on the faces of Phantom Moustache up-close when they lose to Crenshaw House."

They entered the darkened auditorium to find most seats were already spoken for. October's dad and Crown Attorney Salmons had snagged a couple of spots close to the stage, so October scanned backward to see where they could sit unnoticed near the rear of the room, despite Yumi's interest in seeing disappointment up-close-and-personal. As her eyes panned across the seats, one audience member stuck out like a scorpion in a salad bar — the strange man from the cemetery on Sunday night was a Bandwarz fan, apparently. He sat alone, dressed (impossibly!) more garishly than the evening before, having added white platform shoes and a floppy violet hat to his ensemble. And Mr. Santuzzi and he seemed to share a cloak salesman.

Stacey voiced the question on all three's (and, realistically, everyone in the audience's) minds: "Does anyone else see Summertime Count Dracula?"

Yumi just about doubled over in laughter, which went mostly unnoticed in the dark and crowded auditorium. When she recovered, she said, "That's not Dracula." Though maybe that was obvious. "That's Nicodemus Burke, you screwhead."

"Why do you know that guy?" October asked, since the *A&E Biography* of this not-Dracula was of more concern to her than it was for most people assembled at Bandwarz.

"Nicodemus Burke?" Yumi said, repeating the outlandish name again. "He's a local psychic guy — has ads in the *Sticksville Loon* and on the cable-access station. Palm readings, tarot, that kind of stuff. Like a dime-store John Edward."

"But apparently more flamboyantly dressed," Stacey added. Coming from a boy in a mauve and magenta Hawaiian shirt, this was a bold judgment.

October had to admit she didn't read the *Sticksville Loon* (aside from in archival, microfiche form) or watch much cable-access television. Her nights were either spent sleuthing or hanging out with Yumi and Stacey.

"That guy's a psychic?" October asked, somewhat in disbelief. Yumi snorted. "I guess."

"Why would he be here?"

"Maybe he has a kid in one of the bands?" Stacey suggested. "Phantom Moustache does sound a bit paranormal."

"Whatever," Yumi shot him down. "He was probably told to attend by 'the spirits.'"

"Aren't you *afraid* of ghosts?" Stacey asked.

"Shut up!"

Yumi turned bright red. Ever since Morna messed up big-time and accidentally allowed herself to be seen by Yumi, who — unlike most of the other living people October encountered — could see dead people, Yumi had been living in mortal fear of ghost children.

"Whatever reason he has for being here, maybe let's not sit beside him," October said, even though there were plenty of empty seats (for some reason) beside the town psychic.

The gang of three sat a few rows back and several seats over from Nicodemus Burke, who was busy tenting his fingers in anticipation of some kid rock music. (Not to be confused with Kid Rock music.) Shortly thereafter, Principal Hamilton loped up the short flight of stairs beside the stage and took his position at its centre. A drum kit was set in the distance behind him, and amplifiers and mic stands dotted the stage like Lego pieces left by a lazy (or sadistic) child. Hamilton sauntered over to the central microphone. As soon as he opened his mouth, a harrowing banshee squeal pierced the stuffy air of the auditorium, as if God himself were experiencing trouble sending a fax.

As the parents and kids in the audience covered their ears and lowered their heads for the further audio assault that was to come, the student sound tech fixed whatever the issue was so Mr. Hamilton could speak freely without causing the audience's brains to explode into pulp.

"Ladies and gentlemen," he said with such pomp, you half-expected him to unleash bloodthirsty lions into an arena. (He was very unlikely to do this.) "Thank you for joining us in this celebration of student talent, and for supporting our annual summer formal with your ticket purchases. Without further ado . . . let Bandwarz begin!"

☠   ☠   ☠

Let's be real: Stacey, October, and Yumi (did you notice their initials spell "soy"?) were really only in attendance to (a) hate-watch Phantom Moustache, and (b) see if this Crenshaw House was any good, so the first four bands who played their fifteen-minute sets were of no consequence to them or the outcome of this novel. There were six bands in total and — as last year's Bandwarz winner and the most popular band in school — Phantom Moustache would most certainly play last. That meant Crenshaw House was up next, and our trio of misfit teenagers could barely contain their excitement. But before they could play, Principal Hamilton arrived to provide an update on the fundraising situation.

"Before we get to our penultimate band, we have a very special announcement! I've been given an update from Ashlie Salmons and the rest of the Bandwarz committee regarding the funds raised by this wonderful evening. I'd like to thank you all for your generosity, as your combined contributions provided funds for the summer formal of over five thousand dollars!"

The audience erupted into boisterous applause. Clearly a number of people had been paying more than the suggested amount — or Ashlie had somehow convinced them the degenerate loser fee was real.

"Of course, there's still time to donate," Mr. Hamilton reminded everyone. "Especially if you're a fan or — *ahem* — parent of one of the remaining bands, it would be a much-appreciated gesture."

Yumi cocked an eyebrow at October. As Phantom Moustache was assembled from the kids of some of the toniest families in Sticksville, this seemed either a canny or desperate move on the part of their principal. The money talk was followed by a halfhearted introduction that announced the next band as "Columbia House," as its members took the stage and awkwardly plugged in their patch cords. Matilda Coffin adjusted the height of the stool behind the drum kit. Levi Marylebone said nothing at centre stage at first, just stood there, somewhat shaky, but maintaining his solid punk glower at the audience, and appeared ready to beat up his guitar. October was thrilled.

Henry Khan, potentially October Schwartz's one true love but definitely the bassist of Crenshaw House, shuffled up to his microphone and clearly announced:

"We are Crenshaw House and we, uh . . . are here to decapitate you . . . with rock."

This opening statement (because what was about to happen was a trial of sorts) was met with a couple boos, some confused whispers, and the most furrowed brow the student body had yet seen on Mr. Hamilton's forehead this year. Yumi, Stacey, and October were the only ones loudly cheering.

"This is a song we call 'Grave Unto the Joy Fantastic,'" Levi said.

Thirty seconds later, Matilda Coffin hammered on the tom drums as if she were trying to reach the Cadbury creme inside. Levi then unleashed a pulsing sonic beacon through his jagged guitar tiffs, and Henry's thumbs turned into a blur as they ran up and down the neck of his bass. They were heavy, and they were a bit sloppy, but they were good. October found herself pleasantly surprised. Yumi excitedly slapped Stacey's shoulder repeatedly, and his goofy grin only grew.

The song came to a triumphant if abrupt stop. And once the students in the audience realized the song was over, they actually applauded. October could barely believe it herself. Perhaps her fellow Sticksville Central teens weren't clapping quite as hard as if Phantom Moustache were playing, but at least they were willing to recognize talent.

"Thank you," Levi said, a smile almost cracking his serious grimace. He picked up a water bottle that had been placed by the microphone and took a deep pull. "Here's another song. It's also about death and stuff."

The crowd cheered, and Crenshaw House drove headlong into another aggressive but poppy song with a drumbeat that sounded kind of like the theme to *George of the Jungle*. Preston Sinclair, the only member of Phantom Moustache who could reasonably be considered human, paced the aisles and threw his hands up in dismay. By the time they'd hit their fourth (and second-last) song, Levi began to swagger a bit in his leather jacket and black jeans.

"We're so excited to be here with you tonight," he panted, taking another drink of water. "So nice to have an enthusiastic autdience as we triumph over Phantom Moustache."

The crowd *oooohhhhed*, impressed by the sudden bravado that this previously unknown band had developed. Some even laughed. From the wings, October could see Principal Hamilton slowly shake his head in disapproval, but Levi just laughed and tossed his empty water bottle into the crowd. The plastic container landed right at Stacey's feet.

"Did all the bands have water bottles?" October asked. "Why are Crenshaw House the first to properly use them?"

As loudly and magically as they had started, Crenshaw House stopped. By the time they'd ended, Levi, Henry, and Matilda looked sweaty and nearly green, but October supposed rocking so hard took a lot out of you. They had delivered five songs that were all October and her friends could have hoped for. Though they took the stage like nervous kids, Crenshaw House had fused into a real rock band in the course of five songs — though they still seemed a bit unsteady as they departed the stage. They had even seemed to rile up the crowd more than any of the previous bands.

Once a calm settled in, Principal Hamilton returned to the spotlight. "And now, a band that probably needs little introduction," Mr. Hamilton announced. "Your Bandwarz champions, Phantom Moustache!"

The crowd, already in a rambunctious mood and now ready for an honest-to-goodness musical battle, cheered and hooted like the audience in a particularly good episode of *Maury Povich* — most likely a paternity test episode. The four traditionally handsome members of Phantom Moustache took to the stage. Boston Davis stood at the front microphone with his cherry-red guitar slung over his shoulder like a postman ready to deliver as the others — Preston Sinclair, Taylor Young, and Devin McGriff — took their places and studiously adjusted tuning knobs and tightened snares as if they were about to perform in Carnegie Hall.

"I just want to thank all our fans out there," Boston said, running his left hand through a lock of his hair in a way that was surely designed to make his female fans swoon. "This first song is for all of you."

Phantom Moustache played their song, with Devin McGriff starting things off with some riff he probably took from Oasis or Dave Matthews Band or someone boring like that. To be fair, they were perfectly fine songs, but October had heard them all before, six months earlier. And nothing they played or did pulled the lawnmower cord of her heart the same way Crenshaw House's songs had. She, however, seemed to be in the minority, as the rest of the audience was acting as if a bunch of fifteen-year-olds were revolutionizing rock music right there at a high school in Sticksville, Ontario. What did interest October, however, was what happened after they finished their first song.

"We would like to play you guys another song," singer Boston Davis teased. "We would *really* like to . . ."

Most of the crowd began to boo at the very thought of an evening devoid of more Phantom Moustache tunes, but October relished the idea. She might even get to sleep early for once.

". . . but, before we took the stage," he continued, "we received a threat from one of our fellow bands."

The boos and hisses from the crowd escalated wildly as Boston picked up a white sheet and Devin McGriff and Preston Sinclair helped him to unfurl it. Written in red was a sinister note:

Play your entire set tonight and it's curtains.

Oh, it was white curtains, not a sheet. Get it? The crowd went bananas, and not in the good way. October was entirely confused and looked to Yumi and Stacey who pointed at the members of Crenshaw House, who were slouched against the auditorium wall close to the front of the room. As the only other band with a shot of winning Bandwarz — one who'd actively taunted Phantom Moustache — suspicion naturally fell upon them. They looked just as threatened as Phantom Moustache, if not more. More than threatened, they didn't look well — like a punk band popular during the Spanish Flu. October sought out her dad in the audience to see if he could somehow help, but he was clutching his shirt collar and heading toward the door. Panic attack, October thought. This audience-wide distress is not a situation he would want to be part of.

"We want to keep playing," Boston said sincerely, "but we honestly don't feel comfortable with Crenshaw House present."

Some of the crowd — Phantom Moustache diehards — began to chant at Levi, Henry, and Matilda, "Get out! Get out! Get out!"

Principal Hamilton, witnessing the night career wildly out of control, stormed the stage and took the microphone from Boston Davis. He turned to address the band leaning against the wall. "Mr. Marylebone, Mr. Khan, Ms. Coffin," he intoned. "While we won't accuse you of anything, please know that we take threats of this nature very seriously, and we'll be investigating this matter thoroughly."

Some of the more passionate in the crowd booed at the very thought of presumed innocence. October Schwartz glanced over at Nicodemus Burke under his violet hat, who looked mildly amused by the turn of events.

"We didn't do that!" Levi pleaded, which was not very punk.

He looked like he was about to vomit. "That's not my handwriting, I swear, Mr. Hamilton!"

"Nevertheless," Mr. Hamilton raised his voice. "Given your comments about Phantom Moustache earlier this week and during your set, it would be best for everyone if you left for the remainder of the last band's set. We'll sort this out later. But you now have to vacate the school."

Hearing this, Matilda approached the stage, then buckled over to vomit onto its edge. Henry, seeing this, puked as well, but managed to contain the most of it in his palm, which he quickly brought up to his mouth.

What had started out as boos quickly turned to shrieks and cries of disgust as the drama unfolding on the Bandwarz stage had somehow transformed into a musical based on *The Exorcist*.

Principal Hamilton, attempting to seem unfazed by how rapidly a band competition had turned into an ancient Roman vomitorium, continued: "If you don't leave immediately, we'll have to disqualify you from Bandwarz. Now . . . if you'll please follow Mrs. Tischmann, she can connect you with the medical attention you may need."

"Whatever. Don't bother. We're leaving," Levi said, beginning to gag as he shoved past some concertgoers and said a number of words inappropriate to report in a novel intended for this age range.

The rest of Crenshaw House followed their sailor-mouthed frontman, looking wobbly and more than a little seasick. Mr. Hamilton called after Mrs. Tischmann futilely. Within moments, he gave up and returned to the microphone to apologize profusely for the uncommon spectacle onstage, though any parent who had attended a few events at Sticksville Central High School must have realized that spectacles were very much the norm.

"If you'll just bear with us and stay in your seats, the custodial staff should have the stage cleaned up in no time. Then Phantom Moustache can continue their set and our student council can join us to announce the winners of this year's Bandwarz and a five-hundred-dollar credit to Rhythm Impossible Music Store. In the meantime, please talk amongst yourselves and enjoy the background music provided by one Carlos Santana."

"*Oye como va*" coursed through the auditorium speaker system, Santana's fingers smoothly gliding across the six strings of his guitar. Members of the audience alternately expressed astonishment at the band rivalry and gruesome display of reverse digestion, and disbelief when they checked their watches and saw it was merely nine o'clock. Only about ten minutes after the custodian arrived with his mop and wringer, Phantom Moustache continued with their set. And though the crowd was into it, the mood was obviously tainted by the evening's previous events. The set ended to great applause and everyone waited for something else astonishing to happen.

Following Boston Davis's last joyous "Thank you! I feel like we've been through so much tonight," student council president Zogon walked onto the stage to a smattering of applause.

"Thank you, thank you," he said. Despite dressing in a button-down shirt and tie, he maintained the backward ball cap on his head. "What a show! Things really got turnt tonight, didn't they?"

Considering 80% of the auditorium had no idea what "turnt" meant, and the other 20% felt like Zogon was in no position to use the term (and it did not apply at all to the current situation), his evaluation fell flat.

He continued: "I may be courting some disaster here, but if all tonight's musicians could *behave*, I'd like to call up all this evening's bands: Vanity Angel, Computer One, For Nick Cajun, The Breadwinners, and Phantom Moustache. Crenshaw House, pending further investigation, has unfortunately been disqualified."

They all clambered onto the stage, just barely fitting between the student council president and the amassed sound equipment. The members of Phantom Moustache smirked. Boston Davis shot the crowd a thumbs-down to some enthusiastic applause.

"This is wrong," October whispered to Yumi and Stacey. "They can't just disqualify Crenshaw House. There's no proof they left that message! I can't believe they would make a threat like that."

"Right, Henry Khan can do no wrong," Yumi joked.

"Let's get a final round of applause for all tonight's bands," Zogon demanded. "You're all winners just for getting up on this stage and playing your hearts out."

The thunderous applause from parents and classmates dimmed and Zogon continued his announcements: "I mean, figuratively. In reality, most of you are losers, as there can only be one literal winner at Bandwarz. But before we discover who that is, let's get the tally of tonight's ticket sales — all in support of the student summer formal — from our volunteer, Ashlie Salmons. Folks, let's hear it for Ashlie Salmons and her team of volunteers!"

The crowd applauded and cheered again, while October and her friends just side-eyed each other. Yumi took an exaggerated glance at the nonexistent watch on her wrist. (There was no room for a watch, given all the spiked bracelets and what-not.) Ashlie's mom, now unencumbered by the recently departed Mr. Schwartz, rose to her feet and tried — unsuccessfully — to get a standing O started. (The girl collected money for a few hours, lady, she didn't sing *La Traviata*.)

Amidst the applause, Ashlie Salmons entered the auditorium, clutching the metal cash box to her gut. She shuffled along the aisle in her violet dress and pink ballet flats, her feet never lifting from the carpet. And, most alarmingly, Ashlie's face was nearly green. Ashlie Salmons appeared distinctly ill, and October — though not unhappy to see misfortune befall her nemesis — was worried the audience would be treated to a repeat of Crenshaw House's performance. There was only so much vomit one could handle.

"Ashlie, what did the students and parents of Sticksville Central generously donate tonight?" Zogon asked as Ashlie climbed the stage stairs.

Though it was said quietly to Zogon, the microphone still picked up Ashlie saying, "I don't know," and Zogon's response, "What do you mean, you don't know? I thought you were counting the total just now."

Zogon seized the cash box from Ashlie and opened it, at centre stage, causing the audience to gasp once again. Who'd have expected a high school concert to have more twists and turns than an M. Night Shyamalan film?

"What . . . ?" Zogon shouted as he upended the box.

Around his sensible running shoes spilled stacks of bills, but not of legal tender. Instead, novelty bills that were used by garden

and hardware store Canadian Tire littered the freshly mopped
stage. No faces of Queen Elizabeth or Sir Wilfrid Laurier were to
be seen in the tens and twenties falling on the stage floor — they
all bore the face of Sandy McTire, the stereotypical Scottish mascot
of one of Canada's largest retail employers.

"It's been replaced with Canadian Tire money!" Ashlie
shouted.

Panic set in. The audience started to yell and jostle one
another.

"Stay calm," Zogon insisted over the microphone. For all his
backward-hat-wearing, at least he was halfway decent in a crisis.
He pulled out a piece of printer paper and brought it closer to his
face. "Now what's this . . . ?" He read aloud:

I know you think I'm a creep,
It's not a reputation I can save.

Climb in with me, six feet deep.
Babe, it's fantastic in the grave.

"Those are Crenshaw House lyrics!" shouted one helpful Phantom Moustache fan from the audience.

As if Crenshaw House hadn't already been disqualified from Bandwarz; robbing over $5,000 of fundraising money certainly wasn't going to be a mark in their favour.

☠ ☠ ☠

8

A-band-onment

The first thing I did as soon as the police allowed everyone to leave the school auditorium was check on my dad. In retrospect, he was wise to depart when he did. Had he stayed for the theft of the Bandwarz money, rather than just the vague death threats and vomiting, I feel like his depressive episode could have been catastrophic. As it was, he was resting in his bed, staring at the ceiling, when I returned home. His door was open, though, so that was a good sign.

"You won't believe . . ." I began, assuming he'd like to know the bizarre and unexpected way Bandwarz concluded — with a police investigation.

"Nothing until morning, please," he said, still staring at the stucco pockmarks above. Dad knew his limits and the best ways for managing difficult situations, and I didn't dream of double-guessing him.

"That's fair," I said, then whispered to myself, "you'll hear about it from Ms. Salmons soon enough . . ."

With Dad grappling with a depressive episode, escaping the house was easier than usual, though it seemed callous to delight in that. Typically, a small aircraft could crash-land in the backyard and he wouldn't notice. My furtive escape out the sliding glass door and into the cemetery behind my house was like a summer breeze by comparison. And though it was such a stressful night, I felt as if I had played a fifteen-minute musical set and violently puked myself, it still felt important to make the effort to see the dead kids. We had still found no evidence whatsoever about Tabetha's death, and if my moon-watching was accurate, I had less than two weeks until my dead friends disappeared again.

First thing I mentioned when I came across my dead friends was the pandemonium at the school concert. It had been months since I had a story this good to tell them, and Bandwarz had it all: music, artistic jealousy, threats of violence, semi-digested food. For the most part, they were both disgusted and entertained.

"Did all three of them vomit?" Kirby inquired, cupping his chin with his one remaining hand.

"I think just the two," I admitted. Maybe Levi puked on his way out the door, but I had no way of knowing that.

Tabetha, however, seemed disheartened.

"What's the matter, Tabby?" Kirby asked. "It's a funny story."

"Sure," she said. "It's jus' that it sounds like it'll end up another mystery t'solve n' once again, we'll all get roped inta figuring out who stole the money. My mystery will fall by the wayside."

"No," I said, now realizing what I thought was an entertaining story might not be entertaining for everyone. "It's not like that."

"Y'all don't even really wanna solve this mystery," she said. "You don't like me. I'm not brave like Cyril or smart like Derek or sweet like Morna."

"Or handsome like Kirby," Kirby added.

"Ya just think I'm the angry one," Tabetha frowned, kicking a tombstone with her black boot. "Good to break through floorboards and rip off arms."

"You are very angry sometimes," Cyril (very unhelpfully) decided.

"Don't I have reason t' be?!" Tabetha cried.

My stomach twisted into a balloon animal. One of those wiener dogs. As much as I wanted to help Tabetha feel part of the group, I wasn't sure how. Just saying it — especially now

— seemed disingenuous. So, I turned our attention back to her death. (As counter-intuitive as that seemed, I figured it would work. At least it was a problem that I could help solve.)

"We should all just take a breather," I suggested. "Listen, we have two weeks left. Plenty of time to solve your mystery, Tabetha. We'll make it the priority."

"Of course, Tabetha," Morna said. "We'll work round the clock . . . well, mostly at night, because that's when we ghosts are around."

Tabetha didn't respond, but she also had regained her composure.

"Last night you mentioned something about a goat," I said. "Do you remember that? Some sort of goat incident? Can you tell us about that?"

"The Stubborn Goat," Tabetha explained, seemingly exasperated by our foolishness." That's the name a' the tavern where my dad worked. That's where Ms. Yvonne got us in some bad trouble."

"What happened?" Derek asked.

"Usually I got done working at the mayor's house round seven or so. But Dad worked late at the tavern. That's when most people drink — night time. Usually I'd head to the Stubborn Goat right after and stay until Dad was done his shift. The owner didn't like it much, but Dad was cheap labour n' he was good labour, so he dealt with it."

Tabetha then outlined the worst night of her father's tavern career.

☠ ☠ ☠

Thursdays, the Stubborn Goat usually had a band play some songs. This night, Ms. Yvonne was with the band, singing and playing music. Everyone was having a generally good time, according to Tabetha, when two of the tavern patrons started talking nonsense.

"Unfortunate, isn't it?" Virgil Cooper, shipbuilder and one of Cyril's later family members noted.

"What is?" the town pharmacist, Yancey Burnhamthorpe, asked.

"That they can't make serving boys invisible," he said, slamming his tankard on the wooden table right in front of Lunsford.

Yancey exploded with laughter. "I wish those folks would just stay up at the creek," he said. "With the other garbage!"

The two drinking companions guffawed so loudly you could hear it over the band's soaring fiddle.

Lunsford kept tight-lipped. He gathered their empty drinking vessels and turned to shoot his daughter, at the edge of the bar, a quick smile.

"Boy!" shouted the pharmacist. "I wasn't done drinking that!"

Now, it had been a good thirty years or more since Lunsford was a boy, but when he heard the drunken man screaming "boy" at the top of his lungs, he knew who the pharmacist meant.

"Sorry, sir," he said, returning the clearly empty tankard to the table.

"Don't give it back to me, you idiot!" Yancey shouted. "Get me a new one!"

The band, frustrated they had to compete with two rowdy townspeople in the front row, abruptly stopped playing. The way Tabetha told it, it sounded essentially like someone scratched an old vinyl record. Then Ms. Yvonne took to centre stage and started giving the two drinkers a chewing out.

"Gentlemen, if you want to be guest singers in this here band, I'm afraid we're gonna have to audition you," she shouted, then gave Tabetha's dad the slightest wink.

For a little woman, Ms. Yvonne had a booming voice. She also had, maybe, a false sense of confidence. For that one comment — no less that ill-advised wink — caused both the shipbuilder and pharmacist to storm the Stubborn Goat's little stage and begin to rant furiously. What kind of treatment was this? How dare this woman embarrass them in front of everyone? And was she winking? At a Black man? Is this the

kind of thing that hap-
pens in Sticksville these
days? These and other
questions, with a signif-
icant deal of profanity
thrown in for good mea-
sure, were hurled from
the stage by the two livid
men.

Tabetha watched from
behind the bar as Ms.
Yvonne, assisted by the
band's fiddler, attempted
to whisk the two men, who
had quickly made everyone
in the tavern very uncomfortable,
off the stage. And they didn't like that one bit. Virgil put
the fiddler into a headlock, while Yancey shoved Ms. Yvonne
against the wall. The tavern fell into an eerie silence. Not one
of the patrons made a move to help. Tabetha's dad rushed in
where angels — if you could consider any of the tavern patrons
"angels" — feared to tread. Tabetha was almost certain he'd get
himself killed.

"Let me pay for it, let me pay for it!" he started shouting.
He ran to the bar and got the men two fresh ales. "On the
house! Let's just be calm."

The men released the musicians. You could hear a pin
drop. Or rather, a spoon. (One of the other tavern patrons, a
candlestick maker, dropped his spoon in surprise.)

"Somebody get that serving boy out of my sight," commanded Virgil Cooper. He was a man who was used to delivering instructions that had impact.

"Let's go," Tabetha's dad whispered to her, and he dragged
her out the back door. They went immediately home, but Tabetha
could hear Yancey shout after them, "I've got my eye on you, boy!"

I couldn't believe Tabetha had waited so long to tell me
this story. "Have you heard this before?" I asked the other dead

kids, who seemed equally enraptured by this tense standoff. They shook their heads.

"Not a story I particularly like tellin'," Tabetha admitted.

"But Tabetha, your dad saved those musicians," I said. "He defused the situation. He's basically a hero."

"Yeah, n' after that, all a' Mr. Cooper n' Mr. Burnhamthorpe's friends hated us even more. Instead a' jus' ignoring us, they actively harassed us," she said.

October realized how much easier it would have been for one of the white men — a friend or colleague of Cooper or Burnhamthorpe — in the bar to intervene. They could have stepped in and it would have been a wry anecdote between old chums. Instead, it just doubled Tabetha and her dad's pariah status, potentially putting them in even more danger.

"Tha' was such a horrible story," Morna said, visibly shaken.

"I agree. That sounded way worse than the disaster at our band competition."

Cyril had been looking sheepish since the name Virgil Cooper came up in the story. He doffed his tricorn hat and looked into it, as if some sort of fitting response to such a story could be found within. "Oh," he said. "So that's why you hate me."

☠   ☠   ☠

Obviously, I did not look forward to attending school the following morning, though someone who relished going even less was Dad. (Theoretically, the members of Crenshaw House probably dreaded it most, given their lyrics were found in the place of thousands of stolen dollars, and they were accused of issuing threats to fellow students, but I'm no mind reader.) After all, my dad was suffering from the psychological weight of the stress precipitated by some harsh words and bitter rivalries. Now that *actual* theft — technically Theft over $5,000, according to the law — had occurred, I feared he'd be too overwhelmed to teach. But then again, he still didn't know about the theft. Unless

Mrs. Salmons told him.

This fear developed over breakfast. I was starting Dad's coffee and eating my Nutella toast when he shuffled downstairs and across the linoleum floor of the kitchen. At least he was dressed for work. After last night, I wasn't sure I could expect that. Usually if he had changed out of pyjamas, Dad's depression wasn't too, *too* bad.

Spying the imminent percolations of the coffee pot, Dad opened the cabinet and retrieved his favourite mug: *My Other Mug Is a Beaker.*

"Are we sure it's not Saturday?" he asked. "We're definitely certain it's a school day?"

"Mmm-hmm."

"Ashlie's mom told me what happened. Actually, she sent me an email, which I foolishly read first thing this morning."

"Oh, Dad," I sighed. "I'm sorry."

"A couple of those Crenshaw House kids are in my class," he sighed after a gulp of coffee. "Henry and Matilda . . . it really doesn't look good for them. But they're both such good students."

Then he stared into the rich brown pool of his mug for, like, ever, and I started to worry he'd fallen into a depressive coma (though those are impossibly rare, we've been told).

"Dad, are you okay?" I asked.

"Mmm?" he said, rousing from his trance. "What? Oh, yes . . . fine."

"And you're going to work today?"

"Yes, yes," he said. "Don't worry."

At this, I was forced to shoot him my most skeptical "really?" look as I looped my too-heavy backpack over my shoulders.

"Fine. You can worry about me," he agreed. "But this isn't depression — just general dread about going to school when a couple of my students are suspected of threatened violence and robbery."

"All right."

"Depression isn't *caused* by bad things, October. You know that," he explained. "It's a chemical imbalance."

"I know . . . See you in class," I said, heading out the door.

"See you in class," he said, muffled partially by the coffee mug. "And don't be unpleasant to those kids in Crenshaw House, please."

"Why would I be unpleasant to them?" I said. "I think they're innocent."

☠   ☠   ☠

Usually, the first thing that happened at school after I dropped some junk off at my locker is that I ran into Stacey and Yumi, and Thursday was no exception. Naturally, they wanted to talk all about the Bandwarz theft, and — of course — Yumi, the only high school student with an ongoing interest in local journalism, had brought the morning's edition of the *Sticksville Loon*.

"Look at this biased reporting." Yumi was outraged.

As could be expected, the Bandwarz theft was front-page news, with a very compelling photograph of Ashlie Salmons in a mini-cyclone of Canadian Tire money paired with a reproduction of the lines of song lyrics left, Riddler-style, as a cryptic clue.

"How is it an outrage?" I asked.

"Did you even *read* the headline?" she said.

I hadn't, so I did.

HIGH SCHOOL BAND CRENSHAW HOUSE SUS-PECTED IN FUNDRAISER THEFT.

"Who suspects Crenshaw House except total idiots?!" Yumi asked.

"Like, everybody," Stacey answered.

"Exactly," Yumi huffed. "*Idiots*. Why would they leave their own song lyrics at the scene of the crime? Do they *want* to be caught or something?"

Yumi brought up a fascinating point: leaving the song lyrics seemed like a weird thing to do. Why leave anything? Why not just take the cash? Though, as the *Sticksville Loon* informed them, it wasn't just the money that was missing. The cash box had been entirely replaced during the thievery. The old switch-eroo.

"I just figured they were so angry for being disqualified from Bandwarz and puking everywhere, they wanted to get revenge on the school," Stacey said, parroting the prevailing theory, though the Crenshaw House kids had only been questioned, not charged. "They don't seem to love it here."

"Who does?" I said. "But then, did they write the threat on the curtains, too?"

"I don't think so. But the lettering on the curtains and the note with the lyrics apparently match," Yumi said. "So, if they did write both, that's a pretty stupid plan."

"We don't know for sure Crenshaw House is smart," Stacey said, which was another good point. People always assume criminals know what they're doing, but they're usually dumber than you'd expect. Especially teen criminals. "They could have just been really angry."

"Right?" I said. And dehydrated, given how much they each threw up. "Do we know why they got so sick?"

"Some people vomit when they're anxious," Yumi said. And some people, I thought, are anxious when they're guilty. "But Levi thinks someone tampered with their water bottles. Diabolical."

"I don't remember seeing any other bands drink water," I admitted. "But I can't believe Henry Khan stole that much money just to get revenge. Doesn't anyone suspect Phantom Moustache?"

Yumi shot me a look like I was drooling onto my shirt. "What do you think?"

"To be fair," Stacey said, "they never left the auditorium. Crenshaw House left the school before Ashlie found the fake cash box."

"Let's not be fair to those creeps in Phantom Moustache, okay?" Yumi suggested.

A pickle it was, to be sure, but luckily, it wasn't *my* pickle. I had to solve the mystery of Tabetha's death, and that was challenge enough to keep me busy for a long, long time. Yumi was just about to say something hideous, like *Someone should help Crenshaw House out*, or whatever, when the trendily attired girl at the centre of the mystery glided by our locker bay. Though it was my inclination — okay, not my inclination, but my intention — to stay out of this whole band robbery, Yumi had other ideas. We couldn't have cared less if some awful school dance had a lower budget or got cancelled or whatever. But Yumi, she couldn't stand the injustice that Crenshaw House faced.

"Ashlie!" she shouted and hurried after the impeccably dressed menace.

Now even though in the past few months, Yumi, Stacey, and I, especially, had more than a few neutral encounters with Ashlie Salmons, it's not like we were friends, or even people who could get away with shouting her first name and expect her to respond. We were, for all intents and purposes, still Zombie Tramps. Even Stacey.

"Ashlie, wait up!" Yumi continued. Stacey and I chased after her, mostly because we were worried Ashlie would flay her alive.

It wasn't until the three of us were almost literally clinging to her back, with Yumi chanting, "Ashlie! Ashlie!" in regular intervals, that she turned on her heel and leaned back into the lockers behind her.

"Kung Fu Zombie Tramp?" she said, folding her arms across her chest. "Can I assist you with something?"

"I told you," Yumi said, "that name is wholly offensive."

"I wholly apologize then," she said, rolling her eyes. "What do you want? I need to find a copy of the paper to see what photo they used of me."

"I can save you a trip," Yumi said, showing her the *Sticksville Loon*.

"Hmm. Not my favourite, but it's okay."

"This is serious, Ashlie. Come on," I said, not sure why she'd consider my plea.

"You have to tell the police that Levi and Crenshaw House are innocent," Yumi demanded.

"What do I have to do now?" she asked. "What makes you think I'll do *that*? I have no idea if they're innocent. I only told the police what I know, and none of that was about that stupid band that's nowhere near as good as Phantom Moustache. The police — and everybody else — drew their own conclusions about those losers."

"So what *did* happen?" I asked.

"How should I know?" Ashlie said, throwing her arms wide. "You saw everything that I saw — I don't even remember turning my back from the cash box, and neither do Jerica or Ibiza. So I don't even know how they — or whoever — made a switch. Maybe when I went onstage to give the update? But it was *honestly* so short a time . . ."

It took me a few moments to realize Jerica and Ibiza were Ashlie's fellow fund collectors that night. "Okay, thanks."

"Thanks?" Ashlie said, incredulous. "For what? You and your oafish friends hold me hostage in the loser hallway of the school and you think I'm telling you this stuff voluntarily? I am under *duress*."

Ashlie whipped her hair back and fled toward the atrium. Only Stacey waved goodbye.

"You think Ashlie was involved?" Stacey asked. "Was it an inside job?"

"Doesn't matter to me," I said, making a renewed effort to stay out of it. I remembered how Tabetha had looked when I'd even brought up the Bandwarz theft and knew it was best to leave this to the police.

"What are you talking about?" Yumi said, grabbing me by the shoulder of my black hoodie. "You love this stuff. Remember how you nearly got killed trying to figure out how Mr. O'Shea died? This is just like that, only there are no dead bodies. *Ideal!*"

"No," I insisted. Hearing the name Mr. O'Shea and dead bodies within the same minute still stung. "Not my circus, not my monkeys."

As I marched away to English class, Stacey asked Yumi, "What does that mean?"

☠ ☠ ☠

Everything was pretty fine until lunch. We had just started covering *To Kill a Mockingbird* in English, and Dad made it through science class without seeming anywhere close to a breakdown. (He also managed to teach the entire class without once calling me "pumpkin" or "sweetheart," which was especially appreciated.) But whatever schoolwide tension from the Bandwarz incident(s) I thought had eased soon boiled over in the cafeteria.

Stacey and Yumi were again at the far edge of the room, working on the *Loon*'s jumble while (sort of) eating their lunches. Some people really don't ever care about being cool. A bit further down, the only other occupants of the table were in the midst of an Advanced Dungeons & Dragons game.

"How was class?" I asked, slouching into the spot beside them.

"Delightful," Stacey said. "History with Ms. Fenstermacher was — as *always* — a dream."

"Shut up," Yumi grumbled.

In addition to making me physically ill, Stacey's gross thoughts about the school's history teacher reminded me I had to take the bus to the fairgrounds again today to do that fictional English interview with historical Sticksville resident Beryl Gibson. I'd probably need to bring a notebook that wasn't emblazoned with the words *Two Knives, One Thousand Demons* to give myself more credibility.

"Do either of you know an easy way to get to the fairgrounds?" I asked.

"The fair doesn't open until June," Stacey said.

"What do you want to go there for?" Yumi asked, busy somehow unscrambling a series of letters into the word "leonine."

Where that conversation would have led next is a mystery that will never be solved, for within seconds, something best described as a ruckus or commotion erupted near the cafeteria entrance. We swung our eyeballs over to what was happening and saw Boston Davis slapping Levi Marylebone's cafeteria tray out of his hands, sending a blizzard of fries and gravy so far across the floor that a few fries stopped just inches from our table.

"What's happening?" Yumi asked.

We stood up and moved over to the escalating argument,

which had already gathered a crowd, and inadvertently wound up standing behind the other members of Crenshaw House.

"Sorry I knocked over your lunch, Levi," Boston sneered. (I should have known Ashlie Salmons would date a boy who sneers.) "But you should be able to buy a new lunch with all the money you stole."

"I'm not the thief," Levi said, angrily wiping the gravy off his black denim jacket. "Somebody obviously framed us. Most likely somebody who shares a name with a cream-filled doughnut."

The crowd reacted to that insult with a mixture of delight and confusion. (It was a slow burn.) The other Phantom Moustachers began to shove Boston.

"Mess him up, man," goaded Taylor.

While the entire cafeteria seemed to be itching for a good old-fashioned schoolyard brawl (an indoor one), I started looking around for the closest adult. Ideally, a teacher or authority figure; the cafeteria workers didn't seem to care.

"I can't believe they even let a thug like you come to school after last night," Boston shouted, jabbing the air viciously with an index finger.

"Thug?" Levi spat.

"Levi, let's just go," pleaded Matilda Coffin in a meek voice. "We can report him to the office."

"You're like the chair of the Food and Thug Administration," Boston added, which was — while racist — honestly more clever than I though him capable.

"Should I get someone?" Henry Khan asked Matilda.

"Why did you target us, Boston? Pretending we threatened you? Blaming us for the theft? Why did *all* of you?" Levi demanded from everyone chowing down in the cafeteria. "There were four other bands playing last night. Is it because I'm *Black*?!"

A pall fell over the crowd. No one spoke for a moment, then Boston responded: "Are you calling me a racist?"

"If the hood fits," Levi said.

Then, Boston Davis, visibly upset to be called a racist, shoved Levi Marylebone — one of, like, eight Black kids at our school — into the wall.

Levi rebounded and sent his right fist crashing into Boston's shoulder. He continued to swing as the other Phantom Moustache band members tried to restrain him, all while the rest of Crenshaw House tried to restrain the members of Phantom Moustache. The cafeteria crowd exploded into hoots and jeers, but before another solid punch could be delivered (on either side), Mr. Santuzzi appeared in the doorframe like the Phantom of the Opera — only much bulkier. As an expert grappler, within moments he had separated Levi and Boston and started to frog-march them out the doors and toward the principal's office.

"Now, settle down, all of you," he instructed us bystanders, the two fighters still in his death grip. "I notice how none of you came for help once this fight broke out. So if you don't settle down, I'll be happy to march you *all* down to the office."

As unlikely and impractical as him following through on this threat was, it did quiet us down.

With no amateur boxing match left to observe, everyone separated and returned to their tables. Yumi, Stacey, and I made the long trip back to our distant table, but following the fracas, we'd picked up a couple of tails: Henry Khan and

Matilda Coffin. We sat back down by the open Jumble page while Matilda and Henry hovered awkwardly beside the table, not saying anything, just looking very intently.

"Can we sit?" Henry asked.

Stacey MacIsaac, the poorly dressed Boy Scout that he was, gestured to an empty seat. I was a bit hesitant to have a heart-to-heart with two people everyone in school hated, but I realized that wasn't a particularly new phenomenon.

"You doing the Jumble?" Henry asked in a vain attempt to make small talk before asking what was sure to be an unreasonable favour.

"What's going on?" I asked. "You never sit with us."

Yumi, who was about to wax poetic on the Jumble, I guess, seemed taken aback by my direct question.

"Listen, we don't want to bother you . . ." Henry began, but then Matilda Coffin (who really *did* have the coolest name) piped up from underneath that jet-black Dutch boy of hair: "We heard you solve mysteries."

"I . . . don't know what you're talking about."

"That's why people say you're always at the police station," Henry said. "I don't know if it's a stupid rumour, but we need help."

"I'm not . . ."

Matilda continued, "Everybody thinks we stole the Bandwarz money, but we didn't. You have to help us prove our innocence."

This day was turning into the exact opposite of what I'd hoped it would be. Mostly I believed they were innocent, too, but I couldn't sideline Tabetha's mystery. "Listen, I —"

"October," Yumi, my traitorous best friend interjected, "is great at solving mysteries. She's like an expert detective. A real live Carmen Sandiego, if you will."

"I think Carmen Sandiego is a thief," Matilda said.

"Quiet, Yumi," I said from the side of my mouth. But did she listen? *Nooooo.*

Henry stopped biting his nails for a second and returned to the issue of the lunch hour: "This wasn't shoplifting. This was a serious crime. If we get charged with this, I could have a record. That sort of thing would devastate my parents."

"Don't worry," Yumi said, chattering away like an unstoppable juggernaut of talk. "October is really good with problem solving. I'm sure she'll exonerate you in no time."

Yumi started nudging me, leaving me to glare at her, hoping my death-stare might melt the skin from her face, *Raiders of the Lost Ark*–style.

"I'm not exonerating anyone, Yumi!" I said, a bit louder than I'd intended. "I'm not a detective. I'm sorry — Henry, Matilda — but none of those rumours are true. I wish I could help, but I can barely solve a math equation, no less a mystery."

I threw in a few laughs after that for added effect, not that it provided any help.

"Please, October," Henry Khan said, studying his now-bloody thumbnail with his admittedly soulful brown eyes. "You have to help us. We don't know what else to do."

And that was the moment I was railroaded into solving the mystery of the stolen Bandwarz cash box.

☠ ☠ ☠

Sticksvillainy Most Foul

Like any classic detective duo — your Batman and Robin, your Sherlock Holmes and Dr. Watson, your Turner and Hooch — October Schwartz, now saddled with a burdensome mystery she'd tried to avoid, started her investigation by questioning witnesses. And unfortunately, Ashlie Salmons — the person closest to the robbery — either didn't see (or chose not to see) anything and had an airtight alibi provided by the other girls watching the cash box. Other than her, no one was aware the robbery happened until everyone was (when Zogon opened the cash box onstage). That meant there were no witnesses to interview, save the teacher who was overseeing the school parking lot during Bandwarz: Mr. Santuzzi. Given every school entrance save the front one had been locked at the time of the concert, he was the only person who saw every person arrive and every person who left early.

Of course, October Schwartz had no desire to interrogate Mr. Santuzzi. It was a half-baked, impossible task. She might as well have started by interrogating a great white shark. After the cafeteria almost turned into the Octagon, lunch ended, leaving October with very little time to talk to Mr. Santuzzi. And she couldn't put it off until the end of the school day — that was when she intended to conduct her interview with Beryl Gibson over by the fairgrounds.

October sighed with irritation. Every effort she made to help out Henry Khan threatened to steal away time from her more pressing mystery: what happened to Tabetha Scott in the 1800s.

Somehow, she always seemed to get mired in these second mysteries whenever she was *supposed* to be investigating the death of one of her ghost friends. (Funny how that worked.)

With limited time resources, October was forced to visit Mr. Santuzzi's math class between periods. She struggled to stay alert and attentive through Ms. Therieault's social studies class, which was honestly in need of a bit of a *refresh*. She needed to run to the math hall as soon as class ended — ideally *before* — and couldn't risk giving Therieault *any* excuse to hold her after class.

When the between-period tone sounded, October (who had been gradually and quietly sliding her notes and sundry writing utensils into her book bag over the past five minutes) scampered to the back door, nearly bowling over several of her classmates. She hurried down the hall and, paces from Mr. Santuzzi's room, ran into Yumi and Stacey as they exited his class.

"Where are you sprinting to?" Yumi asked, probably confused by all the physical activity October was doing.

"I have to ask Santuzzi about what he saw during Bandwarz."

Yumi elbowed Stacey, who looked harmed. "I told you she loves this detective stuff."

October scowled. She tried not to focus *too* much on how her friend Yumi had pressganged her into solving Crenshaw House's problem for them. She would need to save all her concentration for talking to Mr. Santuzzi. Given there were only a few minutes between classes, she had to make her questions count.

The hulking monster in an (alleged) wig was vigorously swiping at the blackboard, as if he were trying to wear a hole through to the other side. Despite his apparent agitation, October dove right in.

"Mr. Santuzzi," she said. "I know class is starting again soon, but could I ask you a few questions about Bandwarz?"

"Ms. Schwartz," he said, though he hadn't moved his slate-black eyes from the similarly coloured blackboard. The military must have fine-tuned his audio recognition. "I know how you like meddling. But you can be certain the school administration will handle this theft fairly and swiftly."

"I just want to ask you some questions about what you saw in

the parking lot," October protested. She had anticipated some suspicion from her former math teacher, but hadn't really anticipated how reluctant he'd be to speak at all.

"What did I just say about meddling?" he asked, finally turning to face his former student.

"Everyone thinks that Levi and Crenshaw House did it, but I'm sure they didn't," October insisted, a bit more insistent (naturally) this time. "They're not capable of it."

Mr. Santuzzi turned more serious, "Don't assume you know what anyone is capable of."

Well, that was unnecessarily grim and cryptic.

Fully aware that October Schwartz had no plans to leave his classroom without something resembling answers, Mr. Santuzzi sighed. "I'll tell you what I told Principal Hamilton and the police. The school's only unlocked entrance was the front doors. And I only saw three cars leave the parking lot before the police arrived."

"Mmm-hmm," October said, whipping out her composition book.

"The van that your friend in that Crenshaw Home band drives, your dad's car, and a third car I didn't recognize."

October remembered her father leaving early to avoid the swirling mass of anxiety forming at the concert, but didn't realize it might make him a suspect. This was disquieting.

"Can you describe the third car?" October asked.

"Yes."

"*Will* you?"

"I didn't get a great look at it — had I realized the crime of the century was happening inside the school, I might have paid closer attention," he said. "But it was either grey or silver and had fins."

"Like a Cadillac?" October asked.

"Like a shark."

The class tone sounded again and October realized a full math class had, at some point, materialized behind her. That — and she was now late for art with Mr. Muñez. Not that her deformed bust of Vincent Price was going to be helped any by punctuality.

"I truly thought these little conversations would end once I stopped teaching you, Ms. Schwartz," he admitted. "Please leave."

☠   ☠   ☠

Following the school day, October purchased a fresh notebook, free of any graffiti about demons or knives or chemical romances. Once again, she had to embark on an epic journey on the Number 4 Sticksville bus and its anaconda-like route. Once again, she encountered her bearded friend in the beret who this afternoon expounded on Night Ranger, the latest band to be featured in his Discman. However, being already accustomed to the peculiarities and dangers of the Number 4 bus, October found the trip zipped along and she was soon exiting the vehicle's back doors. At the same time, much to October's confusion and dismay, a familiar face was boarding at the front — or so she thought. She caught only a brief glimpse of him, but she was certain it was Nicodemus Burke, black cloak fluttering in the wind to reveal its crimson lining. Was it a simple matter of nearly everyone in Sticksville — both living and dead — residing close to Acheron Creek and the fairgrounds? Or was something stranger at work?

Burke's timing and choice of bus route bothered October for the rest of her walk. Seeing the local celebrity psychic gave her a feeling similar to having a film across her teeth or hearing her dad refer to food as "yummy." Unsettling. Did he do door-to-door psychic readings, like some sort of delivery boy for next year's newspaper? The strange appearance of Mr. Burke lingered in her head as she made her way to Beryl Gibson's front door, untouched spiral-bound notebook tucked under her arm.

Shortly after October mashed her finger into the doorbell, a large, old Black woman in fuzzy slippers, a flowery blouse, and boxy glasses opened the door and raised her eyebrows.

"Are you September Swanson?"

"Uh, October Schwartz?" October asked back, suddenly unsure of everything. "And you're Ms. Gibson?"

"Beryl, honey," she said and shuffled back into her house, apparently unconcerned if it was September or October she was expecting, or whether that girl was following her inside. October was a terrible judge of age. She was thirteen, when everyone over eighteen looks super-old and everyone over forty seems to have one foot in the grave, but she would have pegged Beryl Gibson at sixty until she saw her walk. After that, she figured Beryl was more like a hundred.

Beryl didn't speak a word as she led October through a dark hallway of wood-panelled walls plastered with family photos old and new, featuring grandparents, cousins, and children in every conceivable frame format — ovals, squares, those multi-photo things. The hall opened into a living room that was just as cluttered. The yellow-brown carpet looked as if it hadn't been cleaned in years. It probably wasn't even yellow-brown to begin with. The coffee table was stacked high with copies of *National Geographic* randomly culled from the past few decades, and the television set was covered in an equal number of VHS tapes. Beryl faced the La-Z-Boy chair in the corner as if she were going to dive in face-first, then slowly spun around and sank back with a sigh. She sounded like a storage unit door being opened after twelve months of abandonment.

October looked around for a place to sit, but realized there were no other chairs in the room.

"Grab a chair from the kitchen table," the old woman insisted. "I don't get many visitors here. The room isn't much set up for it."

October walked around the sort of half-wall and counter that separated Beryl's living room from the kitchen, retrieved a white wooden chair, and set it about three feet from her interview subject.

"So you want to talk about dead Black girls, huh?" she asked with a slight laugh.

Firstly, October had — up until now — not known that the dead girl from the 1800s was Black, but that detail did make it slightly more likely to be Tabetha. Secondly, she wished she could explain to Beryl Gibson that she did not *want* to talk about dead Black girls — like, it wasn't a hobby — but it was kind of her duty at this point.

"I . . . guess," October mumbled.

"Don't be shy," Beryl laughed. "I always want to talk about this story. It's nice to finally have a young person interested t'listen."

"Are you comfortable?" October asked, though given Beryl was sinking into her armchair and looked about to fall asleep, she could already tell the answer. Beryl's cat rubbed up against the chair (which appeared as if it doubled as its scratching post), and October's interviewee rubbed it under the chin. October flipped open her notebook. "So, how long have you lived here in Sticksville?"

"Oh, I've been here all my life," Beryl began, and what she eventually revealed to October made her wish she owned a tape recorder. Note-taking, no matter how quickly done, can only capture so much.

☠   ☠   ☠

After some preliminary questions about how Sticksville had grown and evolved over the years, October broached the topic of the tragedy at Acheron Creek. The story flowed freely from Beryl Gibson, as if she were a fountain at a fancy party, and the words, facts, and names were so much liquid chocolate.

"A friend of mine who lives near here says you leave yellow flowers at the telephone pole near the fairgrounds," October said. "Can you tell me why?"

"I leave those flowers for Tabetha, sweetheart," she said, adjusting her thick glasses.

Now October was getting somewhere. Maybe she'd solve the entire mystery just in the course of this one-on-one interview. "And who is Tabetha?" October asked, playing dumb.

"Who *was* Tabetha," Beryl corrected. "She's part of a family tragedy, I'm afraid. Tabetha Scott was a young relation of mine who died in childhood."

Hold the phone, reader! Beryl and Tabetha were related? This was valuable information. October was scribbling frantically, like she was mid-win on a lotto scratch ticket. "Beryl + Tabetha = related???" and so on.

"When did this happen?" October asked.

"Oh, the mid-1800s. About when the American Civil War was taking place down South," Beryl said.

"Were you there when she died?" October asked, not particularly good with math.

"Oh, child, no," Beryl laughed uproariously, which shook October. "How old do you think I *am*? No, don't answer that. She died *long* before I was born. But Tabetha's death is a story passed down the generations."

The gears in October's head spun like Catherine wheels (and generated just as many sparks): not only could Beryl potentially solve her mystery, October could even introduce her descendant to Tabetha — she'd have a link to her family, still alive and well in Sticksville. But their connection did confuse October. Tabetha never mentioned any siblings. If Tabetha died as a child, where did Beryl come from?

"And do you, or your family, know how she died?" October asked.

"That's easy," Beryl snapped.

"It is?"

"This town killed Tabetha."

Of course, this was not the answer October was hoping for, nor did she suspect every single resident ambushed her dead friend with long knives, like a Sticksville reproduction of the death of Julius Caesar. Really, she was hoping more for an answer like, "Old Mr. Jenkins from down the lane." Alas, that was not to be. So, October kindly asked Beryl Gibson to elaborate.

The old woman, fully cemented in her comfortable armchair, revealed the full story to October — well, the full story as completely as she knew it. According to Beryl Gibson, shortly after Lunsford Scott began his job at the tavern and he and Tabetha built a real residence, not far from where the two of them were sitting right then, the town of Sticksville turned against the Scotts. While the white residents of Sticksville, Ontario, had just barely tolerated the Scotts' residing in their town — with some notable exceptions — once Lunsford and the young widow Ms. Yvonne began spending time together, talking out of doors and at the tavern, especially, certain segments of Sticksville society began efforts to push the Scotts out of town. This information more or less corresponded to what Tabetha had already told October.

"Sticksville was fine with the two of 'em so long as they kept to themselves on the outskirts of town," Beryl said. "This was where the dumping ground was in those days. Not many white folks coming up here, 'cept to leave a broken doo-dad or an animal carcass. But once a young white woman started makin' eyes at Lunsford instead of some of the eligible Sticksville bachelors, they about had a fit."

"So you think that musician, Ms. Yvonne, was flirting with Tabetha's dad?" October asked. "Maybe she was just being nice."

In response, Beryl Gibson just stared October down with a look that asked, *What are you? Stupid or something?*

Whatever the woman's motives, Beryl continued, the town made Lunsford unwelcome. He was glared at on the street, couldn't get service at the general store. This was all typical Canadian racism and nothing Lunsford hadn't encountered before. But early in the fall, Tabetha went missing and was never seen again.

"And you think someone killed her or kidnapped her to drive her dad out of town?" October asked, jumping ahead with what she assumed was the conclusion to the story. "Why attack a kid? Why not the dad, if that's who their beef was with?"

"Much easier to kill a twelve-year-old," Beryl plainly stated, which we all know in our heart of hearts to be true. "Lunsford was a big man. Even if one of his hands was busted. And it would have the same ultimate effect: get Lunsford Scott out of their town. He was gone within a month. He met the woman who would become my great-grandma Pearl in Owen Sound. My daddy moved back to Sticksville in the 1950s."

While she now had a second person corroborating Tabetha's memories, October was saddled with still more questions than answers — new ones that she hadn't even considered before.

"But if you're related to Tabetha and Lunsford Scott," October asked, chewing fiercely on the end of her pen, "why is your last name Gibson?"

"Because I married Mr. Titus Gibson, God rest his soul."

"Oh, duh. And you said certain segments of Sticksville society wanted the Scotts driven out of town," October continued. "Can you be more specific? Were there, like, leaders of this effort?"

Beryl Gibson laughed again and rose from her armchair with some effort. "You trying to solve this centuries-old mystery for me, girl? I think you're going a bit above and beyond on this history project. I hope you get a good grade."

"English project. But . . ."

"But *nothing*, child. It's getting close to supper," Beryl Gibson insisted. October checked the clock on the microwave — it was past six. Her dad was liable to freak out when she arrived home after dark. "You can't solve a mystery that can't be solved. My father came back to Sticksville to try to figure it out and it drove him nuts. *Here*."

The old woman tossed a hardcover book on her lap. The dust jacket was missing and a Dewey Decimal code was laminated to its

spine, suggesting it had been purchased at a library sale. October opened the book to the title page:

Sticksvillainy: A Portrait of Small-Town Prejudice and Tragedy

"Self-published, of course. And it never sold much. At least not locally," Ms. Gibson continued, as if October were particularly interested in the book's publication history. "Hard for a town to get behind a book that calls it a den of murderous racists. Can't much sell that to the tourism board. You can borrow it for your school project since you seem so interested."

"Thanks," October said as the old woman hovered close, seemingly waiting for her to hit the road.

"Far as I can remember that book, my dad had it narrowed to three ringleaders behind all the trouble old Lunsford faced." She counted them off on her fingers, names memorized from repeat readings of her father's true-crime opus. "There was Virgil Cooper, one of the big shipbuilding people in town; Noah Sinclair, the town's mayor; and Yancey Burnhamthorpe, who was the pharmacist then."

October's mind reeled. Did Ms. Gibson really just narrow down her suspect list from, say, unlimited to three? Tabetha had certainly mentioned two of them earlier: Cooper and Burnhamthorpe were the central villains in her anecdote about the altercation at the tavern. And the mayor? No wonder Beryl blamed the entire town. Now October was making real progress on this case, and not a moment too soon, given how long she had until the full moon returned. October, rude houseguest that she was, cracked open *Sticksvillainy*, as though she aimed to read it cover-to-cover, before Beryl Gibson gently pushed her out.

"I'm afraid it's dinner time, young friend," she said, gently squeezing October's shoulder. "And this old woman needs her down time. We can talk more when you're done with the book."

"Yes, of course," October said, getting to her feet and rapidly scanning the hodge-podge of photographs on the wall again. Was it possible there was an old photograph of Tabetha among them? Did they even have cameras then? (October didn't know the history of photography super well.) "You don't happen to have any photographs of Lunsford or Tabetha, do you?"

"Photographs?" Beryl barely tried to hide her irritation. "Maybe . . . I'd have to go into the crawlspace to see. I'm sure there are old photos but, really . . . it's getting late."

October stuffed the book into her backpack, returned the chair to the kitchen table, and thanked Beryl Gibson again before heading to the front door.

"Sorry. Thanks again!" October shouted as she exited.

"Send me a copy of your story when it's done, if you don't mind!"

"Of course," said October, though the entire bus ride home, she regretted saying anything. She had no intention of turning her notes into some sort of Sticksville history think piece for Ms. Gibson to read.

☠   ☠   ☠

Great Scott!

Luckily for me, Dad had a late-night meeting with the school athletics department to discuss changes to the volleyball schedule next season, so I somehow — lumbering Sticksville bus notwithstanding — made it home before he did. Dad was none the wiser to my journey across town, where I peppered an old woman with personal questions about her family tragedy. Though having started to read *Sticksvillainy* on the bus ride home, I wasn't sure how I would talk about anything else *but* the various Sticksville family rivalries of the nineteenth century over dinner. Dinner, in this case, being Chinese takeout.

"How come our Chinese takeout never looks like Chinese takeout in the movies?" I asked, rending open some moo shu beef in a plume of steam.

"I think that's an American thing," Dad said, who seemed astonished by the ferocity with which I attacked my meal.

"Really?"

"I don't think it's any great conspiracy, honey," he said. "Just like how our milk comes in bags."

"Now that," I said, talking with my mouth full, I'll admit, "*is* a conspiracy."

Before long, Dad was nodding off in front of some *A&E Biography* of Phil Collins or whoever, which meant it was time for me to quietly slide open the kitchen door and sneak into the cemetery to tell the dead kids the good news — as good as news about a kid's death can get, I suppose. I put on my denim jacket and stuffed thin black gloves into the pockets. Then I tip-toed down the rotten wooden steps of the deck and made my way across the yard with strides that were as quiet and graceful as I could manage.

The dead kids were already awake, though I'm not entirely sure if they sleep or not — it's never been clear to me what they do during the day. My guess: not much. And unlike other times when I'd walked in on them mid-conversation, they were not rehearsing a medley from *Meet Me in St. Louis* or impaling each other with spearlike branches. Instead, they were huddled around Derek and Morna, going over the information they'd uncovered about that weird group, Asphodel Meadows.

Derek and Morna knelt in front of the largest tree in the cemetery, a landmark that often served as our meeting point. Cyril, Tabetha, and Kirby were busy reviewing what they'd written so far and shouting potential additions. Or rather, Kirby was reviewing, and the other two were shouting the additions because neither Cyril nor Tabetha could read.

"Oh, and you forgot to include Alyosha Diamandas as a member of the group," Cyril yelled.

"That's because we don't know that he *is*," Derek replied, snatching the notepad from Kirby.

"Hey," the lone quint protested.

"He must be," Cyril asserted.

"We can't put things in this book that ye just *think* are true, Cyril," Morna insisted.

"Why not?"

"Living girl alert," Derek said, stuffing the coveted notepad into his back jeans pocket.

"Nice to see you engrossed in a mystery," I said, leaning against the massive tree. "Maybe soon you won't need my help to solve them."

"Nun-uh," Tabetha said, wagging her finger. "Don't you try n' get out of this deal. Ya solve a couple white kids' mysteries, n' you think yer done? I know how this works. You've gotta figure out how I died. That was the deal."

"I'm not trying to get out of *anything*," I sighed. "I'm just relieved to know that if I have to leave town or fall in front of a bus, you might be able to do this on your own."

"You never *have* to fall in front of a bus," Kirby quipped.

"Enough jawin'," Tabetha interrupted, obviously already impatient with how little headway had been made in her mystery. "Have you found out anything about the Underground Railroad yet?"

"Besides what we already know? No," I said. "But I did meet a woman named Beryl Gibson who you'll want to know about."

"Who's Beryl Gibson?" Morna asked.

"An old woman who lives over by where the final stop of the Underground Railroad was supposed to be. Right around Acheron Creek. She says she knows *you*, Tabetha."

"Me?"

"Yeah," I explained. "She must be a distant relative of yours, because she claims that your disappearance is her family tragedy. Says her dad was obsessed with solving the murder."

"And what does this Beryl woman say happened?" Kirby asked.

"She doesn't know. Apparently they never found your body, Tabetha."

I shot her a concerned look, which ended up looking more like I was stretching my mouth. She returned the look with a raised eyebrow.

"But she gave me this book, which outlines a theory," I said and held the copy of *Sticksvillainy* in front of me. "And brings suspicion on a few familiar names."

"You know I can't read," Tabetha said.

For the benefit of Tabetha and all the dead kids — just so they wouldn't have to read 250 pages of the fevered writings of Mr. Wilford Scott, an author who somehow managed to make child murder seem boring — I summarized the main idea behind the *Sticksvillainy* book. Namely, that in a racist, rage-induced response to Tabetha's dad hanging around a white woman, someone had killed Tabetha to drive her father out of town. And the book had spotlighted three townspeople as potential culprits, but one made a distinct impression in Tabetha's mind . . .

"I knew it. One of your stupid relatives killed me, Cyril!" shouted Tabetha.

"We don't know that for sure," Cyril reasoned, but still raised his hand defensively, expecting an attack.

He was not, however, expecting the solid punch to the gut that Tabetha delivered.

"You make me sick," Tabetha fumed, and she turned from the other dead kids, her arms tightly folded in on herself. "I shoulda known after rememberin' that incident in the tavern."

"Maybe we should jus' stop looking into these things," Morna said, watching Tabetha's shoulder begin to shake. "They jus' seem to bring up bad memories and things we were better off not knowing."

"Maybe we could get back into musicals," Cyril said, taking off his hat and rubbing the back of his skull.

"Sure," Kirby said. "Now that you two know how *you* died, you want to end things."

"It's not like that," Morna said, becoming more animated.

"Actually, it's exactly like that," Derek interrupted. "You don't want to solve this mystery because it makes you uncomfortable about white people. You know that neither you nor Cyril would talk to anyone like Tabetha or me when you were alive."

"But we're friends now," Morna said.

"Things were different in the past," Cyril said. "It was a different time and people thought about things in very different ways. Society has changed so much."

"That's what I don't understan', Cyril," Tabetha said, looking ashen. "Why do you folks need society or time or whatever to tell ya it's okay to treat Black people like human beings? How long's that supposed ta take?"

I'd never seen the dead kids so angry with one another, and I wasn't sure what to say. I wanted to say that was the past and, now that they were all dead and friends, we should move on. But Derek and Tabetha had a point. Cyril was very much from a world where kids like Derek and Tabetha were treated as less than human. If a relative of Cyril's had, in fact, murdered Tabetha, it would be a difficult thing to look past.

"Tabetha," Cyril said, walking over to the dead girl who had isolated herself from the rest of us and placing a cold hand on her shoulder, "I realize this is difficult for you, and we're going to figure this out together . . . but you can't just run around and accuse my family members of murder."

"Cyril," I pleaded. "Just. Stop. Talking. You don't know what —"

"Get yer hand off me, Cooper!" Tabetha said. "Your family are prime suspects, as far as I'm concerned. Your family hated my dad n' me, just because we're Black," Tabetha said, rigid finger in Cyril's pale face. "I know that fer a fact. I didn't imagine that scene at the tavern. I didn't imagine Virgil Cooper spitting when he saw me in the street. Whether they killed me or not, they *wanted* me dead."

Cyril tried to respond but was only able to open and close his mouth several times like a goldfish that had leapt out of its cloudy bowl.

"I don't know if Virgil Cooper was a killer," Tabetha continued to shout, "but he wasn't no angel."

"What d'ye mean?" Morna asked.

"I told ya how I worked fer the mayor, right?" Tabetha said.

That's when I remembered that Tabetha had mentioned the mayor before. She'd worked for him as a maid or servant or something.

"Noah Sinclair," I said, remembering the name from the book.

Tabetha nodded and described another memory. Working for Mayor Sinclair was never an amusement park ride for Tabetha. She had fourteen rooms, each of which Sinclair liked to see completely spotless. (And given how I imagined the nineteenth century, there were way more spots back then.) Additionally, the mayor was always hosting guests at his home, and Tabetha was on call to serve food and beverages — to basically be at the beck and call of the esteemed guests, whatever a beck was. But one unfortunate night,

Tabetha wasn't informed there was a guest in the Sinclair House, so she was surprised when she walked right into the master of the house's office to find him counting money at his desk, with Virgil Cooper, the not-so-pleasant descendant of Cyril, seated across from him.

"Oh, sir —" Tabetha blurted. She dropped her cleaning rag but managed to hold on to the bucket of hot water.

The mayor turned to the girl servant and his face lit from within as if his skull contained a tiny star gone supernova. "What are you doing in here?"

"I thought you were out. I — I came to clean the parlour . . ."

"Get out!" he shouted, throwing open a drawer and sweeping the paper money inside. "What are you, stupid? I said leave!"

Virgil Cooper's face see-sawed between emotions. He laughed, but without any mirth. "Should I be worried, Mayor?"

"Worried? No . . . what are you still doing here?" Noah Sinclair shrieked once again.

Tabetha bent over to retrieve the rag and quietly left the room.

"That one is as dense as a nickel," the mayor informed the shipmaker, not as quietly as he thought. "I'm surprised she's figured out how to use that bucket. You don't have to worry."

"I wish I could trust you, Noah," Virgil Cooper whistled and, like a rebellious cowboy — the kind that didn't even exist at that time — placed his feet on the desktop. "I wish there were a way to be sure. We can't let anyone know about this little exchange. Even the help."

"I hear you,"

the mayor said, re-opening the drawer. "Sometimes those folks down south have the right idea."

"That sounds like it could be a motive," I said, back in the here and now. "The town's shipbuilder passing the mayor wads of money. It sounds like a bribe of some kind, though I have no idea why." If the mayor ever found out Tabetha wasn't nearly as slow as he assumed she was, that would be good reason to silence her. Beryl was right. This town really did want to kill Tabetha.

Tabetha turned to me. "You say this woman Beryl is related to me somehow? How is that possible?"

"Apparently, after you died, your dad went to Owen Sound and married a woman named Pearl," I said.

Tabetha blinked a couple times, as if temporarily stunned. "Yeah, that's . . ."

"It's okay to be disappointed," Derek said.

"I'm not disappointed," Tabetha said, looking a little disappointed. "What did I expect? Why would I — October, can we go to her home right now?"

"It's really far," I said.

"We got time. What else are we doin'?" she asked, gesturing at the cemetery around her. I know she was talking about her and the other dead kids, but I was planning to sleep at some point. "I want to see this relative of mine. Maybe she can answer more questions."

"We're not waking her up," I warned.

"Maybe she has some old photos of Tabetha or her dad. That's the kind of thing that can jog a memory," Derek encouraged.

"Beryl said she might have some photos, but —"

"Let's go now," Derek said.

"Lead the way, Lady Dracula," Tabetha said.

"Tabetha, I don't know . . . I don't think it's a good idea for you to meet her. I mean, you're a ghost," I said, pointing out the obvious. "She's super old. If she can even *see* ghosts, you'll probably give her a heart attack."

"I promise I won't wake her," Tabetha explained. "You say we're related n' that's great, but mostly I just wanna see her. See if her home, her pictures, even her old Scott face reminds me a' anything. Don't you think we need to search her house sooner rather than later?"

Tabetha presented a decent argument.

☠   ☠   ☠

Though it wasn't clear if it was the mention of Beryl Gibson or my stunning *Cole's Notes* summary of *Sticksvillainy* or our physical proximity to the Sticksville Fairgrounds (and thus, the former site of and endpoint of the Underground Railroad and Tabetha Scott's home), but slowly — nearly as slowly as it was taking us to get to Beryl Gibson's house — Tabetha began to remember more about her last days. Or last *day*, singular.

We were still about a half-hour walk from Beryl Gibson's home when Tabetha started to recall that final twenty-four hours when air still filled her lungs. I was just thankful to have something else to think about, as I was worried that I'd somehow got us all lost by trying a more direct route on foot instead of the maze-like series of switchbacks the bus usually used.

"I think I remember somethin'!" Tabetha shouted just after we'd all scurried across a major intersection. The key was to avoid cars' headlights so drivers couldn't see us pedestrians — living or dead — at all. Not that there were many cars on the roads that evening.

"Do you remember how my family members definitely did *not* kill you?" asked Cyril.

"Don't push me, pirate-boy," she replied. "You are skatin' on the thinnest of ice."

"Don't be ridiculous — it's too warm for . . . oh."

Trying to ignore the ongoing conflict, I asked, "What do you remember, Tabetha?"

"That mornin' wasn't a good memory. First thing I remember 'bout that day was the town pharmacist, Mr. Burnhamthorpe. My dad n' me woke up when we heard him dumpin' a bag of ol' food stuffs n' a couple broken wagon wheels right on our front lawn. We lived near the dump n' all, but this was no mistake.

He basically told us we trash. My dad n' me watched him leave his garbage right there in front of the door. And a couple other Black families came out to watch him, too, but none of us said a thing, 'cuz what could we say? N' this is the man that yer supposed to go to if ya need medicine."

"And then what happened?" Morna asked.

"Then he left. We thought of telling the Quakers on the committee 'bout what happened, but Dad figured we should jus' deal with it. I told him I could take the trash over to the real dumpin' site. He gave me the donkey cart, and I dragged the stuff over there. Passed a couple people on the way, and luckily they were people who were good to us. Ms. Yvonne, out fer her regular hike. The Fergusons, gathering firewood. But because of the firewood, the Fergusons had felled a couple trees in my path. I had to go around a long way to get to the dump. That took me past the old storehouse that my dad n' me first arrived at in town."

Tabetha then outlined a series of strange occurrences that followed her stroll past to the storehouse that served as the terminus of the Underground Railroad. For one, there was no one around, which was not really unusual. With the war in the States, there wasn't as much traffic on the Railroad as there used to be. And while the local Quakers would often be on hand when a new arrival was expected, it wasn't as if the Underground Railroad was a Walmart with an official greeter. The unusual part, according to Tabetha, was the series of lit candles in each of the storehouse's open windows. Daylight had broken hours ago. But the candles remained lit, wax pooling on the windowsills beneath. Tabetha abandoned the donkey cart to get a closer look.

"Did you go inside?" Kirby asked.

"Have you met me?" Tabetha replied. "Of *course* I went inside."

"And what did you find?" I asked. Now we were getting somewhere. Was it possible I wouldn't even have to find any more clues? Would Tabetha solve the mystery herself just by being close to her death spot?

Tabetha looked up to the night sky, struggling to remember. The stars looked like a sugar bowl had been tipped over onto a black placemat. "I don't . . . I don't remember."

"Was somebody there?" I asked.

"I dunno. I said, I can't remember."

Rather than force the issue, it seemed best to leave Tabetha's memory time to recuperate. Besides, when Tabetha's mysterious story time ended, we'd already reached Beryl's street. I told the dead kids to be quiet, as we didn't want to wake her up while we broke into her house. That would prove counterproductive. I pointed out the yellow bungalow, and we crouched behind the hedges while we tried to determine the best way to sneak in. For the dead kids, turning intangible and walking through a wall was nothing, but I was very tangible — some might say *too* tangible — so doors or windows would have to be opened.

"We can just go inside and unlock the front door," Kirby said. "Seems the easiest solution is also the best one."

"But what if she has a burglar alarm?" I said.

"She's *not* going to have a burglar alarm," Kirby insisted.

"She should," I said. "There are no houses on the far side of the street, which makes her a perfect target for burglary."

I know a few things about criminal activity, okay?

Despite my very real, statistically founded worries, when the dead kids opened the front doors to Beryl's yellow house, which basically shone in the dark like a homing beacon for thieves, no alarms or bells sounded. The darkened house interior was quieter than a non-Sticksville cemetery on a Saturday night. Her black cat, who I'd spied dozing before, treated our appearance in the front hallway as if it were a mildly annoying interruption of its sleep. We couldn't even hear old Beryl snoring, but she may be one of the many individuals — unlike my dad — who are blessed with no nighttime respiratory concerns. I slid through the front door and gingerly untied my Chuck Taylors because, as quiet as Chucks are, nothing beats stocking feet for creeping. And who knew how heavy or light a sleeper Beryl Gibson was. Sometimes old people wake up every hour to go to the washroom or take out their teeth or whatever.

"Okay," I whispered. "Let's split up. Cyril and Tabetha, you come with me. We'll head to the bedroom. The rest of you head down the hallway to the living room."

The search presented me with a dilemma. The farther away I could stay from Beryl's bedroom, the better. But Tabetha needed to get a look at Beryl if we thought it might jog her memory, and I wanted to be there to hear what she said. That said, we'd have to be extremely quiet not to wake her, and with the two dead kids who were currently most active in the bickering field, staying quiet was probably going to be a challenge.

"Wait, what are we looking for?" Derek whispered.

"I don't know — anything family related?" I said. "Old photo albums? Didn't Beryl say she thought she might have some photos of Lunsford?"

Everything I said had suddenly become a question. And one the dead kids couldn't answer, having never met Beryl before.

"Do you know what a crawlspace is?" I asked. "If so, see if you can find that."

Tabetha, Cyril, and I crept along the carpeted hall to Beryl's bedroom. We turned the corner and found the room in which she slept was somehow more jam-packed with stuff than the room in which I'd interviewed her just hours ago. (Maybe she'd cleaned up knowing she had a guest. Henry had indicated she didn't get many visitors. As the owner of a less-than-Spartan bedroom, I could relate.) Sinking into the shag carpet felt like we had entered a lost episode of *Hoarders: Southern Ontario*

Edition. Very quietly, we began to inch toward the mass under several layers of blankets. On the nightstand were stacks and stacks of *Hello! Canada* and *Entertainment Weekly* back issues, and tossed in a corner, an endless supply of throw pillows featuring cats and other small mammals. Tabetha sighed heavily.

"What is it?" I whispered as quietly as I could.

"I can't see her face," Tabetha whispered back. "How'm I supposed to remember anythin' if I can't see her face. Wasn't that the idea of bringin' me here?"

"I don't want to wake her up," I said. "Can't you jog your memory by looking at her under all those blankets? What about those photos?"

Tabetha scanned the photos that dotted the wall. "I don't know who those people are! One of you tap her on the shoulder or somethin'. Let me blow in her face."

"No. Cyril, don't do that," I insisted. I didn't want to give Beryl Gibson the shock of her life. "She'll turn or shift eventually. Just be patient."

If I should have learned one thing from working with the dead kids, it's that none of them are overly patient. Maybe it has something to do with only having a lunar cycle to get things done each time I raise them.

"Plus, ya team me up with the guy who probably killed me," Tabetha grumbled, thumbing toward Cyril, who was standing on his tiptoes to angle for a look at the sleeping woman. Hindsight is 20/20 and all that, but I really should have brought Derek or Morna with us instead of Cyril.

"I didn't kill anyone," he said, no longer maintaining our whole whisper rule. "Do I have to remind you that I was *also* killed?"

"Yeah, but by some wizard or something," Tabetha responded, also not whispering. "Not by a town full of hate-mongers. It's not the same."

"My family were not *hate-mongers*, whatever those are," Cyril responded forcefully.

"Shhhh," I interrupted. I didn't want Beryl to wake up to

the quarrelling of two kid ghosts. Hoping to make peace, I said, "Maybe we can discuss this later. Search now?"

Despite all my efforts at maintaining tranquility in Beryl Gibson's bedroom, I failed to prevent the incredible racket that came from down the hall. Something banged. Banged again. And that was followed by a sickly crunch and the sound of glass shattering.

Rather than wait to see how atrophied Beryl's hearing was, I scurried out of the room and clambered down the carpeted hall. (At least Beryl's house didn't have creaky wooden floors!) Cyril followed and we raced to the living room where we found Derek, Morna, and Kirby standing around a massive television set that had met its demise. Though it seemed like nothing short of a wrecking ball or stick of dynamite could have moved a television so large, somehow the three dead kids I foolishly had *not* worried about had caused it to topple from its perch and smash.

"What are you doing? Keep it down," I said. "We can't wake Beryl up."

"Kirby tried to lift it to show how strong he was," Morna said. "But he forgot about his missing arm."

"You rat! I did not," Kirby shouted.

"Shhh!" I warned. "I don't care."

There was no real time to care about who did what exactly. With the dead kids making more racket in Beryl Gibson's living room than a broken cappuccino maker, we didn't have long before Beryl rushed out of her bedroom to investigate. If she thought I was robbing her, she'd probably call the police.

"Now we have to get out of here," I whispered. "And fast! Before Beryl wakes up and finds out what's going on. Somebody tell Tabetha we're going."

Derek helped himself to his feet and said, "I'm not sure we have to worry about that."

"Why not?" I said.

He pointed to Tabetha, solemnly shuffling down the hall in her tattered gingham dress.

"Tabetha," I whispered. "We should go before we wake —"

"That's not gonna happen," Tabetha said.

"What do you mean?" Derek said, dusting off his black T-shirt.

"I got impatient and tapped her on the shoulder," Tabetha croaked. As she got closer, I could see the dark circles around her eyes were wet from tears. (I had never figured out if the dead kids still had bodily fluids.)

"You woke her up?" I asked, already dreading the answer.

"I couldn't," Tabetha said. "I even tried shakin' her awake. She's dead."

☠   ☠   ☠

Girl, You Know It's True (Crime)

Though Tabetha Scott had no training in emergency medical services nor any formal education to speak of, she was correct. Ms. Beryl Gibson had stopped breathing. Her life had come to an unceremonious — although not unexpected, given her advanced age — finale. And unlike the dead kids who feature largely in this book series, the dead Ms. Gibson did not return as a ghost. So if you'd worried this book would rapidly turn into The Dead Seniors' Retirement Community or Canasta Club, your fears are entirely unfounded.

Beryl's death cut their snoopage short, as October (wisely) was none too keen to spend more time around a potential crime scene, having been arrested more times already than most teenage arsonists — especially as her group was not entirely innocent of a crime. While it was entirely likely that Beryl died of old age — or the combination of vague maladies and organ failures that typically get grouped together as "old age" — it was impossible to rule out foul play. After all, who knew how dangerous Asphodel Meadows was, and what lengths they would go to? And who knew if they'd be back or — indeed — weren't still lurking around? So, the dead kids helped October right the broken television set and sweep the glass into the kitchen's dustbin, then left without an entirely proper rummage through the Gibson household. The last thing October did was put on her gloves and dial the police on Beryl's landline. (Unlike most thirteen-year-olds, she knew the number by heart.) She left the telephone off the hook, hoping the police would investigate and poor Beryl wouldn't be left alone too long.

Besides, Tabetha was too sad to rummage. Tabetha, despite never meeting Beryl Gibson in the living flesh, had begun to sob like an Academy Award winner speaking about their estranged parents. (People with actual emotions have told me this isn't odd, given Beryl was Tabetha's only surviving relative.) Though the other kids tried to console her, it wasn't much use. She continued to weep most of the walk home.

☠   ☠   ☠

Given the Gibson house's ridiculous distance from her own, October was considerably less than sharp of mind when she arrived at Sticksville Central the following morning. Her hazy state was only partially due to exhaustion. Another key component was that a secret society was possibly attempting to kill all of October's friends — dead or alive — and one of those dead friends was emotionally devastated from finding her own great-great-aunt (or something) dead. October's mood was not the best state in which to start a Friday, and the synth-pop version of "O Canada" that blared over the P.A. as she stood at attention outside the school library wasn't helping any.

While the Casio key tones hit the "glowing hearts" portion of Canada's national anthem, October spotted her former history teacher checking a few books out of the library.

Readers of the Dead Kid Detective Agency (or "Schwartz-enablers," as I like to call them) should remember that though October was reluctant to befriend Ms. Fenstermacher after what happened to her previous teacher-friend, Mr. O'Shea, Ms. Fenstermacher's unusual amount of knowledge about supernatural things like the occult, ghosts, witches, and (we can assume) tarot cards and healing crystals had come in handy in the past. And while she seemed to regard October with some suspicion — like she was an adult Velma from Scooby-Doo and October was literally the only new character introduced in the episode

— she also had provided October with a lot of background that had helped her solve two previous mysteries and established the legend of historic witch bro Fairfax Crisparkle.

The moment the anthem ended, October ran into the library and confronted the teacher.

"Ms. Fenstermacher, can I ask you a few questions?" she shouted, physically barring the way to the library exit.

"October, we don't have class together anymore," she sighed, blowing her brown bangs from her chunky eyeglasses. "And you'll be late for class."

"It's okay. Mr. Copeland is cool," October said.

Mr. Copeland, October's English teacher, was about as cool as white gym socks with flip-flops.

"Be that as it may," Ms. Fenstermacher responded, trying to edge her way around the student, "I'll also be late for class."

"It won't take long," October pleaded.

Ms. Fenstermacher sighed heavily once again and set her pile of books upon the library counter. She studied her watch. "I can give you five minutes. What is it?"

With that invitation (of sorts), October presented the copy of *Sticksvillainy* she'd borrowed — though it was highly unlikely that Beryl Gibson would ask for it back at this juncture.

"How much do you know about the disappearance of Tabetha Scott?" October asked.

Ms. Fenstermacher inspected the book from every angle — almost as if she had never seen the format before (which was probably not the case, considering she'd just checked out a stack of books from the library).

"She was the daughter of one of the first Black families to settle in Sticksville," Ms. Fenstermacher said hesitantly, "and she went missing around the age of twelve or thirteen . . . but I don't know if this book is the most accurate account . . ."

"Why not?" October asked.

"It comes from the Scott family. I'm not sure how closely they researched this," she said. "Grief-stricken family members aren't always the most objective researchers. The author, Wilford, wasn't a journalist or historian," she continued, skimming over the author bio. "He was a naval engineer."

"Can you suggest another book where I can find more?"

"I can certainly look into it when I have a moment, October. But didn't you have history last semester?" Ms. Fenstermacher didn't answer the question.

"Oh, it's an English class assignment," October expertly lied. "We have to compare two nonfiction books on the same subject or event."

Did Ms. Fenstermacher fall for this ruse? At the very least, she did not shoo October Schwartz away like an overly friendly puppy.

"Could you pick a subject with more written on it?" Ms. Fenstermacher said, returning the book to October's possession and pushing the glasses up the bridge of her nose. "Historical records — no less books — are pretty thin on the Scott family at that time."

"Why?" October asked, pretty keen to find out why her work was going to be doubly difficult.

"As sad as it is to admit, until relatively recently, historians haven't been all that interested in chronicling the lives and times of Black families — or any families of colour — in Canadian history."

October's mood took a cannonball dive. Not only did it appear that racism could be blamed for Tabetha's death, it was also conspiring to keep her from solving the mystery. (Not that these were anywhere near the worst things that could be attributed to racism.)

"Okay," October continued, mostly undeterred, "but what

have *you* heard, as town historian or whatever, happened to Tabetha."

"Tabetha Scott always seemed like one of those urban legends," Ms. Fenstermacher said, lifting the stack of books from the counter. "For a long time, I wasn't sure she was even real. I thought she was a cautionary tale to show how Canada had a history of racism to rival America's, even though we didn't have a widespread system of slavery. The story I'd always heard was that the town tried to drive the Scotts out and someone probably kidnapped or killed the daughter, Tabetha."

October was very aware that Tabetha Scott was no urban legend — she was arguing with Loyalists in bungalows as of last night. But if Tabetha was something like the Sticksville sasquatch to most historians, that wasn't going to make October's work very easy.

"The book suggests there are three main suspects — Virgil Cooper, the town shipbuilder; Noah Sinclair, the mayor; and Yancey Burnhamthorpe, the town pharmacist. Do you think one of them is to blame?"

"I don't know, October," Ms. Fenstermacher said. "Those occupations were essentially held by pillars of the community back in the mid-1800s. Never say never, but I'm not sure if we can pin a murder on any of those men."

"But you just said the whole town was trying to get the Scotts to leave. Wouldn't the pillars be just as rotten as the rest of the town?"

"I suppose so," Ms. Fenstermacher admitted, exhausted by the conversation. "I can imagine them being terrible people, but I have a hard time believing one of them would kill a child with their own hands. Now, class —"

"Wait, just one more question," October insisted.

Ms. Fenstermacher begrudgingly returned her stack of books to the counter. "Okay, let's have it."

"You know a lot about Ouija boards and that kind of thing," October said. "What do you think of Nicodemus Burke?"

The look on Ms. Fenstermacher's face was total confusion, like she was studying one of those optical illusion illustrations and was trying to determine if she was looking at a duck or a rabbit. "Nicodemus Burke?" she asked. "You mean the psychic guy from the bus shelter ads?"

October nodded in enthusiastic agreement. The bus shelter ads *and* the audience at Bandwarz, of course. Not to mention the Sticksville Cemetery and Number 4 bus.

"I mean . . . I don't think I've ever really thought of him," she said, her eyes rising to the ceiling as if there were a Wikipedia entry on Nicodemus Burke printed there. "October, I know a little about witchcraft and that kind of thing," Ms. Fenstermacher said, a bit afraid to use the word "occult" out loud. Sticksville was still a fairly conservative little town. "Particularly when it relates to something historical. The Salem witch trials, for instance. But that Burke guy just seems like a total cheeseball, like Miss Cleo or something."

"I don't know who that is," October said.

"It doesn't matter," Ms. Fenstermacher quickly answered, picking up her books from the counter again. "But if you are looking for spiritual guidance, I genuinely think you're much better off speaking to our school counsellor. Now I really have to head to class."

Before October could say anything further, her former history teacher had been replaced by a swinging glass door. There might as well have been a cartoon dust outline of Ms. Fenstermacher hovering before it. October held the distinct impression that Ms. Fenstermacher didn't have much faith in Nicodemus Burke's magical powers — so, even if she hadn't learned all that much from accosting her before English, she was relieved that there wasn't an actual witch roaming the streets of Sticksville. Just an elaborately dressed hoax.

October picked up *Sticksvillainy* and returned it to her book bag. She then headed off to English, where Mr. Copeland was certainly not having them compare nonfiction titles, but, in fact, diving deep into the most famous young adult novel to focus on racial injustice: *To Kill a Mockingbird*. The synchronicity was not lost on October.

☠   ☠   ☠

At lunchtime, Levi Marylebone was — for the third day running — the victim of high school harassment. By this point, word had spread to the far recesses of the school — from the yearbook staff to the robot engineering team, from the Academic Olympiad hopefuls to the show choir nerds — that there had been a serious theft at Bandwarz, potentially depriving the school of a celebration, and that Levi — and, to a lesser extent, his bandmates Henry and Matilda — was most likely to blame. Suddenly, every inveterate shoplifter, teen bully, and rugby player had no greater loyalty than to their school. Any theft against it inspired them to tape threatening messages to Levi's locker door, shove him between the shoulders, or fake-sneeze "thief" or "thug" whenever he passed in the hall. Nevertheless, Levi persisted in attending school.

October, as she exited the cafeteria line with a tray piled high with Tater Tots, became witness to the most recent and most public of those acts of intimidation:

Boston Davis had made fast friends with some of the popular kids outside the circle of his own band — not defined by a sport or hobby, they were simply *popular*. That lunch hour, this gathering of kids formed, Red-Rover-style (though stopping short of actually holding hands), a wall across the centre aisle of the cafeteria. Levi, who was several paces in front of October, shrouded in a hoodie and air traffic control headphones, looked up at the human fence and made to turn down a row of cafeteria benches.

"Where ya going, Kanye?" shouted Mitchell Webb, an eleventh grader with a face like a ham-coloured cinder block. "Gonna spit some rhymes with your crew?"

Levi extracted his head from the headphones that dwarfed it. "We're not a hip-hop crew. We're a rock band," he said defiantly.

October stopped where she was standing with her precariously balanced Mount McKinley of Tots. With the wall of doofuses (doofi?) also in her path, she couldn't get to the table where she usually sat with Yumi and Stacey, but she was also curious to see how this stand-off would resolve.

"You're a band of *thieves*," yelled Boston Davis, jabbing his index finger toward Levi as if he half-expected a lightning bolt to shoot from the tip.

"The only thieves at Bandwarz are you guys in Phantom Moustache," he said, calmly placing his headphones back on. "You stole the money, then you stole first place by framing us."

"You listen to me!" Boston shouted, yanking the headphones off Levi's head and throwing them to the floor. Now everyone's attention was focused. Henry Khan and Matilda Coffin had assembled behind Levi like some pathetic iteration of the Avengers. In some alternate reality, they must have believed they were somehow intimidating against the figurative rampart of chowderheads Boston Davis and the other members of Phantom Moustache had built. October looked around for a lunch supervisor and only spotted Mrs. Tischmann retreating out the side doors. It was like a Western and all the teachers were closing up their general stores.

"Return the money you stole from Bandwarz to the school by the end of the week, or we'll make sure the next time there's a charity concert, it's to raise funds for your wheelchair or new arms or something . . . because we're going to tear you apart," Boston warned. Why he was suddenly so committed to fundraising was a mystery October might have to investigate.

"We can't return something we don't *have*, Boston," Matilda yelped.

"Shut up, skank," Boston's squeeze and everyone's favourite heel, Ashlie Salmons, shouted from behind the boy wall. "No one cares what you think."

"You can't return something you don't have," Levi repeated slowly, turning each word over in his mouth like a peppermint swirl. "That's good. Listen, Boston — you guys can have that lyric for free. I know you find songwriting *real* hard."

"Shut your mouth," Boston growled. October, who was mesmerized by the prelude of what promised to be a full *West Side Story* rumble — replete with modern dance and finger-snapping — didn't realize until it was too late that the lead singer of Phantom Moustache had broken from the line and made a beeline for her. Without warning, he'd ripped the cafeteria tray from her weak grasp and mashed it into Levi's chest. A paste of Tater Tots and gravy covered his black Megadeth T-shirt.

Surprisingly, Levi did not respond by sending his knuckles

deep into Boston's jaw. Instead, he calmly wiped down his front and retrieved his head-phones from the floor.

"Whatever, Boston," he said. "Like you even care about the stolen money. You just love this because it gives you ample opportunity to torment the Black kid."

"That's not —"

"Or the brown kid," he continued, gesturing to Henry.

"I'm not —" Boston tried to get a word in.

"Or the other brown kid," Levi said.

"You could just say Sri Lankan," Matilda said.

"I'm not a *racist*," Boston shouted, violently grabbing Levi Marylebone by his hood-strings. "So shut your stupid mouth!"

"And the only reason you pinned the theft on us was because it'd be easy," Levi continued. "Who's the school gonna blame for the robbery but the bunch of brown kids."

"Get off of him!" Henry and Matilda yelled in unison, having months of training from doing backup vocals. They grabbed Boston's shoulders, and soon the situation became a veritable collar-grabbing deadlock.

Yumi and Stacey, having realized that October was now embroiled in the cafeteria fracas, rushed to their friend's side moments after she'd lost her Tater Tots to a vicious act of cafeteria bullying. Yumi tapped October on the shoulder to let her know she was there, which helped to break her from her trance.

"Is someone going to get choked to death?" Stacey asked. The potential for strangulation had not managed to keep him from scarfing down two whole Coffee Crisp chocolate bars.

"*Though he's being dramatic, Stacey does have a point," Yumi said. "This can't end well. Should we get someone?*"

"Probably?" October said.

Though it was hard to make out distinct sentences or phrases from the shouting and mouths partially muffled by shirts, Levi shouted: "In fall, an Asian girl was being harassed at this school. Wasn't your bandmate the one responsible?"

The Asian girl in question, Yumi Takeshi, shouted "break it up!" but the mass of dudes and three band members of Crenshaw House were too entangled to be split, like some sort of teenager rat king or one of those zombie stampedes in *World War Z*. The shouting and shoving continued and spiralled until it seemed certain that Crenshaw House would be the first band to be destroyed by a high school mosh pit (*citation needed*).

Into the morass strode Mr. Santuzzi, wearing an olive-green polyester suit two sizes too small and a look of disbelief. Mrs. Tischmann, who had summoned him from his math class, followed behind. In all likelihood, Mr. Santuzzi had seen a lot of nonsense in his days, but nothing quite like this. He cupped his hands around his mouth and began to bellow. "Break it up! Break it up!"

But not even the James-Earl-Jones-esque baritone of Mr. Santuzzi could dissipate the dust-up. The kids all jostled back and forth until, one by one, they stopped shoving and yelling as their attention was slowly drawn to the east side of the cafeteria. There stood Mr. Santuzzi, who had somehow heaved over his head an entire cafeteria table, its awkward length teetering back and forth.

"Since I'm no longer allowed to physically restrain you," Mr. Santuzzi grunted, almost wistfully, "I have to resort to carnival tricks to get your attention."

The He-Teacher pumped the massive cafeteria table in the air once, then slammed it down to the ground with a shuddering bang. Stunned, or maybe confused, by this show of brawn and recklessness from a math teacher, the cafeteria brawlers divided. The panting Mr. Santuzzi walked into the middle of the cafeteria.

"What did we just watch?" Yumi whispered to October.

"I have never been more afraid of Mr. Santuzzi than I am right now," she answered.

"*You're* afraid?" Stacey said. "*We* have class with him."

"All right," Mr. Santuzzi shouted. "All you gawkers, back to your feeding troughs. Levi, Henry, Boston, Taylor, Matilda — all you band people: you're coming with me to the principal's office. You, too, Mitchell. This has gone on long enough."

As Mr. Santuzzi accompanied the main instigators of the Battle of the Cafeteria to visit Principal Hamilton, normalcy returned. Students even sat back down at the very table that Santuzzi had so recently used as a barbell. Yumi and Stacey took aside October, who was still too stunned to move, and sat her down at their usual table.

"October? Hello?" Yumi said, waving her hand before her friend's face. "You okay? Stacey and I want to ask you something."

"Ask me something?" October said, returning to attention. "Sure. What?"

"Stacey and I have been thinking about Bandwarz and . . . we want to form a band."

"A band?"

"Yeah, and we want you to be in it," Yumi continued.

"So, your takeaway from the concert that resulted in grand theft, racial harassment, threats, and a cafeteria brawl just seconds ago . . . is we should start a band?"

"Listen," Yumi said. "Don't get mad at me for trying to turn this into something positive."

"Making lemonade," Stacey added, mouth full of Kit Kat, as if that meant something profound.

"But I don't play any instruments," October said, her eyebrows turning slowly into sine waves. "Just trombone. And badly. And I'm not going to *sing* in front of people."

"*I'll* be singer," Yumi explained. "I can't sing, but I can yell. That'll work better for the band we have in mind. Stacey will be drummer, obviously."

"So what will *I* be doing?" October asked.

"I borrowed my cousin's bass. You can play that."

"I don't know how to play bass, Yumi."

"How hard can it be to learn?" Yumi asked, flattening her hands on the table. "Have you seen a bassist before?"

"So, wait," October added. "We're just drums and a bass? We can't just be drums and a bass."

"October," Yumi explained, as if speaking to a toddler, "there's *literally* a musical genre called 'drum and bass.'"

"That's not —"

"Ever heard of The White Stripes?" she added, throwing her hands up.

"That's a guitar," Stacey said.

"So I have to learn bass?" October said, summarizing the conversation.

"Curling is over. You have time," Yumi said, the portrait of understanding. "We already have a list of band names — Brimstones for Breakfast, Cheesecake Fear Factory, Chill Satanist — though I think we'll probably go with Astaroth Night Bus."

October sat there, her stomach growling. She wished her Tater Tots had not been smashed all over Levi's shirt and the filthy cafeteria floor.

"Okay, I'll join the band," October said. "I'll be bassist for Astaroth Night Bus. It'll give me a chance to hang out with you more."

"Yessssss!" Yumi shouted, slamming her palm repeatedly on the table in victory.

"But I can't start right away," October said. "Remember how you conscripted me into solving the whole Bandwarz mystery?"

"Oh, yeah," Yumi said, her eyes widening with her realization.

"For your boyfriend," Stacey said through chocolate and wafers. He must have just discovered a hidden bag of Halloween candy.

"How's that mystery going?" Yumi said, elbowing Stacey in the arm.

"Not well," October grumbled. "And it looks like my timeline has shortened given today's lunchtime antics. It would be ideal to solve things *before* somebody gets injured."

"We can help," Yumi said. "We can be your detective assistants or deputies or whatever."

"No, thanks," October lied straight into her friends' faces (which she does alarmingly often and well). "I work alone."

☠   ☠   ☠

Behind the Moustache

Of course, I *don't* work alone, and it's really only due to the abilities of the dead kids that I'm able to solve the mysteries I manage to solve, but I wasn't about to tell Yumi and Stacey that. Yumi had already demonstrated that she got a severe case of the creeps around ghosts, and it would just be too weird to introduce Stacey to his long-distant cousin or aunt or whatever relation Morna was. To solve the case of the missing Bandwarz money and exonerate the members of Crenshaw House and (I imagine) reinstate a period of peace and harmony at my high school, I turned again to the corpses just beyond my backyard.

I avoided the cemetery that night because of how heartbroken I knew Tabetha would be. After the events at Beryl's house, I wasn't exactly sure how to face her. But by Saturday, I knew I couldn't keep dawdling. Following another successful late-night escape from my house, I paid a visit to my dead friends. Cyril, Morna, Kirby, and Derek were excitedly discussing some theories regarding Asphodel Meadows, while Tabetha stood on her own under a massive gnarled willow tree, staring into the darkness with a look of resigned sorrow. Like you'd see on a post-op dog with one of those plastic lampshades on its head.

I visited the larger clump of my dead friends first, just as they were discussing what last name among the secret society was most closely connected to "Diamandas." Given he'd been spending evenings hiring cable-access psychics to work faux black magic in cemeteries, it seemed almost impossible that he wasn't involved in a town-wide conspiracy.

"Hey, October," Derek said, looking up from the notepad that acted as their Asphodel Meadows compendium. "Where were you last night?"

"Dad was on guard," I lied, taking the coward's way out. "I couldn't escape."

"But tonight was okay?" Cyril asked.

"Yeah," I said, nodding my head over at the dead girl moping underneath one of nature's saddest trees. "How is she?"

"I'm right *here*," said Tabetha before any of the other dead kids could answer. "It's not like we're in a crowded market-place. This is an empty cemetery. Sound tends to carry."

"Sorry," I said, walking over to her. "How are *you?*"

"How d'ya think?" Tabetha answered gloomily. "When I'm not feelin' sad because my relative died last night – a relative I never even got to see *alive* – I'm worried that yer never gonna figure out how I died. 'Specially not when Beryl's dead."

"Why are you so upset she's dead?" I asked, which is prob-ably the dumbest question I've ever asked someone – and I asked it of a girl who does not suffer fools lightly. Tabetha just glared. The hate waves radiated off her like sonar. "Okay, I deserve that. But Beryl lived a long life. Plus, you're all dead. Is it really all that bad?"

"We're *un*dead, October," Morna said. "It's not the same."

"Maybe she'll become a ghost, too," I said, again unhelp-fully. "She can hang out with the five of you."

"Perfect," Kirby said, eyes rolling so hard they threatened to pop out of his eye sockets. "We can trade recipes for soup and complain about the cost of postage."

"Like you're so cool," Derek said.

"Do you think she'll be buried here?" Kirby added, looking around.

"Shut up! Shut up! Shut up!" Tabetha yelled with her hands cupped over her ears. I worried she was going to wake the neighbourhood until I realized few people other than me could hear her. "I don't wanna talk about Beryl Gibson and if she'll be a ghost or where she'll be buried. I just wanna find out what happened to me!"

Tabetha was on the verge of tears. Her lip even started to do that spasming that happens before people cry. "Can we please go back to Beryl's house to see if we can find somethin'?" she asked. Given she looked like the slightest word could break her, I wasn't very happy to tell her we *couldn't*.

"I'm sorry, but it's way too soon, Tabetha."

Tabetha drove her fists downward, as if she were dangling on some invisible gymnastic rings, and turned to face the tree. "She just died two nights ago. If she didn't die of natural causes, there could be police crawling all over her home. What if someone from Asphodel Meadows did it? They always seem to know what we're doing. We should steer clear at least for a few days."

After making that anonymous call, I had no idea what happened. I just trusted the police to investigate, but it was entirely possible that Beryl Gibson's body hadn't even been found. Maybe I should have actually spoken to the police, but what would I have said? I made a mental note to check with Henry Khan to see if he'd heard any news about Beryl lately.

"Tabetha, I'm really sorry, but I think that tonight we have to focus on the other mystery — the theft at the school," I called to her slowly receding form. "We can get back to your mystery soon."

"We still have Beryl Gibson's book, right?" asked Derek. "What about the three suspects in the book? Maybe we can dig up some information on them?"

"Well, you won't find any scandals in the Coopers' past," Cyril insisted, standing up straighter.

Kirby very weakly attempted to stifle a laugh. "For all we know, the information in that book could be complete fiction."

"What do you mean?" Derek asked defensively.

"It's written and researched by some family relative. Not exactly unbiased."

"It's a starting point," Derek said.

"An' it corresponds t'what Tabetha remembers," Morna backed him up. "We should start with those three suspects. See who we can eliminate."

"Sure, sure," I said, waving my hands around like a majorette with heatstroke. Somehow I had lost control of the conversation. "But tonight, we really have to get started on this Bandwarz mystery."

Tabetha, who had returned to the group, wiped her nose with the back of her hand. "Of course. That's the way it always is. October's problems come first."

"It's not *like* that," I insisted.

"Sure thing, Living Girl," she replied. "How much longer until the full moon? A little over a week? Let's just get this over with. I'm sure the fifty dollars or whatever was taken is worth way more than my life."

"More like five *thousand*," I said, opening my stupid mouth too fast. The actual amount, I realized, wasn't really the point.

Tabetha bristled.

"I'm so sorry, Tabetha," I said. "I didn't mean it like that."

"It's fine," she said."

"Nothing is worth more —"

"I know you didn't mean it like that," she said. "N' if you think it'll be hard to get inta' Beryl's place tonight, I believe you. As long as we go back *soon*."

"We'll make sure we do," Derek insisted.

"Then let's figure out who took this stupid money," Tabetha sighed.

The dead kids began with a series of questions: Did the police check the bags of all the audience and band members? Who left before the police arrived? Was there anyone there who was known to have money troubles? So I told them everything I knew, which — I admit — wasn't all that much. Maybe another secret break-in to the Sticksville Police Station was warranted to see what information *they* had on the theft, even if our first visit to the police station after-hours had been nothing short of disastrous.

Of course, the police had insisted on searching the

belongings of everyone present, which meant, as Cyril astutely noted, the cash box must have been taken by one of the people who left before the theft was discovered. Either that, or it was still hidden in the school, which seemed almost too clever for our Bandwarz thief.

"Let's figure out who our suspects are if the cash box was taken off-site," Derek said. "There's that band you say is being framed . . ."

"Crenshaw House," I added.

"Crenshaw House, your dad, and a third mystery person (or people) in a car with fins."

"If a car has fins," Cyril Cooper, avid if clueless automobile enthusiast, asked, "does that mean it can travel in the water?"

"No," Kirby clarified. "They're just for decoration."

"Do we know yer dad didn't take the money?" Tabetha asked. Part of me realized it was a valid question, but another part of me worried she was trying to irritate me because I'd refused to work on her mystery tonight.

"No, it's my dad . . . he wouldn't," I said. "Besides, it's not like we're poor. My dad has a good job."

"Maybe he owes someone bad a lot of money," Morna said, even though she'd died before the entire genre of *film noir* existed.

"Who else was in attendance that night?" Cyril asked.

"Like, dozens of people — kids, parents . . ." I said.

"Anyone unusual? Anyone who might have an interest in cars with fins?" Derek said, hastily writing down notes in a second notepad. (Where were they getting these pads from? I'd have to ask to review his notes later to see if they matched what I'd already written down.)

"Well, that psychic guy, Nicodemus Burke was there, which was kind of strange."

"Anyone else?" Tabetha asked.

"A lot of parents, Mrs. Salmons, most of the teachers. Mr. Santuzzi was watching the parking lot," I said.

"Did you see him enter the school at any point?" Derek asked.

"Yeah, but —"

"If he was watching the parking lot, he could have made the car with fins up! Invented it," Morna said.

"Guys, as naturally suspicious as I am of Mr. Santuzzi, I don't think he's the thief," I said, almost disbelieving myself as I said the words. "We've suspected him of wrongdoing and even murder several times already this year, and he's always been innocent. I don't want to turn him into Professor Snape and just keep assuming he's a bad guy and always get proven wrong."

The dead kids all looked at one another in confusion.

"Even *I* don't know what you're talking about," Derek said. "Professor who?"

"Never mind," I said. "I just don't think it's Santuzzi."

"He could have hidden the cash box in the school and have access to it any time he wanted," insisted Kirby.

"What d'ye want t' do, October?" asked Morna.

"Given recent events at school," I said, "I really think we need to look into Phantom Moustache's involvement."

"And that is?" Cyril said.

"It's the name of a band at school," I explained. "Remember? The older brother of one of them attacked us with baseball bats at the Crooked Arms?"

Maybe I was bonkers for assuming that was the kind of thing people wouldn't forget.

"Oh," Kirby said. "And you think they stole the money? But didn't you say it happened when they were performing?"

"I still think they're up to no good." Basically an evergreen statement when it came to the members of Phantom Moustache.

"So, how do we investigate 'em?" Tabetha asked.

"I think we should search their band practice space," I said. "I know where it is. It's Boston Davis's pool house."

"Will it necessitate breaking and entering?" Cyril asked.

"Probably."

The dead kids — even Tabetha — were suddenly all smiles.

The Phantom Moustache heartthrob and frontman lived alarmingly close to me. Not so close that I could conceivably run to his home if I was baking (seems unlikely) and needed a cup of sugar. But we could for sure be in the same flood evacuation zone. In any event, the proximity made travelling with a pack of dead kids that much easier than a trip across town.

"Is this the place?" Derek asked.

We were all crouched behind a large hedge, though since the bushes measured about six feet high, there was no real reason for us to be crawling around like soldiers ducking under barbed wire. Though Boston Davis and his family lived only about seven blocks from Dad and me, the houses on his street were about three times the size and featured cars about fifteen years newer in the driveways. Maybe I shouldn't have been surprised. After all, I was aware that Boston's band practised in his *pool house*, a type of structure I'd only seen on the estates of TV millionaires, like in *The Fresh Prince of Bel-Air*. I wondered what Boston Davis's parents did. Probably sold Uzis to Eastern European warlords or something.

"Looks like they're home," Kirby said, pointing to the coloured lights flashing in the front windows. The house was set back from the sidewalk, up a slight incline.

"Somebody's watching television, at least," I agreed.

"So what d'we do?" Morna asked.

"We don't need to get inside the house," I said. "Just the building by the pool." I threw a hand toward the wooden gate that promised to lead into the backyard. A half-deflated innertube was draped over one pillar. Most of April had been decidedly denim-jacket weather (DJW); I was sure the pool hadn't been used yet this year.

"What if someone should be in the yard?" Cyril asked.

"Doing what?" I asked. "Taking a late-night swim in this sweater weather? I'm surprised they're still up watching TV."

We opened the gate to the backyard and used the innertube to prevent the metal lock from clanking when we closed it.

The Davis yard was mostly not yard at all. Instead of grass, the wide expanse featured a square of interlocking stone in which a large kidney-shaped pool was set. Though at this time of year, the pool was covered by what looked like industrial bubble wrap, which in turn was covered by about seventeen pounds of nettles, sticky helicopter plants, and long-dead flies and wasps. Just beyond the floating insect graveyard, on one of the few surviving patches of grass: a structure that must have been the pool house.

No lights were on inside, but when I tried the door, it was clear the Davises locked their pool house to keep out raccoons and vagrants. Though it would have been more satisfying (personally, viscerally) to take a brick and smash out a window, Morna instead ghosted through the pool house door and unlocked it from the inside.

The door swung open and I was met with Morna's flabbergasted expression.

"This is bigger than our entire home was," she said. "It's just for the pool?"

"I guess that won't make searching it any easier," I grumbled. "So many places to hide things — like a cash box."

The dead kids split up and began to root through all of Boston Davis's stuff. And it was — in reality — mostly Boston Davis's stuff. Though it was called a pool house, it seemed more like a rec room for Phantom Moustache, complete with a futon couch littered with mostly empty Doritos bags, a flat-screen TV with an XBox, a drum kit, and several amps and microphones, as well as stacks of *Guitar World* and other such publications.

It's not that I didn't hate Boston Davis, his friends, and his life — I definitely *did*. But I also kind of envied it.

"Can we turn on some lights?" Derek asked. "That would make it much easier to see what we're looking for. Especially if the cash box is black."

For whatever reason, I kept forgetting that the dead kids didn't have night vision like cats. "Oh, yeah. Okay," I said. "But not too many lights. We don't want anyone to know we're back here."

Derek flipped a couple switches and I resumed crawling across the carpeted floor to see if anything had been shoved under tables or chairs.

"How do we know they didn't just spend all the money?" Tabetha said. "What if we're lookin' for somethin' that's already gone?"

Tabetha, as she usually did, had a good point. Would anyone bat an eye if Boston Davis had a few thousand dollars? Even though he was in high school? He could have blown it all on band gear and video games.

"True," I grunted, reaching under an end table piled high with empty Arizona Iced Tea cans. "But he might have left some clues."

"Like the cash box itself," Kirby said.

Yet, after a full hour of searching, no cash box could be found. In fact, we'd found nothing that would be out of place in the average teen band's hangout spot. The pool house may as well have been put together by the set designer of a popular teen drama on The CW. The sole exception was when Kirby,

sifting through a pile of magazines fanned out on a table, found a business card.

"This is odd," Kirby said, flipping the jet-black rectangle around in his fingers.

"Yeah," I said. "Who prints *black* business cards? So tacky. I'm goth and even I wouldn't do that."

Derek, who had taken the card from Kirby, explained, "It's not the design that's the strange part. Look whose it is."

Derek then passed me the card, covered in Doritos thumb-prints:

NICODEMUS BURKE
Medium & Communicator to the Beyond
Payment Plans Available
(Present this card for a 5% discount)

"Isn't that the psychic guy we saw in the graveyard?"

If I hadn't been sure Nicodemus Burke and Alyosha Diamandas were friends before, I was *now*. A five percent discount? Only a friend of Sticksville's most irritating realtor could be so transparently cheap.

The doorknob began to rattle.

"Someone's here!" I whispered.

"I'll get the lights," Kirby announced and turned them off before I could tell him that would only make things worse.

Having spent the past hour scouring the pool house, I was acutely aware there was but one door, and someone was cur-rently trying to open it. Also, there were few places to hide, whether you were a black cash box or a full-size thirteen-year-old.

The dead kids easily split through the pool house's back wall as if it were tissue paper. (More easily, really.) But I couldn't even scramble out a window, as the pool house's only windows also faced the door that someone was trying to enter.

Given limited options, I chose to hide under the futon. From where I was situated on the carpet, I could see the futon frame was partially broken. Moments after I'd stretched out on the floor under the lumpy cushion, the door swung open.

"Weird," said Boston Davis in a muted voice. "I could have sworn there were lights on in here."

"You're being paranoid," came Ashlie Salmons's voice. "I thought you said your parents were cool."

"They let you stay over late, didn't they?"

Ashlie giggled, which made me want to die. Then I felt them both sit down on the futon just above me. Luckily, they were on either side of the missing slats. From where I was lying, I could see Boston's white sneakers and Ashlie's navy blue Keds tapping the carpet. They were just about a foot from my face. Unsure if I was breathing too heavily, I attempted to slow my lungs, but I had no idea what I was doing. Clearly, I should have done training with a Shaolin monk before I took up detective work.

"This is nice," Ashlie said, her voice pitched a full octave higher than I'd ever heard it. Is this how you were supposed to talk to boys? Like you'd just been huffing from a helium tank?

Still, I braved through my irritation since I thought there was an outside chance one or both of them might let slip with some intel on the cash box theft. They had to know something. But instead, something much, much worse happened.

"Do you think your parents would be cool with the two of us being alone in this pool house?" Ashlie asked.

"Yeah, for sure," Boston said, seeming mildly anxious. "Wanna play Xbox or something?"

"No," she said. "I don't."

"Oh," Boston answered, shifting on the futon. "My band practises here, you know. It's soundproof."

Before I could honest-to-goodness start dry-heaving, the shifting on the futon increased and was soon accompanied by wet smacking noises. Boston and Ashlie were making out on the futon directly above me. I thought for sure I would turn to stone. Would I survive the make-out session? And what would be left of me, if I did?

As the kissing intensified, a knee pushed downward into the lumpy futon, through the broken spot, and drove directly into my solar plexus. As I gasped for air, a wider weight pushed down on the futon cushion as a whole and pressed me into the carpet floor. As a result, the back of my thigh pressed into a stray guitar pick on the floor, and it stabbed me so deeply, I was sure it was drawing blood. Boston moaned, the cushion pushed further southward, and the point of the guitar pick struck a nerve — so I yelped.

"What the heck was that?" Boston shouted.

"It wasn't me!" Ashlie said. Her normal unpleasant tone of voice had returned. "Is there someone else in here, *Boston?*"

"The lights!" he said. Then — with a strength that was not unimpressive — ripped the futon cushion from its frame, revealing me beneath, palms facing upward, covered in shards of Cool Ranch chips and dust bunnies.

"Hey, guys," I said, in my most casual voice.

☠   ☠   ☠

Open-Gasket Funeral

At some time that night after Mr. and Mrs. Davis made a telephone call to the police, the sky opened up like a guest on *Sally Jessy Raphael* and giant tears fell steadily and rapidly from the sky. It was in the midst of this storm that Crown Attorney Salmons delivered a sullen and very damp October Schwartz to her father. When Mr. Schwartz opened the door — cautiously, of course, as one is wise to expect trouble when one opens the door at two in the morning — the expression October wore was that of a nearly drowned beagle left on the front porch of the local Humane Society.

"October?" he said, his voice still groggy from sleep. "Crown Attorney Salmons!"

Mr. Schwartz, dressed in pyjamas last seen by the wider public during the original television run of *Father Knows Best*, turned burnt umber with embarrassment and clasped the lapels of his pyjama blazer closed.

"I found something you might want down at the police station," the elder Salmons joked. Though it was at least a few hours past the bedtime of most grownups (who are not rockstars or graveyard shift workers), Crown Attorney Salmons was alert and poised as ever.

"What happened?! Where have you been?" Mr. Schwartz bumbled. He seemed uncertain whether to embrace his child in relief or give her a stern talking to — a decision that was complicated by the

presence of a woman he, to October's unending horror, seemed to want to smooch. Would it look better to her if he was a loving, sensitive dad or take-charge authoritarian dad? Maybe she wasn't into dads at all. Perhaps it would be preferable to cut out the hassle of October's late-night adventures and just dump his troublemaking daughter at the closest orphanage.

While these manifold considerations danced around in Leonard Schwartz's head, all October could think of was how much she resented her traitorous dead friends for ditching her in Boston Davis's pool house. But as Ms. Salmons outlined the evening's criminal transgressions to her dad, and she watched his ashen face dim, like a firefly trapped in a Mason jar without air holes, her resentment turned to guilt and shame. All she wanted to do was roll herself up into a little ball, like a tiny pill bug, and hide herself in the pocket of Crown Attorney Salmons's navy trench coat. Even if that meant she'd be, by necessity, physically closer to her enemy's mom, as well as her spare change, bus transfers, and lip balm.

"I was called to the scene to pick up Ashlie. The Davises are understandably upset," Salmons noted. "They're calling your daughter a voyeur . . . a Peeping Tom. I think I can keep them from pressing charges, but you may want to have a talk to her about respecting privacy."

"Mm-hmm," Mr. Schwartz nodded. October noticed that her enemy's mom kept talking about her as if she were overseas and not directly below her armpit.

"Fair warning: the guys and gals of the Sticksville Police would *love* to get a charge to stick on your daughter," she added. "They think she needs juvenile detention, and that's not an unreasonable suggestion. But as a favour to you, I think we can avoid it this time."

"I appreciate that," Mr. Schwartz said, his disappointment somewhat tempered by the fact that Attorney Salmons was doing him a favour. "And thank you for bringing October back to me safe . . . though a little bit wet."

"I suppose she didn't think to bring an umbrella on her peeping excursion."

This was a bit too much for October. "I wasn't peeping!"

"October!" Mr. Schwartz asserted. "Do *not* yell at Crown Attorney Salmons."

October, her cheeks hot with residual conflict, went silent and looked at her waterlogged shoes, which had formed a sizeable puddle in the front hallway.

"I'll leave it to you to mete out what you see as appropriate punishment," Salmons said.

"October," Mr. Schwartz addressed his daughter, her eyes still downcast. "Go to your room. In the morning, we can decide how many weeks — months! — of grounding will be instituted."

October dragged her particularly sullen and soggy self down the hall to her room, hoping she could get there without bursting into tears or exploding with rage, smashing her fists into the walls or proclaiming she would drink from the skull of her enemy Ashlie Salmons before she finished high school. Thankfully, she was able to successfully contain herself, but — because she was moving in such a dramatically slow fashion — she did overhear her father tell Ms. Salmons that if he had to be woken up in the middle of the night, he was glad it was by her. Then Ms. Salmons said something about him being "adorable" in his pyjamas, and October threw up a little in her mouth.

With a vile taste on her gums that seemed like punishment enough, she lay awake in her bed, staring at *The Crow* poster on her ceiling and wondering how she always managed to get herself tangled up in some school-based mystery that landed her in her poor dad's bad book.

☠   ☠   ☠

Unfortunately, Mr. Schwartz was unconvinced that October throwing up in her own mouth was punishment enough. This much became clear as they had a talk about her "issues" (Mr. Schwartz's air quotes) over breakfast Sunday morning. Mr. Schwartz described his disappointment and his frustration, but also his confusion: "I just don't understand why you were even hiding in their pool house, pumpkin," he said, grimacing as he stirred his oatmeal. "Do you even know that boy?"

"From school, I guess," October mumbled, eyes downcast. "He's in a band."

"Wait, is he in that band that stole the money? Crunch Roll House?"

"That's the problem," October groaned. "Everybody thinks Crenshaw House stole the money, but I know they didn't."

"Honey, they left a note at the crime scene."

"Anyone could have written those lyrics," October shot back, ruffling her hair in frustration. She said it quickly but realized the band's lyrics might not be readily Google-able.

"Hey, watch it," her dad said, protecting his oatmeal from errant black hairs. "I'm eating."

"Crenshaw House have been framed," October asserted. "And I think Boston's band is somehow involved. That's why I was in his pool house."

Mr. Schwartz raised an eyebrow and sucked on his oatmeal spoon for a couple seconds.

"Are you telling me the truth?"

October nodded.

"I guess that's not out of the ordinary for you, given what happened with Mr. O'Shea," October's dad said, referencing the one case of October's he already knew about. "But you have to not get so involved with other people's problems."

"But Dad . . ."

"No buts, pumpkin. This is part of being adult. Maybe Crenshaw House stole that money. Maybe they didn't. But you're not in the band, so this falls squarely in the category of 'not your problem.' Sometimes you have to draw these barriers for your own safety, October."

October frowned and a sharp pain grew between her eyes. Though there was a cold, almost robotic logic to his words, she felt that her father was essentially telling her not to care.

In addition to the unsolicited life advice, October was given six weeks' grounding. She was dumbfounded. Six weeks was a good portion of a school semester. A good number of things she had planned — solving two mysteries, most urgently — were going to prove nigh impossible unless she could somehow convince her dad to relent. Or to take powerful sleeping pills every night. (One or the other.)

☠ ☠ ☠

On Monday, October arrived at school in a mood so dark it could have inspired several popular emo ballads. She arrived at her locker to find Yumi and Stacey waiting for her. Yumi had a piece of note paper in her hands with several drafts of an Astaroth Night Bus logo scribbled across it, which only served to remind October of yet another extracurricular activity that was no longer viable.

"Hey, Schwartz," Yumi said. "Check out these logos. Do you think one is more shirt-worthy than the others? Also, do you want me to bring my cousin's bass to school so you can start practising?"

"About that," October sighed. "Over the weekend, I was doing some, uh, investigative work on the Bandwarz theft, and I may have been caught breaking in to Boston Davis's pool house."

"A pool house?" Stacey asked. "Like on *Fresh Prince*?"

"Schwartz!" Yumi shouted. "I know I encouraged you to take on Henry's case —" ("encouraged" was a mild way of putting it) "— but no one expected you to turn into Magnum P.I.!"

"I take my work seriously."

"Did you get arrested?" Yumi demanded, grabbing October by the shoulder. She seemed both horrified and delighted her friend could be a notorious burglar.

"Almost," she answered. "I'm basically under house arrest with my dad for the next six weeks. This doesn't bode well for the future of our band."

"What a drag," Yumi moaned.

"We can figure something out," Stacey said, with all the confidence of a boy who's rarely ever figured anything out.

Before Stacey could unveil his brilliant, foolproof plan, the band members of Crenshaw House made an unusual, but not entirely unexpected, visit to October's locker wing. Henry had brought the others to check on the state of her investigation. The young Mr. Khan, dressed like a model for L.L. Bean, approached October.

"Not to pressure you, but have you made any progress in looking into the Bandwarz theft?" he asked. "You probably saw from lunch on Friday that things are getting out of control."

"Yeah, I saw. Those were *my* Tater Tots that got smashed into Levi's chest," she answered, then turned to Levi. "Sorry."

"Not your fault."

"I'm doing what I can, but it might take longer than I hoped."

"Why?" asked Matilda.

"October got busted by the cops for breaking into Boston Davis's pool house," Yumi interjected.

"Wicked," said Levi.

"Um, yeah. So, I'm super grounded."

"Is there anything you *can* do while grounded?" asked Henry.

"Listen," Levi said. "Don't sweat it. I know Henry is worried about ruining his perfect attendance record with jail time, but things should be okay as long as we can avoid Phantom Moustache for a while. And I may be missing some school in a few days anyway."

"Why's that?" asked Yumi.

"My great-aunt Beryl just died," he answered. "The funeral is supposed to happen soon."

October's mystery-focused brain began to spin like a rusty exercise bike once again. She had completely forgotten that Henry had mentioned Levi and Beryl were related.

"Your great-aunt Beryl?" she said. "I'm so sorry."

"It's okay. She was pretty old," Levi answered. "I just feel bad because she lived so close to Henry but I barely ever visited her. I don't think I'd seen her since September. She was a bit compulsive with collecting things and my family and I would try to visit to

164

help her clean up every now and then, but we'd been distracted. The police said it was pretty messy. The television was even broken and she never called to fix it."

"October actually left Beryl a note to meet up with her last week," said Henry, who was rapidly losing favour as a potential crush. "Something about an English project. Remember, October?"

Of course she remembered. Why did Henry remember this?

"Really?" Levi said, perhaps hopeful that October had some heartwarming final Beryl anecdote to tell. "Did you meet up with her?"

"No, she never got back to me," October lied. This was among the meaner things she had done in her life, but she reasoned you sometimes had to be cruel to be kind, like in that song her dad often listened to. Also, she didn't want in any way to be implicated in Beryl Gibson's death. "Sorry. I forgot you two were related."

October's mind reeled with a detail she hadn't considered before. If Levi and Beryl were related, this meant that Levi was — distantly, but still — related to Tabetha. He might even know something about the story of her disappearance, though how she'd bring that up was another puzzle. At the very least, she could be relieved someone found Beryl's body in a decent amount of time.

"How did she die?" October said, trying not to sound too morbid, though it was recognized as kind of her thing. "If you don't mind me asking."

"They think it was a heart attack. I guess I shouldn't be surprised, but I thought we'd have her around for longer," Levi said, looking down at his boots and falling speechless.

"Thanks for trying to solve our mystery, October," Henry said, breaking an awkward silence.

"Yeah, thanks," Matilda seconded.

"Thank me once I actually accomplish something," she said. "I have to get to English."

Henry, Matilda, and Yumi accompanied October Schwartz and thus bore witness to what would be her latest indignity as Sticksville Central High School's resident Zombie Tramp. The quartet rounded the corner to the social studies hall and came face to face with a tabloid-sized poster featuring an illustration of what appeared to be October herself. Henry did a double-take from the poster to October and back.

"This is new," marvelled Yumi.

In addition to the uncanny cartoon rendition, the poster featured boldface text that labelled October a "Dangerous Perv Ahead." And there were copies, each emblazoned with other unpleasant labels in boldface.

"Who did this?" Matilda said, mouth agape — not just at the poster they stood before, but at the sheer number of them lining the halls. There were dozens.

"Has to be Ashlie Salmons," said October. But you readers had probably already reached that conclusion.

"But why?" Yumi said.

"One thing I forgot to mention about last night —" October explained, "Ashlie and Boston caught me in the pool house while they were making out."

"Gross," said Yumi.

"So now they think I'm, like, a Peeping Tom or something."

"Maybe nobody will know this drawing is supposed to be you?" said Matilda.

"It's a really good likeness," Yumi, helpful as ever, noted. "Hard to mistake. Who do you think drew it?"

"The bassist in Phantom Moustache, Preston? I think he draws," Henry said.

"Oh, yeah. He's really good," Yumi agreed.

"Who *cares* if he's good?" October said.

"They must have been at school so *early* to do this," Matilda marvelled. "There must be a hundred of these. It's almost impressive."

October glared at Crenshaw House's drummer.

"But, obviously, it's *not*," she corrected.

The morning tone sounded.

"I'm going to be late for Mr. Copeland's class," October fretted.

"But what are you going to do about this smear campaign?" Yumi said.

"Nothing. I don't know. What *can* I do?"

Henry Khan walked over to the poster directly before them and pulled it down, balling it up in his fist. He then strode a few paces down to the next one and repeated the action.

"Henry, there are so many," October said. "You'll miss class."

"So I'll miss class," he said, not wavering from his newly self-imposed mission. "I can catch up in chemistry later. This seems more important."

"Didn't Levi say you have perfect attendance?" October said.

"I don't think so."

"I think I can skip class today too," Yumi said. "Let me go find Stacey. What about you, Matilda?"

"Barely go to class as it is."

By second period, all evidence of October Schwartz as a "dangerous perv" was collected in the dumpster by the basketball court out back. October, in retrospect, regretted being so reluctant to offer her new friends aid. Especially since Levi had been subjected to similar harassment and worse.

☠   ☠   ☠

After being subjected to a full school day of coordinated harassment, October returned home as fast as she could, trying her best
to prove to her father she was taking his punishment seriously.
However, she was also well aware she needed to find the dead
kids that evening and tell them about Levi, about Beryl's wake —
maybe even pay a visit to the local funeral home. Tabetha would
probably appreciate that. She wasn't exactly sure if they would
find anything useful to the investigation there, but it would be nice
thing for Tabetha to see. Maybe there'd even be photographs of her
family on display. So the main issue was how to escape her house
without her dear old pops knowing.

Even though, normally, escape was not an issue, Mr. Schwartz
would be on high alert the night following a visit from Crown
Attorney Salmons, direct from the police station with his daughter.
And October was — as a rule — morally opposed to drugging her
dad. Besides, she had no idea how she'd do it without a degree in
pharmacology. He'd probably have his eyes trained on October's
door all night, just waiting for her to try to sneak out. To October's
mind, there was only one way out: the window.

Trouble was, the window in October's bedroom was not the
most accommodating size. It was a window for looking at things,
not for conveyance. Another problem was that the drop from that
window to her sloping backyard was about eight feet and October
Schwartz was no Olympic gymnast. In terms of physical fitness,
she could barely be considered an Olympic spectator. Still, the
window was — in her mind — the only viable option.

October quietly slid her window open, then — as gently as
she could — removed the screen. As a family of moths rushed
into her room, she took the twelve black shirts she'd tied together,
knotted the makeshift rope to a bedpost, and slowly fed it out the
window. Relying on the material used to make cheap band T-shirts
was a risky move: on more than one occasion, the armpit seams
had ripped when she'd raised her hand too swiftly in class. But the
shirt-rope miraculously supported her weight, and she was soon
jogging through the cemetery to find her dead friends. She only
hoped her dad didn't take a look outside at her window and notice
the cable of shirt lolling out like a dragon's black tongue.

When October arrived in the cemetery, the dead kids were already about, seemingly just waiting on her arrival.

"The Incredible Disappearing Dead Kids!" October announced. "You missed all the excitement last night."

"Sorry, October," Morna said, her pale face gone pink.

"You know we couldn't stick around, given the circumstances," Kirby reasoned.

"Well, I almost got arrested," October said. "And my dad is on high alert. Graveyard visits like this are going to be more and more difficult."

"I'm not sure what we could have done to help you," Cyril said.

"I'm so annoyed, I might not even share the news I learned today about Tabetha," October teased.

"What?" Derek asked.

"Don't mess with me, October," Tabetha commanded, but not harshly. She sounded like the ghost equivalent of a paper clip that's been bent back and forth a few too many times.

"It's okay, Tabetha," Derek reassured, giving Tabetha a small hug. "So, spill, October. What is it?"

"If we head across the street to the funeral home right now, we'll find Beryl Gibson. A boy in my class, Levi, is related to her — we can look into him later — and told me the funeral service is in a few days."

Tabetha gulped. "Can we go there now? I'd like to see her again. Pay my respects."

"Of course we can," October said, relieved to finally be the bearer of good news, finally able to do something to provide Tabetha some relief. "We can go tonight. And if it's not too disrespectful, perhaps we can even do some detective work."

"And what exactly is Beryl Gibson's body going to tell us?" asked Kirby, skeptical as ever.

"You have better ideas?" October shot back. "We could go back to work solving *my* mystery about the band theft —"

Tabetha interrupted. "Let's go see Beryl."

☠   ☠   ☠

Unlocking the Valhalla Funeral Home back door was as easy — for kids who are unhindered by things like brick walls — as unlocking the door at Boston Davis's pool house. The Dead Kid Detective Agency arrived inside the funeral home's kitchen, where light sandwiches and coffee could be prepared so mourners would never have to grieve on an empty stomach. And even with the overwhelming odor of potpourri in two bowls resting on the kitchen counter, it smelled about a hundred times better than Boston Davis's love shack.

"Where should we start?" asked Morna. A good question, as October hadn't given an incredible amount of thought as to what she hoped to find in the funeral home. Given they'd be preparing for Beryl Gibson's funeral, October had thought it possible the place might be littered with personal files and effects of the woman, but that was based on zero knowledge whatsoever. October Schwartz had never been behind-the-scenes at a funeral before. She'd never even watched an episode of *Six Feet Under*.

"I don't know," October said, looking around and seeing one doorway led to a room with muted blue carpeting and watercolour paintings, and the other led to stairs. "We should probably try to find Beryl . . . or, Beryl's body . . . first. Maybe the blue room?"

They all entered the large viewing room, which seemed especially massive with the chairs that were used during service stacked in the corners. Small tables lined the back wall, and a podium, microphone stand, and sound system were at the front, situated underneath a large portrait of what looked like the hotel from *Psycho*, but during a particularly verdant spring. In front of that painting stood an easel displaying an enlarged photo of Beryl Gibson from about forty years earlier.

"Is it strange?" October asked the dead kids as a group. "Investigating your own deaths?"

"Well, *obviously*," Cyril said.

"I was so worried when we were investigating mine," Morna said.

"I can't even imagine what Tabetha's feeling now," Derek chimed in.

"I'm feeling we should do less talkin' and more findin' where Beryl is. The photo is great n' all, but I'd really like t'see her."

"I have to say," Kirby said, because he apparently *had* to, "now that I've seen the LaFlamme name on that Asphodel Meadows list, I'm in no hurry to figure out what happened to me."

"Scared to find out if yer own family ended you?" Tabetha asked.

"Don't be mean," Morna chided.

But October knew exactly how he felt. Since seeing her mom's original name on the very same list, she had feelings about solving mysteries that concerned Asphodel Meadows that could best be described as "mixed." What if her mother had been involved in some dastardly misdeeds?

She almost wished that Nicodemus Burke goof was the real deal — a psychic who could help her find her mother. Maybe Ms. Fenstermacher was wrong. Maybe Alyosha Diamandas had contacted him because Nicodemus actually *did* have abilities beyond what most people would consider "normal." If he did have any precognitive powers at all, it would be worth asking. At the very least, it would be a small gesture toward finding her mom. Whatever other quests she'd undertaken since moving to Sticksville, her efforts to locate her mom had been severely lacking.

October began to wish she'd held on to that business card they found in the Davis pool house.

"I think, after we find Beryl," October said, outlining what might generously be described as a plan, "we really need to investigate the fairgrounds. That's where the Underground Railroad stop was supposed to have been. That's where you lived and where you had your last memory. And that's where you supposedly went missing, Tabetha. It's such a large area, we should start there soon."

"Good thing there are six of us, then," Cyril said.

"Unless they put her under the floorboards, Beryl isn't in this room," Tabetha said grimly. "Maybe we should move on to the next room?"

"Do you think that's where they'd keep her?" October asked. For someone who'd spent her last few months with the dead, she'd never actually attended a funeral (even though she tried her best to get to Mr. O'Shea's). She wasn't sure where you were supposed to pay your last respects.

"How should we know?" Kirby asked.

"You were all dead once. Don't you remember where you were? Your bodies must've ended up in places like this."

"Nuh-uh," reminded Tabetha. "They never found my body. Probably was out rottin' in a ditch somewhere."

October felt the sadness hit her in the stomach again.

"The neighbouring room seems as good an idea as any," Derek replied.

"Shall we?"

"Are you ready for this, Tabetha?" October asked. "I mean, not to be offensive, but what if she's all gross and corpsified in there?"

"We're all gross and corpsified," Kirby reminded.

"Speak for yourself," Morna said.

The dead kids and October pushed through the wooden door and there it was: in the far corner, like a dare, was a chestnut casket set upon a sturdy gurney. Even though the casket was open so they could see it contained Beryl Gibson's remains, they didn't get a close look at exactly how gross and corpsified the body was, because someone else was in the room. Standing before the coffin, peering down into it and moving his left hand up and down the former Beryl Gibson's side, was Nicodemus Burke. Upon hearing the door swing open, he raised his head, lowered his circular glasses, and turned toward October and her friends. When the supposed psychic opened his mouth, October realized their funeral home visit had gone horribly, horribly wrong.

"So," he said with a stroke of his conical beard. "The ghost children are real."

☠   ☠   ☠

14

Burke-Life Balance

Suffice to say, I hadn't expected someone to be at the funeral home at midnight, pawing Beryl Gibson's coffin. Given my experiences in the cemetery, if I had been expecting someone, I wouldn't have expected it to be a living person. If beforehand you'd asked something like, "Out of all the people you've ever met, who would you most likely find in a mortuary, giving a corpse a pat-down," I might have answered Alyosha Diamandas. In fact, if Alyosha Diamandas had been nominated for anything in his high school yearbook, it would be "Most Likely to Disturb the Dead." (Though it's difficult to imagine Alyosha having ever been a teenager.) So, colour me shocked when it was *not* Alyosha Diamandas, but his sometime friend Nicodemus Burke, who was manhandling the dead.

Burke closed the top to Beryl Gibson's casket. He was again dressed for a night out at some kind of Satanic opera, and in his right hand carried a large canvas bag. The dead kids and I all had the dumbest looks on our faces, having just been ambushed by a local psychic, and not even a particularly successful one.

"I see you dead children have brought a living friend with you — October, is it?"

I wasn't expecting him to know my name, but then, I wasn't expecting to run into a psychic towering over Tabetha's dead relative tonight, either. Nicodemus Burke seemed to be everywhere I was — at my school, on my bus.

Nicodemus Burke slid a small flip phone from his jacket's breast pocket (who stores their phone there?) and pressed a single number.

"What is that?" Cyril sputtered. "Some sort of weapon?!"

My head whipped around to him so quickly, I nearly lost a tooth. "No. It's a phone!"

"We've seen phones, October, at the police station and in the Crooked Arms," Kirby reminded her. "Phones have cords. That's no phone."

While I was distracted explaining mobile phone technology and the network of telecommunication towers that made it possible, Nicodemus was busy describing the situation — and us — to his friend at the end of the line.

"Interesting . . . no *five* of them . . . Yes, more than I'd expected too," he whispered. "Yes, just like a hockey team, I suppose . . . and there's also a goalie here. Who is very much alive."

"Who are you talking to?" I shouted, though I wasn't about to move any closer to the guy. When I walked in, he had appeared to be moments away from rummaging through the pockets of a dead body. Who knew what he was capable of. Maybe he did have a weapon.

Burke — surprise, surprise — didn't answer me. He just continued his conversation. "But what I need you to do is . . . you know that canvas sack in the back seat? Take it with you and do what we discussed earlier."

"What did you discuss earlier?" I demanded.

Burke snapped the phone shut. "So the dead ones talk too?"

"He's talkin' 'bout us," Tabetha grumbled and rolled up one sleeve.

"Don't answer him!" I warned, but I don't know why I cared. Maybe just because he wouldn't answer my questions. "Who did you just call?"

Burke slowly slid the phone back into his jacket pocket and

brushed a bit of fluff from his shoulder before finally answering one of my questions. "That's just my ride."

"Your ride?"

"I think you know each other," he said. A lopsided grin grew above his black goatee.

"What is this about some living girl?" came a shout from the far entryway. Soon the body that came along with it filled the doorway, as Alyosha Diamandas, Sticksville's only 24-hour realtor, finished emptying a large canvas bag's contents across the threshold. "Oh, the vampire. October Schwartz."

"Did you know this would happen?" Burke groaned. "That these ghosts and this girl would be here tonight?"

"I never know why anything happens," Alyosha admitted sheepishly, balling up the bag and dusting off his palms. "But this girl and her ghost friends — they do seem to turn up quite a lot."

"The ghosts I can handle."

I wasn't sure what to say or do. The dead kids were keeping stock-still, maybe in the hopes that Alyosha and Nicodemus Burke were like the *Tyrannosaurus rex* and couldn't see them if they made no quick movements. But, from their conversation, it was abundantly clear both men had spectacular vision — so much so, they could see the dead. This, in itself, was weird. Earlier, the dead kids had explained that only a person who had experienced untimely tragedy in their life could see ghosts, and what tragic thing could possibly have happened to Alyosha Diamandas, aside from his moustache?

"Though you interrupted something quite important, I'd still say it's nice to meet you kids. From several different eras, no less, if your clothing is any indication," Nicodemus spoke deliberately, as if he were in a television movie of the week, but there were no cameras were in sight. If cameras *had been* in sight, I would be in even more trouble than I was already. "But my friend Alyosha here tells me you're something of a nuisance."

Rapidly realizing the two men weren't content to let us all go our separate ways, I felt the time had come to stop worrying about why Nicodemus and Alyosha were scoping out Beryl Gibson and to start running.

"Guys, let's make a break for it," I suggested. There was a wide-open exit — the kitchen where we first entered — and both our captors were kind of old dudes. They'd probably get winded after three paces.

Cyril led the charge and dashed for the kitchen door. The other kids and I joined him, Kirby pushing one of the small tables behind him with his good arm to block our pursuers. But out of the corner of my eye, I could see we had no pursuers. Neither man ran after us nor tried to block us on our path. They weren't even calmly walking after us like Jason in the *Friday the 13th* murderfests.

"Cyril!" I shouted. "They're not chasing us!"

"Is that not a good thing?" he called back, clearly not as unsettled by the situation as I was.

Before we could discuss it any further, he reached the back door and threw it open. But as he lunged for the outside, he was shoved backward and landed in Tabetha's arms. She fell into Derek and me. Soon, we were all piled in a heap on the floor tiles.

"What are you doing, you colonial clod?" Kirby shouted face-down on the floor.

"I couldn't run any farther!" he said. "Something held me back!"

"What're you talkin' about?" Tabetha shouted, pushing herself up to one knee.

"The sensation is just like when I drowned — or like when we were in that tomb the other day," Cyril said. "I think the man dressed like a papist is some sort of sorcerer!"

Tabetha was not willing to just believe anything Cyril Cooper told her. (Fair enough, considering another Cooper was currently a prime suspect in her murder.) She got to her feet and stomped her loud boots through the kitchen toward the open door. But when she hit the crisp night air, she fell backward, as if repelled by some kind of ghost chain-link fence.

"What the —?!"

As the rest of us stood upright, the gruesome twosome of Alyosha Diamandas and Nicodemus Burke appeared at the kitchen door.

"I think you'll find that no spirits are permitted to leave this funeral home," Nicodemus said with a smug little grin that made me — for the first time in weeks — want to hit someone. I hadn't even wanted to hit Ashlie Salmons after making those posters. "There's a salt ring encircling the entire Valhalla Funeral Home. You can't escape."

"Enough joking around," Alyosha said, as my stomach dropped. "Think of what we have discovered, Mr. Burke. We should grab them before the living one realizes she can break away."

Alyosha dove at Morna, but she became transparent immediately, and Alyosha's hands grasped at thin air like a sad little crab's claws. He plunged forward onto the tile, sliding face first into the stainless steel refrigerator.

Nicodemus Burke, either more cautious or less buffoonish than his partner, stood in front of the door and took a swipe at Derek, who had also become intangible. But until he moved, I couldn't break the salt circle. Alyosha got up and dove again,

I guess assuming he could leap faster than a ghost could think — this time at Kirby. Again, he passed harmlessly through my dead friend — though it sounded (from the crunch with which he hit the floor) like he inflicted some harm on himself. He also landed very close to where I was kneeling on the ground. Burke was still blocking the kitchen door, so I retreated into the viewing room and the dead kids followed.

Cyril lifted the microphone stand and waved it in front of him like an entirely unskilled Donatello from the Teenage Mutant Ninja Turtles. The rest of us huddled behind him as he kept our enemies at bay.

"You really can't gang up on these guys so we can escape?" I

asked them, knowing full well the ridiculous ghost rules that made so many things so difficult. "They keep blocking the doors so I can't break the salt circle."

"You know the rules," Kirby said. "We're not allowed to harm any living people."

"Even an evil witch?"

"I think he still counts as a human being," Derek said. "Nothing in the rules about the quality of person."

"Then what's he doing right now?" I asked, pointing at Cyril, still sweeping the black pole back and forth in a wide arc, as if he were an undead windshield wiper and Nicodemus and Alyosha were two pesky water droplets.

"He's not harmin' anyone; just keepin' 'em away," Tabetha explained.

She had probably explained too much too loudly. Nicodemus Burke proceeded to walk directly into the path of the mic stand, grasp the slowing pole with his right hand, and toss it harmlessly aside.

"See?" Derek said.

"I'm sorry, October!" Cyril cried, backing with the rest of us into the corner.

"Can't you do that pentagon thing again?" I yelped. "Surround one of them and link arms while I sweep away the salt?"

"Works better when we're not all jammed in a tight spot," Kirby, suddenly a geometry expert, answered.

Alyosha and Nicodemus each chose a viewing room exit and slowly moved toward us in the centre. With the mic stand tossed aside, there were no makeshift weapons within our grasp. Not that anyone but me could use them.

"Unfortunately for all of you, I have plans," Nicodemus explained. "I can't have you ghosts ruining them, which is why I'm afraid you'll have to stay here."

"Scatter!" Cyril yelled, and the six of us scrambled in every direction of that wide, carpeted room.

"Stop the pirate!" Alyosha cried as Cyril ghosted through Nicodemus's cloak like a bull facing a toreador.

"Never mind him," Burke shouted to his companion. "Watch that fat one!"

"Fat one?" Kirby said, mid-run. "Does he mean me?"

"Don't listen to him," I shouted.

"My name is —" Kirby started, but I slapped my palm over his unsettlingly wet mouth. (I guess I should have considered myself lucky he was actually tangible.)

"Shut up!" I yelled. "Don't say your names! The more they know about us, the worse it is!" Neither he nor Alyosha seemed to know much about who the dead kids were or where their gravesites rested, but how much did they already know about me?

The dead kids and I ran around in circles in the big room, dodging tables, a photo easel, and two of the creepiest looking grownups Sticksville had to offer. Given the dead kids were tragically not allowed to just, like, punch them in the faces, I considered trying to take the two men by force myself. Though in a test of physical combat, I imagined literally every adult in town could have easily bested either of them — even both at the same time! — I was less confident in my abilities. These were minor worries compared to the ones I had about Nicodemus's off-hand reference to "plans." Who has plans that a bunch of ghost kids could ruin? Was this proof-positive that the two were members of the secretive Asphodel Meadows? Whatever the case, I sure couldn't turn to Nicodemus Burke now to help me find my mom. Which was too bad, since it seemed like he might be the the real deal. I needed to sneak past one of them to get at the salt.

"Enough of this," shouted a winded Nicodemus Burke, before he nabbed me by my hood and put me in a headlock. Or full nelson. (I'm no expert on wrestling moves, but this was definitely one or the other.)

"It seems like you may be at a disadvantage, girl," he wheezed and flexed his forearms, which tightened around my neck. "This one can't turn intangible."

"Let go!" I rasped.

"No, I think we'll take you hostage and leave your ghost friends to cool their heels at the funeral home."

Alyosha was visibly anxious about this turn of events. "Nicodemus," he said. "The ghosts should be our focus. Think of how famous we can be. Maybe we should let this October Schwartz go."

"October *Schwartz*? Is that her name?" he shouted. I could feel his icky goatee against my cheek.

The dead kids were completely unsure of what to do. Cyril moved toward us, but Nicodemus screamed. "Ah-ah-ah! Any closer, and I'll snap her neck."

"Nicodemus" Alyosha pleaded, looking nearly as worried and confused as the ghosts. "What are you doing?"

It was almost as if hearing my full name had turned Burke more violent, scarier. As worried as the dead kids and that jelly-fish of a real estate agent were, no one was as concerned as me. It was *my* soft, vulnerable neck pressed between the radius and ulna of some creep psychic. Maybe he was just trying to scare me, but maybe he had already killed a bunch of kids in his life. After all, he was a witch. Isn't that what witches do? Kill kids? Eat them, trap them in gingerbread houses — that kind of thing? My worry turned to real fear when I saw how helpless the dead kids looked. I couldn't rely on a save from them, and the town's supposedly fraudulent psychic was already dragging me to the front door.

I dug the heels of my Chuck Taylors into the carpet, to not much effect.

"Burke, good sir," Alyosha asked again in that weird cadence he had. "Don't do this."

"Do you even *want* these ghosts out of your hair?" he asked, loudly, right in my ear. "No more interruptions. Desperate times, Diamandas."

He continued to drag me, past the hallway table that held the guest book. Remembering the general setup of the room and sensing a very brief opportunity, I shot my arms out and grabbed hold of the large foamcore print of young Beryl

Gibson, pulling it off the easel. With all my strength, I heaved it back into Nicodemus Burke's face. When I brought my arms back down, there was a big hole in the Beryl Gibson portrait and a bloody tooth embedded just above her eyebrow.

Howling in pain, Nicodemus released me for just a moment — a moment in which I was able to stomp my heel on his foot and make a mad dash for the front door.

"Follow me!" I yelled to the dead kids.

"October!" Morna shouted. "The salt circle! We can't get out that way."

"But I can," I said.

I swung open the heavy wooden door, letting the cold night air sweep in. Spotting the line of salt at the bottom of the concrete steps, I kicked a hole in the ring, scattering granulated salt across the parking lot. I continued to kick at it, widening the hole as the dead kids ran down the steps and into the parking lot without the slightest encumbrance. From inside, the howling stopped and I heard Nicodemus Burke ask, "Where did they go?"

Alyosha and Nicodemus (now one tooth lighter) ran to the front door, then the top of the stairs at Valhalla Funeral Home. By the time they made their appearance, like the least coordinated, most flamboyant undertakers alive, the dead kids and I were clear across the parking lot.

"Maybe next time, make your protective circles from a substance stronger than salt!" I yelled. It was bratty, I'll admit. Then I picked up a loose chunk of concrete and aimed it at the Yaris in the parking lot. There was a real danger in what I was about to do. On the one hand, my house wasn't very far from the funeral home, and any loud noise could potentially wake my dad and notify him of my absence. On the other hand, two dudes were trying to kill me and I could potentially draw the police's attention to that.

"You'll live to regret this, girl," Nicodemus warned.

"Tabetha," I whispered. "Is it against the ghost rules to damage someone's car?"

"Heck, no," she said with glee.

I passed her the chunk of concrete and she hurled it through the car's passenger window, making a sound that we all thoroughly enjoyed.

"What are you doing?!" Alyosha Diamandas screamed, clutching the sides of his head as if the window smashing caused him acute physical pain. But he didn't move from the top step. "That's my car!"

"I had kind of hoped there would be a car alarm," I said.

"There is," Alyosha moaned. "It is *very* inconsistent."

Finding another stone of similar heft, I passed it to Tabetha, who aimed it at Alyosha Diamandas's Yaris.

With a riotous crash and spider web of glass engulfing the front windshield, Alyosha's car let rip with a panic alarm that sounded like doomsday was imminent. Knowing — or hoping — the police would soon be on their way, the dead kids and I absconded into the cemetery. I only hoped the graveyard was wide enough for the alarm sound not to carry. There could be no worse way to end an evening when my life was threatened than to come home to find my dad awake, filling out the papers to enlist me in boot camp.

One thing was certain. The dead kids and I barely talked to one another as we sprinted through the cemetery. We were all thinking the same thing: a magic man with a dastardly plan now knew we existed. We could no longer trust that we could solve our mysteries in relative safety.

☠   ☠   ☠

Rehearsal
Dispersal

October Schwartz spent most of the following school day in a state of panic, as if she were a Chicken Little who shopped at Hot Topic. But there was no one for this Chicken Little to proclaim "the sky was falling" to. Two adult creeps were aware October was friends with ghosts and trying — for some probably super-nefarious reason — to capture them. And they seemed to be working on some indubitably evil plan that involved the dead body of an elderly resident, Beryl Gibson. And who could October tell *that* to? Not her father, not her moderately hip former history teacher, Ms. Fenstermacher. Not even her best friends (and now bandmates) Yumi and Stacey, whom she greeted with a half-hearted wave as she seated herself at their cafeteria table. In short, October was stressed out.

One small mercy: October hadn't seen any more posters that proclaimed her some sort of deviant. Ashlie Salmons had, in fact, ignored her for most of the day, simply pouting with her arms tightly crossed from the other side of the cafeteria while her friends told jokes. *Hilarious* jokes, if her friend with a big distinctive laugh was any indication.

October noted the lack of posters as she peeled back the lid of her yogurt container.

"Crenshaw House has been hyper-vigilant," Yumi said. "They've been tearing down any new posters they find, patrolling the hallways."

"Like Dementors," Stacey said.

Yumi glared at him.

October sighed. "I guess I should really get to work solving their case. Prove they're innocent and everything . . ."

"If they *are*," Yumi said.

"Where's this suspicion from?" October asked. "Weren't you pushing me to get married to Henry Khan a couple weeks ago? Now you think he's a criminal?"

"As a detective, you have to keep all options open," she said, delivering some sage gumshoe advice.

"Whatever," October said, stabbing the yogurt with a plastic spoon. "I can't do much detective work of any sort until my father decides to let me leave the house."

"Sounds rough," Stacey said, attempting to commiserate.

"If you can't do your detective work, that means you'll have plenty of time to start rehearsing with Astaroth Night Bus," Yumi claimed.

"What part of 'grounded for weeks' sounds negotiable to you, Yumi?" October asked.

"You don't have to *go* anywhere, Schwartz," Yumi explained. "Let the Astaroth Night Bus come to you!"

"Should that be our band slogan?" Stacey asked.

After Yumi and Stacey seriously and intensely argued over whether bands had slogans, Yumi explained her plan: the three of them could hold their first practice (and any necessary subsequent practices) in the Schwartz family garage. Yumi would ask her parents for a ride, and they could pick up Stacey and his drum kit along the way.

"I don't know," October said, feeling the acute sting of peer pressure. "Do you think my dad will go for it? The idea behind a grounding is punishment. Having fun with my friends seems counter to its spirit."

"I'm sure you can smooth things over with him," Yumi insisted.

"Isn't a drum kit heavy to move?" October continued down her laundry list of concerns.

"Kind of . . ."

"Stacey'll be fine," Yumi declared. "Look, I've already started putting together some killer lyrics."

Yumi dug into her book bag, patterned with skulls and crossbones, and unfolded a sheet of paper that — while it once must have been crisp and white — now looked like it had been unearthed from the Sticksville Cemetery.

"Let me know what you think?" she asked, sliding the creased paper across the cafeteria table.

October let her eyes run along the tightly scripted lines.

"Looks great," said October. Not even one of Yumi's best friends had the heart to tell her that "disembowelling" and "rock-and-rolling" didn't actually rhyme.

"And I've been working on some new drumbeats," Stacey said, slapping his palms against his thighs. "Maybe something that uses the cowbell in an interesting way?"

Though there is literally no way to use a cowbell that could be deemed "interesting," October smiled and nodded. She couldn't, at the moment, fathom what sort of band Astaroth Night Bus was supposed to be. Some sort of disco death metal? Yet, because

it was difficult for a teenage detective with a clinically depressed father and a reputation for being a perv to keep friends, she agreed to have them over for band practice, hoping she could convince her dad it was a good idea beforehand.

Other mystery essentials would have to wait until she figured out how to hold a bass guitar.

☠   ☠   ☠

Smoothing over a band practice with Mr. Schwartz, however, proved not to be as easy as Yumi's blasé attitude would suggest. For one, Mr. Schwartz was understandably suspicious of October's new band, given that she had no ability to play a musical instrument outside of a trombone, and had never once previously mentioned said band.

"Yumi is bringing her cousin's bass, and I'm going to learn it?" October mostly asked, though the game plan was a bit foggy for her as well.

"Don't you think you should do that *before* starting the band?" Mr. Schwartz was moving back and forth from the fridge to the kitchen table, ferrying ingredients. October followed his movements like a naval convoy.

October sighed. "I didn't *start* the band. I'm just *in* it."

"Due to your phenomenal ability to shred on the bass, I assume," Mr. Schwartz joked. "You're probably a natural Bootsy Collins."

October frowned. "I don't know who that is. But I'm not sure I like your sarcastic tone." October's father was a bit of a pretentious music snob, despite being a Phil Collins fan.

"Dad, we'll just be in the garage," October pleaded.

"You know, part of the grounding concept is that you don't get to pal around with your friends."

Though October would never in a million years have used the phrase "pal around," she had used essentially the same logic with Yumi hours earlier.

"Dad, I don't know how to play bass. Stacey is bringing a cowbell. Our band name makes no sense whatsoever, and Yumi's lyrics sound like pages from the diary of a child poisoner who can't rhyme. I *swear* this is not going to be fun at all."

Eventually, as Mr. Schwartz and his daughter sat down to an early dinner, he relented and allowed the band to rehearse in the garage. (It was likely the child poisoner comparison that won him over.) This was good news, as October had never called her friends or notified them in any way to suggest rehearsal might not happen. Shortly after dinner, the fun began. And that's "fun" in the most facetious sense of the word.

☠   ☠   ☠

October was sitting on her father's workbench, scanning through the index of *Sticksvillainy* — how bad could a book be if it had an index? — when she heard the crunch of tires in the driveway. October had opened the garage door, as she wisely realized the three of them playing music in a closed garage would likely result in hearing loss or suffocation. The drawback was they'd have under two hours of practice time before running afoul of neighbourhood noise bylaws. (Sticksville does *not* appreciate rocking and rolling all night — nor partying every day, for that matter.) As the sun fell, they also realized the well-lit garage would be something of a bug magnet.

October glanced up from her book to see the emotionless face of Mr. Takeshi behind the wheel, and — beside that face — the beaming one of Yumi, who was waving like she hoped to wind up on a baseball stadium Jumbotron. The side door of the van rolled open, and lanky Stacey MacIsaac began to unload his drum kit, piece by piece. Yumi clambered out and the three of them carried the various drum parts into the garage while Mr. Takeshi remained planted in his seat.

"Everything work out with your dad?" Yumi asked. "Is he okay with band practice happening here?"

"Yes," October huffed as she lugged the bass drum from the minivan. "We just have to seem like we're not having fun."

"We've already started," Yumi grunted as she carried a tom inside.

Once the drum parts had been fully transported to a corner of the garage, Yumi and October took out her cousin's bass and its amplifier. The bass guitar was, improbably, olive green, as if it had been camouflaged for funk bands infiltrating the Cambodian jungle.

"This looks weird," October said, in a clear understatement.

"I mean, it works," said Yumi.

"How long is that going to take him?" October asked, shoving a thumb toward Stacey, who was hunched over a snare drum, tightening and loosening screws like a medieval torturer.

Before Yumi could answer, a shadow darkened the brightly lit floor of the garage.

"Levi!" October shouted.

Levi, shoulders turned inward in a charcoal-grey hoodie, glanced around at the garage setup. "Do you guys have a band or something?" he asked.

Beyond the multiple shovels and the half-hidden Rubbermaid container of October's mom's old clothing, something resembling a band practice space was definitely being established.

"No," October said.

"Yes," Yumi countered.

"Well, not yet," October explained.

Levi looked at the members of Astaroth Night Bus with suspicion.

192

"Because I've just been too busy trying to prove your inno-cence . . ." October stammered. ". . . Obviously . . . that takes time . . ."

"Stop," Levi insisted. "It's fine if you're starting a band. I don't care. I don't own the copyright on all music. I came to see you, October."

An awkward silence fell upon the garage. The buzzing of the fluorescent lighting was somehow more overwhelming than the sound of Stacey tinkering with his drums.

"Wait," October broke the silence. "How do you know where I live?"

"Everyone knows," Levi said. "Creepy goth girl lives beside the cemetery. It's a whole thing."

October looked over to Yumi, who nodded.

The two girls scooted over to the scratched and torn couch that occupied most of the side of the garage that Mr. Schwartz's car didn't occupy and Levi joined them, flipping back his hood.

"I know you're working on a mystery and those things take time . . ." he said. "But do you have an ETA for answers? A few days? A week? You may have noticed that tensions are high at school. If I get into any more fights with the guys from Phantom Moustache or their friends, I'm gonna be suspended or expelled. So far, I've been able to keep my parents somewhat in the dark because they've been occupied with Beryl's funeral, but that won't last much longer. The school's just waiting for an opportunity to get rid of me."

"I know," October said.

"It's not just that," he continued. "Listen, not a lot of people know about this, but something happened at the funeral home last night. My great-aunt Beryl — her body . . . was disturbed. Her casket was opened. And there was salt all over the floor, tables overturned. The police said it looked like a break-in. It has to be connected. Someone's messing with my family, but I don't know why."

October wasn't about to inform Levi of the exact circumstances that left the funeral home in shambles. The truth might have alle-viated some of his concerns, but would have also led to a series of questions impossible to answer. And, truth be told, October still had no idea what Nicodemus was planning with Beryl's body.

"It's urgent, I get it. But I'm grounded because of my detective work. You think you can talk to my dad about commuting my sentence?"

Levi considered the request seriously. "I'm not all that good with parents."

"What if I did some investigating of my own?" he asked.

"That's up to you," October said, like a little goth Pontius Pilate. "Given how most people suspect you of the crime and that it looks like the school is on Phantom Moustache's side, it could make things worse. You'd have to be careful. It's safer for me to do the investigating"

"I'm not sure it can wait. I feel like things are getting worse," Levi confessed. "Like, I used to be pretty chill. I wasn't so angry all the time. You like to think your skin colour doesn't matter — you have a great punk band, you're getting along at school — but then Sticksville just swats you down to remind you. These Phantom Moustche guys push all my buttons."

"I swear I'll get to the bottom of this," October promised. "But

194

you'll need to lie low in the meantime. Stay cool. Don't get into any fights."

Levi nodded sagely.

Of October's many flaws, chief among them were (1) her keenness to make unfulfillable promises in the blink of an eye, and (2) her inability to follow her own advice. Where was the girl who advised people to "stay cool" when her face was smeared with tear-stained eyeliner or when she was viciously tussling with Ashlie Salmons within her first few weeks of high school?

Speaking of the high school villainess, her mother, Crown Attorney Salmons, was at that moment pulling her sensible four-door sedan in to the Schwartz driveway. Levi took the arrival of another guest at October's as an invitation to leave. He disappeared nearly as suddenly as the Batman. If Batman were a tad more polite. After all, October and Yumi did hear him say, "Thanks, October. I owe you," before he evaporated into the night.

October had barely peeled herself from the couch before Ms. Salmons entered their rehearsal space. It seemed like they would never get around to jamming. (For the record, I am against jamming and would advise Astaroth Night Bus to think thoroughly before taking any action that might lead down the treacherous path to becoming a jam band.)

"We're never going to get this band started," Yumi sulked, though this truth wasn't entirely Levi Marylebone's or Ms. Salmons's fault. Stacey was still in the process of arranging his drums.

"Is your father home?" Ms. Salmons asked.

"He's inside," October answered, pointing toward the front door.

With that, Ms. Salmons quickly strode out of the garage.

"What was that all about?" Yumi asked, perching cross-legged on the edge of the couch and pulling her feet up.

Though October was well aware it could have been a social visit — that her dad and the matriarch of the devilish Salmons clan could be scheming for a date or even for a smooch in her very home — she opted to give Yumi the less traumatic explanation: that her dad was likely under suspicion for robbing a teen charity fundraiser.

"They seriously think that was your dad and not some kid at the school?" Yumi was in disbelief.

"I don't know how seriously," October said. "He hasn't been arrested or even questioned by the police, but his car was one of the few that left the concert early. I think they called him a person of interest."

"No way," Yumi scoffed. "Your dad is like the dad in *To Kill a Mockingbird*."

"Atticus Finch?"

"Yeah. I mean, I trust your dad more than I'd trust *my* parents," Yumi declared.

October had always considered her dad a trustworthy and honest person, but she realized she might have to consider the alternative. After all, her mother's last name was on that Asphodel Meadows list. If her mom was possibly part of some nefarious secret society, who was to say her dad wasn't too? Maybe he'd dragged October to Sticksville so he could be closer to his secret society friends. What other reason was there to relocate to Sticksville?

October shook the thoughts away like they were pesky spiderwebs, stood, and slung the strap of the bass guitar over her shoulder.

Stacey hammered on the pedal of his bass drum. "What about my dad?" he asked. "Do you think he's more or less trustworthy than October's dad?"

"Your dad?" Yumi said, weighing Mr. MacIsaac on the dad trust scale as she unfolded what was presumably the beginning of a set list and picked herself up from the couch. "From what I know about your dad, he could be the head of organized crime across the Atlantic seaboard."

Frowning, Stacey took a seat behind his now-assembled drum kit. "Should I count us in?"

"Count us in to what?" October panicked. "What are we playing? I don't even know how to use this yet."

"Just play what feels right," Yumi cooed. "Let the bass tell you what notes to hit."

"What? No," October said. "Give me a minute to test this out."

Yumi sighed heavily. "Fine. Stacey, work on some fills. I'll do a few vocal warm-ups."

Unsurprisingly, Yumi, who had never taken vocal lessons nor sang in a choir, knew a sum total of zero vocal exercises. So instead, she began singing "Do Re Mi" from *The Sound of Music* as if she were all the von Trapps rolled into one, while October noodled around on her borrowed bass. Just as Yumi hit the line about jam and bread, she stopped, spotting the book that had tumbled out of October's backpack.

"What are you reading?" she asked.

October, realizing the veritable can of worms that book would open (about the literal worms that sometimes burrowed through the corpses of her pals), felt her heart sink.

"Oh, it's nothing."

"Just tell me," Yumi said.

"Is it a Harlequin?" Stacey asked.

"One Direction fan fiction?"

"No, it's just some local history book."

Yumi forgot her vocal exercises and picked up the book. "Wilford Scott. *Sticksvillainy*," she read. "I like the title."

"Yeah, I don't know why I borrowed it."

"Listen," Yumi said. "I have to do a report for Ms. Fenstermacher's class."

"Ms. Fenstermacher?" asked a clearly lovestruck Stacey.

"Knock it off, Stacey," Yumi chided. "We have to read a history book, write a thousand words, blah blah blah . . . And knowing Ms. Fenstermacher, she'll probably love it if I read a book of local history. She's always going on about the Sticksville Museum or whatever."

"I should probably read it too," decided Stacey. He was thinking strategically.

October figured that Beryl Gibson certainly wouldn't be expecting her book back any time soon, and the fewer of Yumi's questions she had to answer, the better.

"Take it, with my blessing," October said.

Once Yumi's upcoming history project was squared away, the newly formed band gave *actual* practising a whirl. An auspicious beginning, it was not. What at first resembled a full dishwasher being thrown down a rocky hill (in audio quality), eventually morphed into an off-time, crummy knock-off of "Another One Bites the Dust," in which Yumi repeatedly shouted "so scandalous" and "no calculus."

The infant song forming from the primordial music ooze that October, Stacey, and Yumi were pumping out was cut short by the arrival of yet another car. Though the Schwartz household was typically quiet on a weeknight (and weekend, for that matter), this evening it rivalled the activity of twenty-four-hour Tim Hortons in a small town. A white sports car pulled up behind Ms. Salmons. (I'd tell you what kind of car, but I don't know cars very well. What is this? *The Lemon-Aid Guide*?) When the engine died, not one or two, but all four members of Phantom Moustache emerged from within. And one didn't need to study their facial expressions to realize this wasn't going to be a fun meeting of bands, like when Aerosmith broke in to Run-DMC's practice space in the classic "Walk This Way" music video.

The members of Phantom Moustache moseyed into the garage (for there is no other accurate way to describe their movements) and surveyed the practice space of Astaroth Night Bus.

"What, are you guys starting a band now?" asked Taylor Young.

"Don't we already have a loser band at the school?" Preston asked his bandmates. "Scrimshaw House?"

"Crenshaw House," Yumi corrected.

"Whatever, loser."

"What are you guys doing here?" Stacey asked, rising from his kit stool.

"We were just in the neighbourhood," Taylor explained, "and wanted to show Miss Schwartz here our gratitude for spying on Ashlie and Boston."

And as the four boys in Phantom Moustache began to trash

October's garage, she came around to Levi's line of thinking: time *was* of the essence in solving the case of the missing charity money.

☠ ☠ ☠

Break Stuff

The members of Phantom Moustache treated my garage as if it were a hotel room and they were The Who or some other old band that probably only my dad and other men who wear tan shorts with brown belts and Teva sandals care about. Which is just a very long way of saying they destroyed the place. Phantom Moustache unleashed violence in our temporary practice space, and I was honestly scared for my life. Taylor Young lunged at the couch and began to pull open the cushions with a frightening rip. Devin McGriff yanked Yumi's cousin's bass from my hands and promptly hammered it against the concrete floor until the green body separated from the neck and went coasting into the driveway. Stacey moved toward the four vandals to . . . do something, I suppose. (Poke them in the eyes with his drumsticks?) But before he could extract himself from the drum kit, Boston Davis shoved him with both hands, which sent him crashing into his kit, toppling the hi-hat and the snare drum he'd so carefully arranged.

Yumi and I scrambled over to Stacey to help him to his feet, mistakenly leaving our backs turned to the angry crew of Boston's friends. Surprisingly, we weren't thrown flat on our faces. Once our drummer was upright, Yumi and I attempted to stop the boys or call my dad for help, but Devin kept wildly swinging the neck of the bass back and forth, turning himself into a deadly miniature golf course obstacle.

"Help! Dad!" I yelled, though I had no idea why all the noise hadn't already brought him running.

"Shut up, you baby!" Boston yelled. "Calling for your daddy?" He and the other band members continued to toss around garden tools, cushions, stored newspapers, and upend our backpacks, but I noticed they steered clear (pun) of damaging my dad's car. (It was almost as if they'd calculated replacement costs and realized a car was in a totally other price range than the rest of the junk in our garage.) The guys found a few of our shovels and started wailing on the other tools and containers with them.

"Preston, start the car," Boston instructed. The lanky bassist, who was a year older than his bandmates, returned to the vehicle and started it up. Were they going to ram us with their car?

"I'm gonna take those puka shells from around your neck and feed 'em to you," Yumi warned, but it was a threat without substance. Phantom Moustache had the implements of destruction, and we were helpless. The only small mercy was that they'd stopped short of actually wailing on us with the guitar neck or rake. And yes, Devin McGriff *was* still wearing a puka-shell necklace decades after that trend had run its course everywhere that was more than five kilometres from a beach.

Stacey tripped over some fallen garden tools, bringing the remaining upright cymbals down around him in an explosion of bright sounds.

"Stacey!" Yumi shouted.

Before the Phantom Moustache crew could damage much else, we heard my dad from around the corner. "October, what is that racket?!" he yelled. "What is going on out here?!"

Before either of the adults appeared or was able to see what was, indeed, making the ruckus, Phantom Moustache hopped back into their idling car — each taking one of our shovels with them — then sped off into the night. We were left in the disaster zone of the garage as my dad and Ashlie's mom arrived looking very confused. Needless to say, the inaugural practice of Astaroth Night Bus was not off to a great start.

My dad ran into the garage and pulled me into a tight hug.

"Who was that?" Ms. Salmons demanded, almost as if the drive-by vandalism were my fault. "What's happening?"

"It was the creeps in Phantom Moustache," Yumi answered, wiping her palm across her nose. "They trashed our stuff."

Crown Attorney Salmons turned on her heel and stalked back to the house. "I'm calling the police. This band nonsense is out of control."

Had I not been recovering from the trauma of a Phantom Moustache attack, I would have questioned what "nonsense" meant. This wasn't a friendly band rivalry that got out of hand; this was targeted harassment. But I imagined there would be time to discuss that with Ashlie's mom later. Crown Attorney Salmons moved very quickly when she was motivated.

"Pumpkin, are you okay?" my dad asked, turning my face to look me right in the eyes. When I nodded, he checked with Yumi, who was also merely shaken (and covered in couch stuffing). Dad then visited with Stacey to help him up and reset the drum kit. Taking a closer look at my dad righting toms and whatnot, I noted his shirt appeared to be unbuttoned a bit further than it had been before. Had he and Ms. Salmons been making out while we'd been holding band practice? Is that why it took them so long to come to our rescue? A deep shudder ran through my body. I should have checked him more closely for the smell of perfume when he brought me in for a hug. A detective must *always* be observant!

My dad, Stacey, Yumi, and I were assessing the damage in

the garage and starting to set stuff back in its proper place. A few weeks' worth of the Sunday *Loon* covered the concrete floor as if we were paper training a panther, and hoes, trowels — all sorts of garden tools — were scattered across the ground like we were in a life-sized version of Mouse Trap. Not that it wouldn't be cool under different circumstances. More troublingly, Phantom Moustache had taken a few of the extra shovels I'd purchased for official detective grave digging purposes.

"Are you sure you're okay?" Dad asked again, his hand on my shoulder. "You and your friends were attacked."

"By a bunch of losers!" Yumi shouted, tossing a ruined throw pillow back onto the couch.

"This may not seem like a big deal now, but the effects can linger," Dad advised.

Obviously, my dad meant well, and I'm not going to fault him in the least for that, but he also didn't realize that in the list of most traumatic events that had happened to me in the past month, tonight's attack ranked, like, fifth. Last night, a middle-aged psychic in Harry Potter glasses threatened to snap my neck!

"The police should be here soon," Crown Attorney Salmons announced, returning to the garage. "They said — what are you doing?!"

Ms. Salmons was horrified. She looked as if she'd come across us playing Slip 'n' Slide in sacramental wine.

"Cleaning up?" my dad said, pretty obviously.

"Sweetie, this is an active crime scene," the crown attorney reminded my dad. (And, yes, I noted the "sweetie," too, but couldn't be sure if it was a romantic thing or a totally condescending thing. Like, "Sweetie, have you ever heard of a napkin?") "Drop everything. Leave it all where you found it until the police have the chance to document."

Stacey dropped the ride cymbal as if it were on fire, and the resulting crash set everyone's teeth on edge.

"Good, good," Ms. Salmons said reluctantly. "I can't believe how this band stuff has escalated."

"Actually —" I started.

"You kids take this Bandwarz thing so seriously. I know that Moustache band — my Ashlie loves them, for some reason — was very concerned by the theft, but I tried to assure them the authorities are working on it. I mean, can't you just play music and have some fun?"

"That's what we were trying to do when your daughter's boyfriend broke our instruments." Yumi, God bless her, was still driven to speak the truth.

I glanced over at the olive-green bass — or what was left of it — and despaired.

"Yumi, your cousin's guitar . . ."

"It's okay," she said, "I think. She never uses it. And we'll just get Devin to pay for a replacement. Stacey, how does your drum stuff look?"

Stacey cocked his head like a spaniel hearing its name. "Hard to say before I try it out. But the bass drum looks intact. And most of the other stuff can take a pounding. I mean . . . that's what it's supposed to do."

We stood in our separate spots for a few minutes beyond that, suddenly concerned that a wrong footstep or turn could upset the crime scene that we'd already compromised a dozen times over. Then a police cruiser rolled into the driveway, its lights flashing but siren off.

Ms. Salmons went to the car to greet two officers: a moustached man whom I'd encountered before — the one who resembled an extra in a silent film — and a Hispanic woman I'd never seen, which was something of a surprise. At this point, I figured I'd met nearly all the police in Sticksville. In the rear of the cruiser, wedged in like subway commuters during rush hour and looking twice as sullen, were all four members of Phantom Moustache.

Seeing Boston Davis among the perps packed into a police car, Ms. Salmons had to admit her daughter's boyfriend was — all evidence would suggest — up to no good.

Ms. Salmons talked with the officers for a few moments before I began to worry. Was I supposed to trust Ashlie's mom with providing the police with the full story? I needed an advocate,

so I asked my dad to join the conversation. Dad shrugged, as if Ms. Salmons were a totally trustworthy witness even though she hadn't seen any of the things that had happened, and walked over with me to the police car. Then it occurred to me that my dad hadn't witnessed the attack either. Why was I letting the grownups tell *my* story? Facing the virtual daggers the Phantom Moustache crew were shooting in my direction with every step, I approached the old-timey moustache cop (Officer Grenouille, by his name tag) and his new partner (Officer Machado).

"Excuse me," I said. "I don't know what Ms. Salmons told you, but my friends and I were just having band practice when these guys showed up and started smashing our stuff. It was completely unprovoked!"

"The crown attorney informed us of the sequence of events," Officer Machado said.

"She wasn't even there," I insisted.

"Band practice?" Officer Grenouille asked, then took a theatrically slow look at his wristwatch. "A bit late, don't you think? Aren't you worried about noise complaints?"

Once you have a few interactions with the law, you realize police officers are, like, the all-time experts on missing the point.

"Okay, okay," the other officer said. "I think we've heard enough. Let's take a look at the damage to the garage. All of you steer clear, and don't talk to the kids in the back of the cruiser."

The police officers slowly strode into the disaster area that once was our garage, and Yumi and Stacey were politely shoved out. Even though the bare fluorescent tubes in the ceiling illuminated everything more brightly than a hospital surgery theatre, they still brought out their black-handled flashlights and pushed stuff around, prodded other things, and took more photos using their phones than kids at school did during a dance.

"I'm sorry your visit ended this way," my dad apologized to Ms. Salmons. I was outraged. As if he — or more accurately, I — were somehow to blame for a bunch of mouth-breathers dropping by to bust up part of our house. I glared at him pretty hard, but he was still locking eyes with Ashlie's mom.

"Don't apologize, Leonard," she said. "It's not as if it were unexpected. Trouble with the law seems to follow your daughter around."

I exhaled as loudly as I could and stomped over to Yumi and Stacey.

"Please talk to me before I set Ms. Salmons on fire," I demanded.

"Do you think those guys are going to get arrested?" Stacey asked.

"Pfft," scoffed Yumi, eyeballing Sticksville's finest, who were currently studying something in a couch corner. "Forget it, Stacey, it's Sticksville. The losers in Phantom Moustache will probably be elected to student council, if not just straight-up become the mayor."

"You can't have *four* mayors," Stacey reasoned.

"Whatever."

"Sir," shouted Officer Grenouille. "We need to speak with you."

The officers returned to the driveway and we civilians gathered around them.

"Mr. Schwartz," said Officer Machado, "can you explain why we found *this* shoved beneath the cushions of your couch?"

Held between her hands was a black cash box. Just above the keyhole in white ink was an imprinted label designating it property of Sticksville Central High School. She popped open the black box like a clamshell to reveal it was totally empty. The original stolen cash box from the Bandwarz night, and it was hidden in my garage. On the plus side, the kids in Crenshaw House would be glad they were no longer under suspicion.

☠   ☠   ☠

Interrogation Situation

The police interrogation of October Schwartz, such as it was, was not what she'd expected after a lifetime of watching television programs. There was no bad cop or good cop, just a moustached cop who probably had elements of both. There was no cold metal table or bare light bulb hanging from the ceiling. The police weren't even using the interrogation room — a room that October *knew* they had, because she had been inside it when the dead kids and she had broken into the police station months earlier. No, disappointingly, she was sitting on a moderately comfortable wooden chair in Officer Grenouille's office, having a relatively casual conversation about the events of the Bandwarz evening. And, given her age, October's dad, looking as exhausted and wrung out as a year-old loofah, was seated right there in the corner of the room, having insisted on being present.

October fiddled with a paperweight in the shape of a salmon on the cop's desk, glanced over at her unimpressed father, and repeated her story about the battle of the bands — how she, Yumi, and Stacey were shocked (if somewhat dubious) when Phantom Moustache claimed that Crenshaw House had threatened them, how they were just as surprised as everyone else that night that the fundraising donations had been swiped, and how she had submitted herself to the police's likely-unconstitutional search that night. Late night had progressed to morning. The early sunlight revealed all the hovering dust particles in Officer Grenouille's office;

it was positively Tony-Scott-esque. The long night was taking its toll on both the conversationalists and the dutiful dad trying his best to make sure his daughter wasn't being unduly influenced. Mr. Schwartz stifled a yawn while October rubbed the dried out mascara around her eyes with her knuckle and wondered why this interrogation couldn't have happened during regular hours. After all, it wasn't like she'd secreted time bombs around the town set to go off at daybreak; she was suspected of stealing a few thousand dollars. And beyond that, the dead kids were probably wondering what had happened to her. They probably thought Nicodemus Burke or Alyosha Diamandas had kidnapped her.

"I'm going to take a walk," Mr. Schwartz announced and slowly pushed himself out of the chair.

"You expecting someone?" the police officer joked.

"Yes, actually," October's dad answered.

October and the police officer both looked at each other as if her father had become delirious through lack of sleep. (It's a real concern.) The two remaining occupants sat in silence.

"Want to go to the washroom and wash that guck off?" a bored Grenouille asked, seemingly about October's eyeliner.

"Like, never," she answered.

"Fine," he yawned, no longer interested in stifling such things.

A minute later, Mr. Schwartz returned to his seat but seemed not the least bit refreshed by his constitutional.

"So you insist you never touched the cash box, but you've also talked at length about disliking the young men in that other band," the police officer repeated.

"Yeah, so?"

"That, little lady," the officer said condescendingly while tenting his fingers, "is what we in the police biz call a motive."

October tried to hide the complete disdain on her face. How could she communicate to him that, despite their very different ages, clothing, and feelings about facial hair, they were essentially on the same side? October was trying to solve the same mystery, and she had eliminated herself as a suspect almost immediately.

Mr. Schwartz snapped his fingers and shook his hand across his throat. "Can we cut back on the 'little lady' stuff? I don't think that's appropriate."

The police officer exhaled. Likely, he preferred interrogating suspects who were the age of majority, whose dads didn't horn in on the process. "Fine. Now you say you stayed at the concert the whole time. You didn't duck out early."

"Yes," she confirmed.

"Can anyone corroborate this story? Did anyone else see you stay for the entire concert?"

"Like a dozen people," October said, exasperated. "Yumi, Stacey, the guys in Phantom Moustache, about six teachers . . ."

Officer Grenouille was furiously jotting down this list of further interview subjects in his notepad when the imposing figure of October's former math teacher, Mr. Santuzzi, blotted out the sunrise with his entry. October's unlikely corroborator had arrived.

"Officer," he greeted Grenouille. "Mr. and Ms. Schwartz."

The officer looked up at the teacher who looked like an MMA fighter dressed in vintage knits.

"Mr. Santuzzi, you made it," October's dad smiled.

"Who are you?" Officer Grenouille asked the man in his doorway.

"I'm one of Ms. Schwartz's teachers," Mr. Santuzzi said.

"Why are you here?" October asked. The sergeant didn't seem to mind that she had become the asker of questions.

"Your father called me," he said, nodding to the rumpled man in the corner. "He sounded somewhat pathetic over the phone, so I thought I'd come down to the station before classes start to see if I could help clear some things up."

"Sir," Officer Grenouille said, pen at the ready, "can you confirm this young lady never left the building during the Bandwarz concert held at your high school?"

And once again, Mr. Santuzzi — whose own moustache outshone the police officer's in terms of sheer majesty — became October's unlikely saviour, corroborating (there's that word again — it means "verifying") her story of being on site the entire night of the theft. Of course, this being a crime interview, Mr. Santuzzi was asked a number of questions about October's version of events, and the stolid math teacher answered them all, robot-like, never wavering. He noted he was out in the parking lot for the duration of the concert, much as he had informed police in an earlier interview, so he was not privy to a number of the evening's details — the searing rock songs and the like — but he was still very aware of who came and went.

Naturally, in the midst of exonerating October, Mr. Santuzzi was impelled to repeat his anecdote about how all the school's exits were locked, save the front entrance, and how only three vehicles left the premises early during the concert: the car containing the members of Crenshaw House, Mr. Schwartz (solo), and a strange shark-like car with fins. Which only drew further suspicion to the other member of the Schwartz family in the room: October's dad.

"You're free to go," the police officer told October, folding his notebook closed. "Seems your story checks out. But I *will* have to keep your father here for a few more questions."

Somehow, even when Mr. Santuzzi helped out, he made things worse.

"Mr. Santuzzi, would you mind giving October a ride to school?" her dad asked with the saddest head tilt you can imagine. October wondered if he even knew Santuzzi's first name. After spending several hours at the police station, Mr. Schwartz faced more questioning in much the same manner as an eighteenth-century French aristocrat faced the guillotine after spending all day in a queue. "Pumpkin, this will be resolved in no time. I'm sure I'll be there in time for our science class."

Mr. Santuzzi — of *course* — did not mind. Though October had spent the first several months of school carefully avoiding car rides to school with her dad to protect against potential embarrassment, her work was now about to be entirely undone by a ride with her math teacher. She only hoped they'd arrive so early no one would spot them together. Hopefully, he didn't want to stop for coffee or something.

The unlikely pair exited the police station and crossed the parking lot to Mr. Santuzzi's car, which seemed to have been purchased in the same era as all of Mr. Santuzzi's wardrobe. For inexplicable reasons, he had parked in a far corner of the lot, though there were literally *no* other vehicles in sight.

"Mr. Santuzzi," October paused a moment before opening the passenger-side door. "Thanks."

"There's no need, Ms. Schwartz," he said matter-of-factly. "You shouldn't have to thank people for telling the truth or doing what's simply right."

Then he got into the driver's seat and they began their awkward, silent drive to Sticksville Central High School.

☠   ☠   ☠

Aside from being delivered to the high school by the strict, possibly bewigged math teacher whom everybody loathed, there were a number of other issues with October's journey to school that morning. Most notably, October was still wearing yesterday's clothes and had no chance to shower or brush her teeth or even complete her verging on obsessive deodorization routine. She was arriving at school with bad breath and body odour and greasy hair (and not the *good* kind of greasy), and the situation would only deteriorate as the day wore on. If she'd been an outcast at Sticksville Central on her best hygiene day, she shuddered to think

213

what might happen to her social standing after a fitful sleep-free night at the police station.

Conventional wisdom suggests one must experience rock bottom to undergo real growth and change, but in reality, October Schwartz had never *not* been at rock bottom.

Mr. Santuzzi parked his car in the mostly empty lot and the unlikely duo walked to the school's front doors. About forty minutes remained until the opening bell, so few students (or any people, really) were present. October still expected she would drive anyone inside away with the waves of stench she assumed were radiating out from her body like a Spirograph design. But before she could hightail it to the washroom for a dry shower, October and Mr. Santuzzi (who refused to hang back or turn a corner so the two wouldn't be walking conspicuously together) were intercepted by history buff Ms. Fenstermacher.

"Good morning, Mr. Santuzzi," she said. "Do you mind if I borrow October for a minute?"

"Ms. Fenstermacher," he answered. "By all means. My business with Ms. Schwartz has concluded."

Ms. Fenstermacher looked at Mr. Santuzzi as if he'd been speaking in Tagalog, which — for all intents and purposes — he might as well have been. She then beckoned October to follow her to her classroom. As if the two of them were in a deadly boring new Aaron Sorkin television show about public schools, Ms. Fenstermacher started the conversation as they walked.

"Remember you asked me about that psychic, Nicodemus Burke?"

October felt like three lifetimes had passed since she'd spoken to her former history teacher about that. There had been so many revelations and police interactions since. Nicodemus Burke had been patting down corpses and had even tried to attack her! She just figured Ms. Fenstermacher had forgotten all about him — why would she look into him any further? Unless she thought there was something strange about him too.

"Of course," October said, careful not to open her mouth too widely in case the bad breath seeped out.

"Did you know he was at the concert night?" she asked,

throwing open her classroom door. "I met with him last night. Even got a reading."

"You did?" October said. Since Ms. Fenstermacher was alive, October assumed Burke hadn't tried to murder or maim her, too.

"Butterscotch candy?" Ms. Fenstermacher asked. At first, October thought she was having a stroke or speaking in code, but then saw her former teacher was holding out a bunch of Buxton's Original Butterscotch Candy, usually something only grandparents purchased. For some reason, October assumed Ms. Fenstermacher was too young to truck in such depressing candy choices.

"Oh, thanks." October normally despised the candy — a far cry from a decent bonbon like an Everlasting Gobstopper or Tic Tac, but she figured it might help her breath situation.

"So, the Burke guy seems legit," she said, approaching her blackboard and inscribing it with a few words. "Or as legit as these supposed clairvoyants get. It's hard to tell, but he wasn't an *obvious* fraud. Despite his hokey appearance."

"Really?" October wasn't that surprised, as he seemed to know his way around a salt circle.

"Really. The things he was doing all check out with what little I know about magic and wiccan stuff," she said. "I could hardly believe it either."

"Hmm," October said, looking downward in a stance that aimed to combine thoughtfulness with a subtle nose check of her armpits.

"Yeah, he told me if I wanted a follow-up session, I should book it soon. Apparently he closes his little shop for the summer and heads over to the fairground," Ms. Fenstermacher continued. "He said he does a lot of business there. Which reminds me: remember you asked about an Underground Railroad stop near the fairgrounds?"

"Yeah," October said, suddenly perking up. "There's supposed to have been a terminus there."

"Guess whose historical society just successfully delayed a permanent fairground ride construction until a full archaeological dig of the site can be done?" Ms. Fenstermacher stood there, grinning like she'd had a canister of nitrous oxide for breakfast.

"Yours?" October ventured.

"Yes!" she shouted. "More accurately, the *Sticksville* Historical Society was responsible, but we're one and the same. Starting in June, the university will undertake a full archaeological investigation into that spot where they were building the Sharktacular Plunge ride."

"But they hold the fair every summer, don't they?" October asked. "What made the city change their minds this time around?"

"It's the ride itself," Ms. Fenstermacher said, proudly unveiling a copy of the day's *Sticksville Loon*. The construction delay had made the front page. October wondered if it was just wishful thinking to hope she wouldn't make a future edition's police blotter with the petty thieves and public drunks. "The Sharktacular Plunge, because it's some sort of water ride, involves actual digging on the site, potentially damaging historical artifacts. All the other fairground stuff is just tied down with water barrels and stakes. There are no backhoes ripping up the ground. So, the fair will happen this summer as it does every year — just without a shark ride."

"Oh, man. I know so many people who were looking forward to that ride," October lied. She was secretly having other misgivings about the dig.

"They've been advertising it everywhere. I almost feel bad," Ms. Fenstermacher said with a grin (that suggested she didn't exactly feel terrible). "But a proper archaeological dig must be done."

October was thinking, hopefully, that an actual historical investigation into the fairground site could uncover clues that would really help in Tabetha's mystery. But she also assumed a thing like a "proper archaeological dig" took a long time — months, maybe years! — and October didn't have that kind of time. Tabetha and the dead kids had less than a week

216

before the next full moon. Then they'd disappear for a month. And Tabetha, October felt it safe to assume, wasn't keen to wait around for several months before someone else's literal digging helped to uncover what they'd been figuratively digging for. October thought maybe the Dead Kid Detective Agency might have to do some proper archaeological excavations of their own — now that she knew the proposed site of the Sharktacular Plunge was an ace place to start.

"That's great news, Ms. Fenstermacher," October smiled. "Local historical society gets action! Congratulations."

"Thanks. I'll keep you posted on what the study uncovers, if you're interested."

"Please do," October said, leaving Ms. Fenstermacher's room for her own class, though, really, she hoped she learned anything there was to know about the site before her history teacher did.

☠   ☠   ☠

After the extended conversation about local amusements and oracles, October barely made it to English in time, so it was lunchtime before she saw Yumi and Stacey again. Both friends were relieved she was not imprisoned.

"I couldn't believe it!" Yumi shouted, punching her graffitied binder with her fist. "Phantom Moustache trashes our band stuff and they arrest *you*. Never trust a cop, I tell you."

"Isn't your uncle a police officer?" Stacey asked.

"Yes, and I trust him as far as I can throw him," she confirmed. "And that's not far at all. The man is a refrigerator. An *untrustworthy* refrigerator."

"Anyway, glad you're out of the joint," Stacey mumbled.

"Yeah," October agreed. "I never thought I'd be so relieved to be at school. But I'm a bit worried about my dad now. I had to leave him at the station. The cops wanted to know why he left the concert early that night."

"Don't worry," Yumi assured. "The swift arm and hammer of justice will come crashing down on whoever really stole the money — *Phantom Moustache* — soon enough."

As the three made their way to the cafeteria, October pulled Yumi aside, leaving Stacey to stroll along while obliviously blasting his archaic Walkman, and said, "Speaking of arm and hammer, can you smell me?"

"Smell you?" Yumi looked like October asked her to break into the Smithsonian and steal the Declaration of Independence.

"I was at the police station all night and never got the chance to go home. Smell me. I need to make sure I don't reek."

Yumi, who was already basically at October's armpit height, leaned cautiously forward and inhaled deeply.

"You're safe," she said.

"For real?"

"Arid extra-dry," she added.

It was while the two good friends were in the midst of this pit-iful display that their good enemy, Ashlie Salmons, came across them in the hall. Upon sighting October, Yumi, and — at a distance, lost in his portable music player — Stacey, Ashlie Salmons's face bloomed into a fuchsia rage. She stormed right up to the trio, elbowing other schoolmates aside, and invaded their personal space.

"I am so mad at you primordial monsters right now, you should probably leave the school before I go atomic," she warned in an outside voice.

"Atomic like *explosion* or like *very small*?" asked Yumi. October felt less flippant about Ashlie's mood. She'd been on Ashlie's bad side before and was in no rush to see what new and inventive revenge she had planned.

"Because of you idiots and your loser band, my mom says I can't see Boston anymore!" she shouted, her slender finger waving back and forth among the faces of the (former) members of the short-lived Astaroth Night Bus.

"That's not our fault, Ashlie," October insisted.

"Yeah," Yumi chimed in, folding her arms and thrusting her chest out like a tiny silverback gorilla. "If your homicidal boyfriend hadn't shown up and smashed all our gear, this never would have happened."

"Don't change the subject," Ashlie said.

"This is *literally* the same subject!" Yumi noted.

And while October would have liked to help defend her friend Yumi in this skirmish of words with Ashlie Salmons, she spied a fellow student one hallway over and felt the need to escape the conversation. Levi Marylebone was in the building and she needed to have a word with him.

"Hey, Levi!" October shouted and left the tense hallway conversation with no preamble.

"Bye." Stacey waved to October's swiftly escaping figure.

"Shut up, you goon!" Ashlie commanded.

There was a lot of semi-witty repartee back and forth following that exchange, but as narrator, I must direct your attention, dear readers, to another conversation: between October and the lead singer of Crenshaw House.

"Levi, wait up!" October shouted, annoyed that Levi was making her jog.

Levi seemed somewhat in a hurry, distracted in his conversation with October, as if he hadn't just dropped by her house late last night. Suddenly this guy had all sorts of appointments like he was the executive producer of *Everybody Loves Raymond* or something.

"What is it?" he said.

"What is it?" October repeated. Then, turning momentarily into her dad, "How about 'hello'?"

"Sorry. *Hello*," he added. "I just got catcalled in the parking lot this morning. I'm not in the best mood."

"I'm sorry. I'm in a bad mood, too," October said. "I haven't slept."

"What do you mean?" Levi asked.

"After you left, Phantom Moustache dropped by and trashed the garage," October said. "Then I got to spend all night with the police because they found the cash box in the couch."

"Phantom Moustache must have put it there when you weren't looking," Levi fumed. He turned back and forth, seemingly looking for a phone book (ask your parents) to tear in half.

"Well, *I* certainly didn't steal that cash box, and my dad didn't steal it, though the police saw fit to interrogate him for some reason," October complained. "But how can I prove anything?"

"They're weirdly clever," Levi chewed on his lip. "For a bunch of idiots."

October outlined the central bugaboo with accusing Phantom Moustache. "The issue remains that they were onstage when the cash box was stolen, and they never left the school. So how would they have even got hold of the box in the first place?"

"Maybe the moustache isn't the only thing," Levi said, pulling his hoodie over his head, "that's phantom."

October scowled. "What, they're ghosts now? And a sheet of your lyrics was left in the cash box . . . which is weird."

"Not if someone was trying to put the blame on us," Levi insisted. "Someone who is racist and unpleasant."

October's mind returned to that unpleasant thought: Where would someone else even find Crenshaw House lyrics? It's not like they were Rick Astley. Who had even heard their songs before Bandwarz?

Levi saw the doubt slowly appear on October's face. "Don't even think it, Schwartz. Not *you* too. We trusted you to help us."

However, no matter how sincere Levi seemed, or how much she wanted him and all of Crenshaw House to be innocent, she couldn't entirely rule him out as the thief. Not that she'd ever tell him that out loud. But she didn't have to, because Crown Attorney Salmons, the skinny arms and hammers of justice herself, made an unpleasant appearance in their school hallway to do that very thing.

"Ms. Salmons?" October asked.

"October," she said with a curt nod. "Mr. Marylebone, I've been looking for you. Your first-period teacher said you never made it to class."

Levi looked down at the floor. "I know . . . I."

"I'm not a truant officer, Levi," she said. "But I would like to speak to you . . ."

"Okay, about what?"

". . . down at the station," Crown Attorney Salmons continued. "According to Miss Schwartz's police report, you just popped by to say hi to her less than an hour before the cash box was found in her garage. Odd, isn't it?"

"October," Levi groaned as if she'd slid a sharpened awl between his ribs.

"No — Levi didn't do anything, Ms. Salmons," October protested.

But the Sticksville crown attorney was already escorting Levi Marylebone to the office. "We'll have to notify your parents before we take you for questionioning, Levi. You understand, we just like to be sure in these matters, October."

☠   ☠   ☠

Can You
Dig It?

Dad, I'm relieved to say, arrived for science class just a couple minutes after the national anthem. But I left school ignorant of Levi's fate. And though he seemed like a nice enough guy, we weren't really friends — we'd hardly spoken before the other week — so I had no way of contacting him or his family. I thought about getting in touch with Henry, but the awkwardness I envisioned from that conversation deterred me. Left with nothing to do about Levi until morning, I shifted focus to Tabetha Scott and the new revelations about the fairground.

If I were to believe Ms. Fenstermacher — and I had no reason to *dis*believe her — it was only because construction work had begun on the Sharktacular Plunge at the fairgrounds that her historical society was able to get the area designated as a historical site. Apparently a backhoe or whatever — I'm not Bob the Builder — uncovered some sort of wooden structure they weren't expecting to see. Some of the older settlements near Acheron Creek had been buried and built over decades ago to make way for the fairgrounds. Ms. Fenstermacher and her volunteer group were able to convince people that it was a location of historical significance: potentially a portion of the Underground Railroad.

For me, this meant the dead kids and I now had a starting point for searching the ruins of the Underground Railroad site. All I had to do was figure out the best way to sneak myself and six shovels out of the house. But as I sat in school, waiting for the final period of the day to conclude, I realized I no longer had six shovels. Phantom Moustache had taken three. I was a few short. Plus, getting new shovels and getting to the fairground both seemed impossible. After all, I was technically still grounded — being arrested and falsely accused of a crime hadn't garnered me any sympathy from Dad. Leaving the house for any reason besides school was strictly forbidden.

But I had a plan: challenge Dad to a competitive game of Scrabble immediately after dinner — a challenge Dad could seldom refuse. Most of our Scrabble matches would go far into the night, but Dad had been up the night before talking to the police. He'd probably tap out by eight, falling asleep confident that his daughter was good and wholesome and interested in nothing more than family board games. She wasn't hanging out with corpses or desecrating heritage sites. That would be ghoulish and ridiculous. And if he was asleep by eight, that gave me just enough time to get to the hardware store and buy a few more shovels. The only drawback was that I, too, spent all night awake at the very same police station. I'd be lucky if I didn't fall into a coma by last period.

My carefully crafted plan (okay, maybe it wasn't *that* careful) proved totally unnecessary. My dad was not having one of his better evenings. I went home straight after school, as per the conditions of my grounding, but Dad didn't cross the threshold until closer to six. And when he did, he said hello, mentioned he was late because he had to return to the police station following class to answer more questions, and then closed himself off in his room. Well, that wasn't entirely accurate. Dad left the door open a sliver so that I knew not to worry. He was just in the midst of a mild-to-severe depressive episode (I say "just" as in "the landslide *just* killed four people"), but nothing I should be concerned about unless this state persisted for another few days.

I set to work making myself a healthy meal of Kraft Dinner while the sounds of Fleetwood Mac's "Gold Dust Woman" blared from my dad's bedroom down the hall. What the song had to do with my dad's mental state was beyond me: Was Ashlie's mom the Gold Dust Woman? What exactly did being a Gold Dust Woman entail? Whatever it meant, the song was going into its sixth rotation when I knocked and left a plate of Kraft Dinner by his door.

In the beginning, when Dad had just been diagnosed with clinical depression, I found these phases of my dad's illness frustrating to the extreme. Every time, I worried he'd never get out of the depression — this would be the one that broke him — and all I could do was feel helpless. And with each downturn, I blamed myself. He was depressed because Mom left. He was depressed because I was spending all night in the cemetery. Most recently, he was depressed because some stupid band fight had made him of interest to the police. Even though there was very little I could do besides make sure he got fed and got help when he really needed it, I'd preoccupy myself with how I could be helping more.

But now, as much as I hated to admit it, Dad's depression often provided a very convenient opportunity for me to sneak out and work with the dead kids. Though I made sure I only took advantage of this opportunity when it seemed safe to do so. Dad picked up the KD and thanked me before apologizing and retreating to the recesses of his room again.

A few minutes later, I decided it was safe to make an excursion to the hardware store. I crept quietly, easing the front door open with the gentlest push, but the truth was, I could have dragged a garbage bag full of chandeliers down the hall and Dad wouldn't have left the bedroom.

☠   ☠   ☠

The entry chime of Beaver Lumber sounded as I slid through the front door, just about ten minutes before close. To be honest, I wasn't even sure if the hardware store was open during the day. I only frequented it as late as possible. And, as per usual during evening shifts, Goth Hardware Clerk (his

225

real name was Percy, like he was the secret son of Poseidon or something) leaned against the front counter, looking bored as could be. Though he was wearing fingerless black motorcycle gloves, he was busying himself embroidering a square of fabric with what appeared to be the Misfits logo.

"Look who's back," he said, which was strange. I had literally visited the store a grand total of three times. Like, I'd been to Niagara Falls two times already, and nobody there would say, "Look who's back," if I went again.

"Hi, Percy?" I said it as a question, as if I could ever forget *that* name. "I'm just . . . I need a shovel."

"You know where they live," he said, not breaking his concentration on his needlework.

I turned to head down the far aisle, when Percy raised his head from his craft to talk music. "You go to Sticksville Central, right? Do you know Crenshaw House?"

As I might have expected, the Goth Hardware Clerk knew all about Crenshaw House and was a big fan — despite the band having only what could be deemed mild goth leanings. Percy lamented that they allegedly had stolen a significant amount of money, and while I have to admit I really did enjoy talking to Percy, I was also very aware the store he worked at was closing in about five minutes.

But then Percy's position as the gothest Beaver Lumber stock boy and cashier gave me an idea. "Hey, in the past month or so, did anyone buy a cash box?"

"Like, about a thousand people," he said. "We sell at least one a day. Some high school kid from student council bought, like, five of them the other week."

Scratch that idea. Too many cash boxes being purchased.

"I should go get my shovels," I said.

That's when Goth Hardware Clerk leaned in conspiratorially and gestured for me to do the same. For a hot second, I thought he might give me a shovel for free. (Such were the wild fantasies I harboured.)

"There's a creepy John Waters–looking guy in the last row," he whispered. "Consider this a heads-up."

226

My blood ran cold — an expression I hadn't really understood before. I thought it might feel refreshing, but it wasn't pleasant at all. Alyosha Diamandas — because who else in Sticksville fit that description? — and I were in the same hardware store, late at night. And it had been just days since he'd trapped me in a funeral home where his psychic friend had tried to kill me. I was faced with a difficult choice: skip the shovels and see how quickly the dead kids and  I could dig with three, or confront one of my least favourite people in town. (It was a growing list, with a lot of jockeying for position.)

"October Schwartz," the realtor said, drawing out the z. (In case it's not clear, I decided on the confrontation.) "Shopping for shovels? I wonder why that could be."

"Listen, we both shouldn't have been at that funeral home," I said. Already I worried I'd made the wrong choice. "We don't even need to talk about it. Just don't throw salt on me or whatever."

I gently edged past Diamandas, who was wearing a black button-down shirt with little white polka dots, to reach the shovels.

"I am glad to see you, actually," he said to the back of my head. "I wanted to apologize."

"You wanted to apologize?"

Though I know it's not possible, I swear Alyosha's thin moustache twitched in response.

"Two minutes until close!" Percy shouted from somewhere near the front cash.

"My associate, Nicodemus, was out of line," Alyosha continued, his head lowered and palms facing upward in supplication.

"He nearly killed me," I said.

"I would like you to know that, since the evening in question, I have broken ties with him."

That was something, at least. But why was I even having this conversation with Alyosha Diamandas? "Who is that guy? Why are you friends with him?"

"I don't need to tell you that I do not enjoy the . . . *ghosts*." He whispered the last word and picked nervously at a tag on a garden spade. "Ghosts scared me when I was growing up in the old country. Now they plague me in my work. Believe me, I take no issue with you, as a vampire girl or whatever you are. But Nicodemus — he was to help me get rid of the ghost children."

"You need help back there?" yelled Percy, who must have been at least a bit alarmed that I had engaged in a dialogue with Gomez Addams.

"But why were you there?" I asked Alyosha. Best, I figured, to stop talking about ghost children, before he asked me a whole bunch of prying questions about them.

"Let it be known that I love a deal," he almost chuckled. This was an understatement. If someone told me that Alyosha Diamandas did his own dentistry, I wouldn't doubt it. "Nicodemus, he offered to help me with the ghost children — keep them out of my business — if I could drive him on some errands."

Some errands? What was this, some sort of twisted *Driving Miss Daisy*?

"He wanted for me to drive him around," Alyosha explained. "Be a chauffeur. He could only borrow the car from his work every once in a while."

This confused me, as I was pretty certain a town psychic was typically self-employed. Was it possible he worked for the town? Was my dad's property tax paying for that?

228

"But what errand, exactly, were you doing at the funeral home?" I asked.

Alyosha sighed and scratched where his scalp met his hairline, which was nearly at the back of his skull. "He was looking for something. He said the deceased woman — she took something that belonged to him."

"Closing time," Percy announced. "Don't make me sing the song, you two."

Alyosha and I made our way to the cash register with our separate purchases. Alyosha was buying a planter, but then told Percy he'd pay for my three shovels as well. Goth Hardware Clerk gave me a look to check that this weird transaction wasn't putting me in any sort of danger, but I let him know with a nod it was fine.

"Perhaps we can call this a truce," Alyosha Diamandas suggested as he left the lumber store. "Enjoy your shovels."

I watched as Diamandas went to open the passenger door of his Yaris outside, but instead slid his planter in through the broken window. He took a seat behind the shattered windshield. It made me regret telling Tabetha to break it. And, in retrospect, he really should have picked up a window repair kit while he was at Beaver Lumber. Nevertheless, shortly before trying to dig my way to the Underground Railroad, I made a truce with Sticksville's weirdest real estate agent.

☠ ☠ ☠

When I arrived at our usual meeting place near the large willow tree, the dead kids couldn't help but notice the pile of shovels I was hauling. (It probably didn't help that I was panting and nearly collapsed in a heap when I arrived, dumping the heavy load on the cemetery ground.)

"What's with all the shovels?" Derek asked. "We already told you Tabetha's not even buried here."

"Yeah," I said between deep breaths, my hands on my knees, "but I have news. Construction crews uncovered a structure they think might be part of the Underground Railroad site at the fairgrounds, so we've got to check it out and see what we can find before anyone else does. It could be that store-house where your last memory is from, Tabetha. What if we find something? We could even find your body! This could be the key to solving your mystery."

"Checkin' it out involves diggin'?" Tabetha asked.

"Yes," I said, "and *all* of us digging. There are *six* shovels here. No 'supervising' like last time, Kirby."

"But my left arm *just* grew back," he pouted.

"How *much* digging?" Cyril asked.

"I don't know . . . depends on what we find."

"I thought this Underground Railroad wasn't supposed t'be actually underground," Morna said.

"True," I agreed. "But this is a different situation. The land it was on got filled in and built over."

"And it took hours to get to the fairgrounds last time," Morna pointed out. "Are we even gonna have time t'dig?"

My Scottish ghost friend made a solid point. This is the main reason we stole — or rather, *borrowed* — a car: to make our way to the fairgrounds much, much faster.

Breaking into a car is the easiest thing in the world for the dead kids — simple as getting past any other locked door. Sadly, hotwiring a stolen vehicle wasn't yet in their skill set. (I made a mental note to look into it before our next caper. I wondered if there was a sort of training academy for enterprising juvenile delinquents.) So, the only logical remaining choice was to steal my dad's car.

The dead kids followed me back to my house, shovels in hand. They waited outside as I slipped back inside through the sliding glass door and retrieved the car keys from a repurposed ashtray on the hallway table. The vocals of Stevie Nicks mer-cifully disguised the jingle of the keys and, before long, I was standing in the driveway with my dead friends.

As dissociative as my dad could sometimes be during a depressive episode, I still feared the sound of a car ignition right outside his window would rouse his suspicion. So I popped Dad's car into neutral, and we slowly rolled the car down the driveway and into the street. I wasn't comfortable starting the engine until we were at least six houses away from home. And luckily, no one else was out and about on our street, as I doubt they'd have believed I was able to push a two-ton Volkswagen by my lonesome. (The five invisible dead kids, their various levels of physical strength aside, were a significant help.)

Cyril took the driver's seat, with me riding shotgun and the others and shovels in the back. Though Sticksville's streets were pretty deserted any given night — the exception being when there were big social events like Bandwarz or the fair during the summer — it was important for me to sit up front so I could hop into the driver's seat if we spotted anyone else on the road. As a frequently arrested police suspect, I had no desire to draw any undue suspicion. And as suspicious as it was for a thirteen-year-old to be driving, it was *way* more suspicious for a car to have no driver at all.

And so, Cyril — the only enthusiastic driver amongst us, despite dying over a hundred years prior to the internal combustion engine even being a thing — drove us shakily, but without real incident to the site of the Sticksville Fairgrounds.

☠   ☠   ☠

Cyril pulled my dad's Volkswagen Golf into the fair's mostly deserted parking lot shortly after ten. The moon in the sky provided some decent light to augment the streetlamps, but also reminded me how little time I had left before the next full moon, when the dead kids would disappear again. The moonlight was a big advantage, but I'd packed a few flashlights in my bag, just in case. There was no way I could rely on there being any light at the fairground when the fair was at least a month from opening. And with the flashlights, I could guarantee we could see what we were digging.

Cyril parked a few spaces over from a bizarre vehicle, obviously some kind of promotion for the new ride that Ms. Fenstermacher and friends had delayed. It was a sports car, steel-grey, made to look like a shark. Fins and sharp teeth had been painted along the sides, with bold blue lettering that read *Sharktacular!*

"It's a car with fins!" I shouted, pointing frantically, Mr. Santuzzi's description now clear to me.

"Yes, and it looks ridiculous," Kirby assessed.

"Straight-up ugly." Derek, for once, was in total agreement with LaFlamme.

"No, it's a clue that I'd been missing," I tried to explain, "from my other mystery — the one about the stolen money." I turned to face the dead kids in the rear of the car and immediately saw Tabetha's expression, eyebrow raised and eyelids narrowed to show she was the opposite of impressed.

"Sorry," I said. "I'll try to focus on the mystery at hand."

Still, as we exited my dad's car and made our way to the diggers and bulldozers in the distance, I could only wonder who at school had a parent or older sibling who worked at the fairgrounds. It now seemed undeniable that the only other car that left Bandwarz early — besides those carrying Crenshaw House and my dad — was promoting the fair's Sharktacular Plunge. And that was the odd thing. Given the sudden arrival of the cash box in my garage, it seemed certain someone in Phantom Moustache stole the money. But they all seemed like spoiled rich kids. It was difficult to imagine any of them as the children of carnies.

The dead kids and I trudged through grass that hadn't been mowed since last summer until we came upon a rectangle of land that had been dug about four feet deep. The northwest corner of the dirt square was guarded by a golden construction vehicle. (Not, like, *gold* golden. Just a darker shade of yellow.) In another corner of the rectangle was a shabby-looking half-excavated wooden structure, the roof of which had been rotted through. Clearly, this is what the crew building the Sharktacular Plunge had found that caused them to stop.

"This is it," Tabetha said, moving toward the corner occupied by the shack as if hypnotized. "I remember this storehouse. This is where my dad n' me were dropped off. It's where I saw those candles that last day."

She hopped down into the massive hole, carrying her shovel. "Be careful!" I called.

Tabetha continued to move forward, now inches from the dilapidated structure, gently caressing it with her hand.

"I think this is the place," Kirby deadpanned.

Derek hopped into the monster crater to join her, but instead of gazing deeply at the partially uncovered building, he began to dig.

"We should get started," he said.

I took my shovel and made my own less-than-sharktacular plunge into the hole, nearly twisting my ankle in the process. The ground wasn't very even. The other dead kids joined us and began to haphazardly stab the ground with their shovels.

"Wait," I said. "We can't just dig up this entire square! We need a plan."

"Yes, but what would that be?" Cyril asked. He dragged a clammy hand across his forehead, smearing it with a fresh splotch of dirt. I'd forgotten how messy digging could be.

"Tabetha," I asked, resting my foot on the blade of the shovel. "Is seeing this place bringing back any more memories for you?"

It was a dumb question. Tabetha had been staring wide-eyed at the shanty for the past minute.

"Yes, I remember seeing the candles . . ." she began. "When I went to dump the trash that Mr. Burnhamthorpe had left on our lawn."

"You actually entered this rat trap willingly?" Kirby asked, disgusted.

"I'm sure it looks much worse now, Kirby," Morna said. "It's been buried underground fer years."

"Candles were set out and still lit, even though it was morning," Tabetha continued as if she couldn't hear the other kids running rifftrax over the tale of her untimely death. "Who would light candles during the day? I'd been in the storehouse before — it's where my dad n' me came t' town. Where the Quakers found us n' told us we'd made it to Canada."

"And what happened when you came back here, Tabetha? On the day you were going to the dump?" I asked. She was remembering a lot — and in detail. This was way more vivid than what Morna or Cyril had remembered. Maybe contact with the actual structure was having a positive effect.

"This is where I died," Tabetha announced. "I know it."

"Are you sure?" Derek said, still insistent on digging, despite a lack of plan.

"I died here," she repeated. "I remember it was hot that mornin', n' the garbage smelled. I knew I was gettin' close to the dump because it smelled so ripe. But I saw the candles n' thought that was weird, so I came inside. The place hadn't been used for the Underground Railroad for a while, but there was still bedding, a couple wooden chairs, a mug. Almost as if someone had been livin' there. I remember there was a big, thick book n' a ring on the table."

"What book?" Derek asked.

"I dunno. I can't read, *remember?*" Tabetha snapped. (She'd heard *that* comment, at least.) "I just remember it looked big. N' old. I think it had gold on the pages."

"Like gold leaf?" Kirby asked.

"What's that?" Derek asked.

"Shut up," Tabetha said. "I'm rememberin'."

"What was the ring like?" Derek asked, hauling up more rocks and dirt.

"Was it a wedding ring?" Morna asked.

"No, no," Tabetha insisted. "It wasn't a plain thing . . . it had some kind of weird jewel in it."

"So, like an engagement ring?" I said.

"No, not like that, either," she said, though none of us knew what that meant.

"Was it an *ear*ring?" Derek panted.

"No. I know it was green," she said. "Or the stone was green . . . I remember I stuck it in my boot when I heard someone coming."

"You stole it?" Morna asked.

"Stole it from a murderer!"

"An emerald?" Cyril asked.

"Somethin' like that. The ring looked like a . . . like a spider."

"So tacky," Kirby decided.

"Shhh," Tabetha said. "I was still lookin' at the book, suddenly worried I'd busted inta somebody's new home. How'd I know someone hadn't escaped from some plantation in South Carolina t'come up here? But the sun was high n' I saw the shadow of a person blot out the sunlight on the back wall."

"Who?"

"That's all I remember," Tabetha said, exhaling heavily.

Derek dropped his shovel, and he and Morna started flipping through their notepad.

"Did it look like the shadow of a mayor or a pharmacist?" Morna asked.

"What?!" Tabetha shouted, finally turning to face the rest of us. "What's a mayor's shadow look like? Or a pharmacist's?"

"Maybe it was holding a vial of something?" Morna asked.

"Noah Sinclair, town mayor; Virgil Cooper, shipbuilder; Yancey Burnhamthorpe, pharmacist," Derek recited from the page where he'd written down the names and occupations of the three suspects the author of *Sticksvillainy* liked best.

"Well, we can be pretty sure it wasn't the shipbuilder," Cyril asserted, laying the shovel across his shoulders.

"Pfft," Kirby spat. "What we can be pretty sure of is that that book and ring were things important to Asphodel Meadows."

"Ya think?" Morna said and winked. (It was odd.)

"I dunno, guys, I just don't know," Tabetha moaned. "I jus' know that whatever happened after I saw that shadow is what killed me."

Tabetha seemed on the verge of tears. The memories flooding back — not to mention the gruelling (and just plain annoying) interrogation we'd just subjected her to — were obviously taking their toll.

"Let's slow down," I said. "We don't need to ask any more questions right now. We know for sure this is where Tabetha died. So let's let her sit with those awful feelings and just keep digging. And maybe we can move *inside* the storehouse?"

"Inside that?" Kirby seemed in mild disbelief, though I'd certainly asked him to do about a hundred things more unpleasant.

"It's pretty dark, October," Derek agreed. "I don't know how we'd see what we're digging."

"That's why I brought these," I said, retrieving the three flashlights from my backpack. "What, do you think I'm new to this?"

☠ ☠ ☠

Tabetha and I took a break after a couple hours of digging. This was solid digging, too — no loafing around (this brief break aside). I had no real idea of when and if the construction crew would be back in the morning, and I really didn't want them to find a bunch of corpses messing up their site. We had managed to affix the flashlights onto the roof rafters, so the dead kids and I had a good view of what we were excavating, but we hadn't uncovered any of the stuff Tabetha had mentioned earlier — no candles or chairs or mugs.

"The others aren't gonna like that we're taking a break," Tabetha noted, staring into the portion of the field where tents and rickety amusement park rides had already been erected. I have no idea if Tabetha had ever seen a ride before. When had the Ferris Wheel been invented?

"We're looking into your death," I shot back. "They can cut you some slack."

"Yeah, I guess," she relented.

"And since when do you care what any of them think?" I asked.

"I dunno," Tabetha said and strolled off into the tall grass.

This wasn't the Tabetha I was used to. She wasn't kicking through floors with her boots and insulting Kirby in new, exciting ways. She seemed uncertain about everything. Remembering the events that led up to her own death was rattling her something fierce. But given the circumstances, I'm not sure why I expected something different. As far as we knew, she'd been killed as part of a nineteenth-century hate crime and her body never found. Maybe I shouldn't have been surprised that, underneath her tough exterior, Tabetha Scott was a girl who had been grievously hurt.

"Tabetha, are you sure you want us to keep at this?" I asked, following her into the grass. From my experiences with my dad, I was used to asking when things were too much. "Is this too weird or painful?"

"Nah," she said. "It's not that. I know I'm dead. I've gotten used to the idea somebody would kill a kid. I think we all are."

"But?" I asked.

"But . . . this is different. It's not just like some murder mystery. It's not some Asphodel Meadows plot."

"We don't know that," I said. I guess I was missing something. It seemed pretty clearly like an Asphodel Meadows production to me.

"The other kids don't understand slavery," she said. "What it was like to grow up in that. And to get here, where you think it'll be safe, only t' find the town's full a' racists who want us all dead or gone. They're throwin' bottles n' dumpin' trash at our front porch."

"I'm sorry, Tabetha —"

"Even if it was some Asphodel Meadows member who actually killed me, it wasn't him, y'know? It was this place. This *town*. This *country*."

I wasn't sure what to say to that. There *was* nothing to say. She was born into slavery and escaped to a place where virulent racism was still the norm. And, if we were lucky, we might find her body buried under this summer fair, where she was murdered by some deranged follower of a witch. I could apologize. But it's not like I could find a greeting card that matched the sentiment.

"Tabetha, I'm not sure how to make things better," I confessed. "I'll never know what it was like for you. I won't even know what it's like for my friends Levi or Yumi. But you're my friend, and anything I can do to help . . ."

"I s'ppose that's a nice offer, but there are some things ya can't make better," Tabetha answered.

"I guess you're right. I know I've been impatient and flippant at times," I continued. "But —"

That's when we were interrupted by a shout from Cyril

emanating from within the walls of the rotting house: "We found something!"

Tabetha and I dashed inside the wooden structure to see our dirt-covered friends huddled around a giant old guitar case embedded in the dirt. That's what it looked like at first, but upon closer inspection, it appeared to be the case for a double bass. The leather that covered the case was peeling, but the box shape held.

"Well, open it up!" Tabetha commanded. "What're we waitin' for?"

I was about to warn everyone that we had no idea what could be inside, but it was too late. Cyril had already flipped open the clasps, and when he raised the lid, there was no bass to be seen. Instead, it contained a small skeleton, mostly intact, save for the skull, which had been completely caved in. And it was wearing a dress and boots identical to Tabetha's own.

"Maybe you don't want to see this, Tabetha," I said, trying to angle my body between her and what seemed to be undeniably her own abused remains.

"October, it's okay," she said, pushing me out of her way to get a closer look.

"Okay, maybe I don't want to see this."

The sight of the skeleton wasn't the issue. The smell, however — or the *stench* — was unholy.

"That has to be you, right, Tabby?" Kirby said. "Does this look familiar?"

"How's she supposed t'know what her skeleton looks like, dummy?" Morna said.

"Kirby, if you keep asking dumb questions, I'll show you what *your* skeleton looks like," Cyril threatened.

While the other dead kids squabbled, Tabetha crouched down to the skeleton crammed uncomfortably into the case and removed its faded leather boots. She turned them over and out into the double bass case fell a ring. Tabetha picked it up and brought it close to my face. It was the ring, just as she had described it from her memories. A green jewel set in a silver ring in the shape of a spider.

239

"Now we know they didn't kill you to take the ring," Kirby said.

"And now we also know who the murderer was," Derek said, turning the guitar-case-turned-makeshift-coffin slightly so the monogrammed clasps could be seen in the flashlight from overhead. "A 'Y' and a 'B,'" he said, "for Yancey Burnhamthorpe."

"The pharmacist?" Morna asked.

"I still don't understand what that is," Cyril said, adjusting his neckerchief.

"What did they call them in Cyril's era, Tabetha?" Derek asked. "Chemists?"

But Tabetha was not answering. Just staring at the skeleton in Tabetha Scott cosplay.

"And I suppose the cause of death is head trauma," Kirby said, somewhat callously, I thought. "If he was a pharmacist, maybe he used a pestle."

"Kirby," I said. "Be quiet."

Thankfully, Kirby did — for once in his entire un-life — listen to me and stopped talking. I ushered Tabetha out of the shack and she handed me the ring.

"You should stay outside," I said. "We can take it from here."

I left Tabetha and returned to the Underground Railroad terminus, where I instructed the rest of my dead friends to re-bury everything we'd uncovered.

"Let's see if we can put this all back before daylight," I said. "Derek, can you keep Tabetha company?"

Derek nodded and went outside.

"I don't want anyone to know we were here," I said.

"I think the archaeologists will be able to tell," Kirby said.

"I guess as long as they don't know *who* was digging," I said, securing the skeleton in its grim container once again. "We should be fine."

"What about the ring?" Morna asked, just as I was stuffing it into my front pants pocket.

"We don't have to bury *that* again," I said. "It could be a clue."

Morna looked at me with great disappointment. As if I were the person who had stolen the charity cash box.

"This ring obviously belongs to a murderer," I explained. "Probably a murderous pharmacist. So I'm keeping it."

As I heaved the first shovelful of dirt back onto the double bass, Cyril brought up an interesting point: "I know he was a prime suspect with his behaviour in the tavern, and the case has his initials and all, but it all seems . . . I don't know," he said, throwing dirt into the hole. "Anti-climactic?"

"Not for me," Kirby said. "Finding a skeleton in an instrument case is the definition of excitement."

"Are we so certain that because we found Tabetha's skeleton in an instrument case marked Y.B.," Cyril reasoned, "that some Y.B. is the one responsible?"

"And the pharmacist has no connection to Asphodel Meadows," Morna added, struggling with her shovelful of earth. "At least, none that we know of. That name isn't on our list. Maybe his name changed?"

"Or maybe that list is wrong?" Cyril suggested.

"No, it feels strange," said Tabetha, who surprised us all as she and Derek returned to the shed. She seemed to be calmer, even though her face was puffy, as if she'd just been crying. "I agree. Everything feels strange."

"What do you mean?" I asked.

"I thought it would feel different when we solved this mystery. I know we don't disappear or see a glowing light or anything, but I thought there'd be some kind of different feeling. Morna, Cyril, do you know what I mean?"

"Yes," Cyril said.

"I think so," Morna said.

"I thought I'd feel *relief*. But I don't."

☠ ☠ ☠

Crisparkle
and Shine

Despite Tabetha Scott's entirely non-scientific "intuition" (which remains ludicrous even in a world where ghost children exist), October considered the Case of Who Killed Tabetha Scott entirely closed. The culprit: pharmacist and hobbyist double-bass player Yancey Burnhamthorpe, a man so twisted by racist indignation, so threatened when a Black man stood up to him in a bar, he killed that man's thirteen-year-old daughter. As October was rapidly learning, the more one learned about Canadian history, the more injustice, oppression, and tragedy one found.

After doing a rather pathetic job of covering up their late-night dig, the dead kids drove October Schwartz home in her father's car. The complete lack of traffic incidents meant that unless her father kept a close eye on the odometer like that Cameron fellow's father in *Ferris Bueller's Day Off* (which he did *not*), no one would be the wiser of the unauthorized joy ride. The dead kids and their live leader, October, parted ways with Tabetha still feeling a niggling doubt that stuck in her head like a poorly thrown dart in a crowded bar. But all signs pointed to Burnhamthorpe — he hated the Scotts, led a town campaign against them, just about killed them in a tavern in front of a crowd — and Tabetha's body was found in what was most assuredly *his* double-bass case.

As October quietly slid open her back door, she discovered her father's music was still playing. But the volume was much lower and the lights in his room were out. Mr. Schwartz was most definitely asleep, and using the classic rock of the 1970s the way others used white noise or whale sounds to guide them to slumber. Taped onto the outside of the bedroom door, a note for October: *Please wake me @ 7*. Though Mr. Schwartz was, undoubtedly, in the depths of a serious depression, he was also adamant about not using any more of his sick days at work.

October decided her closet might be a better place to store her digging equipment — her dad would notice them in the garage sooner or later — so she shuffled into her bedroom as quietly as one can while lugging several shovels. She had some misgivings about putting the dirt-caked shovels into her closet, but, then again, most of her clothing was pretty dirty already, and black, to boot. She carefully leaned them against the back wall, slid into her pyjamas — basically softer versions of what she was already wearing — and drifted off for a couple hours' worth of sleep.

☠ ☠ ☠

Though October was a bit grumpy about the wake-up instructions left on her dad's door — she did not relish being treated like an employee at the Holiday Inn — she followed them perfectly, because that was a concrete thing this daughter could do to help out her depressive father. When awakened, Mr. Schwartz apologized.

"Sorry, pumpkin," the rumpled father said. "Yesterday was a bad day. I hope the music didn't keep you up."

"No, it was fine, Dad," October answered. She did not, of course, reveal the reason it was fine was that she wasn't home for most of the evening.

"You need a ride today?" her dad asked, as he began the elaborate process involved in making coffee.

"No," October said. "I'll walk, like usual."

As soon as October stepped out the front door, however, she regretted not taking her dad up on his offer. Having spent the night digging up, then re-burying a historical site, and not getting much rest afterward, October felt like her entire body had been repeatedly beaten by rolling pins. Each step wore her down more, and she looked forward to taking a seat in class.

And though her pasty flesh was weak, October Schwartz's mind was energized by the completion of a two-hundred-year-old murder mystery. With that tidied up and squared away, she could renew her focus on the school theft and figure out how to prove Phantom Moustache's involvement in the crime. All she had to do, she figured, was sort out which of the weaselly young musicians had a relative that worked at the fair. She felt like a phoenix, rising from the ashes — if that phoenix were an exhausted, teenaged detective.

Energy quickly turned to deflation when October walked through the front doors of Sticksville Central and her eyes were assailed by the tableau of quiet Matilda Coffin being tormented by Boston Davis. October had arrived in the front atrium just in time to witness Boston overturn Matilda's schoolbag and send the contents — pens, notebooks, makeup, earbuds — skittering all over the tiled floor.

"What are you doing?" she shouted, louder than anyone at school had ever heard Matilda speak offstage. "My stuff!"

"Should've thought about what would happen to your stuff *before* you started drumming for Crenshaw House," Boston retroactively warned. "Too late to do anything about it now."

"You're a real tool, you know that, Boston?" Matilda said, glaring up at him from the floor as she began to gather her things.

October strode over to the mini-drama unfolding in the centre of the atrium to help Matilda retrieve all her personal effects.

"Don't you have lyrics to butcher, Boston?" October said, squatting and picking up several full packages of Chiclets.

"I can't think of anything more important than making this thief pay," he said. Boston dug into the pocket of his baggy jeans and extracted a butterscotch candy. He popped open the candy's wrapper and dumped it (the candy, not the wrapper) into his big, stupid, grinning mouth to momentarily stop it from saying terrible things. "Unless it's watching the girl who ruined my relationship with Ashlie pick crud off the floor."

October, from her vantage point on the dusty ground (some

of its "vantages" were more apparent than others) took special note of the butterscotch candy Boston Davis was enjoying — partially because he chased that first candy with three others (all well before 9 a.m.), and partially because she'd never seen anyone under fifty-five enjoy those candies, save Ms. Fenstermacher (who was essentially fifty-five in her mind).

"What're you looking at?" Boston shouted through a mouth full of butterscotchy saliva, and shoved October's shoulder with his foot.

"Leave her alone," said Henry Khan, entering from the social studies hall. He gently pushed Boston Davis back a bit from the two girls cleaning up the bag spill. Khan — perhaps unwisely — then got to his knees to assist October and his bandmate.

Boston seemed certain to retaliate for the minor shove, nearly spitting his candy juice out as he charged toward Henry. He was only stopped by Principal Hamilton, who appeared like a genie in a bad suit at his side.

"Mr. Davis, can you tell me what is going on here?"

Mr. Hamilton probably wasn't going to be convinced the mess all over the atrium floor was part of some student council project or team-building exercise.

"Uh, Matilda dropped her bag . . . I guess?"

Boston Davis was about as good a liar as he was a vocalist.

"Well, either help out or get to class," the principal insisted.

Boston, seeing the opportunity to escape without being admonished for his bullying, skedaddled. Hamilton, meanwhile, groaned as he squatted low to the ground and asked Matilda if he could assist in the cleanup.

"It's fine," she mumbled.

His black loafers making crisp taps along the floor, Principal Hamilton returned to his office, leaving October and two members · of Crenshaw House to tidy up the seemingly unlimited supply of Matilda Coffin's tchotchkes.

"Were you planning to run away?" Henry, on all fours, asked.

"Ha ha," Matilda groaned. "I have a lot of stuff, okay?"

"I can see that," he said. "It's a school fact now." As if "school facts" were a term human beings used.

246

"I just want this to end," Matilda said.

October grimaced, beginning to feel some shame that she had yet to find a culprit for the Bandwarz theft. She actually had a culprit, but no real evidence. This morning's atrium incident made it abundantly clear she couldn't just ask Phantom Moustache directly if one of them had some connection to the fair. They weren't going to answer her questions. They were more likely to spit in her face.

"I know, I know," October said. "I'm following some leads . . . I should have this case solved soon."

"When's 'soon'?" Henry asked.

October knew Yumi thought Henry was cute — like a stockier, younger Dev Patel — but she couldn't see it. He was, however, annoyingly persistent. But October wasn't being entirely fair. She didn't have to bear the brunt of the consequences while the case remained unsolved.

"Henry," she said, changing the subject and scooping up $2.57 in coins from the tile, "do you know anyone at school who works at the fair? Either students or maybe one of their parents?"

"The fair?" he repeated, leaning back on his heels and spreading his palms against his thighs. "Who works at the fair?"

"I thought all those guys came in from out of town," Matilda added. "The fair travels around."

"Clowns and carnies," Henry added.

"It was just an idea," October said, a little discouraged. She handed the last of Matilda's stuff back to her. "I'll be in touch about the case."

☠   ☠   ☠

During lunch, October realized Ashlie Salmons would also be of no help determining which, if any, Phantom Moustache members had relatives working for the fair. Their on-again, off-again mild friendship was decidedly in the "off" mode. This point was driven home when Ashlie "accidentally" dumped a banana smoothie on October's head as she passed by her table.

"Sorry," Ashlie fake-cringed, extending the last syllable of the word out to nearly a full minute.

"I bet," October said, yellow ooze inching its way down her black hair.

"Walk much?" shot Yumi, who was seated across the way when this banana smoothie snafu went down.

Ashlie departed mercifully fast, leaving October, Yumi, and Stacey to clean up and discuss recent events. Alarmingly, Stacey pulled a beach towel from his bag and tossed it to October, who used it to dry her now banana-scented hair.

"There are worse things to smell like," Stacey said, embracing positivity like a lunatic.

"Stacey, why do you have a towel?" Yumi asked. A more than reasonable question. "Are you on the swim team or something?"

"I always have a towel," he said. "Haven't you read *The Hitchhiker's Guide*?"

Rather than invite a boy to talk about *The Hitchhiker's Guide to the Galaxy*, October altered the subject of the conversation.

"Yumi, do you still have that book, *Sticksvillainy*?" she asked, wiping clean her bangs. "Can I look at it quickly?"

Naturally, October was hoping to find a photo or illustration or detailed description of the pharmacist, Yancey Burnhamthorpe. October had only skimmed the book quickly, TBH, and didn't remember what the book had said about him. So when Yumi produced the true-crime book from her bag, October immediately searched for mentions of Tabetha's murderer in the book's index.

"What do you need the book for?" Yumi asked.

"Just looking up something," October sort-of explained and flipped to the italicized page number. "Wait. Why does Yancey Burnhamthorpe have no fingers?"

October *really* hadn't read this book carefully. In the sole photograph of Mr. Burnhamthorpe, he was proudly standing beside some of the retail items on his sales counter, and was clearly missing all the fingers on his left hand. What remained was a perfectly fine trapezoid of flesh that he seemed to be waggling at some of the peppermint sticks and soap bars on display.

"The pharmacist? I thought you read this," Yumi said, maybe even a little judgey. "Remember he had that accident early on in his work? When he passed out from ether and his hand fell in a vat of lye? They had to amputate his fingers."

"Do you think he could play the string bass?" October asked hopefully, though (a) she was pretty sure she knew the answer to that question, and (b) what was Yumi, an expert in the abilities of amputees to play various musical instruments?

"Seems unlikely," Yumi said. "*Now*, for sure. But in the olden days? I don't think he could play *any* stringed instrument."

This was a bit of an issue: the case that October was certain was airtight suddenly had some very compelling holes punched in it. Of course, there's no reason Yancey couldn't have bludgeoned Tabetha Scott with something and stuffed her into that instrument case — back to the mortar and pestle theory — but why would he even own a double bass? Unless it was a double bass case from before his tragic lye accident. Or it was someone else's case. And if they'd placed blame on the wrong suspect, it would explain why Tabetha was still unsettled.

"Why do you care if this long-dead druggist can play the bass?" Stacey asked between massive gulps of chocolate milk.

"Y'know . . . Now that I play one, I like to learn about bassists through history," October said, stuck without a reasonable explanation. "And I just know how much joy learning an instrument can bring."

"Maybe he learned the drums," Stacey helpfully suggested. "Like that guy in Def Leppard."

"Who cares if this racist dude played an instrument?" Yumi interjected with a valid sentiment. She grabbed the book back and started to flip through the pages. "The real musical talent was that white lady the family knew. She could sing, play the cello

— I feel like I found a role model from the mid-1800s, which is not easy to do!"

October searched her memories from her cursory scan of the book and her conversations with Beryl and Tabetha. (It probably would have been too conspicuous to consult her *Two Knives, One Thousand Demons* notebook.)

"What lady?" she asked. "Miss Yvonne?"

Yumi opened the book to a photo of an attractive young woman with raven-coloured hair and a cotton dress that was patterned with musical notes.

"Miss Yvonne?" Yumi scoffed. "Who are you, Mr. Rogers? It's Yvonne *Burton*."

October's head started to spin. Not in reality — she wasn't Beetlejuice or Linda Blair in *The Exorcist* or something. Her head merely *felt like* it was spinning. Yvonne Burton was Y.B., too. And she was known to play the cello! (Maybe that was a cello case instead?) She played in a band in Lunsford's tavern. But why would she want to kill Tabetha? She was a friend of the Scotts. Basically, the only white friend they had in Sticksville.

"I have to go," October said, leaving her tray, quite rudely, on the table instead of depositing it in the area where used trays should be collected.

"What'd I say?" Yumi asked Stacey after October had departed.

"Maybe she didn't like that Mr. Rogers crack."

"Listen, Mr. Rogers is a saint. We should all be so lucky to be compared to Mr. Rogers."

October jogged to her locker and threw it open. Partially obscured by the door, she pulled out *Two Knives, One Thousand Demons* and flipped to the list of names associated with Asphodel Meadows. One of the six names was — you guessed it — Burton.

250

Yvonne Burton: she had the same initials as the instrument case where the body was shoved, she had a name associated with the nefarious secret society in town (not that there are *benevolent* secret societies), and she played the cello. Tabetha had even mentioned seeing her on her way to the storehouse. October had to tell Tabetha this new theory as soon as possible. She slammed the locker shut, angry with herself for not connecting the clues earlier. What else had she missed? What clues was she not connecting in the Bandwarz mystery? This was shaping up to be a real lesson about the importance of careful reading and not dismissing your friends' intuition. Then, just as she was mentally beating herself up for her sloppy detective work, October made a connection in the Bandwarz case and suddenly had a new strategy. She knew where she and the dead kids needed to search next.

☠   ☠   ☠

After nightfall, October Schwartz practically ran to visit the dead kids, and she was not the biggest fan of running. Her dad, though still going to work, was on the same schedule after-hours, it seemed. Again, he sequestered himself in his room, though he had progressed to songs by Carly Simon. October didn't know enough rock music history to understand if this was a good or bad sign, but she did know it was a good opportunity to visit the dead kids more or less as she pleased. She left him a plate of sesame chicken and rice before making her escape.

As she raced into the dark cemetery as if it were the final segment of the *Supermarket Sweep* game show, she spotted her dead friends playing tag by their favourite willow tree. She shouted, showing no caution about who might still be alive and on the cemetery grounds. (After all, it wasn't particularly late.)

"Tabetha!" October called. "We were wrong! It wasn't the pharmacist or druggist. It wasn't Yancey Burnhamthorpe!"

Tabetha looked both pleased and unhappier than ever, somehow, and dug her fists into her hips. "I knew it!"

"What do you mean?" Derek asked. "He hated Tabetha. He has the same initials as the double-bass case."

"But he doesn't have hands," October explained. "At least, not the kind of hands that can play a stringed instrument. He lost his fingers in an accident. But Tabetha's friend — the white lady who visited — her name is Yvonne Burton."

"Wait a second . . ." Tabetha said.

"And Burton," October panted, now out of breath, "is an Asphodel Meadows name."

"Oh my goodness," Morna shouted, though it was not October's words that alarmed her as much as it was Tabetha's face. Tabetha was having a revelation, a breakthrough. "I remember," Tabetha said to no one in particular. She was fixated on the night sky as if the memory was being re-enacted there — as if the stars were a television screen playing an *Unsolved Mysteries* episode about her Civil War–era murder.

"She was the one who found me with the book. I asked her if it was her book. She said it was. She was smiling the whole time," Tabetha said. "Very friendly."

"Do you remember what happened next?" October tentatively asked.

"Then she asked me 'bout the ring. I lied n' said I hadn't seen any ring. Ms. Yvonne asked if I knew how ta read, n' I admitted I didn't. But she didn't believe me."

"Why not?" Cyril asked.

"Said I worked in the mayor's house. Musta been one a' them smart servants. That I shouldn't be bashful 'bout being smart. She asked what I thought a' the book, and I couldn't say. Then she put down her cello case, n' opened it up. Still smilin'. Even smiling when she lifted the cello over her head . . . and she . . ."

Tabetha couldn't continue, but October and the others all knew how it ended. Derek patted her on the shoulder, unsure if a hug was appropriate in the situation, but Morna — unfettered by ideas of propriety — just crushed Tabetha in her arms.

"She musta picked the storehouse as a hidin' spot because no one ever visited," Tabtetha reasoned, breaking free of Morna. "Nobody used it anymore, n' it was so close ta the dump."

"Explains how nobody ever smelled your dead body," Derek added.

"I'm just assuming it was a spell book, right?" Kirby added. "With the witch and all. It wasn't a songbook?"

"I'm so sorry, Tabetha," October said.

"It was a long time ago," Tabetha croaked. "Now we figgered it out, so . . ."

"Even though it was long ago," Morna said. "It doesn't make it less awful."

"I don't know if I feel better or worse that it wasn't a racist plot, just a secret society usin' racism as a smokescreen," Tabetha lamented. "But at least I know what happened."

"Tabetha, please accept my condolences and apologies," Cyril said as he doffed his cap.

With everyone soaking up the sadness, pondering the commonplace existence of evil, October felt truly awful for ending the moment.

"Friends, I'm so sorry, but I have to ask you all another favour," October said. "We need to investigate the office of that psychic, Nicodemus Burke."

"The one who tried to capture us?" Kirby said. "That's dangerous. If I had a death wish, October, it has already been fulfilled."

"Why?" Cyril asked, still looking over at Tabetha with concern.

"I want to check something out," she explained. "He was at

our concert even though he doesn't have any kids in our school, as far as I can tell. And he works summers at the fair, where that shark car lives. And given what happened at the funeral home, we know he's up to something involving Tabetha's family. He's probably in Asphodel Meadows. Maybe he even stole the money."

"He can see all of us," Derek warned, "and he seems to know magic."

"I know it's a lot to ask," October said.

"We'll do it," Tabetha announced, looking grave. "If this guy is trying to catch us, 'specially if he's part a' this secret society — a secret society that killed me — we should stop 'im."

"But we can probably wait until tomorrow," October said, reasoning it was a kind decision to leave this evening to mourning. "No need to rush out now."

"Thanks," Tabetha said.

"How will we find him?" Morna asked.

October produced a recent edition of the *Sticksville Loon* from her bag and opened it to a page featuring a print ad that read *Nicodemus Burke: Psychic Readings and Spiritual Healings*.

"Luckily, he advertises," October said. "And he takes walk-ins."

☠   ☠   ☠

Psychic
Break-in

There's the old joke about psychics that would have applied to our break-in and following snoopfest: if Nicodemus Burke were actually a psychic and could see the future, then why didn't he know we'd break into his office and set a trap for us? People who believe in psychics typically explain that's not really how it works, but whatever. Ms. Fenstermacher seemed to think he was legit. Psychic or not, Nicodemus Burke certainly *seemed* to have some sort of magic or supernatural powers. But he was also not present in his office that Friday night. Maybe he did see us coming.

Given it was Friday, I was somewhat relieved I wouldn't have to face school the next morning. I'd had a few too many late nights recently and wasn't feeling my sharpest. Additionally, I had no real joy about seeing what fresh and innovative torment the band members of Phantom Moustache had cooked up — either for me or for Levi, Henry, and Matilda. I used to think a couple of those guys were okay, like Preston Sinclair, the bassist, but now I thought of them all as, like, a start-up for high school bullying.

Travelling to Nicodemus Burke's office was the easy part of the evening. Predictably, he lived close to the cemetery, and, by extension, me. While it made sense for someone so concerned with ghost and paranormal activities to work so close to Sticksville Cemetery — the spiritual energy was probably better for his readings or something — it still creeped me out. He was just a short stroll from my house. The office itself was pretty non-supernatural looking from the outside, though it's probably difficult to look supernatural while situated between a Tim Hortons and nail salon in a sad-looking strip mall. Nicodemus's full name was arched across a large window shrouded with deep red curtains. What I imagine could only be an occult or Illuminati symbol was painted underneath his name, as well as a short list of the services he offered: tarot reading, healing crystals, aura photos. The atmosphere was, however, way different after Cyril walked through the glass front door and let us in.

"What is an aura, and why do I want a photograph of it?" Kirby asked.

Sometimes it felt like a curse that some of the dead kids could read.

Inside looked like a psychic's proper place of business, instead of a place that sold travel insurance or bail bonds. The motif of floor-length crimson curtains continued throughout the dark, carpeted room. A large circular wooden table that looked heavier than a truck sat in the middle of the room beside a majestic armchair that could properly be called a throne. The opposite side of the table featured a more modest pair of chairs.

"This is where that guy in the opera outfit lives?" Morna asked.

"It's where he works," I corrected.

"At least he doesn't have a crystal ball," Derek noted.

Cyril, meanwhile, was transfixed by a small marble bust of someone who appeared to be the Phantom of the Opera. It seemed like the kind of thing that I, a modern person living in the present time, should have been able to explain to him, but — like so many of the objects and trinkets in Nicodemus's office — I had no idea what it was all about.

"What're we s'posed t'be lookin' for?" Tabetha asked.

"Can you explain this?" Derek asked, pointing to a dream-catcher in the corner of the ceiling. "Is this guy Ojibwe?"

"It's kind of a fad for, like, New Age people to put these in their bedrooms and their cars," I said, suddenly ashamed for all of North America.

"I don't know how to feel about that," he said.

Morna called out from behind the far red curtain. "There's another room!"

We gathered around Morna, and I felt some relief this hidden room existed. I wasn't, to be quite honest, sure what we were looking for, but it was probably stored here.

"Open it up," Kirby insisted.

The door behind the far red curtain led to a much smaller room that looked exactly like any office cubicle. It could have doubled as the desk for a school administrator. No magic crystals or dark fabrics to be found in here. Just an outdated photocopier, stacks of invoices and bills, and yet *another* bust. This one was of another dude I didn't recognize — an angrier-looking Alfred Hitchcock. Two more busts and this psychic could make his own Mount Rushmore of homely looking weirdoes.

"Who is this?" Tabetha asked, lifting the bust of the intense bald man.

"I don't know," I admitted. "The base says *Aleister Crowley?*"

From the way the dead kids looked at me, I might as well have read "Harry Styles" or some other celebrity who rose to fame after they'd all died. If this guy were in a boy band, he'd definitely be considered "the bad boy."

"It doesn't matter who that is," I said. "We just need to find some evidence in this office. Something that ties Burke to the school theft, because I'm almost one hundred percent sure he's involved."

The dead kids started rummaging through the desk drawers, shelves, and garbage bins. Derek eventually produced a crumpled paper that, when unfolded, was clearly a memo to someone from Burke outlining the proper feeding and care of his two black Siamese cats.

"Does this note help?" he asked.

Kirby took a long look at the wrinkled notepaper. "Maybe the high cost of sodium-free cat food could be considered a motive for the theft."

"No, you goof," I said, snatching the paper from him. "The note is in Burke's handwriting. We can see if it matches the song lyrics left at the scene of the crime. And the threatening note on the curtain too."

"Didya bring the paper?" Morna asked, but I was already on my knees, digging out from my bag that front-page story from the *Loon*, complete with photos. The photo of the note wasn't the best quality, but holding it side-by-side with the memo about Nicodemus Burke's (probably) innocent cats, it was impossible to deny the similarities.

"I'm no handwriting expert," I said, "but it looks like a match."

"Let me see," Kirby insisted, snatching the note and paper from me. Kirby was pretty certain he was an expert in most things. Or, at the very least, more accomplished than I was. "It *does* look like it was written by the same hand."

"Guys," Morna called, staring at the bookshelf tucked in one corner of the shabby little office. "I can't read, but I know I've seen *that* thing before."

We all turned to see what Morna was talking about, and boy, was it *ever* familiar. We'd seen it first in my own house. But soon it seemed like we'd found a needlepoint, with text in German, declaring loyalty to alleged witch Fairfax Crisparkle, in the residence of nearly every family or person we encountered who had a connection to the group Asphodel Meadows. So Nicodemus Burke and Ms. Yvonne, who killed Tabetha, had something in common. And knowing the interest Asphodel Meadows had in Fairfax Crisparkle, I just assumed the book and ring had something do with him.

"Seems clear our psychic friend is behind the theft," Cyril noted. "And by friend, I more accurately mean 'fiend.'"

"Ya think?" Tabetha said. "So now we know who did it, can we get outta here? I'm gettin' the creeps."

The note and the framed needlepoint on the bookshelf were two strikes against Nicodemus Burke, and enough to convince us that he was behind the concert theft, but since we were in his office and no one else was around, I figured it would be ideal to uncover some

real evidence and make my case against him airtight. Police probably wouldn't see a German needlepoint as a smoking gun. "Not so fast," I said. "We have time, let's see if we can find anything else. Tabetha: you, Cyril, and Kirby go to the main room and see if you can find anything there. We'll keep searching here."

The three of them grumbled but headed out to the area where I assumed the readings and "healing" happened. While Morna, Derek, and I searched through his papers, I couldn't help but worry. A member of some sinister local secret society had supernatural powers that could affect ghosts? How were we supposed to deal with that?

"Morna and I have read that list of Asphodel Meadows names about two hundred times," Derek noted, going through the books on Burke's shelves. "And Burke isn't one of them."

"I know," I admitted. That was another part of my worry. "But maybe he changed his name? Maybe Nicodemus Burke is a professional name, like Criss Angel. I mean, it *sounds* made up."

"All names are made up," said the literal-minded Derek.

"Or maybe Asphodel Meadows is bigger than we thought," Morna said.

Morna managed to encapsulate all my worst fears about Sticksville in one statement. We didn't even know what the goals of Asphodel Meadows were, really. Just that its members were into Fairfax Crisparkle and all seemed very active in murdering children for some reason. And it seemed like membership numbers were high.

I was opening my mouth to provide some reassurance to Derek and Morna that I didn't even really believe when we heard a crash like a clumsy cater-waiter had fallen on his face from the other room. We rushed through the office door.

The circumstances behind the scuffle in the other room were never really confirmed, because depending on who I asked about it, there was a completely different story. But whatever started it, the squabble ended in a slap fight of sorts with the three of them managing to knock over the two smaller chairs, pull down the dreamcatcher, scatter tarot cards all over the carpet, and completely upend an end table I hadn't previously noticed by the front door, sending all its contents flying.

"It wasn't me!" all three dead kids said in unison.

Unfair as it was to pre-judge the situation, I was pretty confident this catastrophe started with Kirby LaFlamme.

"What happened?!" I shouted.

"There was a disagreement, and — as you can see for yourself," Cyril explained, removing his tricorn hat in supplication, "things got out of hand."

"What a mess," I said, surveying the damage and trying to estimate how long it would take the six of us, sans horseplay, to clean it all up. "Burke is going to come back here at some point, and it's better for us if he doesn't learn we've been pawing through his stuff."

"I guess so," Tabetha said.

"Let's just fix this mess," I said with resignation, heading over to the overturned table. "I think we found everything we're going to find."

That's when I noticed — among the contents that were originally on the table — a porcelain bowl that had thankfully not cracked but had vomited out its contents: dozens of those stupid butterscotch candies old people love. They were all over the carpet, their golden wrappers glittering in the light from the hidden rear office.

"These candies are more popular than I thought," I remarked, mostly to myself, because what did the dead kids care about candy?

Then I remembered the first time that candy stood out: Ms. Fenstermacher. Then I saw Boston Davis downing a bunch of them. What kid buys those voluntarily? Stood to reason he got them from Burke — likely where Ms. Fenstermacher came by hers — but probably *not* after a psychic reading. Could Boston have worked with Burke to swipe the money? Maybe Burke handled the actual theft and kept Phantom Moustache with a squeaky clean alibi. But why would Nicodemus Burke do favours for Boston Davis? Or any teenager, for that matter? Parts of the story were a bit of a stretch, but I was beginning to feel the pieces locking into place, like a particularly satisfying game of *Tetris*.

"Something wrong?" Morna asked, as she joined me in the candy cleanup.

"No, I — " but I didn't finish my comment because we all heard stirring above. We glanced at each other.

"We're all here, right?" Tabetha asked.

I counted six of us.

"Does he live upstairs?" Derek asked.

"It's a strip mall," I answered. "I don't think there *is* an upstairs."

"Maybe there are mice?" Cyril suggested.

"We need to go," I insisted.

The dead kids and I scrambled as quietly as we could, taking the cat care note with us. Kirby, Derek, and Tabetha exited through the wall of a Tim Hortons, Morna and Cyril through the adjoining nail salon, and I, the only one of us cat burglars (or cat-note burglars) governed by the law of physics, scooted out the back. The back door of the office led into an alley full of garbage containers and cardboard boxes.

The dead kids joined me in the alley. Tabetha had scrounged a box of doughnuts from the Tim Hortons.

"I found snacks," she said, throwing open the lid. "Circle pastries!"

"They're called doughnuts," Derek corrected.

"Those must be at *least* a day old," Kirby said, refusing Tabetha's offer with a wave of his hand and a projection of his tongue. "And we don't even need to eat."

"My apologies, your highness."

"Be quiet," I insisted. "Shut up until we get back to the cemetery."

We dashed off down the street, Tabetha dropping crullers and honey dips along the way (no real loss). When we reached the intersection with Riverside, I turned back just in time to catch the lights inside the psychic reader's office blaze on. Which was all kinds of bad news. It was possible Nicodemus Burke thought he just prevented a robbery, but it was just as likely he now knew exactly what the dead kids and I knew. If he didn't want us dead (relatively speaking) before — and he more or less told us he did — I'm sure this incident helped him overcome that personal hurdle.

☠   ☠   ☠

Boston
Dead Sox

Having established a very credible link between Boston Davis and the other members of Phantom Moustache — as credible as any candy-based evidence is — October Schwartz was unsure how to proceed prior to class on Monday. Being able to search Boston Davis's house (and pool house) uninterrupted would have been ideal, but that didn't work out well the first time, and October feared being found inside the Davis's home at this point would result in her immediate imprisonment.

October did have one idea, but it would require wheels. So she called her friends Stacey and Yumi to set up a Saturday afternoon movie marathon. Though their hopes of forming a band were as demolished as Yumi's cousin's bass guitar, they still had plenty of good reasons to hang around each other. And what better reason than watching as many *Friday the 13th* movies in an afternoon as physically possible?

Of course, Yumi's parents would tolerate no R-rated movies on their watch, and Yumi's house was so pristine and neat October felt like a coal miner walking into an art gallery whenever she visited. Having Stacey and Yumi over to her place would be beneficial to her plan, which (spoiler alert) involved her borrowing both Yumi and Stacey's bicycles, but even Mr. Schwartz's deepest depression couldn't prevent him from harassing three teenagers into "spending a beautiful spring day outside," even if the weather was just *okay*. So, as usual, Stacey of the fairly hands-off parents would have to host.

October knocked on her dad's door to inform him of her lazy Saturday plans. Mr. Schwartz sat on his tartan bedspread, analyzing a page of a Malcolm Gladwell book.

"Did you forget about your continued grounding?" he asked. "I feel bad about that band attacking you and your friends, but that doesn't undo your earlier misbehaviour."

October's face fell. Her (hastily crafted) plan relied on her being able to leave the house. She'd sort of fantasized her dad would grant her amnesty after all she'd been through lately. There was no way she could see Stacey and Yumi or procure their bikes if she was grounded.

"What if Stacey and Yumi came here?" October asked.

"I don't think that's in the spirit of grounding," Mr. Schwartz noted. "I know I made an exception before with your band practice, but this doesn't seem like a productive or creative pursuit."

October grumbled. "I would argue enjoying *Friday the 13th* involves a *great* deal of creativity."

"I'm not crazy about you watching those movies, either," Mr. Schwartz added, slipping a receipt into his book. "Aren't they a little violent for you?"

October refused to provide her father with any further information about the content of *Friday the 13th* and its many sequels. As she desperately tried to devise a practical way to see Stacey and Yumi — or at least get their bicycles — the doorbell sounded. Young October was shortly to discover that, as in the bestselling self-help book *The Secret*, she had willed a solution to her dilemma into existence. But, as in the classic short story "The Monkey's Paw," she got what she wanted at a terrible price.

When October answered the front door, she saw their Saturday morning visitors were the duo of police officers who had been in their garage just days ago. To be honest, the police officer with the moustache visited more than anyone else. He might as well keep a spare toothbrush in the Schwartzes' washroom.

"Hello?" October said. With last night spent prowling, she expected the officers to be there to arrest (or at least reprimand) her. So she was a bit surprised to learn they didn't want to place her in handcuffs.

264

"Is your father home?" Captain Moustache said.

"He's just in the other room," October said, her eyes trailing to the bedroom. "Dad!"

Mr. Schwartz came to the front entrance, depositing his book on a side table and rubbing his day-old stubble. "Yes?"

"Mr. Leonard Schwartz," Officer Machado announced, "we're holding you on suspicion of the theft of over five thousand dollars in school fundraising. We don't have enough to charge you just yet, but I'm sure we will in about forty-eight hours."

Officer Grenouille chimed in: "We'd recommend you keep silent until you've spoken to a lawyer."

Though Mr. Schwartz looked resigned, October was beginning to panic. How could they arrest her dad? Technically, the police weren't arresting him, but holding him until they could gather enough evidence to charge him, but October was largely unaware of the vagaries of the criminal justice system. Didn't they realize he was totally innocent? That he was literally one of the few non-sketchy adults in existence? Her dad was going to have a criminal record, and somehow Nicodemus Burke did not.

"This is a mistake," October said as the police ushered her dad out the front door.

"Honey, it's going to be okay," he said.

"Should I call Ms. Salmons?" October called after her dad as he was escorted down their front steps.

"She's a crown attorney," her dad said, way calmer about this than October was. "She's probably building the case against me. I don't think she'll be much help."

"I'll come with you," October decided, rushing out the front door, at which point the male officer blocked her path.

"I'm afraid you can't come

with us, miss," he said. "We have to speak to your father alone. You can visit him later this afternoon. "

"Do you have someone you can stay with?" Officer Machado added, realizing they were leaving a minor on her own.

"Yeah. My friend Yumi." October answered.

The two police officers helped her father into the back of their police cruiser and rolled off without providing any further information. It was fair for them to assume October knew where the Sticksville police station was located, but she was still a bit alarmed by their lack of concern. Not that she expected to be handed a pamphlet — *So, Your Father's Been Arrested* — but she also didn't think a pamphlet was a bad idea.

October was home alone, much like that blond Kevin McCallister child who maimed those poor burglars in that children's movie. The police expected her to head to Yumi's. But given her dad's bouts of depression, she had plenty of experience in caring for herself, and — last she checked — the refrigerator was full. She was more concerned about her father. October feared, given the current circumstances, he could fall into a pit of depression that no dosage of classic rock could propel him out of.

As the police wouldn't allow her to see her father for hours and as the best way she knew to resolve this situation was to complete the task she'd already started — find out who *really* took the Bandwarz money — she went ahead with her Saturday plans. Callous as it may have seemed, she invited her friends over to watch horror movies while her dad was probably languishing in jail. And when she called both Stacey and Yumi to invite them over, she also asked to borrow their bicycles for a few days.

As expected, Stacey asked no questions about October's unusual request. October got the sense she could have asked him to bring anything from a set of golf clubs to a mannequin's head to a Baked Alaska, and Stacey would have shrugged and said, "Sure."

Yumi Takeshi was another story entirely. Naturally inquisitive, she had a whole barrage of questions about this bicycle barter.

"What do you need my bike for? Don't you have a bike?" Yumi asked. "Not that I'm *not* coming over — I need to watch Jason kill some people."

"My dad wants to go on a trail ride next week," October said. "But we don't actually have bikes."

October was lying. And if Yumi had a good enough recollection of the Schwartz garage (which had briefly served as the Astaroth Night Bus practice space), she would have realized that. October was also only guessing there was a viable trail to take a bike ride nearby.

"Your dad isn't going to fit on my bike," Yumi said.

"Yours is for me. My dad is going to use Stacey's bike," October explained.

"This sounds suspiciously wholesome." Yumi's suspicion wouldn't subside. "Why would your dad plan a trip using a vehicle neither of you own?"

"We used to have bikes but had to leave them when we moved to Sticksville," October explained. "I guess he's feeling sentimental."

October's impatience was growing. She wished Yumi would either bike over or give her time to put together a backup plan.

"Your dad won't be watching *Friday the 13th* with us, will he?"

"No."

"As much as I like your dad, I don't want him raising an eyebrow at us when, like, someone gets stabbed through the face."

"He has other plans this afternoon," October said, which technically wasn't a fib.

Eventually, Yumi did bike over, and she, Stacey, and October watched both *Friday the 13th* and *Friday the 13th Part 2* while Mr. Schwartz was occupied with his important "other plans." And while October couldn't fully enjoy the moment — a nice period of relaxation after solving an important mystery, some time spent eating all-dressed potato chips and drinking Grape Crush with her best (living) friends — she tried her best to act as if she did, to keep up appearances. She didn't want Stacey and Yumi to discover she was potentially the child of a future convict. Not that, had she thought about it, either friend would have judged her for it.

After spending the perfectly pleasant Saturday indoors, it was with a twinge of guilt that she waved goodbye to her friends and planned her visit to the police station. Not that there was anything she could have done for her dad. They wouldn't even allow her to visit until the late afternoon, and she was already planning to go to great — most outside observers would call them "unreasonable" — lengths to prove her father's innocence. Still, October couldn't escape the lingering feeling that she should have been doing more. Like baking a file into a pie. But October was no good with pastry.

She had one more task before visiting her dad. She found a black Sharpie in a kitchen drawer and tore a piece of paper from the notepad resting beside the telephone. She retrieved a metal shish kebab skewer from another kitchen drawer and marched to the backyard with all her implements. October walked with purpose to the large tree in the cemetery. She checked the horizon for weekend grievers — always a risk on a Saturday afternoon — then drove a note into the tree with her skewer (which required much more arm strength than she anticipated). The note nailed into the tree detailed instructions for the dead kids:

CYRIL, TABETHA, MORNA, KIRBY, DEREK:
MEET ME AT THE BACK GATE AT 10.

☠   ☠   ☠

Shortly before dinnertime, October made a rare voluntary visit to the Sticksville police station. She almost didn't know what to make of it. She'd been dragged there by police officers (including her moustached new best friend) before, and had broken in after-hours with the help of the dead kids, but never visited as a (mostly) invited guest. Desks of police officers across the open pit of a main room overflowed with accordions of undone paperwork. A few police officers sat at their desks, desperately searching for needed punctuation marks on their keyboards, and two kids whom October recognized as eleventh graders sat sullenly in wooden chairs by the reception desk. From the looks of the paint stains, they must have been caught vandalizing — magenta-handed, as it were. October approached the solid-looking oak desk and the disinterested-looking woman behind it.

"I'm October Schwartz," she said. "I'm here to see my father?" She still wasn't entirely sure they'd let her see him.

Without a sound, the woman consulted a clipboard, then pressed a button on the intercom.

"Grenouille," she called into the telephone receiver. "There's a little girl here to see that Schwartz perp."

The woman placed the phone back into its cradle and said someone would attend her shortly. October didn't like how she'd called her dad "the Schwartz perp." Maybe because "perp" was just a single phoneme away from "perv." Or maybe because he hadn't *actually* perpetrated anything. "Suspect" seemed a more accurate label. Or even just his first name, Leonard.

Grenouille appeared and escorted October to a holding cell. He told October she could have fifteen minutes with her dad, but that he (Grenouille) would be the other side of the Plexiglas, watching the whole time, as if her dad were a master criminal. A master criminal who swiped a few thousand dollars from some band kids.

October entered the office and there was her dad, looking more deflated than a week-old balloon. He sat in a wooden chair, not even handcuffed.

"Dad!"

"October, pumpkin," he said, slightly reinflating and giving October a massive hug.

October took a seat in the not-very-comfortable wooden chair across from her dad. "Are you okay? How are they treating you?"

"Fine, fine," he said. "I should be able to go home early tomorrow morning. Possibly even later tonight if they can get ahold of a judge on the weekend."

"Is this about Bandwarz?" October asked. "They can't think that you did it! What evidence do they have?"

"Nothing much more than what we already knew . . . the cash box in our garage, me leaving the concert early . . . I guess they decided to bring me in to see if I might just confess."

"That's so sketchy," October said. "That evidence is nothing."

"Also, a few of the band participants have come forward to say they saw me lingering around the donation table that night," her dad continued, rubbing his face as if he were in a very sad Noxzema commercial.

"Yeah, right," October mumbled. She knew exactly *which* band members would have said that. "Dad, I *know* that someone in Phantom Moustache did it. First they tried to frame Crenshaw House, and now they're trying to frame you. I can prove it."

"No, I don't want you to prove anything, honey," Mr. Schwartz said in one long, deep sigh. "No mysteries, no criminal investigations. You're only thirteen."

"Dad, I literally just need one more night and I can prove —"

"No, October. You remember what happened last time you thought there was a mystery to solve. You nearly got killed by Mr. Page."

Mr. Schwartz was under the impression that the last mystery his daughter had investigated was a full two mysteries ago.

October rolled her eyes. "Arguably, that would have happened if I was playing detective or not."

"That's not true at all," her dad argued.

"Okay, fair."

"October," Mr. Schwartz said, leaning forward and placing his palms on his daughter's knees, "you are forbidden from looking into the band theft."

This would be when Grenouille barged into the office, mistaking Mr. Schwartz's intense fatherly lean-in for intense criminal intimidation.

"Everything okay in here?" he asked, more as warning than genuine question. As in, if everything were *not* okay in here, he was going to start busting skulls.

"Yeah, great," October said, rising from her seat. "So, you think you'll be home by morning, Dad?"

"Most likely by morning . . . afternoon at the latest. You'll be okay on your own . . . at Yumi's?"

October shot her dad a look that said, "Really?" and gave him another hug.

"And can you do me one more favour, October?" her dad asked.

"Yeah, what?"

"Can you call Mr. Hamilton and let him know the school may need a substitute for my classes tomorrow?"

Hours after an awkward weekend telephone conversation with her school principal, October even more awkwardly retrieved three bicycles from the garage where she'd stashed them and walked them to the cemetery gates. Though she didn't like the idea of her dad spending the night in the police station, (a) it wasn't anything she hadn't done before, and (b) it certainly made sneaking off the property with three bicycles much easier.

As she'd requested on her ominously stabbed note, the dead kids were all waiting for her on the other side of the fence.

"I believe this is yours," Kirby said handing a metal skewer to October.

"Thanks," she said and stuffed it into her backpack.

"What is all this about?" Cyril asked.

"Tonight, we're going on a stakeout at Boston Davis's," October answered. "And every stakeout needs wheels."

"And what type of wheels are these, exactly?" Cyril asked.

Kirby slapped Cyril so hard on the back of his skull, his tricorn hat popped off.

"It's a bicycle, you ninny."

"Wait," October said. "Do some of you not know how to use these? I just assumed bikes had been around forever! Who knows how to ride a bicycle?"

Derek and Kirby's hands went up, and Morna made a lopsided grin and wobbled her hand in a "so-so" gesture.

"That's enough riders, at least," October said, resigned. "Kirby, Derek, and I will drive; the rest of you have to double us on the handlebars, I guess. But first, I'm going to take the lights and reflectors off your bikes."

October crouched down and pulled off the very important safety gear.

"If anyone sees us biking, I just want them to see *me*. If they can't see your bikes and they can't see ghosts, maybe we'll be okay."

"This seems like a really dumb plan already," Tabetha decided. "And I like it."

Derek hopped onto Stacey's banana seat and gestured for Morna to join him. (It was long enough for both of them.) "So where are we following you to?"

"Boston Davis's house, remember?" October repeated. (Clearly Derek wasn't paying attention.) "I have a hunch he's going to lead us to the stolen money."

"N' why's that?" asked Tabetha, clambering onto October's bike's handlebars.

"My dad just got sort-of arrested for the Bandwarz theft," October said, "so the heat's off Boston. He'll probably go to the location he's hidden the money or meet with his accomplices."

"I'm so sorry about your dad," Morna covered.

"Thanks, Morna."

"Yes, *quelle tragédie*," Kirby said. "But don't you think whoever's stolen this money — this Boston or whoever else — has spent it by now?"

"Maybe," October allowed, and began pedalling toward the road. "Maybe not. Either way, I suspect it'll be worthwhile keeping an eye on Boston."

The bicycle convoy of October and her ghost friends — a veritable *Tour de Mort* — soon arrived at Boston Davis's near-mansion

of a house. The Davises and Schwartzes did not refer to the same page in the federal tax instructions. The dead kids had been here before to witness October's most recent teenage embarrassment — the (entirely purposeful) snooping session that got her branded as some sort of goth voyeur. So, naturally, she was acting the voyeur again, stashing bicycles behind a transformer and hiding in the bushes outside the Davises' living room window. The Dead Kid Detective Agency hid in the bushes for a half-hour before starting to mutiny.

"How long are we gonna stay here before we admit nuthin' is happening?" Tabetha asked. "I wanna get these Asphodel Meadows guys more than you, but we have no way to know if anything's gonna happen tonight."

"Relax," Kirby said, which had the exact opposite effect of relaxing Tabetha. "We already solved your murder. Now it's time to show some patience for solving this mystery."

"You gonna show patience for havin' yer face pounded in?"

"Tabetha does bring up an important question," Cyril said. "How long should we stay here if nothing is, indeed, happening?"

"I'm happy t'stay here however long it takes, October," Morna said.

"I'm givin' it about five more minutes," Tabetha said, though it was an empty threat. She didn't know how to ride a bike, nor did she know where she was.

As they bickered, the front door opened and the spiky-haired silhouette of a teenage boy emerged from within, then carefully, quietly closed the door behind him.

"Is that him?" asked Derek.

"That's Boston," October whispered.

"Where's he going?" Tabetha asked.

Boston crept around the side of the large brick house to retrieve his own bike. He mounted it and turned out of his driveway, zipping south down the road, away from where October and her friends were huddled in the bushes.

"Grab your bikes and follow him," October whispered as loudly as she could while still maintaining a volume that could be considered whispering. "But not too close! We can't alert him to our presence."

"Where's he going this time of night?" Kirby asked.

"I don't know," October said. Already she could feel her thighs burning from trying to keep up with Boston Davis's breakneck cycling pace. Following him too closely was proving to be a non-issue.

Though October said she didn't know what Boston Davis's destination was, she had a sneaking suspicion (you know the kind) he was headed toward Nicodemus Burke's home office. However, as she pumped alongside the dead kids through the coal black, empty streets of Sticksville for longer and longer, she realized she was mistaken. October stifled her urge to pant with the ongoing moderate exercise and started to pay attention to where they were. Fewer streetlights, more modest homes.

"I know where we're going," she said to Tabetha, busy gripping October's shoulders. "That's Henry Khan's house."

"The fairgrounds," Tabetha said.

Farther ahead, they spotted Boston Davis turning down the dirt road into the fairgrounds and slowing down. At the bend, October stopped and suggested they walk their bikes from there. As they quietly made their way through the fairgrounds, they were drawn to a solitary light near the future site of the Sharktacular Plunge, shining through the window of a construction trailer. The dead kids and October ditched their bicycles beside a dormant front-end loader and progressed quietly. A conveniently placed bulldozer provided a good hiding spot. The six night-riders crouched in the dirt behind the dozer's shovel, from where they had a pretty decent view.

"What's happenin'?" Tabetha asked. "I can't see with Kirby's big head inna' way."

"I can see Boston, and he looks really agitated," Derek said.

His description wasn't inaccurate. Boston Davis was pacing in circles, clearly talking to someone and gesturing wildly with his hands. Unfortunately, given this animated conversation was happening inside, October and the dead kids couldn't make out anything he was saying or who he was saying it to. Tabetha decided to change that.

274

Tabetha found a rock like a golf ball — though much greyer and more jagged — and raised it with her fist.

"What are you doing?" October said, with a twinge of fear in her throat.

"We gotta get them outside, don't we?" she said.

"Okay, but that's way too big," October warned, but she was too late. Tabetha had already hurled it at the window.

Luckily, Ms. Tabetha Scott was not much of a pitcher, and like a celebrity throwing out the opening pitch of a baseball game, her arm sent the rock sailing awry, just narrowly missing the window and bouncing off the sill with a thunk.

Boston, framed in the lit window, stopped pacing to look outside. Then he walked out of the frame. Next time the kids saw him, he was outside. Then, his late-night conversation partner strode into view: Nicodemus Burke, clad in full cloak and regalia.

"It's — " Morna started, but Derek, realizing the severity of the situation and the supernatural mojo of Burke, clapped his hand over her mouth.

"What are you doing?" Burke asked.

"I thought I heard something," he said, looking back and forth.

"Out here?" Burke replied. "It's probably just your friends. You're being paranoid."

"The fairgrounds aren't that far from people's homes," Boston answered. "Including the homes of two of the band members we're scamming."

"You speak as if I care about this ridiculous high school

drama." Burke joined Boston and did a half-hearted scan of the darkened construction site. "It doesn't matter. We got away with the robbery. All that matters now is the ring. And I'm sure the Schwartz girl knows where it is. It wasn't on Beryl, so she must have taken it."

Schwartz girl? October Schwartz was a Schwartz girl.

"I don't even understand why this ring is so important," Boston grumbled.

"Colour me astonished," Nicodemus Burke sighed. "The things you don't understand could fill an encyclopedia."

The two guys were talking a *lot* about a ring. So much so, one would half-believe them to be rehearsing for a stage production of *The Hobbit*. Hidden on the dark side of a bulldozer, Kirby elbowed October in the gut and raised an eyebrow. The other dead kids all looked to her with the same unspoken question. October ever-so-slowly opened her backpack and showed him the emerald ring they'd found in Tabetha's boot. Or her corpse's boot. Then she raised her own eyebrows. October had to admit, it seemed like this was the ring they were after, given they were looking for it on Beryl's person and Tabetha was one of her ancestors.

Boston Davis and Nicodemus Burke had admitted to thieving the money and were now (seemingly) looking to rob a ring. Possibly from October herself, never mind that she had grave-robbed the ring. However, October wasn't sure what to do with this information. She wasn't wearing a wire, she didn't have a tape recorder or video camera. How would she turn this newfound information into hard evidence? This was exactly the issue October was tackling when she turned around to see the bespectacled bass player, Preston Sinclair, holding an acoustic guitar aloft by the neck, which he then brought crashing down on October's head.

☠   ☠   ☠

22

Scream If
You Wanna
Die Faster

Fortunately for all of us, the guitar to the head didn't kill me.
Maybe I was just lucky. I seemed kind of lucky, current pre-
dicament notwithstanding. The one hope I always held on to
was that if I was murdered in the course of one of my mystery
investigations, I could always be certain I'd have at least five
friends in the afterlife.

Those five dead friends were nowhere to be seen when I
returned to consciousness. I couldn't be sure how long I'd been
out, but it was enough time for my attackers to tie me to the
front plow (or whatever it's called) of a bulldozer. The sky was
still dark, so morning hadn't arrived yet. The vision in my right
eye wasn't the best, and it took me a while to figure out that
was because my face was bleeding. I had already determined my
wrists were bound to the bulldozer with rope — how every crook
I tried to stop had ready access to, like, sailor's ropes is a mystery I'd love to solve later — but my legs were free. I was looking
forward to the opportunity of perhaps kicking someone hard.

As my sight cleared — in the one eye, at least — I could see
nearly my entire rogues gallery before me: Nicodemus Burke,
standing in his starched collar and dark cloak, and the members of Phantom Moustache, who seemed a bit uncomfortable
standing next to Blackstone the magician.

"Miss Schwartz, you're awake," Burke said, trudging
through the sand to be closer to the bulldozer, but tragically

not close enough to be within kicking distance. "Did you bring any of your friends?"

"I'm telling you, Mr. Burke," Preston answered while still holding the broken guitar like it was an inverted umbrella and we were all mid-thunderstorm. "She was alone when I found her."

"We'll see about that," he replied.

My mind was working slowly — which possibly had something to do with being bashed in the head every other month — but I soon realized the dead kids hadn't abandoned me. They were in hiding because they knew Nicodemus Burke could see them.

"Mr. Burke?" Boston Davis asked, pulling back and forth on the toggles of his hoodie. "I still don't understand how you know October. She's just some garbage loser from our school."

"Yeah," Taylor added. "One who likes to watch Boston makeout with his girlfriend."

The Phantom Moustache guys all started giggling then, which was one of the scarier things I've seen.

"October is much more than just a high school outcast, though I admit she may be that, as well," Nicodemus began, adding insult to injury. "She's very connected to your plans. In fact, with the ghosts she controls, she may be the only one who could possibly prevent what's coming."

"Ghosts?" Taylor spat. "You're joking, right?"

"I don't control them. They're more like friends," I said, which I intended to sound really cool. Mostly I just spat blood.

"What is she talking about, Burke?" Devin asked.

"You haven't seen them?" he smiled broadly.

"Ghost aren't real," Taylor insisted.

"You need to discuss some things amongst yourselves," Burke said, losing patience with his teen hooligans' reactions. "We are joined in this enterprise to raise a witch from the dead and you're having trouble with ghosts?"

Raise a witch from the dead? I only knew of one dead witch (maybe) and that was Fairfax Crisparkle. Was that Asphodel Meadows' endgame? And if so, why? Digging my heels into the dirt, I tried to see if I could spot the dead kids anywhere, but they had vanished, along with any semblance of a normal life in high school, should I survive the night.

"So, you're all members of Asphodel Meadows?" I asked, trying to stall for time. Maybe the dead kids were working on a really stellar rescue operation. One that'd make *The Great Escape* look like a tea party.

Mr. Burke let out a supervillain laugh, which was fitting because he was also kind of dressed like one.

"Oh, goodness, *yes*," he bellowed. "These young men are dyed-in-the-wool Meadows men."

That phrase, "dyed-in-the-wool," meant almost nothing to me.

"We're all fans of a certain old witch. But I know the occult and these boys, sadly, do *not*. At least not to the degree they need to know it to achieve their plans —"

"Shut up, Burton!" Boston Davis shouted. "You don't need to tell this goth skid our life story! What is this, a James Bond movie?"

Nicodemus Burke looked less than impressed to be chided by a sixteen-year-old. "As if she hadn't already figured it out."

I waited quietly, hoping to learn more about Asphodel Meadows, like how many members there were and how far along they were in resurrecting Fairfax Crisparkle, the town's most notorious former resident. I mean, Nicodemus Burke was pretty good with a salt circle, but resurrection seemed pretty advanced. I struggled against my ropes, but my wrists felt like they'd been walloped with a belt.

"Suffice to say, young lady, these gentlemen needed my . . . *spiritual* help . . . and the movement needs money. You can't just dig up mandrake root nowadays. Do you know how much that costs to order online?"

"Which is why you stole the Bandwarz money," I completed the thought.

"They said you were something of an amateur detective," Nicodemus said, removing his evening gloves from his vest pocket. (Who wears evening gloves?)

"But how did you steal it? The whole band was in the auditorium when the cash box was stolen," I said.

Nicodemus edged a tiny bit closer, dangling one of his white gloves from his forefinger, then drew his hand up, making the glove evaporate into the ether. "In addition to my arcane knowledge of the occult," he said as he retrieved the missing glove from his vest pocket, "I am also a gifted illusionist."

"So, wait," I said. "You tricked Ashlie and her friends with sleight-of-hand? Then what did Phantom Moustache do?"

"We told him *how* to steal the money," Devin explained.

"And," added Taylor, "we created a solid diversion."

"You guys," Boston interjected. "Shut up and stop telling her everything."

"Plus, *we* came up with the idea to pin it on Crenshaw House," Preston added. "We knew how readily people would blame the Black guy and his brown bandmates. It was a team effort, if you think about it."

While Burke gave the Phantom Moustache boys a serious death glower, I decided to take my chance. I swung forward with my right leg, but the guitar blow must have made me woozier than I'd noticed. My head swam and my leg went akimbo.

Nicodemus deftly lunged backward, leaving me to harmlessly kick a stray length of his stupid cloak.

"Does Alyosha know?" I asked with some effort. The kick had made me dizzy. "Is he part of Asphodel Meadows?"

"Who?" said Taylor.

"Oh, the real estate agent?" Burke laughed. "No, he just sees ghosts. I figured I could use him to drive me around and do my bidding if I trapped them, since he was so bothered by their existence. But if I could capture you and ghosts in the process, so much the better."

I smiled to let Burke and Phantom Moustache know I was fathoming the depths of their terribleness.

"Wait till Ashlie finds out she was dating pure evil."

"I'm afraid it won't be you who gets to tell her, October," Burke said, putting his gloves on. When a stranger puts on gloves and it's not chilly outside, that's typically a red flag. "You know too much."

"But that's *your* fault!" I shouted, realizing now why I was tied to heavy construction equipment and going into full panic mode. "You're the one who wanted to talk so much!"

"Be that as it may," he said, beginning to circle the bull-dozer, "we can't let you leave here with that knowledge. So we're going to make you have a little construction accident. Don't worry. We'll remove the ropes later so it looks more authentic."

The faces of Phantom Moustache showed a spectrum of emotions, almost like those phases people go through when someone dies: Boston had reached acceptance and Devin seemed to be experiencing depression. Preston seemed ready to bargain and Taylor was still in denial.

"We can't just kill her, can we?" Taylor asked, but no one volunteered an answer.

"Maybe we can, like . . . do something else," Preston suggested. "Like, um, cut out her tongue."

"That's worse!" Taylor shouted.

"How is that worse? I mean, it's gross . . . and probably won't work."

"This is no time to be squeamish, you wimps," Boston

shouted at the others. "We're on our way to unleash, like, ancient evil on this stupid town. You can't poop your pants because we've gotta kill some chick no one even cares about."

Things were looking more and more grim. Like, if I was going to be murdered by some crummy band, I'd have hoped it would at least be someone famous, like the Spin Doctors. At about this point, I was starting to get really annoyed my dead kid cavalry hadn't arrived yet.

"Need I remind you boys that Devin's brother tried killing this girl once before?" Burke called from the elevated seat of the dozer. "He had no qualms about it."

"That was her?" Devin said, now broken from his sad resignation.

"Or that over a century ago, a girl was killed in this very spot by Asphodel Meadows," he continued shouting, throwing on the bulldozer's lights. "Isn't that why we are here? To retrieve the Crisparkle ring that went missing with that girl's murder?"

I was half-impelled to be a pedantic jerk and point out that Tabetha had died more like a hundred feet away, but I figured it wouldn't be wise to antagonize the guy in the driver's seat of the construction vehicle I was strapped to. Was the ring in my bag once a powerful witch's? Or is that something only the zealous members of Asphodel Meadows truly believed? I held out hope that there were no other current members besides the band and their older siblings. With even five members, the secret society was causing all sorts of trouble.

"But our friend already knew about that death, I'm guessing. Didn't you, October?" Burke called. Then he hopped off the idling bulldozer and circled the vehicle to face me. "What exactly do you know, October Schwartz?"

"Aren't you gonna run her over?" exclaimed Devin, seemingly disappointed.

"Me? No," Burke snorted. "I've done all the work so far. I think it's time for the younger generation to get their hands a little dirty."

"But you have to!"

"Do it, Burton!" Devin shouted.

"My name is Nicodemus Burke, you little goon."

"Sure thing, *Ned Burton*," Devin spat back.

"That's not my name!" Burke screamed. Then, calmer: "Now one of you cowards needs to kill this girl."

"You want *us* to kill her?" Preston shouted.

"Do whatever you want," Burke said, folding his arms across his chest in a way that made his cloak billow and swirl. This could have been my opportunity to escape, if only my dead friends had been paying attention. "But she knows what we're up to. And worse, she knows ghosts."

"She doesn't know ghosts," Boston scoffed. "She's just a chubby goth who wants us to *think* she does."

"She probably knows about the ring too," Burke continued. "The bulldozer is already on. One of you just needs to pull that lever."

"I'll do it," Devin exhaled, and trudged toward the vehicle's side ladder.

Well, this was it. My dad was in a holding cell, and when and if he was released, he'd discover his only daughter was killed in yet another tragic teen construction site accident. And worst of all, it was a bunch of racist teen boys who were going to crush my bones between a wall and a multi-ton vehicle. But I could delay my death briefly, at least. Because when Burke started talking about Crisparkle's ring, my eyes — or the eye that wasn't caked over in blood — drifted over to my bag, which had fallen off near the corner of the construction trailer.

"Her backpack!" Burke shouted.

"What?" Devin shouted. "I can't hear you over the engine."

"Never mind," he said. "You others. Boston, Prescott — whatever you're named — get her backpack!"

Boston and Preston scrambled to my bag and brought it back, going through all the pockets, even dumping my *Two Knives, One Thousand Demons* book on the ground.

"Is the ring inside?" Burke shouted.

"I don't see anything," Preston said, adjusting his glasses with a free hand.

"Wait!" shouted Taylor as he pointed at the steps into the trailer. "Is that it there?"

Like everyone else, I followed Taylor's finger and saw a tiny green sparkle. *Something* had certainly fallen there. But unlike everyone else — or unlike the band members, at least — I also saw the heads of Tabetha Scott, Morna MacIsaac, and Kirby LaFlamme just peeking beyond the corner of the trailer. I guess I wasn't completely deluded to think the dead kids had some sort of plan for my rescue. Hopefully a good one.

Almost immediately, Nicodemus Burke, apparently the only other living person in attendance who could see ghosts, started yelling warnings and admonitions.

"Stop!" he screamed at Preston and Boston, who were already mid-sprint toward the ring. "Can't you see the ghosts?"

"Ghosts?" Preston shouted, while his sprinting partner reached down for the ring just as it was yanked away. The dead kids had rigged the ring with fishing line or dental floss or something. To the band, it must have seemed like the ring zipped off on its own. Boston fell to his knees as the ring flew from his grasp. The ring escaped around the corner, tugged by Tabetha. Preston and Boston — not heeding the only adult there — chased after it. Taylor and Devin joined them on the hunt.

"You idiots!" Burke shouted and jogged after them. "Can't you see this is a trick?"

All my attackers were soon lost in the dark night, scrambling after a green ring that seemed to have a mind and flight pattern all its own. Before too long, I could feel hands at my wrists, working on the ropes.

"Thanks for the rescue," I said. Derek and Cyril were at

work on my bindings. "That rule about not harming living people is a real pain, you know."

"After you die," Derek deadpanned, "you don't get a lot of choices."

"These knots are embarrassingly simple," scoffed Cyril, who had already freed my left hand. "It's as if these people have never been on a ship."

"This may shock you, Cyril, but that's entirely possible," I said. "I'd never been on a ship before that one we burned down."

"What now?" Derek asked after undoing the knot on my other hand.

"We need to get somewhere safe. We can't take on all five of them, especially with your enforced pacifism," I said. "But we also need to make sure they don't get that ring."

"Why not?" Cyril asked.

"I think it belonged to Crisparkle. You know, the witch who killed you?" Add that to the list of phrases I never thought I'd say. "They need it for some reason, and it's safe to assume it's a bad reason."

"Tabetha has it now," Derek said. "She's the fastest of any of us, so it should be safe."

"We need to catch up with her," I said, reclaiming my book and backpack.

"Can't we just use this machine here and destroy the trailer?" Cyril suggested, indicating the bulldozer, which had been left idling.

"Fun, but maybe another time."

So, like first responders hurtling headlong into a burning building, we raced toward the group that had just tried to turn me into me a bloody street pizza (or, more accurately, fairground pizza). Tabetha, Morna, and Kirby were running around in circles and figure eights, keeping the ring on a tight lead. The four band members and their spooky adult partner were hopping around like amateur basketball players trying to guard Harlem Globetrotters who also happened to be invisible.

"Okay, Burke," panted Preston Sinclair. "I'm willing to concede there might be ghosts. Something supernatural is definitely happening."

"Here comes October," Boston spat. "How did she escape?"

"There are more ghosts!" Burke cried in desperation. "Five of them. I warned you. She controls them. We never should have left her unattended."

Tabetha dashed toward us and hastily jammed the ring into my sweaty palm.

"Take this!" she shouted. "Shove it in your pocket and follow me!"

Tabetha sprinted toward the fair rides and stalls. The other dead kids and I haplessly raced behind her, our far-too-quick pace bunny.

"Why did you give this to me?! You're much faster!" I shouted.

"The more the boys doubt we exist," gulped Kirby, who was also *not* into all this track and field, "the better!"

Some distance behind us, Nicodemus Burke hunched over for a breather. "Get them. If you ever want the Crisparkle ring, you have to stop the girl from leaving," he gasped. "I have bad knees. I can't keep up."

"What *them*?!" asked Taylor, still not buying the ghost thing. "It's just October."

"Bro," Preston replied. "How did that ring move on its own then?"

"Not ghosts," Taylor said.

"Hurry, you morons," Burke interrupted. "You can still catch her. Look at her; her knees are probably worse than mine!"

The guys in Phantom Moustache were having some sort of scrum with Burke, which gave us enough time to fully enter the midway area of the fair. The absence of blinking lights gave everything a haunted quality, with food tents, test-your-strength booths, and a mid-sized Ferris wheel all sleepy-like in the moonlight.

"Over there!" shouted someone. Phantom Moustache were back on the hunt.

"Hide in here," Morna whispered, and led us onto a darkened carousel. We quietly crept past the plastic horses, their dead eyes frozen open in terror, and I settled in a two-seater carriage that was turned toward the ride's centrum.

"They can't see you," I whispered. "Stay outside and keep watch for me."

Almost a second after I delivered my instructions, the platform of the carousel sank with a heavy weight.

"Too late," I said. "I think they've arrived."

"Run!" shouted Derek. "They're here!"

The six of us bolted from the platform with Taylor and Devin fast on our heels. We ducked into a row of game booths, but Boston was already waiting for us at the end of the aisle. He'd overturned a water barrel and, with some help from Preston, rolled it on its side toward us. It thundered through the games booths like that boulder in *Raiders of the Lost Ark*, and I heard glass shattering as the large silhouette of a drum hurtled our way.

"Jump!" Cyril shouted, leaping over the booth's tabletop. The other kids followed and Tabetha grabbed me by the backpack to drag me over the booth counter like a reluctant dog hauled into a car by its collar.

The boys sprinted toward our spot on the lawn, converging from the north and south. Derek rushed east and we all scrambled to our feet to race after him. He hopped over the fence into a ride named the Polar Express and beckoned us to follow his lead.

"This seems like a bad idea," I gasped. If I was going to be running from teenage boys regularly in my detective work, I was going to have to work on my stamina. Or not get caught in these situations in the first place.

The Polar Express looked like a giant Wheel of Fortune game wheel, tilted at a twenty-degree angle, with little roller-coaster cars attached to the edge. The backdrop was an airbrushed scene of snowy mountain peaks, with an angry Yeti splashed at one end. The other dead kids followed, and I, not being quite as nimble as Derek, rolled into the ride over the uncomfortable metal gates.

287

I dusted off my jeans and followed Derek to where he and the dead kids had gathered atop the wheel.

"Get in a car and strap yourselves in," he shouted. "Tabetha, man the controls."

Tabetha hopped off the massive disc and over to a board of buttons and levers. I joined the others, seating myself in an electric blue car and pulling my seat belt tight. The boys were now (literally) at the gate, and soon leapt over it.

"Turn it on! Turn it on!" Derek shouted.

"I don't even know what this thing is!" Tabetha barked back.

"Just push buttons until it starts moving!"

Tabetha had only mashed a few buttons before the cars began to move, slowly revolving around the wheel, gradually gaining speed. The ride's lamps blasted on, momentarily blinding me and imprinting the words "Polar Express" on my retinas. Grating music accompanied the revolutions: Cher's problematic anthem, "Gypsies, Tramps, and Thieves," which I only recognized because it was Yumi's cell phone ringtone back during the brief period when she had a cell phone.

"I'm going to be sick," Kirby shouted as the speed of rotations increased.

"How can you be sick?" I shouted. "You don't even eat!"

"Can we slow this down?" Morna said, bracing her arms against the sides of her crimson car.

"Slow down?" shouted Cyril as he held onto his hat. "No! Go faster, Tabetha!"

Whatever Tabetha said was lost in the rotations and overpowering vocals of Cher.

"How is this supposed to help us, Derek?!" I shouted.

As if in response, Devin McGriff, gathered with his three bandmates at the edge of the Polar Express, reared back and took a running leap onto the fast-moving ride. Astonishingly, he landed on his feet atop the edge of a gold car just two lengths away from where I'd strapped myself in. But within a second, centripetal force (see? I pay attention in Dad's class) hurled him from the ride and sent him splayed onto the pavement.

"Like that?"

Devin got to his feet. The throw didn't seem to have hurt him badly, but neither he nor anyone else in Phantom Moustache looked keen to jump onto a moving amusement park ride again. Boston pointed to the ride's controls, and they rushed over to turn it off, but Tabetha stood fast in front of them, effectively blocking their grasping hands. From the brief glimpses I could get of their faces as I spun at forty kilometres an hour, they looked completely befuddled. After thirty seconds like that, they gave up, resigned that the controls were protected by some sort of invisible force field.

"Okay, great," I admitted. But, fully aware that all rides, like lives, end, I asked, "How long do we stay here?"

"All night if we have to," Derek shouted from his lime car behind me, way too enthusiastic about the concept. "We keep riding until someone shows up in the morning. These dudes will have to leave before that happens."

"You mean you want us to stay on this death trap all night?" shouted Kirby. "No, no. I'm out. I'll help Tabby."

In the silver car ahead of the gold one, Kirby released the seatbelt safety and was sent coasting in the same direction as Devin, but he landed with a troubling crack that left his left arm bent sideways at the elbow.

"Oh no," I gulped. In a second, I'd decided that staying on the Polar Express was by far the better option.

And so, the three other dead kids and I continued to spin through the airbrushed Arctic mountains over and over. The Cher song transitioned to some electronic dance hit while the Phantom Moustachers discussed something amongst themselves and scratched their heads. Kirby dragged himself out of the dirt and stood at Tabetha's side. Then, out of the gloom that surrounded our beacon of a ride emerged Nicodemus Burke, calmly striding to the gate and allowing himself in. From what I could see, from my constant 360 spin, he assessed the rapidly twirling ride, briefly consulted with the teen musicians who were trying to kill me, then walked right up to the controls and — instead of trying to turn them off, scooped up Tabetha in his arms and held her with his left forearm pulled tight across her throat.

Kirby, seeing the deathly fear in Tabetha's watering eyes, stepped back from the controls. With his free right hand, Nicodemus Burke powered the ride down.

The rotations slowed and the music ended. The lights dimmed, but remained partially illuminated, like a resto-lounge after seven. When the Polar Express finally creaked to a halt, my blue car and I were on the far edge of the disc, away from Nicodemus Burke and Phantom Moustache, who cautiously approached the dormant ride. That was when I realized I was probably going to die.

My looming and inevitable death worried me — mostly because it was happening much sooner than I'd hoped. But I tried to comfort myself with the things I'd managed to accomplish in my brief time on earth. After all, I'd solved a number of mysteries in the past year alone, without any formal training in crime investigation or even very good marks in critical thinking.

"What were you going to do, just stand there like pylons all night?" Burke shouted, still keeping Tabetha in his sleeper hold. "I have your dead friend, Miss Schwartz, as I'm sure you can see. Why don't you get off that ride so we can talk?"

I unbuckled my seat belt. The dead kids eyed me and let themselves off the ride first. They fanned out around my tormenters but were helpless to do much other than watch.

"That's good. Now come down here," Burke suggested. "Obviously, as your friend is dead. I can't really threaten her life, but you know I have certain abilities. After all, she's not able to just go intangible right now, is she?"

That *would* have been the easiest way to escape this situation. I slowly crept to the edge of the disc and let myself down.

"Maybe I could put this ghost girl under my mind control. Make her a zombie. Could I do that? Only one way to find out . . ." He grinned, now just a few paces from me. The boys weren't far behind. "Or you could just give me the ring and we can all go home, pretend this didn't happen."

Phantom Moustache protested.

"What?!"

"Dude, she's gonna tell on us. We'll be expelled!"

"We'll be arrested!"

"Quiet!" he responded. "You think that matters? With the ring — if you complete your plans — it won't matter within a week if you were expelled or what your permanent records say. Why can't you think?!"

The entire crew kept edging closer to me, as if they were stealthy ninjas and I couldn't notice.

"Stay back," I warned. "I can control ghosts and . . . I can make them kill you!"

The boys looked startled, but Nicodemus Burke just patted Tabetha's head and called my bluff. "You know ghosts can't harm the living, girl. Who do you think you're talking to?"

Oh, yeah. Burke knew all about ghosts.

"No," I stammered. "These are . . . different kind of ghosts. Super dangerous."

"He's touching her hair," Kirby said out of the side of his mouth. "Tabby's not gonna like that."

"She doesn't like bein' called Tabby either," Tabetha answered through gritted teeth. "Do somethin', October!"

Derek glanced at me, completely at a loss for plans.

"Yeah, October, do somethin'," Burke snorted. "Help poor Tabby Scott, the girl that got killed by one of our order."

"It's *Tabetha!*"

"Just reach into your bag, give me the ring, and this will all be over," Burke cooed.

"Okay," I sighed.

Slowly, methodically, I pulled the bag from my shoulders and unzipped the main compartment.

"Good, good," he said, just a metre or two away. "Now, just throw it in this direction."

Tabetha coughed and, in that split second, I pulled out the shish kebab skewer and drove it as hard as I could through Tabetha's neck — and deep into the soft torso of Nicodemus Burke.

As Burke screamed in pain and dropped to his knees, I shouted "Pentagon!" Before the evil band members could even figure out what was going on, the dead kids, minus Tabetha, had surrounded them in a circle and locked arms.

"What's pentagon?" Taylor shouted, clearly alarmed by people yelling out random shape names.

"There's only four of us," Kirby, holding hands with Morna and Derek on either side, corrected.

Tabetha pulled the skewer from her neck as she walked away from the howling, wounded psychic rolling around on the ground, a puncture wound in his stomach. She wiped the splash of blood from her throat and joined the circle, putting her bloody palm in Cyril's hand.

"*Now* it's a pentagon," she said.

"I thought we'd agreed penta*gram* sounded better," Derek said.

"October," Tabetha added, "never stab me in the neck again."

"I'm really sorry," I grimaced.

Preston, who was not keen to get skewered, I guess, ran and collided with Kirby, then fell back on the pavement.

"What's happening?!"

Taylor, panicked, tried to walk away and was also repelled.

"Why can't we move?!" he shouted.

"It's the *ghosts*," Boston said.

"Shut up! They're not real!"

"Why is he still screaming?" Devin shouted.

Nicodemus Burke, Sticksville's master of the occult, was, in fact, still shrieking, still clutching the bloody spot on his belly.

"Maybe he's being tormented by ghosts," I smirked. The dead kids closed their pentagon or pentagram or whatever they preferred to call it around the members of Asphodel Meadows as I approached. The four boys looked like spotted deer that had just heard a gunshot. "Now, can I borrow one of your cell phones? While I call the police, you can work on your confessions."

☠   ☠   ☠

23

Carnival
of Trolls

Did the members of Phantom Moustache, like Usher Raymond the Fourth, work on their confessions? You shall soon discover the truth. But after a killer action-movie line delivery like the final sentence of our previous chapter, we need to jump ahead in our story. I'm afraid it doesn't work any other way.

You'll be relieved to know that both local psychic and recently perforated master of the occult Nicodemus Burke and Phantom Moustache lead singer Boston Davis were arrested — by the one-and-only Officer Grenouille, no less — for the theft of the stolen Bandwarz donations. When the police found that Burke's handwriting matched the note, that his Sharktacular Plunge car matched the vehicle Mr. Santuzzi had identified, and — most importantly — the actual cash money had been stashed with Davis's guitar magazines in the pool house, neither crook had much recourse. However, the other members of Phantom Moustache (and Asphodel Meadows) went home freer than a rich white man (which, in essence, the three of them were). Boston took the fall, claiming the other members had nothing to do with the robbery. And there wasn't enough proof to charge them with anything more than trespassing on the fairgrounds. Though October claimed all five conspired to kill her, she was the only one who had stabbed someone with a barbecue tool. This is not to say Sticksville Central High School didn't discuss expelling all three for their alleged attempts to murder a schoolmate. But allegations can, the school administration reasoned, often prove false.

Imagine the surprise to Mr. Schwartz when he ran into his own daughter — bruised, dishevelled, covered in both her own and others' blood — at the police station in the wee hours of the morning. Obviously, October's return to the pursuits of crime prevention and detection gave him pause. One expects a daughter with heavy eye makeup and spiked bracelets to run afoul of the law here and there, but October was making it her preferred extra-curricular activity. And college admissions do not favour amateur sleuthing over debate club or volleyball. But there were benefits, he reasoned, to a detective for a daughter. After all, October's work was the primary reason for his release from custody.

So, instead of grounding her or chiding her for getting involved in matters that didn't directly concern her, he did what felt right and just hugged October. He brushed her bangs from her bloody forehead and asked the police if he could take her home to get cleaned up before they took her statement.

Even though it felt like several days had been spent on the Polar Express, it was merely Sunday morning, so father and daughter went home, got cleaned up, and had an obscenely large breakfast of bacon and eggs. Then her dad made an attempt to watch the third *Friday the 13th* with his daughter, as she said it was the thing she most wanted to do that afternoon.

"Are you sure you want to watch something so violent?" he asked, opening up the plastic DVD clamshell. "On the Internet Movie Database, it says a man's head is squeezed so hard his eyeball shoots out, and I feel like you've already been scared enough."

"This helps," October said, settling into a couch nook and embracing a big throw pillow. "I know this isn't real. Think of these horror movies like your seventies rock music."

"I'll try," he said, taking a seat at the far end of the couch.

Mr. Schwartz made it twelve minutes before wondering aloud, "What kind of movie am I watching?" then slinking out to the kitchen to continue his reading of some pop psychology that had been earlier interrupted by the police. When the two members of the household reconnected post-movie, they had a dinner of delivery pizza and root beer, and, for a short while, everything seemed like it would be all right.

☠   ☠   ☠

Just a few hours after the pizza, that calm normalcy experienced its first setback. In the light of a nearly full moon — moon experts (or astronomers — see, this book is educational) would call it waxing gibbous — October met with the dead kids and gave them one final task before they vanished for a while.

"While you're still around, I'd like us to search Boston Davis's pool house," October said.

"Didn't we have enough excitement last night?" Tabetha protested. October found it difficult to look right at her, as she still had a quarter-inch hole in the middle of her neck.

"I have to agree, October," Morna said. "Maybe we can just relax . . . n' play a fun game."

"Or since we're doing my mystery next," Kirby hinted, adjusting his tie, "it might not hurt to get a headstart. I'm sure my mystery will prove the most complex one yet."

"Please," October begged. "The police found the cash there. Boston is part of the secret order. I think we have the opportunity to find out way more about Asphodel Meadows. Who else is a member besides Nicodemus Burke and the band?"

"I think you mean Ned Burton," Derek corrected October with the psychic's real name.

"It's not like any of those guys in Phantom Moustache are going to talk to me ever again," October added. "And think of what you could add to your Meadow Files."

"She has a point," Morna agreed.

"That's not what we call the files," Derek pouted.

And so, as the waxing gibbous moon (remember?) slunk under some heavy cloud cover, October Schwartz and the dead kids arrived at the Davis pool house. The pool house, naturally, was entirely cordoned off by yellow police tape. Tabetha ghosted through the front door first and opened it for the rest of the group. October ducked under the tape and joined them.

"This is *very* illegal," Morna announced, following close behind her.

"How many illegal things have we done in the past day alone, Morna?" October reminded her. "I stabbed a psychic."

"True," Tabetha said.

"Tabetha, in all the excitement, we haven't asked how you are feeling," Cyril said, weirdly empathetic for a moment.

"Like *you* care, slave owner," she said, opening up a cabinet in the pool house living area.

"Hey, *guys*," October said.

"No, I understand," Cyril said. "My family didn't own slaves, I suppose, but that doesn't mean they were kind to people of your race. In fact, I believe we've established some of them were down-right cruel."

"That's an understatement," Tabetha mumbled.

"Aw, Cyril's growing," Derek smiled and rifled through a book case, which begged the question: Boston Davis reads?

"It wasn't even racism that killed Tabetha," Kirby corrected. "It was some weird secret society. The racism was just a red herring."

"Now, now," Cyril said. "Don't be dismissive. Maybe that wasn't the motive of the murderer — this Yvonne person — but that doesn't change the fact that most of the town — my family included — tried to drive Tabetha and her family away, that they showed no compassion when she died, that Tabetha was once legally *owned* by someone, that this entire nation was established on the erroneous concept that white Europeans are somehow . . ."

"Okay, I get it," Kirby said, throwing up his hands in surrender.

"Fine then," the suddenly woke Cyril said, errantly glancing around at October and his fellow dead kids mid-search. "I just wanted to apologize on behalf of the Cooper family, Tabetha."

"That's very nice, Cyril," October said, finding a cigar box full of coins.

"Yes, thank you," Tabetha said. "I do feel a little better now. A little."

"I want to apologize, too, Tabetha," October added. "I was so distracted by the other mystery, I didn't treat you the way a friend should be treated."

298

"What about you, Kirby?" Tabetha asked. "You got anything ta say?"

"Apologies are for the imperfect," he groused.

"I found a filing cabinet," Derek said, moving a stack of pillows that had been obscuring the office shelving. "Why is there a filing cabinet in a pool house?"

"Search it," October instructed. "Did you and Morna add the new information we learned last night to your Meadow Files?"

"Yes," Morna, who was less concerned about the title of their notebook, replied. "'Looking for ring found by Tabetha. Want to resurrect a witch — Fairfax Crisparkle?'"

"And we added the names of those band members," Derek said. "Wait a second . . ."

Derek Running Water extracted a file folder from the metal cabinet and began to go through it.

"What did you find?" Cyril asked.

"A folder labelled F to C," he said. "That's strange because that's not how the alphabet goes."

"They can't read, but they must at least know the *song*," Kirby insisted.

October was less interested in whether Cyril, Tabetha, and Morna knew the alphabet than she was in what Derek had found.

"What's inside?"

"Something that I think should go in our Meadow Files," he said, holding out a few sheets of paper stapled together. "Even though that's not what they're called."

Kirby grabbed the papers from Derek. At some point overnight, he must have set his arm back in place, as it no longer jutted out at a frightening angle. Kirby had experienced a lot of arm trauma lately. "Names and dates . . . Schlangegriff, Burton, Crookshanks."

"Those are Asphodel Meadows names," Morna exclaimed. She had them well memorized.

"Shh," October shushed.

Derek read more: "Edmund Burton, 1862. Dorothy Crookshanks, 1871," then he passed me the paper. "Look at this, on the third page. Meredith Fairweather. Is this your mom? What is this year?"

October stood transfixed by the printout of her mother's name, just waiting to be discovered in Boston Davis's stupid pool house.

"That's the year she disappeared."

☠   ☠   ☠

Both Schwartzes took Monday as a sick day, but by Tuesday, they returned to thir regular duties at Sticksville Central High School, as science teacher and student, respectively. Following a brisk stroll to school through a very light drizzle, October wasn't inside for forty seconds before being tackled by Yumi. She was joined by Stacey, as well, who did not tackle her in a hug — unless you mean that hug metaphorically. And even then, not really.

"Schwartz, is *everyone* trying to kill you?" she said, releasing October from her death grip. "You're going to need Stacey and me to act as bodyguards. And if that's the case, we're going to have to start working out."

Stacey's face, usually impassive, broke into a very slight, almost imperceptible smirk. "I don't like the sound of that. Can't be *too* ripped as a drummer. It hurts the drums."

"We're glad you're not dead, October. But you need to be more careful. How's your head?"

"Better. I'm hoping it doesn't scar."

300

"Forehead scar — like the Boy Who Lived," Yumi pointed at October.

"More like the Girl Who Nearly Died."

"I feel a bit responsible, Schwartz. I assume you were spying on Boston Davis and his creep-tastic adult friend because I pushed you into helping Levi. I feel like I keep pushing you into things and don't provide much support," Yumi said, staring at her dirty shoes (which seemed mere moments from total disintegration). "So, I'm sorry."

"I probably would have done it anyway, even without your peer pressure," October said.

"They're always warning us about the dangers of peer pressure," said Stacey.

"Next time you need to undertake a dangerous adventure, give us a call, huh? So we can support you?" said Yumi, punching October in her shoulder. She so desperately would have wanted to be a member of the Dead Kid Detective Agency had she known it existed. "We'll start training, if that helps. We can be backup."

"I would definitely take a bullet for you," Stacey offered.

"That's sweet, Stacey," October smiled. "But it was a guitar."

Yumi escorted October to her locker. Both friends flanked her a bit more carefully now, as if she were a foreign dignitary marked for death.

"I hope Levi appreciates all of this," Yumi added. "You should get danger pay."

"I don't think I'm getting paid at all," October said. She was really going to need to monetize things if she wanted to continue playing detective.

"Total Spider-Man," Stacey marvelled. "Justice is your reward."

"Besides, he shouldn't *appreciate* anything," October said, turning serious. "This whole school was willing to write him off."

"Yeah, this place kind of sucks," Yumi began, but paused mid-thought when the members of Crenshaw House turned the corner.

"October!" Levi shouted.

The two trios stopped a couple paces from each other, just like when Alvin and the Chipmunks first met their female counterparts, the Chipettes.

"Can we talk with October alone for a second?" Henry asked.

Yumi turned to gauge October's feelings about this, and October put her mind at ease: "I'm fine, Yumi. Don't worry about me."

Stacey and Yumi scampered off down the arts hall to history class. Levi approached October in such a formal way, she felt like Crenshaw House was going to knight her or propose marriage.

"October," Levi said. "We can't thank you enough for proving us innocent. We owe you, big time."

"Yeah, it was a pretty cool thing, October," Matilda said from behind her shag of hair.

"I'm so sorry it put you in so much danger," Levi continued. "If we'd known —"

"We never meant —" Henry added.

"It's okay, really," October tried to calm them down. They looked like they'd accidentally entered the code sequence to launch a missile attack on Saint Petersburg. "Last night was scary, but it turned out okay. We're all good. Really, it never should have come to this. People were so quick to accuse you."

The trio of Crenshaw House looked mildly confused. As if they expected more self-flagellation would be necessary.

"Okay . . . then . . ." Levi Marylebone stuttered, taking October's right hand firmly in both of his and pumping it vigorously. "If you ever need any sort of help in the future . . ."

"We're already working on a song about you," Matilda said, brushing the bangs from her eyes. "It's called 'October Rain.'"

"Like 'November Rain,'" Levi added.

"Thanks, I get it," she nodded.

"Thank you so much, October," Henry said, and pulled October into a hug she was not prepared for. There was a lot of stealth hugging on tap this morning, and October didn't particularly like being touched this much. However, Henry Khan's hug wasn't so bad. It was kind of warm. "I can't believe you were just down the block when Phantom Moustache attacked you. If . . ."

Henry left the imaginary scenario unspoken as the hug lingered. In fact, it was only the sound of the morning tone that interrupted it. Otherwise, the embrace could conceivably have persisted through several class periods.

"Gotta go," she told them. Matilda had to grab Henry by the shoulder to get his attention.

"Oh! Of course," he said, blushing.

October ran down the hallway and stole a look at the members of Crenshaw House retreating from view. She should have been paying more attention to what was directly ahead of her, for she ran headlong into one of the deceitful but fortunate members of Phantom Moustache, Preston Sinclair. October fell backward onto the floor, uninjured but stunned. This was, after all, the boy who'd attacked her with a guitar just one night prior, despite what the authorities believed. That kind of thing lingered in the memory.

Preston, as you'd imagine, did not apologize. He did, however, help October up from her turtle-like positon, but the aid came with a vague warning. Barely speaking above a whisper, Preston Sinclair locked his grey eyes on our favourite teen detective. "You know you're only delaying the inevitable. I don't know why you bother."

"I'm just trying to get to class on time, Preston." October shrugged.

"Sure, sure," he said, unwilling to break his gaze. "Asphodel Meadows is all around us. We are legion. And we are unstoppable . . . especially now that we know where to find the ring."

October felt her throat dry up like the Gobi Desert.

"Before long, we're going to make those horror movies you like so much look like a Disney cartoon."

"Mr. Sinclair," said Ms. Fenstermacher in her sternest librarian voice. "I think you have a chemistry class to sleep through right now."

Ms. Fenstermacher, clad in a grey military-style shirt, had swooped in to October's rescue, though October doubted she knew how lucky she was to see her.

"October, I need to borrow you." Extracting her from the situation as if she were a one-woman SEAL Team Six, Ms. Fenstermacher pulled October into the library and over to the computer bay. With a row of beige computer terminals to her back, she retrieved her passenger bag.

"First: are you feeling okay?" she asked. "Sounds like you had a serious ordeal."

"You're not going to hug me, too, are you?"

"What?" she said, wrist-deep in her papers. "We're not allowed to do that, I don't think."

At least there was that small mercy.

"But check it out," Fenstermacher continued and held out the front page of the latest *Sticksville Loon* as if it were a hard-won college degree.

October scanned the headline story about criminal accomplices Nicodemus Burke and Boston Davis being arrested for a school theft.

"Yeah, I was there," October noted. "Remember?"

Fenstermacher adjusted the glasses on her face. "Oh, not that. Sorry. Look lower on the page, at the very bottom."

The headline at the very bottom was about an archaeological discovery: a child's skeleton had been found in a cello case. So the Sticksville Historic Society had finally found Tabetha Scott.

"Isn't it amazing?" Ms. Fenstermacher beamed.

"Oh, wow! A dead kid?!" October did her best to seem astounded by the existence of dead kids. "On the fairgrounds? I wonder what *that's* all about."

"So cool and eerie, right?" Ms. Fenstermacher gushed. October wasn't sure what Stacey was so into. Her history teacher was like a diehard Backstreet Boys fan, but drooling and shrieking over grim archaeological discoveries instead of Brian and A.J.

"Do you think the kid was *murdered*?" October gasped, trying to play the part as best as her limited acting abilities would allow. She was a Melissa Joan Hart, not a Meryl Streep.

"Good question," Ms. Fenstermacher said, and her affect had changed. She removed her glasses and rested them on the big computer desk. "But I think you already know the answer to that."

"Wait . . . what?"

October hadn't prepared for the 200% increase in hugs this April morning, and she was most assuredly not prepared for this. Whatever *this* was.

"Sit down, October," her history teacher insisted, pulling out an orange desk chair. "I think it's time we have a frank discussion about Asphodel Meadows."

Derek and Morna were going to have to add a second volume to their Meadow Files.

☠   ☠   ☠

Appendix
A: Cast of
Characters

October Schwartz: she's the protagonist of the book. If you're having a hard time keeping track of which one she is, you should probably put the book down right now. She's like a master detective (probably) and in nearly every sentence of the book.

Mr. (Leonard) Schwartz: October's dad and a teacher at Sticksville Central High School. He teaches auto repair and biology and probably important life lessons to October, or whatever. He's suffered from bouts of clinical depression ever since October's mom left the both of them.

Yumi Takeshi: October's best friend at Sticksville. She shares October's interest in black clothing, eyeliner, and horror movies. She also comes as part of a two-friend package deal with Stacey.

Stacey MacIsaac: friend to October and constant companion to Yumi Takeshi. A lanky boy with an affinity for mismatched vintage clothing and percussion instruments. Book Two (*Dial M for Morna*) revealed he was related to October's dead friend, Morna MacIsaac.

Ashlie Salmons: terror of the unpopular ninth-grade girls at Sticksville Central High School. Loves include belts, boots, bangs, and bullying. She leads a small crew of mostly unpleasant young ladies. Her mother is Crown Attorney Salmons.

Ms. Fenstermacher: October's cool history teacher (perhaps a little too cool to be a teacher), who replaced the sometimes homicidal Mr. Page. (See Book One for that story.) She also works at the Sticksville Museum (former home of Cyril Cooper) and is Sticksville's biggest fan of *Battlestar Galactica*, which doesn't come up much in this book.

Mr. Terry O'Shea: October's former (and formerly living) French teacher. He coached the girls' curling team and was encouraging of October's whole writing thing and was pretty important to her. So when (spoiler alert) he died in Book One, it was *très* tragic.

Mr. Santuzzi: stern mathematics teacher at Sticksville Central High School, noted for his tight leisure suits, alleged toupée, and military past. He says things like "roger" and "lock 'n' load" when going over the ways to determine the volume of a cone.

Cyril Cooper: unofficial leader and oldest of the dead kids. He was from a Loyalist family who fled to Canada during the American Revolution and had a possibly promising career in shipbuilding cut short by one Fairfax Crisparkle, as was revealed in Book Three, *Loyalist to a Fault*. Cyril is fascinated by automobiles.

Morna MacIsaac: youngest of the dead kids, Morna was a Scottish immigrant who came with her family to Canada in 1910 for work and affordable land. Instead of finding much of either, the MacIsaacs lived in a boarding house called the Crooked Arms

until Morna was killed outside a local pub by a man named Udo Schlangegriff (who was posing as a *Titanic* survivor named Dr. Alfred Pain), as revealed in Book Two, *Dial M for Morna*.

Tabetha Scott: dead kid who had to escape slavery in the American South before arriving in Sticksville. She left Virginia via an ornithologist who helped them access the Underground Railroad and settled in town with her dad. Bickers endlessly with Kirby and never hesitates to share her opinions. Who brought about Tabetha's untimely end? You'll just have to read this very book to find out.

Kirby LaFlamme: dead kid and one fifth of the not-so-famous LaFlamme quintuplets. During the Depression, he and his siblings were the inspiration for the LaFlammetown theme park. He was outlived by all his brothers and is fluent in both French and English.

Derek Running Water: the most recent death among the dead kids, Derek lived with his mother in Sticksville but became politically committed to the Mohawk Warrior cause with the 1990 standoff in Oka, Quebec, the events of which are somehow connected to his death. Derek can be relied upon to provide explanations to the other dead kids for modern technology and terminology. But he's not great with directions.

Alyosha Diamandas: one of Sticksville's most persistent realtors. Alyosha feels a healthy real estate market is indicative of a healthy democracy. He's a fan of all houses, save the haunted kind. (He's had a few run-ins with the dead kids over the years and is well aware that October Schwartz is somehow linked to them.)

Crown Attorney Salmons: mother of Ashlie Salmons who shares her daughter's taste in fashion but also shares October's thirst for justice. (After all, she spends her days prosecuting criminals and such.) Has recently been romantically linked to Leonard Schwartz, much to the chagrin of his daughter, October.

Phantom Moustache: the most popular band in Sticksville Central High School, a couple of its members have been romantically linked (ooh-la-la) with Ashlie Salmons. The popularity of this mediocre rock band has not waned, despite one member being the brother of a dangerous, bat-wielding felon.

Crenshaw House: a mysterious new band, consisting of lead singer and guitarist Levi Marylebone, bassist (and a boy that a computer thinks October should date) Henry Khan, and drummer Matilda Coffin. They're the only real competition for Phantom Moustache as far as school bands with oblique names go.

Nicodemus Burke: Sticksville psychic who advertises in the local papers and bus shelters — never mind that he's never appeared in the book series prior to this book. (He knew you'd bring that up.) Burke is known for being garishly attired, like a Met Gala attendee when the theme is The Occult.

Fairfax Crisparkle: historic and controversial figure from Sticksville's past, who may or may not have been a witch. (That's the controversial part.) Crisparkle has been closely associated with a secretive group or organization called Asphodel Meadows, and — witchcraft or not — was revealed as the murderer of our own Cyril Cooper in Book Three, *Loyalist to a Fault*.

Appendix B: Passing References (Important Cultural History!)

Advanced Dungeons & Dragons: the grandmammy of all tabletop role-playing games. Developed by Gary Gygax and Dave Arneson in the 1970s, this is where things like "experience points" and "chaotic neutral" and many scenes from *Stranger Things* come from.

Aaron Sorkin: screenwriter, filmmaker, and dialogue enthusiast probably best known for writing *The West Wing* and *The Social Network* and for the "walk and talk," where characters do those two things (together).

Aleister Crowley: famous English occultist from the late nineteenth, early twentieth century who dabbled in a little black magic and new religion creation here and there, which got him sometimes labelled "The Wickedest Man in Britain." Coming from the nation so heavily involved in the Transatlantic slave trade and colonialism, that's really saying something.

Amazon: massive online shopping company that manages to combine conveniently quick shipping of nearly anything you could want with the wholesale destruction of the retail sector and avoidance of nearly every labour and tax law in existence. (Maybe you got this very book from them!)

Archie Andrews: somewhat thick-headed but adorable red-headed protagonist of several comic book series that follow the romantic adventures of a group of clean-cut American youth. Also the name of the protagonist of television series *Riverdale*, which takes that premise but adds some abs, motorcycle gangs, and violent stabbings.

The Avengers: loosely knit group of superpowered beings in both the Marvel Comics Universe and the Marvel Cinematic Universe (or MCU) who defend the planet from Asgardian trickster gods and killer robots. Their membership consists of characters like Captain America, Thor, Iron Man, Scarlet Witch, and — occasionally — lesser-known folks like Doctor Druid.

The Backstreet Boys: Orlando-based boy band supreme of the late 1990s. They were a demanding group, insisting "I Want It That Way," "Show Me the Meaning of Being Lonely," and that you "Quit Playing Games (with My Heart)." Though they may not have invented choreographed dancing with a chair, they certainly perfected it.

***Beetlejuice* (1988):** Tim Burton movie about a recently deceased couple who employ a dirtbag ghost named Beetlejuice (Michael Keaton, in possibly his finest role) to help them scare a new family out of their former home. At one point in the film, his head spins around faster than a blender. (See also The Exorcist.)

***Biography*:** long-running A&E documentary television series that delved into the life stories of everyone from Mao Zedong to Helen Keller to Muhammad Ali. The half-hour show was a staple of seniors' households and the classrooms of tired history teachers.

Black metal: subgenre of heavy metal music for only the most extreme headbangers amongst us. Songs may feature fast tempos, shrieking vocals, and an emphasis on dark atmosphere, and bands often appear in makeup (like KISS, but cooler). A *Big Shiny Black Metal Tunes* compilation (as unlikely as that is) would probably include bands like Gorgoroth, Cradle of Filth, and Bathory.

Blackstone: either Harry Blackstone Sr. or Jr. — they're both famous stage magicians and illusionists, though at the time of writing, neither has been accused of witchcraft. (Curious, no?)

Bob the Builder: animated character from children's television who is essentially a less-butch Mike Holmes for kids. Though he relentlessly repairs buildings and structures for other people, who will fix Bob's broken insides?

Bootsy Collins: a.k.a., Casper the Funky Ghost, a.k.a., Bootzilla, the flamboyantly dressed pioneer of funk music and one of the most famous and talented bass players in music history.

The Boy Who Lived: nickname for Harry Potter in the book and movie series of the same name. None of the other kids get similar epithets: Hermione Granger is not the Girl Who Does the Homework. Cedric Diggory is not — spoiler alert — the Boy Who Died.

Canadian Tire: Canadian retailer that's kind of a cross between a Walmart and Home Depot (though you can also sometimes get gas or your car fixed there). Instead of a loyalty card, the store uses its own Canadian Tire money that can be exchanged for retail discounts.

Canasta: I think it's a card game that began in South America? But I'll be honest: I don't really know what it is. Cards are definitely involved. (See also *Old Maid*.)

Carlos Santana: the guitar king of popular music who fused rock and Latin American sounds and made it big in the 1970s with hits like "Oye Como Va" and "Black Magic Woman" (which was apparently not about Stevie Nicks). But to modern audiences, he may be best known as the guy shredding with Rob Thomas in the summertime jam "Smooth."

Carly Simon: singer-songwriter most popular in the 1970s who wrote the original subtweet track, "You're So Vain." Speculation has surrounded the single since its recording about the identity of the narcissistic subject, which was thought to be Mick Jagger, Warren Beatty, David Bowie, Cat Stevens, and others. (No shortage of vain celebrities, apparently.)

Carmen Sandiego: she's a "sticky-fingered filcher from Berlin down to Belize." First in a series of video games, then a game show and animated series, Sandiego was an international thief who robbed treasures and led detectives on a wild chase around the world, inadvertently teaching them valuable facts about world geography (or how to use a *World Almanac*) along the way. Has been known to both "ransack Pakistan" and "run a scam in Scandinavia."

Carrie: title character in both a novel by Stephen King and film by Brian De Palma who is relentlessly bullied by her classmates and puritanical mother. At her high school prom — spoiler — mean kids pull a prank on her, dousing her with pig's blood, and she retaliates by using her telekinetic powers to bust up the joint, killing nearly everyone.

Coles Notes: before you could just look up explanations of Shakespearean plays and complex works of literature on the internet, you could purchase guides that served as long cheat sheets to classic works of literature. (The American equivalent is *CliffsNotes*.)

The Cranberries: sometimes heavy, sometimes radio-friendly rock band from Ireland noted for their dearly departed lead singer Dolores O'Riordan's vocal stylings that were variously described as "ethereal" or "like a cat in its final death throes."

Criss Angel: the Marilyn Manson of illusionists, Angel (born Christopher Nicholas Sarantakos) rose to frame with his show, *Criss Angel: Mindfreak*, during which he dazzled unsuspecting rubes with his mind-blowing (and sometimes violent) illusions. Like if Harry Blackstone shopped only at Hot Topic. (See *Marilyn Manson, Blackstone, Hot Topic.*)

The Crow: simultaneously the most '90s and most goth super-hero ever, the subject of a comic book and series of movies, the Crow is a musician who is killed (with his fiancée) right before his wedding but rises from the grave as a supernatural avenger. The film was all the more goth as the lead actor, Brandon Lee, was killed during filmmaking.

The CW: television network that has — since 2006 — been a reliable source of teenage dramas of questionable content, from *One Tree Hill* and *Supernatural* to *Gossip Girl* and *The Vampire Diaries*.

Darth Vader: one of the main villains of the ubiquitous Star Wars movies. Big guy with a deep voice that dresses in black. You probably have seen him. Carries a lightsaber and (spoiler alert) is the dad of that Luke Skywalker kid. (See also *James Earl Jones.*)

Dave Matthews Band: wildly popular jam band active since the 1990s that is a go-to musical choice for people who don't really like music.

The Decline of Western Civilization, Part I and Part II (1981, 1988): documentary movies by Penelope Spheeris (director of *Wayne's World!*) that looked at the Los Angeles music scene. The first film looked at the punk scene of the late 1970s and early 1980s. The second, more notorious film looked at the rock-star excess of the glam metal scene of the later 1980s.

Dementors: the spooky, soul-sucking wraiths that act as prison guards in the Harry Potter books. Easily the most problematic aspect of the wizarding world's prison-industrial complex.

Discman: before you could have literally thousands of songs on your mobile phone, people used portable music players that used CDs (compact discs) and skipped about every thirty seconds. The Discman was first released in 1984 but gained popularity in the 1990s. (See also *Walkman*.)

Donatello (of the Teenage Mutant Ninja Turtles): traditionally depicted with a purple bandana, Donatello, as the song goes, "does machines." For the purposes of this book, it's more important you know he also fights with a bo staff, which is more or less like a long broom handle.

Dr. Ellie Sattler: portrayed by the incredible Laura Dern in the Jurassic Park films, a paleobotanist whose specialty is prehistoric plant life and who is very, very excited to see a real live Brontosaurus.

***Driving Miss Daisy* (1989):** Oscar-winning movie in which a Black chauffeur drives around an elderly Jewish retiree, and the viewers all learn vague, feel-good lessons about racism in America.

Everybody Loves Raymond: improbably one of the most successful sitcoms of all time (everybody did *indeed* love Raymond), it follows the family-friendly comedic misadventures of a sportswriter, Ray Barone (Ray Romano); his wife, Debra; his subtly menacing cop brother; and meddling parents (who live next door).

***The Exorcist* (1973):** widely held as one of the scariest films ever made, it concerns the efforts of two priests to exorcise a young girl, Regan (played by Linda Blair), seemingly possessed by the devil. Among the many memory-scarring scenes of horror is one where our possessed girl vomits pea soup with the force of a Super Soaker.

Fangoria: popular horror film fan magazine and bane of parental figures. Known to feature such articles as "*Living Dead II*: Back for more brains" and "Toxic Monster Makeup."

Father Knows Best: overly wholesome sitcom from the 1950s that featured an idealized family — the type of family whose members might wear semi-formal nightwear rather than a dirty T-shirt and boxer shorts.

***Ferris Bueller's Day Off* (1986):** classic teen comedy about a self-interested boy who tricks his school and family into believing he's ill so he can spend the day having a blast in downtown Chicago. He also convinces his friend Cameron to borrow his father's beloved Ferrari (against his express wishes), and they later run the car in reverse to return the odometer to its original number, which — fun fact — will not work on cars nowadays.

The Fresh Prince of Bel-Air: early '90s sitcom starring hip-hop MC Will Smith as a street-smart Philadelphia teenager who got in one little fight and his mom got scared and said, "You're moving with your auntie and uncle in Bel-Air." The show explored issues of race, class, and actor Alfonso Ribeiro's dance skills. In season four, Will and his cousin Carlton moved into their mansion's surprisingly spacious pool house.

Friday the 13th: a never-ending franchise of horror films that (mostly) star hockey-mask-attired killer Jason Voorhees (mostly) terrorizing teenagers who congregate at Crystal Lake (mostly) by dismembering them in horrible ways. Film reviewer Gene Siskel was so disgusted with the first film that he gave out the address of both the chairman of the production company and film's star in his review.

George of the Jungle: animated television show (and later film) about a Tarzan knockoff that was mostly remembered for its drum-heavy theme song.

"Gold Dust Woman": beginning with instructions for the titular Gold Dust Woman to take her silver spoon and dig her grave, this song by rock band Fleetwood Mac seems to bear no goodwill towards Gold Dust Women, whoever they may be.

Gomez Addams: moustachioed patriarch of the creepy and kooky Addams Family (as seen in comics, television, and film). His interests include throwing knives, crashing his model trains, and hearing his wife, Morticia, speak *en français*.

The Great Escape (1963): classic film (based on true events!) that chronicles the escape of Allied POWs from a German prison camp during World War II. Highlights include a pretty rad motorcycle jump.

Grey's Anatomy: long-running medical romance-drama featuring the life and times of Meredith Grey, a Seattle surgeon, as well as a bevy of other attractive doctors given nicknames such as "McDreamy" and "McSteamy" (despite none of the character names beginning with "Mc").

The Harlem Globetrotters: basketball team that plays exhibition games that blend theatre and comedy with pure athleticism. They're also a staple of popular culture, having famously appeared in their own animated series, visited North Korea, and even solved mysteries with Scooby-Doo. (See also *Scooby-Doo*.)

Harlequin novels: hugely successful brand of romance novels, often featuring painted covers with barrel-chested men embracing traditionally attractive heroines. Some sample titles include *Married by Mistake*, *Princess's Secret Baby*, and *An Honorable Seduction*.

Harry Styles: tousle-haired British singer and Anglo heart-throb who rose to fame as a member of the boy band One Direction. The face that launched a thousand fan fictions. (See also *One Direction*.)

Hawkwind: psychedelic space rock band that really only long-haired dudes with handlebar moustaches know.

The Hitchhiker's Guide to the Galaxy: comedic novel by Douglas Adams beloved by many a nerd, it features an average British man, Arthur Dent, who is brought into deep space by his friend, Ford Prefect (secretly an alien doing research on Earth for an intergalactic travel guide). Dryly humorous capers ensue. In the book, a towel is revealed as the most "massively useful thing an interstellar hitchhiker can have."

Hoarders: a painful (and sometimes exploitative) documentary television series that examines individuals who obsessively collect stuff and/or refuse to throw out anything they've ever acquired.

The Hobbit: from the dude who brought you *The Lord of the Rings* (J.R.R. Tolkien) comes this earlier (and significantly shorter) novel about a hobbit, Bilbo Baggins, who embarks on a quest to lift some treasure from a dragon named Smaug.

Hot Topic: if you ever find yourself in need of a Panic! at the Disco hoodie, Stewie from *Family Guy* high-tops, or literally anything with Jack Skellington on it, this go-to retailer for emo and goth kids in suburbs around North America has you covered.

The Illuminati: clandestine society that secretly controls and guides . . . I've said too much already.

James Earl Jones: respected, bass-voiced actor who is most recognized as the voice of Darth Vader, Mufasa in *The Lion King*, and CNN. (See also *Darth Vader*.)

Jericho: city located in modern-day Palestine. Biblically, it was a heavily fortified city, but its walls tumbled down after the Israelites marched around the city blowing their trumpets. As with most stuff in the Bible, you can bet God was behind some of this. Not to be confused with the short-lived post-apocalyptic TV show starring Skeet Ulrich.

John Edward: alleged medium from the television show *Crossing Over with John Edward*, in which he connected audience members with dead relatives and friends who sent vague and general messages from "the other side."

John Waters: bizarre filmmaker from Baltimore, Maryland, best known for his cult films, love of kitsch, and pencil-thin moustache.

Kevin McCallister: Portrayed by Macaulay Culkin, protagonist of the first two *Home Alone* films, who — abandoned and neglected by his affluent and undeniably fertile parents — proceeds to maim and mangle a duo of cat burglars one Christmas Eve.

Kid Rock: Michigan-born musician who mixed rock, hip hop, and country as well as he mixed white tank tops and fedoras. Has, among other things, inspired people on the internet to earnestly ask such existential questions as "What is the meaning of the song 'Bawitdaba'?"

La Traviata: an opera (in three acts) by Giuseppe Verdi about a courtesan's romance with a nobleman whose love is interrupted by an inconvenient bout of tuberculosis. It's also apparently the most performed opera in the world, so if you've never heard of it, you need to watch some more opera.

The Lemon-Aid Guide: started by former journalist Phil Edmonston over forty years ago, this annual guide rates new and used cars and provides insider information to prospective car buyers. Kind of like a cheat code for buying automobiles.

L.L.Bean: retail clothing chain that specializes in outdoorsy clothing. Earth tones and flannels need only apply.

Luke Skywalker: bratty young desert dweller who, through the guidance of wise mentors, learns to use the Force to become a Jedi master and stop kissing his sister on the mouth in the

Star Wars film franchise. Child and sometimes enemy of Darth Vader. (See also *Darth Vader*.)

M. Night Shyamalan: master filmmaker of such thrillers as *The Sixth Sense, The Village, The Visit,* and more. Known for his trademark twist endings that will have you going, "Say WHAT?!"

Magnum, P.I.: Thomas Magnum, a Hawaii-based private detective who wears his state patriotism on his floral shirts. He lives on a reclusive author's estate and butts heads with the estate's stiff-upper-lip British caretaker Jonathan Quayle Higgins III, and pals around with helicopter pilot T.C. and bar owner Rick Wright. The theme song is a real jam.

Malcolm Gladwell: if you know a man who's only read one book in the past twenty years, you can bet it has a fifty percent chance of being a book by this gentleman (most likely *The Tipping Point* or *Outliers*), who writes popular social science books about broad phenomena and changes around the world.

Marilyn Manson: the Criss Angel of music. (See also *Criss Angel*.)

Mason–Dixon Line: an imaginary line that separated the American states of Pennsylvania and Delaware from Maryland and — more broadly — the North from the South in the Civil War (and, in 1820, it separated those states with institutional slavery from those where the practice had been abolished).

Maury Povich: television host best known for his slightly-more-respectable-than-Jerry-Springer talk show *Maury*, which traded in such intellectual fare as shocking on-air paternity tests, out-of-control teens (who are often then shipped off to some sort of boot camp or prison), and — who could forget — obese babies.

Meet Me in St. Louis (1944): musical film that follows the Missouri-based Smith family through four seasons in the early

1900s and has inspired dozens of parents to sing, "Clang, clang, clang went the trolley!" whenever they step inside a streetcar.

Megadeth: heavy metal band immortalized on millions of headbangers' T-shirts around the world. You've gotta respect a metal band whose debut album is named *Killing Is My Business . . . and Business Is Good!*

Melissa Joan Hart: Disney actress who has essentially been on-screen since tweenhood, starring in such family-friendly shows as *Clarissa Explains It All* (the best), *Sabrina the Teenage Witch* (still pretty good), and *Melissa & Joey* (you can skip this one). Totally passable as a television actress, but you're never going to mistake her for Meryl Streep. (See also *Meryl Streep*.)

Melissa McCarthy: gifted comic actress with a talent for slapstick, known for *Ghostbusters*, *Bridesmaids*, and *The Heat*. But for many of us, she'll always be Sookie from *Gilmore Girls*.

Meryl Streep: widely hailed as one of the best living actresses, Streep has portrayed Julia Child, Margaret Thatcher, and Sophie (the one who had to make that choice). She only has one significant hater on record. (See also *Melissa Joan Hart*.)

The Misfits: American band who blended punk rock with horror film themes and imagery. They write songs about needing skulls and their band patches (featuring skulls — it's a recurring motif — with underbites) live on forever on punk kids' jean jackets.

Miss Cleo: spokeswoman for a psychic telephone service ("Call Me Now!") who claimed she was a mystical shaman from Jamaica (she was not), and who turned to shilling dubious psychic readings following an unsuccessful career in live theatre.

Mister Rogers: Pittsburgh-area children's television entertainer who hosted the PBS show *Mister Rogers' Neighborhood*, which — for decades — taught kids the importance of kindness, sharing, indoor shoes, and cardigan sweaters.

"The Monkey's Paw": famous supernatural short story by W.W. Jacobs in which three wishes are granted to the owners (the Whites) of a mummified monkey's paw from India. The owners do get their wishes, but they are granted in the most horrible, terrible ways possible. Possibly a colonial revenge fantasy with Whites (literally) punished for taking resources out of India for personal gain.

Mouse Trap: "the craziest trap you'll ever see," the television ads promise of this Rube Goldberg–esque board game contraption. Given it involves hitting a man into a pan (all in pursuit of the capture of one mouse), you know the theoretical vermin infestation is dire. A classic case of a board game looking way more fun than it actually is.

MMA: shorthand term for mixed martial arts, a combat sport between two individuals that allows use of techniques from a multitude of martial arts (boxing, wrestling, Brazilian jiu-jitsu, Muay Thai, etc.). (See also *The Octagon*.)

Neil deGrasse Tyson: decorated astrophysicist and host of the science-themed TV shows *NOVA ScienceNow* and *Cosmos: A Spacetime Odyssey.* Also, the kind of science nerd who just *has* to remind you in the middle of a *Star Wars* movie that there is no sound in space.

Nickelback: Canada's hugely successful answer to the question, "What would a skeezier version of Creed sound like?" It's statistically impossible they haven't been mentioned in this book series already.

Night Ranger: rock band most popular in the early 1980s best known for the power ballad "Sister Christian," which you might erroneously know as "Motorin'."

"November Rain": only the most soulful and devastating heavy metal ballad of all time. Guns N' Roses recorded this haunting song in 1991. In its equally affecting music video, you witness both a face-melting guitar solo played outside a lonesome desert mission and a doofus who dives headfirst through a wedding cake to avoid the titular November rain.

Noxzema: facial-cleansing product popular among teenagers of the 1990s who wished to avoid facial acne.

Oasis: Manchester rock band that was often seen as the 1990s version of the Beatles. Led by often-feuding brothers Liam and Noel Gallagher, who are noted for their creative insults: "I've had more fun with a tin of sardines," Liam has said of Noel. Their hit "Wonderwall" remains a reliable favourite of frat-boy guitar jams.

The Octagon: the arena in which Ultimate Fighting Championship mixed martial arts (or MMA) bouts take place. (See also *MMA*.)

Old Maid: another card game. Like canasta, but way more people have heard of it. (See also *Canasta*.)

One Direction: Harry. Liam. Zayn. Louis. Niall. *The* English-Irish boy band of the early 2010s with a rabid fanbase of Directioners (and their somewhat alarming fan fiction) produced a string of Brilliam, Amazayn, and 1Derful hits like "What Makes You Beautiful" and — personal favourite — "Best Song Ever." (See also *Harry Styles*.)

Phil Collins: possibly one of the most famous drummers in history and the computer-sounding voice behind songs like "In the Air Tonight," "Sussudio," and the *Tarzan* soundtrack hit "You'll Be in My Heart."

Pig-Pen: Charlie Brown's extremely filthy friend in the *Peanuts* comic strips. In retrospect, we can probably assume Pig-Pen was the product of either extreme poverty or parental neglect. (Not so funny now, is he?)

Pontius Pilate: in the Bible, he's the Roman governor who allegedly refuses to decide whether or not to execute Jesus Christ and leaves it — as all good politicians do — to the will of the people. He is quoted as having "washed his hands" of the matter, which is — long story short — why we now have Christianity.

Professor Snape: instructor at Hogwarts in the Harry Potter book series who is frequently a villain to our hero Harry but always has a convoluted-yet-sort-of-heroic explanation for his seemingly nefarious actions. Played by Alan Rickman in the films, who had a voice that just about matched James Earl Jones's for coolness. (See also *James Earl Jones*.)

Psycho **(1960):** psychological horror film directed by Alfred Hitchcock about the highs and lows of managing an independently run motel. The influential film warns audiences about the dangers of (a) showers, and (b) getting *too* close to one's mother.

Raiders of the Lost Ark **(1981):** the first installment of the adventure films starring dashing archaeologist Indiana Jones (played by Han Solo), as he expropriates sacred artifacts from Indigenous tribes and battles Nazis. (He contains multitudes.) Though ostensibly a PG-rated film, it does include a climactic scene of face-melting burned into many an '80s child's retinas.

Rick Astley: small English man with a deep, soulful voice. You can be sure Mr. Astley will never give you up, let you down, run around and desert you, make you cry, say goodbye, or tell a lie and hurt you. So, he's got a lot going for him in the romantic partner department.

The Riddler: nemesis of Batman who maintains a consistent style preference for green, purple, and question marks, and uses various puzzles to baffle the caped crusader. Essentially, he's an escape room in human form.

Rifftrax: humorous audio commentaries produced for various films and television shows, to be listened to in unison with the films or programs they mock.

Ryan Seacrest: smarmy blond television host best known for *American Idol*, red carpet interviews at the Oscars, and harrassment allegations.

Sally Jessy Raphael: former talk show host noted for her large red glasses who was one of the more popular television presenters during the talk show boom of the 1990s.

Science Diet: a brand of cat and dog foods that uses veterinary science and nutrition to provide your pet with the best fuel possible. Basically like the Freshii of dog food.

Scooby-Doo: clearly the spiritual predecessor to The Dead Kid Detective Agency, this immortal Hanna-Barbera animated television series follows the Mystery Gang (Fred, Daphne, Velma, Shaggy, and talking dog Scooby) as they cross the country in a quest to debunk all supernatural mysteries, apprehending scores of crotchety old carnival owners and ruining their schemes along the way.

SEAL Team Six: highly trained American counter-terrorism unit that is the military's go-to team for the most high-risk and specialized missions. They rescued Captain Phillips from pirates, killed Osama Bin Laden, and likely committed hundreds of terrible war crimes. But very professionally.

The Secret: bestselling self-help book by Rhonda Byrne that claims by thinking about certain things hard enough, you can will them into existence. For instance, you probably thought really hard about a fourth Dead Kid Detective Agency book.

Settlers of Catan: popular German-made board game that normalizes colonialism as you compete against your fellow players in attempt to make the most industrialized settlement possible, using resources like wheat, wood, and sheep as you see fit.

Simone Biles: four-time Olympic gold medal winner and the most decorated American gymnast in history. There isn't a back handspring or Yurchenko she hasn't perfected.

Six Feet Under: heart-rending HBO dramedy series about a family who owns and operates a Los Angeles funeral home. So, if you're into death — specifically what happens after your death — it's a good show to watch. But really? It's about *family*.

***The Sound of Music* (1965):** a musical by Rodgers and Hammerstein based on the real-life experiences of Maria von Trapp and the von Trapp family singers. A nun Maria leaves the convent, becomes an au pair for an Austrian military man, and teaches his kids to sing, but then they all must flee due to the rise of Nazism. That old story. The movie version stars Julie Andrews (Mary Poppins) and Christopher Plummer (General Chang).

Spirograph: strangely popular drawing toy for children that looks like a series of plastic gears and produces curving designs and patterns that look pretty neat.

Starbucks: ubiquitous Seattle-based coffee chain that can be found on every third block in most North American cities. Known for forcing coffee consumers to replace size labels with terms like "grande" and "venti," and misspelling the name of every customer who darkens their doorstep.

Stevie Nicks: tenth-level sorceress and sometime vocalist in the rock group Fleetwood Mac. As of yet, unconnected to Asphodel Meadows. (See *"Gold Dust Woman."*)

Supermarket Sweep: game show that combined all the excitement of high-stakes gambling with a visit to your local grocery store. Most of the half-hour program was a boring preamble to the intense "Big Sweep," during which contestants madly dashed through the aisle of a mock-supermarket and filled their shopping carts with the most expensive stuff possible.

Tagalog: national language of the Philippines.

Tetris: notoriously addictive puzzle video game in which a series of seven tiled shapes drop from the sky while Russian folk tunes play.

To Kill a Mockingbird: novel by Harper Lee about racial injustice and the unimpeachable integrity of lawyers. Has been part of most school curricula for decades.

Tony Scott: film director and brother of Ridley Scott. Director of *Top Gun*, *True Romance*, and *Crimson Tide*, who somehow managed to fit venetian blinds into nearly every film he made, even those ones that largely take place in submarines.

Turner & Hooch: crime-fighting duo of a young police investigator (played by an equally young Tom Hanks) and the slobbery dog he is saddled with (played by Beasley the Dog). In the film that bears their names, the two initially hate each other but become close friends and partners who solve a murder investigation and uncover corruption in the police force.

Usher: recording artist Usher Raymond IV, who you might remember from such jams as "U Got It Bad," "Yeah!," and "U Remind Me." But, for this book, just know he is the singer behind "Confessions" and "Confessions, Part II," both of which involved his infidelity.

Unsolved Mysteries: the television program most likely to give you nightmares, the program documented real-life unsolved crimes, conspiracy theories, and supernatural phenomena via interviews and re-enactments. For most of its run, it was hosted by Robert "Flying a plane is no different than riding a bicycle" Stack.

VHS tapes: before the age of Netflix or even DVDs, people watched films at home using these plastic boxes, then had to rewind them to the beginning after viewing.

Vincent Price: totally creepy actor who starred in countless horror movies over his career. His money-maker was his distinctive and authoritative voice. If you've ever heard Michael Jackson's "Thriller," Price provided the spooky voice during the bridge.

"Walk This Way": a song originally released in 1975 by rock band Aerosmith, it was covered in 1986 by early rap group Run-DMC. The two groups then produced a classic music video (through the 1980s and 1990s, bands sometimes produced short videos for singles) in which they share neighbouring studios and eventually break down the wall between them to fuse rock music and hip hop together. And the world was never the same.

Walkman: back before iPods and MP3 players, even back before CDs, but after vinyl records, people listened to music on cassette tapes. They could play these cassettes on a portable cassette player, more commonly referred to as a Walkman. But if you've seen *Guardians of the Galaxy*, you know all about these. (See also *Discman*.)

West Side Story (1961): film adaptation of a musical that told the story of Romeo and Juliet via contemporary street gangs — the Irish-American Jets and Puerto Rican Sharks. Even though it's honestly one of the best musicals ever made, for some people it's best remembered as "that movie where local toughs snap their fingers and pirouette."

Wheel of Fortune: if you've ever been over your grandparents' at 7 p.m., you know this game show, in which contestants compete in a fairly easy large-scale version of Hangman.

The White Stripes: Jack White and Meg White (no relation) formed an iconic low-fi garage rock duo that rose to fame in the early 2000s with songs like "Fell in Love with a Girl," "Icky Thump," and "Seven Nation Army." Notably, a musical group that primarily just makes use of two instruments (guitar and drums) and three colours (black, white, and red).

World War Z (2013): unsuccessful zombie movie starring Brad Pitt based on a successful zombie novel by Max Brooks that introduced the idea of "zombie stampedes." They're like cattle stampedes but smell worse.

Evan Munday is the author and illustrator of the Silver Birch shortlisted Dead Kid Detective Agency Series, which includes *The Dead Kid Detective Agency*, *Dial M for Morna*, and *Loyalist to a Fault*. Evan works as publicity manager for children's books at Penguin Random House Canada. He lives in Toronto, Ontario.

The Dead Kid Detective Agency Series

The Dead Kid Detective Agency
Dial M for Morna
Loyalist to a Fault
Connect the Scotts

Get the
eBook free!

At ECW Press, we want you to enjoy *Connect the Scotts* in whatever format you like, whenever you like. Leave your print book at home and take the eBook to go! Purchase the print edition and receive the eBook free. Just send an email to ebook@ecwpress.com and include

- the book title
- the name of the store where you purchased it
- your receipt number
- your preference of file type: PDF or ePub?

A real person will respond to your email with your eBook attached. And thanks for supporting an independently owned Canadian publisher with your purchase!